Building Trust in Your American Dream

Also by Paul Mullin

PLAYS

Tuesday

Louis Slotin Sonata

An American Book of the Dead – The Game Show

The Sequence

The Ten Thousand Things

Ballard House Duet

MEMOIR

The Starting Gate

Seattle TRUST

Paul Mullin

Ⓢ Ⓐ
Sweet Air Publishing

SEATTLE TRUST

Copyright © 2020 by Paul Mullin

All rights reserved, including the right to reproduce this book,
or portions thereof, in any form.

Design and layout: K. Brian Neel
Editor: Brendan Kiley

Sweet Air Publishing
www.paulmullin.org

ISBN: 978-0-9970747-1-0

First Edition: Nov. 2020

0 9 8 7 6 5 4 3 2 1

Contents

For Heather

1.
The Interview

It's a great building. That's what Tom thinks. It's what a lot of people think. With its neoclassical lines, granite and glass curtain walls, and inside, that gorgeous, brass-accented cherry paneling all through the lobby and elevators, it's a classy standout among boxes of architectural bullshit.

Tom feels good, confident. The lightness in his chest as he pushes the 16 button in the elevator isn't so much anxiety as anticipation: gently electric, not at all uncomfortable. Here's what it is—what you need to know about Tom in this situation. He's got this. Or at least he's got it as good as it's gonna get got. No sense jinxing it. It is April Fools after all. But even that's fine. April Fools is his lucky day. The whole city seems to have brightened with promise in the last week. The cherry trees are bursting pink and white. The sun's shining. The air's gone gauzy, gently hinting at summer. Yup, in just the last few days, Seattle's been sucking a whole lot less.

Tom's got this. This can be done.

Oh, and listen to that. It's a Brandenburg playing—the one with the trumpets. Even the elevator music in the SeaTru Tower is classy.

Of course, nothing's guaranteed. It's just the first interview in a likely series of them; but he's up for a permanent position at the bank, which would be the choicest gig he's ever landed. No more temping. Just imagine the sort of bennies the permanent employees here enjoy. Healthcare? First class. Vacation days, sick days, 401Ks—the works. Try getting any sort of bennies temping. It's a sucker's gig, and he's done with it.

Sure, he's desperate. He's not gonna tell you he's not a little desperate. Things are tight and getting tighter. Absolutely, if he lands this, it changes everything drastically for the better; but he knows he can't let any of that hope and fear play inside of him when he interviews. He just has to exude confidence. Assertiveness. Bold humility, if there is such a thing. Let this Brandenburg set the tone. Stately and taut. Every line and flourish, crisp and necessary somehow. Let every move Tom makes, every answer he gives, have the same stately grace and perfection.

Tom's wearing his gray suit—his *only* suit, his marrying-and-burying suit—seemingly cut to flatter his slim, but no longer skinny, six-foot-two frame (Of course it's off the rack, not actually tailored.) He's wearing a freshly bought shirt, bold blue, with a subtle sheen in the material and a grey tie, almost silver, with that classy crosshatching pattern—herringbone? He thinks it's herringbone, but he wouldn't swear to it. He thought of buying himself a pocket square to match but decided that was a bridge too far. Might make him look like his Uncle Gil, who sold Buicks. His shoes are classic black Oxfords: slender, pointy, and buffed to a midnight gloss last night so his hands wouldn't smell of polish today. His black mane might be a bit too shaggy and fall a bit too far past his collar for him to be mistaken for an executive, but his shave is impeccable. Not a hint of shadow.

The elevator doors open on a waiting area decorated in muted greens and blues. To Tom's right is a formidable set of pale green, frosted glass doors. Etched across the opening is the SeaTru logo—an anchor "T" with a bank note font "S" wrapping around it. Tom pushes open the right-side door and finds a wide reception counter topped with the same spearmint-tinted frosted glass. A bearded man with tightly curled black and silver hair sits primly erect behind the counter. He wears a vest over a conservative tie. Eyes bright, smile measured, he greets Tom with: "Welcome to Seattle Trust, can I help you?"

"Hello," says Tom, displaying his high-beam smile. "My name is Tom Kavanagh and I'm here to see Maddie Dennett."

"Of course, Tom. I'm Count. Why don't you take a seat in the waiting area and I'll give Maddie a jingle?"

"Thanks, Count. I appreciate it." *Always use a name once you've been offered it,* his brother had taught him. *Goes further than you think.* Tom takes a seat on one of a pair of modernist, white leather sofas angled to a view of Elliot Bay.

"Tom?" Count calls quietly from the counter after a moment. Tom stands, as if summoned. "Yes, Count."

"No, no. Don't get up. Maddie says she needs to wrap up an emergent situation and then she'll be out in five minutes."

"No problem," says Tom, still standing. "Do you think I might use your restroom in the meantime?"

"Of course. It's back the way you came in, past the elevators and to the left."

"Thanks so much," Tom says softly as he passes. Count gives him a friendly smile.

Inspecting himself in the restroom mirror, Tom feels like he looks good. Hair combed but not too slick. The very small patch that's running thin right at the back on top is completely invisible the way he's styled it. Good shave. Suit falling just so. Hell, he could practically double for a Men's Warehouse model, though maybe, just maybe, he's a couple years too old.

Too old. Fuck. When did that *happen?*

Somewhere in New York. Sometime between when he first arrived there with Kirsten (Seattle-born-and-bred, but blonde-certain she would make it as a supermodel) and seven years later, when he took that flight back to Seattle, his tiny infant daughter swaddled on his lap in her blue turtle blanket, and her mother (his wife!) Kona, looking wistfully out the plexiglass oval. New mom and dad both scared, but certain that Seattle would offer them a better chance than Manhattan after the Towers fell.

It was Kona's idea. "Seattle just makes sense. My sister lives there now, and you've got your best friend J."

"Why not Hawaii then? Just move in with your folks?" Tom had countered, disingenuously. They both knew Hawaii was too far, and Tom was reluctant to leave New York at all. He was just making inroads with an off-Broadway theatre that had a big grant to develop plays about poets. Their hot young associate artistic director had seen Tom's one-man show about William Carlos Williams, *This is Just to Say...*, and had asked him out afterwards for beers. She had chatted him up with smiling eyes, smelling lightly of patchouli. For sure he could have gone home with her that night. That's how good his show had been. He was at his best and most successful with women after a show. He glowed, they told him. He was glowing when he first met Kirsten in that grungy garage theatre on Seattle's Capitol Hill.

Fuck. Rich-titted Kirsten. Haven't thought of her in forever.

Damn, but hadn't she bitched him over? And even so, just the thought of her makes his dick swell as he stares himself down in the SeaTru Tower's men's room mirror.

Kavanagh, you, of all people, should've known better.

By now rich-titted Kirsten was certain to have those three kids she wanted, with that venture capitalist she tossed Tom over for, or she's found someone else, even higher up Manhattan's high-finance food chain. Kirsten had cut Tom loose mere weeks after arriving with him in the city, realizing he was never going to be able to take her where she needed to go. Still staring at himself, Tom recalls the moment she goodbye-fucked him in her new boyfriend's Tribeca loft, wearing nothing but that asshole's Dartmouth sweatshirt, tears streaming down her face as she rode him.

Tom sucks in some air and blinks. He can't go back into the lobby like this.

Get in the game, Kavanagh! Your father fed and housed a family of eight on a teacher's salary.

He breathes. Counts to ten. Forces himself to recall the homeless woman pushing her cart up Capitol Hill this afternoon as he walked in the opposite direction, catching her sour reek as he passed.

Breathe. Think of the filth and the poverty in every direction as you step out of your apartment building. You have to get this job.

He looks around, embarrassed, and then smiles at his lack of a reason to be.

4

No one's around. No one cares about your sentimental memory boners. Tom smooths his tie, pulls his jacket taut and buttons it.

Back in the waiting area, he takes a seat, this time closer to the window so he can stare out at the city and Puget Sound, currently gleaming gold in the afternoon sun.

God, he needs this job. Kona's reaching her limits in her legal secretary gig. She and Tom agreed that whoever got the best paying job would work while the other stayed home with the baby, but the situation is deteriorating. Kona says she cries every morning on her walk downtown. And Tom knows they need to get out of "Crack Alley": their nickname for where they live. It didn't take longer than a week to realize that, cute unit or not, their apartment was smack in the middle of one of Seattle's roughest blocks: two halfway houses, and a '60s-era complex full of temporary housing just across the street from Poma's bedroom. It seems like every other night a fight breaks out, or some junkie sprawls unconscious on the sidewalk beneath their window. Tom has the police precinct's non-emergency number written on an index card magneted to the fridge.

Catching himself, Tom turns away from the view of the shimmering Sound and checks the reception desk, but Count appears otherwise occupied. So he waits.

Most recently there was his Oprah sex offenders discovery. In the afternoons, after Poma's nap, they would watch *Oprah* together, which one day was about sexual predators, and what you could do to protect your family from them. At the end, Oprah gave a website where you could plug in your zip code and even your street address to find out how many registered felons you had living around you. Mostly as a lark, Tom went back to the computer in the bedroom and typed their Crack Alley address. He went cold when the results came up. The website said there were 60 sexual offenders in their zip code and 13 lived on their block. (Fucking halfway houses.)

What was he gonna do? Tell Kona? She'd freak. She'd want to move the very next day, and they simply didn't have the money. He had to get a job, so they could save up and get off Crack Alley.

Tom's gaze had drifted back to the Sound, but he pulls himself away from the window just as a pair of well-sculpted calves descends the lobby's internal stairway. A silverish skirt and white blouse follow. When the face appears, Tom realizes he interviewed with this woman three months before. *Dammit. What was her name? Carrie? Nah. Erin? No. It was W-something. Wendy.* She worked for the president of the bank directly: his executive assistant. She had interviewed Tom for the position of EA to the chief financial officer, but he never heard back, even though he thought he'd made a pretty good impression. Wendy says something at the reception desk, and Count nods crisply. Her mission accomplished, she returns to the stairs. A few steps up she looks over at Tom and seems to recognize him, but then goes blank, as if deciding she'd rather not be obliged to offer conversation.

How old is she? Tom wonders, as he watches those heels—just barely on the proper side from "fuck me" pumps—climb the last few steps.

Would I?

He smiles to himself and shakes his head slightly. *Like that's an option.*

Still, the ancient snake brain persists in witless speculation, operating on standby: *current circumstances notwithstanding.* Those sculpted calves have to be maybe ten years Tom's senior, but does Ben Franklin's theory about older women hold true? Aren't they always more grateful? How would Wendy show her gratitude?

What the fuck, dude?

Tom shakes his head vigorously. Then checks to see if anyone noticed.

Jesus, man, chill.

Tom looks at his watch, which he almost never wears now, but believes it gives him a more executive look. It's been about ten minutes.

Crack Alley is starting to stalk his psyche. In his worst recurring nightmare all the streetlights go out, turning Summit Avenue pitch black. Menacing shapes lurch through the darker shadows.

Ah, how's that for poetic?

Piss poor, frankly. Asinine assonance.

Forget about poetry today, Tommy. Today's the day you finally get right with the Corporate Lord. Forget about the implausibly long-limbed black guy you've nicknamed Marfan Man, who sits on the Siamese standpipe across Summit from your living room window. Forget about how he sits there for hours, day in and day out, and sometimes deep into the night, too, coughing the whole time. Sometimes stopping only long enough to pull a drag from his ever-lit cigarette. He's so obviously sick, so skinny you can see the hollows and protuberances of his skull. What's that Counting Crows lyric?

> *I got bones beneath my skin, mister...*
> *There's a skeleton in every man's house.*

But AIDS can't explain his arms and legs, like a spider crab's. Tom figures that has to be Marfan syndrome.

"Hello!" Tom called out as he approached one day in the drizzle.

"Hello there," said Marfan Man, with an earnest attempt at a friendly smile, but the effort seemed to cost him. He started coughing, and his gaze dropped to the cigarette in his hand.

Tom plowed ahead. "Listen, can I get you anything? A cup of coffee or something? A little extra cash?"

"Oh bless you," said the man, twisting his head to meet Tom's eyes. "I'm fine. Just waiting on a friend."

> *Beneath the dust and love and sweat that hangs on everybody*
> *There's a dead man trying to get out.*

Tom tugs his focus back again to the lobby. *How long is this gonna take?*

Kona's at her job right now, literally just one block south in the 1201 building. Her boss, Marty, refuses to keep a computer on his desk: makes her print his emails so he can read them, arranged in order of arrival, in a red file folder, which he insists she replace every few weeks after it becomes "too worn." Marty should have retired 15 years ago.

As often as he can, Tom pushes Poma downtown in her stroller, so they can have lunch with Kona outside at Westlake Center if the weather's nice enough out, which it's usually not. He remembers that one day in February when the sky was bright and the sidewalks were dry. He handed Poma off to Kona and went and sat on a plaza bench about 50 feet away, reading the paper while they played, a small respite from his long days with the baby. A few minutes later, attempting to puzzle out a crossword clue, he happened to look up. Poma was laughing as she bobbled toward Kona, delighted at her newfound, but wobbly, walking skills. Two punkish street kids stalked past. One of them, in a long, greasy, black trench coat brushed against Poma, toppling her on her bum. Kona was up in a flash, bitching him out. But the skinny, pimply fuck wasn't backing down. "You should watch your kid, lady!" he spat at her. His mohawked buddy tried to calm him down, but Trench Coat wasn't having it. "Stupid bitch should watch her kid." With a thrill in his gut, Tom got up and walked over, slowly, calmly—

"Tom?" It's Count at the reception counter. "Maddie just called to say she will be right out."

"Great," Tom replies. *Wait. What am I doing here?*

You're here to interview, dumbass, because you need this goddamned job. Now. Tom nods to himself again.

I'm good. I've got this. Because if I don't—if I don't get this job, and if Kona can't help quitting her shitty gig printing old-school Marty's emails, then... Then they've got maybe two months left living on Crack Alley before they can't even cover the rent. And then what? "Well, there's always Hawaii," as Kona often says, in consolation.

Hawaii.

Meaning, living in her parent's mother-in-law apartment above the garage. Imprisoned in paradise. Marginalized as a non-provider, forever indebted to Kona's ex-hippy parents, Dan and Mayumi.

You don't come back from that. Land of the Lotus Eaters. At least not without being forever changed. Happiness must be pursued, not retreated to.

Suddenly, in front of him is a squat, well-dressed woman, her head barely above his, where he sits. "Tom Kavanagh," she says in a worn, ex-smoker's voice: a statement, not a question.

"That's me." Tom stands. She openly appraises him as they shake hands, her grip firm and dry, the creases in her face detailing experience and guile. Without more clues Tom can't decide if her eyes twinkle with humor or glint with menace.

"Maddie Dennett. Thanks for coming in."

"Thanks for having me."

"Let's head back to my office and chat."

"Okay. Perfect."

"Here, let's take the long way around, give you a little bit of the lay of the land." Maddie leads him past the reception desk. Tom nods a "thank you" to Count, who nods a "you're welcome" in return. Tom has to take two long strides to catch up with Maddie as she turns a corner.

"That corner office is Ashok's. He's not here much. He handles acquisitions. Terry's office is just one floor above." She stops at the next office, "This is Michelle Fleischer's office. She's got her door closed, so she's probably on the phone. Probably talking to Wall Street. And this is her EA, Amy Verducci."

"Hi, Maddie," Amy chirps.

"Amy, this is Tom. He's interviewing for my EA position."

Amy stands, smiling with a vapid happy bird's face. She extends Tom a limp hand, as if something firmer might be somehow threatening. On her desk is an oversized Starbucks mug and a Jacob's ladder, obviously fashioned by a child, with: "I ♥ Aunt Amy!" carefully scrawled across two of its fat wooden slats.

"Nice to meet you," says Tom.

"Nice to meet you," says Amy.

Tom looks to Maddie, who, he could swear, makes a quick face as if to say Amy isn't worth her time, or his. Then she actually says, "Amy's boss is a very important figure at the bank. Deals with our market risk."

Amy says, "That's right."

"Well great," says Tom. "I look forward to meeting her."

"Oh, well, she's on the phone right now," says Amy.

"Of course. I meant... maybe later, someday. If that should happen to happen."

Amy nods, looks around blankly, like a canary.

Maddie moves on. "This is Eileen Standley's office. She's SVP in charge of retail. But I believe she's in Chicago. We're opening big there soon. Five Occasio branches if I'm not mistaken."

Over his shoulder Tom says, "Amy, I'll see ya around maybe."

"Okay, thanks," she replies, then sits back down at her desk, still oddly smiling.

"That's a small conference room," says Maddie, continuing as Tom catches up. "And that office next to it is vacant but is sure to get scooped up soon by some SVP."

"SVP?"

"Senior Vice President," Maddie explains with a dab of derision. "*I'm* an SVP. As is everyone with a window office on this floor."

"Of course. I just didn't put two and two together, and link your title to the… I'm bad with acronyms."

"That's my office." Maddie points to a door opening onto a sizable space, warmly lit, with loud music coming from inside. *Really? Springsteen's* Nebraska*?*

Maddie continues making the circle, passing several doors, some closed, some opening onto variously sized conference rooms. At a cubicle across from an open office door, she says, "This is Darlene, she works for Louis Saks."

Darlene moves to get up, but her phone rings. She taps her headset. "SeaTru, Louis Saks' Office."

From the office a man shouts impatiently, "Dar! Who is it?"

"It's London, Louis," she shouts back, then makes a silent face to them: *"See what I have to put up with?"* She's Tom's age, maybe a couple years older, with a skeptical face. Her khaki slacks and purple blouse are like something a dental hygienist might wear under her smock.

"Good, put 'em through," her boss shouts.

"Hold on for one second," Maddie says.

Darlene looks disinclined to obey, but Maddie's breezy menace is not easily gainsaid. She turns and walks into Louis's office, leaving Tom no choice but to follow.

"Lou, before you get on that call, let me just introduce you to someone." Behind a huge desk sits a large, paunchy guy with glasses, reddish hair running thin on his crown. When he looks at Tom, the fluorescent lights bounce off his thick, squarish lenses. "This is Tom Kavanagh," Maddie says.

"How ya doin'?" says Lou. Tom steps up and offers his hand. Lou slides his feet off his desk and leans his chair forward to shake.

"Lou is acquisitions," says Maddie. "He came to us from New York."

"Guilty," says Lou. "Who are you?"

"Tom's in for my open EA position."

"This shaggy-haired dude? Shouldn't you be playing drums in a band or something?"

Tom smiles. "I play keyboards."

"Ah, well that explains it. Who ever heard of a Seattle grunge band with keyboards?"

"Right?"

"Well, welcome to the team, I guess."

Maddie chimes in, "Well, I haven't hired him yet."

"What? You got me holding up my London call for a *candidate*? Jesus *Christ*, Maddie."

"Oh, Lou, you can afford to take a pause. You're on Pacific time now."

Lou blows a raspberry of disgust. "Whatever. Hey, look, good luck… Tom, right? Nice meeting ya. I gotta take this. It's 9:00 p.m. for these smug Limey pricks." He kicks his feet back onto his desk and shouts out the door, "Dar! Tell 'em I was in the can, then put 'em through."

Maddie and Tom step out as Darlene purrs into the phone, "I'm sorry. Mr. Saks was away from his desk for a moment."

"'Away from my *desk*'?" shouts Lou. "Christ, Dar. Makes it sound like I wasn't working. I told you tell them I was in the can."

"I'm not gonna tell them you were taking a crap, Lou."

"You think the English don't crap?" he shouts back. "I got news for ya."

Maddie takes Tom's elbow and guides him back in the direction of her office. "Lou brings a distinctly East Coast flavor to the floor."

"So I gather."

"But really most of the executives on both 16 and 17 are very down to earth, very Midwest and Pacific Northwest. Most of us are very comfortable living the values of the company." She points to a framed poster next to the door to her office that says in bold words, each a different color. "Fair, Caring, Human, Dynamic, Driven."

A young man in a dark blue suit, snug at the shoulders, approaches from the direction they first walked. Maddie says: "Ah, Jake. How are you?"

"Afternoon, Maddie."

"Jake this is Tom, interviewing for the open position as my executive assistant. Tom, this is Jake, who is—"

"A very small part of the team," he interrupts affably, offering Tom his hand. His firm grip, and the way he stands, shoulders squared and slightly sprung on the balls of his feet, gives Tom very little doubt as to his role. Even so, when Jake excuses himself and continues his circuit of the floor, Maddie confirms in a whispered aside: "Jake heads up executive suite security."

She leads Tom into her office, which is lit with three green-shaded bankers' lamps placed strategically around the room. She's killed all the overhead fluorescents. It's on the dark side of the building, the windows facing the old Seattle Tower, with its bricks the color of old pennies. Maddie picks up a small remote control, points it at a Bose CD player, and the Boss's "Johnny 99" goes silent. Once seated behind her desk, she puts on a pair of readers to look at the copy of Tom's resume resting in front of her, squared to the edges of her leather blotter. "Kavanagh. That's Irish."

"Oh yes," says Tom.

"My maiden name is McCreedy," she says.

"Nice," says Tom, all Gaelic gregariousness. It seems insipid, but what else is there to say? Isn't everybody a little Irish?

"Now this is interesting." She reads from the resume, "Creative writer and performer, 1990 to present. Creative CV available on request." She leafs through the packet. "But I don't see that in any of these."

"No, I didn't submit that."

"Why not?" She looks over her glasses at him. "I'd like to see that."

Tom mentally kicks himself for not deleting that line months ago. What possessed him to put it there in the first place? Nothing but a red flag, screaming: *This job I'm applying for will never be my first priority.* He explains, "Well, I was thinking it's not very germane to the position I'm seeking."

"I think it's very germane to this position. For instance, how many executive assistants casually and properly use the word 'germane?'"

Tom nods. "Good point."

"What sort of writing do you do?"

"Well, all kinds, really. Short stories, poems, plays, essays. Never anything as long as a novel, though I have half an outline for one I'll get around to one day."

"Okay, great. Would a job like this get in the way of that?"

There it is. "Not at all. I don't really write much anymore. There's no money in it and I need a job that can support my family."

"A job should be more than just a means to money. Someone like you should relish the challenges of the work they do to support their family."

Oh no. She's a true believer.

"Agreed. Completely. It's just…writing for me is a hobby. Like ballroom dancing, or…"

"Some people make a lot of money ballroom dancing these days."

"Very true. See? What kind of a writer would offer such an inept metaphor?" Tom laughs, trying to ease the atmosphere. But Maddie doesn't smile. Instead she stares at him over her glasses, deadpan.

"Tell me about your writing. I'm asking. I'm interested. My husband Harrison is a professor of English at the University of Washington."

"Well, I guess the work I'm best known for is a one-man show I wrote and acted in about William Carlos Williams."

"'Red Wheelbarrow'"

"Right, right." Tom nods.

"And the thing with the plums."

"Right. 'This is Just to Say,'" says Tom, and thinks, *And that's about all anybody knows.*

"And *Paterson*."

"That's *right*." Now he *is* impressed.

"Those lines about women always bothered me."

"Which ones are those?"

"'A man like a city and a woman like a flower/—who are in love. Two women. Three women. / Innumerable women, each like a flower. / But / only one man—like a city.'" *Shit. She's word perfect.* "Always sounded like crap to me."

"Yeah," Tom tries to agree. "I guess it's a part of the poem… that makes you want to dig a little more."

"And didn't he cheat on his wife?"

"Once maybe. But they say his remorse over it led him to write what I consider his masterpiece, 'Asphodel, That Greeny Flower.'"

"Hmmm," she says, but she seems unconvinced, and a split second later, uninterested. "Says here you worked for Morgan Stanley.

"That's right."

"What did you do for them?"

The honest answer would have been "nothing." Tom spent over eight months there and worked maybe a total of 25 full hours. Some temp gigs were like that. They could be a grand opportunity for someone who liked to write, but they could also be a vast time suck, when one found oneself uninspired. "I worked on the edge of the trading floor, helping to maintain an experimental database of active letters of credit."

Maddie nods. This seems to impress her. Less impressive would be the truth: Every day he hand-entered foreign exchange rates into a spreadsheet. It took him maybe ten minutes, tops.

The spreadsheet fed a database designed by a Russian guy named Pavel, who spent most of his hours day-trading tech stocks on E-Trade. Pavel and another Russian programmer were constantly cajoling Tom to invest in stocks. "Guys, I'm a temp," he'd protest. "I have no money."

"So borrow," they'd say. Pavel adding, "I took out a second mortgage on my condo in Brooklyn. You're losing money if you're not investing."

To which Tom would reply, smugly, "Dudes, I'm *from* America, remember? I know our markets are amazing and all, but if you knew our history, you'd also know they do occasionally crash."

"Internet stocks don't crash," said Pavel's friend. "They only go up."

Tom took long, *long* breaks during which he would wander all over lower Manhattan, until the assignment finally got canceled.

Maddie asks, "You worked in one of the Twin Towers?"

"Yeah. South."

"Says here you left Morgan in 2001."

"Yeah. July of."

"Ah. So you dodged the bullet, then."

"Yeah. I dodged the bullet."

Pavel's face was in *The New York Times* a week or so later, along with hundreds of others dead or missing, but by that point, "missing" would only ever mean "dead." At least Pavel never had to see the internet bubble burst.

Fuck! Focus, Kavanagh.

Maddie is saying: "Your title will be 'Executive Assistant' because your primary responsibilities will be in reporting to me. You understand?"

"Absolutely, if hired I would organize my work with that understanding."

"Well, I'm glad you understand, because you're hired."

"I am?" *Whoa.*

Maddie finally smiles, albeit tightly. "I pretty much knew on sight."

"Great." *Weird.*

"You can start Monday."

"Monday? That soon?"

"Is that a problem?"

"Not at all. I had no idea the bank could move that fast."

"I run Enterprise Risk Services. We prepare for and respond to all exigencies that impact bank operations. We have to work faster than most."

"Got it. What time should I be here?"

"Well, I like to be here by seven," she says. "Unless I have a gym class, and then I'm a little later."

"Okay." *Frickin' ass-crack of dawn, then.*

"Of course, I don't expect *you* to be here that early, but eight would be too late. Remember the stock market opens at six our time, so we begin every day behind."

"Right. I can be here by seven-thirty for sure."

"Good."

They chat some more: small talk, pleasantries. Then Maddie walks Tom to the elevator. He comments on how much he loves this building. She says she's glad to hear it as he's going to be coming here for a good long while. A wave of relief and gratitude wells up as the elevator dings and the doors open. He steps in, turns to Maddie, and she nods as the doors close. His reflection appears only slightly fuzzy in the brushed steel of the elevator door. Vivaldi's "Winter" plays.

A good long while.

2.
The Bible

When Tom shows up at 7:15 a.m. Monday morning, his new boss is sitting at what he thought was *his* desk just outside her office. "Good morning," he says.

"Good morning," Maddie replies without looking away from his computer screen, blurry twin reflections of which swim in her bifocals. "There were some problems getting you a login quickly. Usually takes two weeks for a new hire, but I know people." She finally looks up and winks. Then, striking one final key, she announces, "There. You're good to go. I set you up with a password "ERS2004," but feel free to change it. I do appreciate my EAs letting me know their passwords, however, in case I need to get at something under their login."

"Of course," Tom says, but he thinks, *Well, that's kind of weird.* He's worked for execs who have given him *their* passwords, for convenience's sake, but he's never been asked to cough up *his.*

With some effort Maddie pushes herself up from Tom's chair and gestures toward it, announcing, "It's all yours."

"Thanks," he says, easing past her and sitting at the computer. *This is good,* he thinks. *The angle of the screen is such that no one passing by can see it.* Directly in front of him rests a white binder with a printed insert cover sheet that reads "Enterprise Risk Services: Maddie's EA Bible."

"I sort of hate the word 'bible,'" says Maddie, just over his shoulder. "I've had some EAs who were a bit too eager to take it as some sort of embrace of religion on my part, but I know *you'll* recognize the sarcasm. Why don't you take some time to peruse that and explore your computer and then we'll have our kick-off one-on-one at eight. I already put it on your Outlook calendar. We'll have to cut it a little short this morning since I have a meeting across the street with Jerry and his other directs at nine. In the future, we'll meet at seven-thirty on Mondays."

Seven-thirty on Mondays, Tom thought. *Great. And who's Jerry?*

"Jerry's the CIO," says Maddie. "I'm one of his solid-line directs. For now."

She heads into her office. Moments later the Goldberg Variations stream out her open door loud enough for Tom to catch Glenn Gould softly caterwauling his counterpoint.

He flits his thumb through the neatly tabbed pages of the thick binder.

> How to Calendar for Maddie
> SOX Reports
> Basel II Reports
> TPS Reports
> Maddie's System of Filing

A flash of panic runs through him—*this is a shit-ton to take in*—but he shakes it off and turns to the computer. The mouse is old and sticky, but happily he finds the standard suite of Microsoft Office apps on his desktop, all nicely up to date: Word, Excel, Outlook, and PowerPoint—the last not his strong suit. Well, he'll learn on the fly as needed. His assigned email address is TKave@SeaTru.com. *Cool enough.* In his calendar he sees the 8:00 a.m. meeting Maddie mentioned and then scrolls forward and clicks in to see that she's created a 7:30 a.m. Monday recurrence with no end date. There's another standing one-on-one for the two of them on Wednesdays at the same time, and then another at 3:00 p.m. on Friday, subtitled "Weekly Debrief (as necessary)."

He pulls up Maddie's calendar. It's stacked with meetings of various colors. He's willing to bet there's a key to them somewhere in the bible. He sees a two-week block in June marked "Vacation – St. Johns." *Maybe I'll get a little break then, and maybe the Caribbean will mellow her out a bit.*

He's kept an eye on the time and goes to her door at 7:55 a.m. She's facing her computer screen, which is placed on the credenza behind her broad desk, the polished expanse of which is covered only by an oxblood blotter fronted with two pens resting in a stately holder. He knocks softly on the open door, hoping not to startle her. "Hi, Maddie. Are you ready for our one-on-one?" She turns to look at him over her glasses with a confused frown. She swivels to consult an antique ship's chronometer on her credenza.

"I thought we were meeting at 8."

"Right."

"It's 7:56."

"Oh. Right. Sorry. I'll come back.

"Well, you're here now. It's… fine. Have a seat." Tom sits in the visitor's chair across from her. "So you have the bible entirely by heart then?" She doesn't smile, but she must be kidding.

Tom decides to roll with it. "Memorized, word for word."

"I don't need for you to memorize it. It's a living document. I need you to know it completely, and then change it when you're ready to better suit your methods to mine. I expect us to always be evolving together."

"You bet. Evolution trumps the bible every time."

She nods and this time smiles grudgingly at the joke. "You're clever. That's the show biz in you. I'm sure we can use that."

"Well, just let me know when I start to annoy you with it."

"Don't worry. Shall we start with travel?"

"Sure."

"I travel a lot. I try not to make last minute changes, both because I know that's stressful on all involved, including my EA, but also because unnecessary change breeds chaos, and chaos, of course, breeds what?" Tom leans back, assuming this question is rhetorical, but Maddie asks again. "What does chaos breed?"

"Uh…" *Will she be like this forever or will she cut me a break once I've learned the ropes?*

"Chaos breeds risk," Maddie finally answers herself. "And in this division, that's what we manage: risk.

"Of course." *Roll with it.*

"I'll be traveling some in April, even more in May, and then in June I'm taking some personal time to see my son graduate from St. John's in Maryland."

"The Great Books School."

"That's right."

"Man, that's a tough program."

"He's a tough kid. Takes after his father."

"And his mother, no doubt."

Maddie looks up with a particularly unnerving gaze. Her irises are sharp pale blue, the whites shot with red. *Stress? Insomnia?* "Of course he takes after me. I'm his mother. But academically, he's much more like his father."

Tom decides to take a chance and points to a photo of a family. It's Maddie and what must be her husband, a portly, stern-staring, long-bearded fellow, standing in a line with two adult women. Seated in front of them are Maddie and a teenage boy who looks uncannily like a tall skinny version of her with auburn hair. "And are those your daughters?"

"My step-daughters. Harrison was married once before." Maddie plows on: "I keep my calendar pretty booked. And I want you to continue in that vein. Though I might be looking to adjust that in the summer. My executive coach says I need to reserve more time for just thinking. So does Jim."

"Jim?"

"Jim Verhoeven? My boss?"

Fuck. I thought she said Jerry the CIO was her boss. Chill. You'll catch up eventually. Just buy yourself time. Shift gears. Show interest in everything.

"Looking through your calendar I was gratified to see precious few double bookings." Maddie raises her eyebrows as if to say, *Go on.* So he does. "I hate when I call another admin trying to set up a meeting and they tell me their boss is double-booked. I'm like: 'Well, then you're not doing your job.'"

She nods. "That's exactly right. No one can be at two meet-

20

ings. When you don't know how to decide between them, you can ask me. I don't need to impress anyone with how busy I am."

"Perfect."

"Did you get a chance to look over the org charts in my bible?"

"Briefly."

"Look over them in depth. I want you to understand our team structure from top to bottom. I'm only two levels down from the President and CEO."

"Terry Torgerson."

"Very good," but her tone says, *No shit, Sherlock.* "So that places you, as my direct report, only three steps down from the enterprise leader. It shouldn't be daunting. It's why I hired you."

"Thank you."

"I'm the head of Enterprise Risk Services. ERS is part of the Risk Management Group, which is led by Jim Verhoeven. He's the CRO, and thus an EVP of course." Maddie notices Tom's momentary blankness. "Which acronym lost you?"

"CRO."

"Chief Risk Officer."

"Okay, got it."

"Now, we're at a bank so it's going to seem like everyone above branch manager is some sort of vice president. For instance, with the exception of you, I have nothing but vice presidents reporting to me. There are AVPs, FVPs, VPs, SVPs, and EVPs. And I may be leaving a level or two out."

"So Jim…"

"Verhoeven."

"He's an EVP, and he's your boss."

"Yes. But he's not my *only* boss. I also report to Jerry Croft. He's the CIO."

"Chief Information Officer."

"Yes. That one you should know already. And a lot of the rest you're going to have to teach yourself."

"Of course. Are either of those reporting lines dotted?"

"Good question." She seems relieved. Her expression seems to say, maybe she *hasn't* hired an utter dumbass. "I used to be solid line to Jerry and only dotted to Jim, but recently Jim insisted I go solid to him as well."

"Ah, okay."

"Frankly, I feel like it was a vote of confidence for my team."

"Good."

"And also, perhaps something of the opposite for Jerry."

"I see."

"That doesn't leave this room."

"Of course not," Tom gravely replies.

"Jerry was brought in to sort out the mortgage tracking systems mess and has not, as of yet, managed to do so."

"So most of your team's work is computer-related."

"No. Most of my team's work is *systems*-related. We make sure that the bank's systems work as they are intended and are not vulnerable to unmitigated threats. I own Emergency Preparedness, Change Control, Cyber Security, Information Systems Compliance, and the Office of Continuity Assurance. You will need to get yourself up to speed on all of those areas."

"Understood."

"Also, you should know that Jim Verhoeven has put me on a senior executive track. I am receiving weekly coaching, with an eye to moving up a level, ideally within the next three years." Maddie makes an inscrutable face. "I'd rather not think of Jim as going anywhere in that time. But his wife *has* already moved down to Arizona."

Tom looks at his watch. "You have 15 minutes before your meeting with Jerry"

"That's good. That's what I want." She grabs her purse and a leather portfolio. "Do you have any questions so far?"

Tom suppresses a mad cackle. His head is swimming. He has nothing but questions. "How do you like your phone answered?"

"That's in the bible."

"Okay, good. I'll look at that more closely."

"But it's a good question. I don't think I've put in there yet that when I'm at my desk I like to answer my own phone. You're not here to be a gatekeeper like some of those ladies a floor above."

"Right."

"And again, editorial comments like that do not leave this office."

"Of course not."

•   •   •

Maddie's back at her desk a little after ten. At 10:30 a.m. she gets on a conference call. Tom finds it in her calendar: "Change Control (weekly recurrence)."

Change control. There's a trick.

Maddie chimes in regularly via speaker phone, asking pointed questions and admonishing someone named Jeannie, who seems to be leading the call. Tom can't hear exactly what Jeannie's saying, only her tone of voice, which sounds beleaguered. At one point Maddie breaks in to say, "Obviously I understand all that, Jeannie, but I have to remind everyone on this call that we *have* to get this right. No excuses. No do-overs." Jeannie's response is curt, but affirmative.

After the call ends, Tom gives Maddie a few minutes, then goes to the door and softly knocks. She looks up at him with a puzzled expression, like she's forgotten who he is, then smiles as if genuinely pleased to remember. "Do you have any particular time you'd like me to take lunch?" Tom asks.

"Not really. That's your time. My only hope is that you don't make a habit of taking it at your desk."

"I feel the same way."

"Oh, and speaking of lunch," Maddie turns to her credenza and rummages in her purse, pulling out a five-dollar bill. "Do you know Mel's downstairs?"

"The deli just above the Nantucket?"

"Yeah. Can you go down and get me a Cobb salad, Italian dressing on the side?"

"Sure." Tom takes the five. He's fine with it. He's known admins who balk at this sort of thing, but he's gotten lunch for plenty of executives. It honestly doesn't bother him.

At Mel's he gets 27 cents back in change after buying Maddie's salad, then buys a sandwich, a V-8, and a pack of Kettle chips with his own cash. After delivering the salad and change to Maddie, he heads back downstairs to the Tower's outdoor courtyard, where the cherry trees are shedding the last of their blossoms in the midday brightness. He gives himself half an hour to eat and read a couple sections of *The Seattle P-I* he found on a bench. Then he heads back upstairs to his desk. Maddie has her door closed.

He sits and closes his eyes. He's got a job. He's making more an hour than he has ever. This job is going to change his life. In a few years, he and Kona are going to be able to buy a house. That was the goal when they left New York. Maybe not in Seattle proper, but somewhere close.

He checks Maddie's calendar. She has this quarter hour blocked out for "Thought." At 1:15 p.m. her door opens and she stands at his counter. With a mischievous smirk she asks, "Shall we visit our other offices?"

"Other offices?"

"Things get stuffy up here on the executive floors. So..." She pulls on her light overcoat: "Let's go see how the other half lives."

•　　•　　•

A block south on Second Avenue, walking past the marble columned main entrance of an older building, Maddie tells Tom: "Through those doors is the lobby of the original Seattle Trust Bank, circa 1890. It's quite beautiful inside, but not long for this world. Occasio branches are being rolled out everywhere."

Tom is resigned to not understanding a lot until he catches up on the SeaTru lingo. Just past the old bank they walk through a much plainer door into a modernist 1960s elevator lobby, white marble floors with a grid of gold lines. Once inside the elevator she starts typing into her Blackberry and tells Tom, "Push five, will ya?"

Five is a cramped, windowless gray box of a lobby, glowing in the corners with indirect lighting like the deck of some drab starship. Maddie digs a lanyard of key cards from her purse and shuffles through them until she finds the one she's looking for, which she touches against a black square next to a black door. The tiny flashing red light remains a flashing red light. "Well, shit." She shuffles through the cards again and finds another, exactly identical. "This is a problem I look forward to solving."

"I hear ya."

She looks up with an expression that says, *You hear* what *exactly?* then she touches the second card to the pad. This time the flashing red light turns solid green, and something clicks. "Open that, will ya?" she says, zipping her purse closed. Tom pulls open the door and holds it for her to pass. She talks to him over her shoulder. "My departments are currently spread out in buildings all over downtown. Once we're in the new SeaTru Center we'll be coalesced on one floor." They pass through a narrow, wan blue corridor into a wider hall of cubicles. Maddie stops next to a closed office door. "This is Compliance, headed up by Kathy Smith Johnson. She's also got change control for the moment, but I'm thinking I might need to peel that off and have it report directly to me." Maddie knocks twice sharply, then opens it. Inside Kathy looks up from her desk, annoyed at first, but then wide-eyed upon seeing Maddie.

"I gotta go," she says quickly into her phone. "Yes, yes... that's fine. I *have* to go." She hangs up. "Hello, Maddie." She shoots an anxious look at Tom.

"Kathy. This is Tom. He's my new EA. Tom, Kathy is Assistant VP in charge of Operational Risk Compliance. She's also the interim owner of Change Control." A cloud passes over Kathy's face at the word "interim." "I didn't mean to pounce on you, but I wanted Tom to have a physical understanding of the scope and spread of my team." Even though there's a chair, Maddie remains standing.

"Yes," says Kathy, finally seeming to catch up. "It's a lot. I think we're in what? Four different downtown buildings?"

"Six," says Maddie.

"Oh." Kathy's face is flushed. Her glasses and blouse seem straight from the 1980s. Her mousy hair forms a sort of lumpy helmet on her head.

Tom stands at ease but alert as Maddie gives her critique of the morning's call. Kathy, her fleshy cheeks blushing even brighter, plaintively attempts to interject, but Maddie persists unfazed, her voice soft and low, her analysis cool and harsh. Finally she wraps it up. "I'll let you go. I know you have a lot of work to do."

"Thank you, Maddie," says Kathy, in precisely the tone of a girl who longs to be the teacher's pet and knows her case is hopeless.

"Nice meeting you," says Tom.

"Nice meeting you," she replies, without looking at him or meaning it. Following Maddie, Tom turns to see Kathy close her office door as they leave.

•   •   •

Next is Second Avenue and Seneca, or what everyone in Seattle calls the "Ban Roll-On Building" because of its blue-green dome. Just inside the sixth floor's secure door, Maddie points at an open cube. "That's your desk." It's empty except for a monitor, an ancient CPU tower, and pencil holder with one eraser-less pencil in it. "Seventy-five percent of my team is housed on this floor," Maddie explains. "So I keep an office here, and now so do you. Or cube, whatever. We used to have a receptionist sitting here but her position was eliminated in the last RIF."

"RIF?"

Maddie sighs. "Reduction in force. Let's see Mary first. She heads up Info Sec." Cubicles line the corridor at about neck height, but so far Tom hasn't seen anybody. Maddie goes into an interior office with a nameplate: "Mary Saskell." The windowless wall space is filled with tacked-up printouts and white boards covered with long lines of inscrutable code and colorful detailed schematics, both hand-scrawled and crisply printed. One board displays an exceptionally well-drawn cartoon of an obviously female Bigfoot, a tiara on her head. Beneath, in Old English script, the caption reads, "Lady Sasquatch." The desk is crammed with stacks and stacks of papers, file folders, binders, CPU towers, and tangles of cables. A mouse and keyboard occupy the only clear space. Three monitors of different sizes face away from the entrance.

"Dammit." Maddie turns and barks at the cubicle wall opposite, "Eric! Where's Mary?"

A balding, red-bearded head pops up. "Oh, hi Maddie. She's not in her office?"

"Would I be asking if she were?"

"Uh… She was in there a minute ago."

"Forget it. I'll catch up with her later. How's the data obfuscation coming?"

"Great." He pauses, as if unsure if it's wise to say anything more.

"Okay. Get back to it," she tells him. The head drops back below the cube wall. Maddie mutters as she moves on, "She's out on the deck smoking, I'm sure."

An older black man steps out of an office farther down the hall, wearing a cream Kangol cabbie's hat and a light jacket that matches perfectly. Seeing Maddie, he smiles widely. "Well, hello there!"

"Hiya, Al. You heading to lunch?"

"Oh that can wait. Come on in."

"I want to introduce you to Tom, my new EA."

"Al Sherman," he says, extending his hand. "Pleased to meet ya."

"My pleasure," says Tom. Al's palm is warm and dry, like a cozy robe.

"Come on in," he says, tipping his head toward his door. They all sit, and Maddie and Al commence catching each other up in mostly strings of acronyms. Tom looks around at the diplomas, certificates, and plaques on the walls. Prominently displayed on the desk is a picture of him and his wife with their arms around a beautiful young woman, clearly their daughter, in a royal blue graduation gown.

"What do you think, Tom?" Maddie asks. She and Al are looking at him expectantly.

Dammit! You can't relax, jackass.

"I think…" he shakes his head as if dizzy. "I think I have a lot to learn. I get lost in the alphabet soup."

Maddie narrows her eyes, but Al laughs. As they all stand, he pats Tom on the back. "Don't worry, son. You'll get there. I can already tell Maddie likes you."

•   •   •

Back on the 16th floor of the Tower, Tom digs into Maddie's "bible." The text swims before his eyes and there's a faint, high-pitched ringing in his ears. He's doing his best to breathe normally. To his surprise and relief, Maddie appears at his counter at 4:00 p.m., jacket in one arm and purse in the other, saying, "I've got an errand to run before going home. I'll see you tomorrow."

Tom lingers until 5:00 p.m., half reading the bible, half trying to figure out how to manage his panic. Finally, he decides, *Fuck it. Been here since 7:15 and I only took a half hour for lunch.* He catches a number 11 up Pike and surprises Kona with being early. He flops down on the futon sofa as she changes Poma's diaper on the living room floor. "So?" she asks.

Tom plays dumb. "So… what?"

Kona shakes her head. "How'd it go?"

"It went. It could be… maybe great. My new boss is uh… challenging, but I've been looking for a challenge."

"Okay, well good." If Kona's reading his anxiety, she's keeping it to herself.

"And fuck it! It feels so good to finally be bringing money in again that I'm taking everybody out to dinner." Her face goes blank. "Bad idea?" He reaches out to brush a strand of her long black hair behind her ear.

"I'm just wiped is all. And getting Pomaika'i ready to go out is just another chore I'd rather not do tonight."

"No problem. Totally get it. How 'bout Bimbos?"

"Sounds great."

"Cool. I'll go get it right now."

"Why not call it in first?"

"Nah, I wanna look at their menu."

"We always get the same thing. Chicken burrito for me. Carne asada for you."

"Maybe it's time to shake things up."

Tom changes into jeans and a T-shirt, then heads out. The Gits are playing over cheap speakers as he steps into Bimbo's. A white girl with dreadlocks takes his order: one chicken and one carne asada. "How long will that take?" he asks, nice as pie.

"Don't know. Cook's new. Fifteen minutes, maybe?" Tom understands he's not remotely hip enough to merit her respect.

"Totally cool. I just need to run a quick errand and I'll be back."

He heads out, turns left, past The Cha Cha Room with its "No Assholes" sign. *Drinking without threat of assholes is un-American.* Instead, it's one more storefront to Kincora's on the corner. He grabs a *Stranger* from the stack at the door, orders a Maker's neat and an IPA, and leafs through the paper without reading it. Each sip of whiskey and each follow of beer untightens his chest a little bit more.

There are no options, Kavanagh. You gotta ride this out.

He drains both drinks with enough spare time to duck into the bodega across the street and pick up a six-pack before grabbing the burritos.

I can afford it.

3.
Brand Rally

Tom is a little worse for the wear when he hits the 16th floor the next morning. He blew through the six-pack by himself. Kona didn't even nurse one. Instead she turned in at nine, just after *Joan of Arcadia*. Happily, the walk into work was brisk enough to blow some of the cobwebs out, though at the corner of Pike and Boren some asshole bike messenger on a fixed-gear ran the light and nearly took him out. "Start seeing bikes, asshole!" the dude shouted, no helmet, black poker chip thingies dangling in his ear lobes. Tom's heart thudded so hard, all he could think of to shout back was "FUCK YOU!" The biker just lifted his middle finger in the air and waved it over his head without turning around.

Now Maddie is looming at his counter even before his computer has fully booted up. "You see that Brand Rally I have at ten?"

"Well, Windows hasn't quite opened yet," he replies cheerfully enough. "But I do remember it from reviewing your calendar before leaving yesterday." A politic lie which seems to please her.

"Good, good. I want you to forward it to yourself. You're coming with me."

"Okay." *Oh boy. Another tour.*

At 9:30 a.m. Maddie comes out of her office with her keys in hand and purse over her shoulder. "My knee's acting up since my workout this morning. We'll drive over."

In the elevator she explains that while most SeaTru execs have their perk parking spaces in the SeaTru Tower, she prefers to keep hers one block north in Benaroya Hall. "Say something happens to the Tower—fire maybe, earthquake, whatever—taking it off-line. When all those cars are inaccessible, I'll still be mobile. Risk management.

"Smart."

"Yes, and I'm going to need you to start thinking more like this, too."

"Absolutely."

She drives them in her sporty black BMW the five blocks to the Convention Center parking garage. "I need you to play along with a little lie," she tells him. "I wrangled you a special invite to this, even though strictly speaking ERS is not part of the Sales or Retail divisions. I wanted you to see Terry speak. So if anyone asks, you're one of my direct reports."

"But *aren't* I one of your direct reports?"

"Well, yes, of course. But not…" Maddie struggles to be tactful. "You're not on the executive track."

"Right."

The lobby is filled with booths offering a variety of SeaTru swag: coffee cups, key chains, stress balls, even action-figure dolls of SeaTru tellers, in both attractive Caucasian female and clean-cut African American male. "Oh, look. They've got Terry Dolls," Maddie points at some molded in the image of SeaTru's CEO, Terry Torgerson, a wide, white smile painted on his plastic face. "Are these free?"

"$14.95, actually," says the woman, smiling, but wary of Maddie's bluff aggression.

Maddie shakes her head. As they walk away, she says, "I'll just get one free from Eileen Standley."

"Heads up retail," Tom declares, proud student of the bible.

"Exactly," says Maddie.

At the sign-in table outside the presentation hall, Tom writes his title as FVP while Maddie nods conspiratorially next to him. Before they head in, she says, "I need to sit up front. Do you mind finding yourself something farther back?"

"Not at all." In fact, he's happy to not have her hovering at his elbow.

Inside the vast hall the seats are arranged wider than deep, such that the huge screen above the stage looms large even for the back rows. Tom takes a seat a few rows from the back on the inner aisle, so he can stretch out his long legs. After a while the house lights dim to half and the giant screen starts to shuffle through close-ups of smiling faces, carefully assorted for an optimal gender, age, and ethnic variety. The crowd quiets and the last stragglers take their seats. The house lights go full dark, and as the screen fills with SeaTru's logo, a woman's voice speaks, with the slightest hint of a Latina accent. "I feel like we're bringing something different at SeaTru, something of value." A pretty teller appears, smiling behind a bank counter. Letters tumble together to form a caption: *Carla Peralta, Las Vegas Branch Teller.* Her face morphs into a middle-aged African American woman's.

"Let's face it. People like me don't get to hope to own their own homes. Except I do!" The caption: *Veronda King, Chicago Homeowner.*

Another morph. "I care about our customers so *much*! It's a little crazy!" *Peggy Scanlon, Pasco, WA Branch Manager.* Peggy's wide eyes make her seem, indeed, a little nuts.

"I get to choose. Every month I say what I can and cannot pay. SeaTru gives me the choices I need. Who else does that?" *Vivian Castenada, Fort Worth, TX.*

"I'm building myself. I'm feeding my soul." *Bruce Dooley, Northridge, CA Database Administrator.*

Now on the screen it's just words: no voice, no face. "If someone's willing to give a piece of their heart and their life, there's really no limit to what you can do." A caption flies in, different font. "Can you guess who said this?" The crowd murmurs. Everyone's making guesses. Was it Eleanor Roosevelt? Steve Jobs? John Lennon? Somewhere in front of Tom a woman opines loudly, "I know it's not Jesus, but it sure as heck sounds like Him."

Overhead, a man's voice asks, "Anyone care to guess?" Somehow, it's clear that the voice is live, from somewhere in the room. The crowd grows electric.

"Anyone?... Okay. Here's another question... Are you ready to get pumped?!" The crowd cheers. "I'm sorry. I said... are you ready to get *pumped?!*" The crowd cheers louder. "Hmmm." The man still sounds disappointed. "I am really having trouble hearing you."

Now the crowd explodes, as if desperate to convince this disembodied voice that they are, indeed, *pumped*: more pumped, in fact, than he ever thought they *could* be. "Let's get on our feet, y'all!" the man hollers.

The crowd stands—Tom, too, if only to see what's happening. A spotlight roves over the audience. People wave their arms and scream whenever the blinding, blue-white ellipse touches them. Finally, it hovers over a spot about 20 rows ahead of Tom. A man in a shiny gray suit climbs up on his chair. He's youngish, well-tanned, his dark hair slicked back from a sharp widow's peak. His shirt, open at the collar, is a rich purple. He's holding a microphone, smiling and waving, turning to either side and behind him, making sure everyone knows he's waving right at them. Finally, he hops down and begins pushing his way through the crowd, slapping backs, shaking hands, giving hugs. He jogs up onto the stage, trades his microphone for a headset, and coyly asks: "Am I live?"

The crowd gently roars the affirmative.

"I'm sorry. I said: '*Am I LIVE?!*'"

The crowd goes nuts, everyone around Tom is screaming some variation of "YES!... YES, BOB!... YOU'RE LIVE!"

Bob nods, smiling, laughing, clearly loving this. "That's good. I mean, I *thought* I was, but I needed some help making sure."

"For those of you who don't know—and really, does anybody here *not* know?" He frowns and wags his finger, a parody of a scolding teacher. "If so, I'm gonna want their name and employee number!"

The audience laughs, and Bob laughs, shaking his head: He's only kidding of course. "I'm Bob Ramirez and I head up the SeaTru Home Loans Group." Big applause. "Oh, and can I just say that I think I have the best job in the world? No offense to our next guest." The audience roars approval. "Know why I started in the audience today?" He waits for them to think about it, then says: "Because I am one of you. A true SeaTrulian. I bleed forest green and Pacific blue, just like all y'all."

They love this. They're smiling and clapping and hooting. "Okay, okay. Take your seats." Bob smiles and rocks back on his heels, waiting to be obeyed. People sit, almost reluctantly, like fans at a rock concert. Once they do, he continues: "I have a couple pieces of news before we bring out Mr. Big Guns. Can you bear with me?" The crowd applauds affirmation.

"Item one: SeaTru is the fastest-growing issuer of home loans in the United States of *America*. How 'bout *that?*" Somebody whoops. Somebody whistles. General applause. Bob nods sagely, holding up his hand up for quiet. "Two: At our current rate of growth we are poised to become the *largest* initiator of home loans in the country!" Even bigger applause. "Three—and really I think this is actually the most important—as of this quarter we have financed more first-time home buyers than any other lender. Now what does that mean?" He waits for a response, riveting them to him. "That means we are embracing minority, low-income, and underserved communities and we are... what?" He pauses again. The audience rumbles. "Simple. We are making. People's. Dreams. Come. *True!*"

Eruption. Tom looks around. If he didn't know better, he'd think he was at some sort of mega church. *Is that woman across the aisle crying?* She is. She's weeping like she just won on *The Price is Right*. Bob happily waits, grinning, until the crowd finally calms down enough for him to speak again. "Now... how did we do this? Well, to explain that, I need to get a little business-y. I need to show you a new org chart." The crowd quiets. Ramirez points his controller at the screen, which lights up with: "SeaTru Corporate Org Chart."

"Bear with me," he says. "I know this is boring stuff, but these rallies can't be all fun and games, right? I mean, we are a *business* after all, right?" The audience murmurs reluctant agreement. Tom wonders: *Shit. Is he losing them?* "This chart illustrates a re-org which is already underway from the top levels of the bank to the lowest." Noticing how quickly the room has chilled, Bob pauses. "What? You worried about a little re-org?" He points at someone in the front row. "How 'bout you? How do you feel about another re-org?" Tom can't see or hear the person, but he hears Bob say: "She's thinking, 'Uh-oh.'" Bob clicks at the screen and the skeleton of an organizational chart appears: just a pyramid of boxes, empty of text, but connected by lines.

Bob turns back to the woman in the front row. "What if I were to tell you this is a *good* re-org? Would that be okay?" He drops his head in laughter. "She's nodding, but she's not buying it. Okay. Fair enough. Let me walk you through it. At the top of the company we have our president and CEO, right?" He clicks at the screen and the top box fills with "President/CEO." We all know who *that* is, right?" Happy applause, but somewhat muted. Everyone's wondering where he's going. "Now let's fill in the lower levels." He clicks and the next five boxes down all fill with the word "Sales." "Hunh," Bob says inspecting the screen. He clicks at it again, the next subordinate tier has maybe ten boxes which again all fill with "Sales." "Well, *that's* interesting."

The audience starts to smatter with applause as a few folks begin to catch on. "What's the next level?" Bob asks, and then clicks at the screen to show "Sales" filling every box. Laughter and applause. Everyone's caught on now and appreciates the gag. "Turns out no matter what you do for SeaTru, we're all in sales."

Now Bob shifts into an insistent chanting rhythm, like a candidate on the stump. "It doesn't matter if you write mortgages for a living, or if you write the software code that approves those mortgages. It doesn't matter if you're a branch teller in small-town Oregon, or the executive vice president in charge of acquisitions. We are *all* responsible for advancing the SeaTru Brand. No! Strike that. Forget I said 'responsible.' Makes it sound like a chore. SeaTrulians don't do chores, do we? *No!* SeaTrulians are on a mission. To take this brand and make it one of the biggest and best known in the nation. And then? Who knows? The world!" Bob basks in the surge of applause, then puts out a hand to quiet it.

"Folks, I know you're not here to see me. And trust me, I'm

not the least bit sad about that. Fact is, *I'm* not here to see me either. I get to see me in the mirror every morning." He waits for the laughter. "You're here to see the guy at the *top* of this org chart. So let's fill that box in with the only name that *could* fill it. Ladies and gentlemen, fellow SeaTrulians, I give you…" and with Bob's final flourish, the box that reads "President/CEO" expands, while shining gold letters fly in from all directions to fill the space above the title, until it reads "Terry Torgerson." Simultaneously, Bob bellows the name out loud and long, like an announcer at a Vegas prize fight. "Terrrrrr-reeeeeeeeeeeee Torgersooonnnnnnn-nnnnnn!"

The room goes completely dark except for the green, glowing exit signs. Somewhere behind Tom, but close enough to make him jump, a brace of snare drums cracks out a cadence. Rumbling tom-toms and bass drums join on the next measure. Then cymbals crash along with the rhythmic cacophony. The spotlight starts to roam the room again; then a second beam joins the search; then another. The drum corps starts marching up the center aisle led by a middle-aged man in a business suit wearing a drum major's hat. He jerks out time with a silver baton wrapped in green and blue tassels. The procession takes the stage. Someone swaps Torgerson's baton for a trombone, and breezily he jumps in on the next measure playing "When the Saints Go Marching In." On the last note of the verse, the drums cut out abruptly and the players simply clap their hands to the beat. The audience immediately joins them. Finally, the spotlights all merge on Torgerson, who blasts into an impressive solo, sliding so high into the trombone's register that it almost sounds like a trumpet before finally swooping down to land the run of notes.

The crowd is stunned silent.

Torgerson lowers his horn, smiles shyly, and bows.

The crowd goes bonkers. The three hot spots manically scan the thousands of faces. Blue and green glitter falls from above. Torgerson finally has to gesture for the audience to be quiet, and even then it takes a while before everyone settles down enough for him to speak. "I play a little trombone," he says, shrugging. The audience erupts again. He gestures for quiet. "It's true. For a while there, when I was a very young man, I thought I might go pro, but then someone told me the joke about the trombonist and the snake."

Someone hollers out: "Tell it, Terry!"

"Okay. I will. Why is running over a snake in the road worse than running over a trombonist?" He waits with a goofy grin, then answers. "The snake might be on his way to a job."

General indulgent laughter.

"I know, I know. It's pretty corny, but back then I was happy to find out that there *was* something else I could do!"

Bigger laughter, louder applause.

"Just a few miles northwest of here at Ballard High School, we had the best band director in the country. Maybe some of you who grew up here might remember him? His name was Hal Torgerson. And he was my dad."

Several women, and at least one man, simultaneously exclaim, "Awwww!" And then everyone applauds.

"Hey, let's thank Blue Thunder for coming out and joining the brand rally today!" He gestures to the Seahawk's drumline, provoking thunderous applause, whistles, hoots, and even one guy shouting, "Go Hawks!" as the percussionists file off the platform. Terry calls out, "See you guys at the stadium in September!"

When the room quiets a bit Terry says, "Okay, can I be serious for a second?" In what strikes Tom as a rehearsed moment, the CEO looks up at his drum major hat and shrugs, "Maybe not with this thing on, right?" He hands it, along with his trombone to his assistant, Wendy, of the sculpted calves, who deftly hustles both items offstage.

Terry runs a hand through his hair, thinning on top and cut in a sort of bowl-shaped comb-over. He's average looking with big teeth and a shy demeanor. His institutional blue suit is well-fitting but nothing fancy, more like something you might find in the men's department at J.C. Penney. Torgerson's stage presence, in contrast to Ramirez's before him, feels carefully practiced, like someone who's spent time with Toastmasters. He wipes his brow with a handkerchief and continues: "I have an important announcement to make, which I have saved for this occasion, the home city brand rally. Today, here and now, we make it official. From this moment forward, Seattle Trust Bank will be known in all public relations and marketing materials as SeaTru, since this is what our customers like to call us and it's what we like to call ourselves."

The audience cheers.

"We're casual with our customers, comfortable. But we are not casual with their money, and we are not comfortable with our place in this industry. We want to grow, so that we can offer this new kind of banking to everyone in the nation."

The screen comes alive again behind Torgerson as he walks the audience through a PowerPoint about the bank's recent expansion into new markets. He talks about converting old-style branches, with their marble counters and slotted windows, into freshly envisioned "occasios," where the teller stands side by side with the customer at a very modern-looking kiosk as, together, they manage the transaction. Slides display tellers wearing their new uniforms: casual khakis and blue denim shirts. *Literally blue collar*, Tom thinks. There's a photo of an occasio kids' area, where boys and girls of mixed ethnicities play with brightly painted wooden Scandinavian toys while Mom and Dad do their banking. Another shows an occasio espresso bar. "Hey, we are headquartered in Seattle after all!" Terry exclaims, to happy laughter.

Famous logos swoop onto the screen, and as each appears Terry calls out the company's name: "Starbucks. Home Depot. Wal-Mart. Costco. What do all of these companies have in common, besides massive brand recognition?" He pauses as if waiting for an answer, but everyone understands he'll provide it. "These companies are category-killers. They have exploded the marketing space around their business line, completely setting themselves apart from their competitors. In doing so, they have utterly altered the landscape. I want SeaTru to become the category-killer of banking, and I know in my heart we can do this in a relatively short period of time.

"Imagine banking being something fun to do, like going to a

Starbucks. Imagine it being easy, offering a vast variety of products, like Home Depot. And imagine it being affordable—no checking fees, no transaction fees—just good, friendly customer service that isn't fancy, but works, like you get at Wal-Mart. In ten years, banking will be fundamentally different from what it is today, and SeaTru will have led that change."

He nods, eyes glowing, as the flood of applause washes over him. When it finally recedes, he continues. "We are going to do all of this without changing who we are at our core. I'm very serious about this. Let's take a moment to review our core values. Will you say them with me?" He turns to the screen. The word "Fair" flies onto the screen. Terry says it out loud. At first, the audience is reluctant to join in, but when it's clear this is what Terry wants and expects, they come in loud on the second word: "Caring." Then: "Human."

"Good!" Terry says. He lifts his hand like a conductor for the next word as it comes in dancing. "Dynamic... And finally...Nice and loud and proud now!" Terry prompts. "*Driven!*" The word, chanted by thousands in unison, booms off the convention hall's walls.

"Fair, Caring, Human, Dynamic, Driven," Terry repeats. He grins, shaking his head in admiration. "Geez, these are such great values! Combined with our great new slogan—'The Power of Yes!'—these are going to make SeaTru unstoppable in the years to come."

He frowns to indicate seriousness. "But as we look to the future, I want to take some time to honor the past, and the great men and women who brought us to this amazing point in our history, when we are uniquely positioned to do such great things for our customers, our shareholders, and, frankly, our fellow Americans. In as much as he needs any introduction, please allow me to introduce my predecessor, Bill Piper!"

The screen switches to display a jowly, rosy-faced old man, sitting uncomfortably in a high-backed leather chair, in what appears to be someone's actual den. The old man glares at a spot just slightly above and off-center from the camera's point of view. "Hello?" he says, huskily.

Terry Torgerson shakes his head and smiles, like a loving son, at once charmed by, and slightly embarrassed for, his dad. "Hello Bill!" he calls to the screen. "It's Terry Torgerson in Seattle."

"Well, ahoy there, Terry! Are you uh… are you ready to get this booster rally started?"

Terry laughs, kindly. Clearly he loves this old man. "The brand rally has already started, Bill. I'm speaking to you live from the Washington State Convention Center, in front of an audience of…" He puts up a hand to shade his eyes from the bright lights. "Well, we had seats for two thousand and it looks like a pretty full house."

"So I'm live?" the man asks, somewhat alarmed.

"You're live, Bill!"

"Okay. Well, hello everyone." The audience laughs and murmurs. Applause gradually gathers.

"Bill," Terry says. "We were hoping you'd share your thoughts on our core values."

Bill nods. "Well, values are important. When I was running the bank, I always told folks: 'Be nice to one another. Work hard at your job. Be pleasant. You'll succeed in business and you'll succeed as a human being. It's a nice way to live your life.'"

"Terrific," Terry says. "Just terrific." He's clearly hoping, however, for something different, something scripted. "I'm wondering if you can't tell us more about specifically the five corporate values you helped develop."

Piper stares blankly slightly off camera. The effect is unnerving, like he's attending fairy voices. After a moment, Terry prompts him: "The values, Bill?…"

"Well, yes, of course. The corporate values. I have the list right here. Fair, Caring, Human. We came up with those in the mid-'80s."

"Yes," says Terry. "I remember it well. I sat in on that committee." The audience laughs indulgently, but they've grown quieter, tense.

"And then there's these other two." Piper squints at a piece of paper. "Dynamic and Driven. I didn't have anything to do with those. Those were added after I retired."

"Yes, we added those three years ago," Terry says helpfully.

"Well, I'm not sure about them, frankly. I looked up 'driven' in my desk *Webster's* and I wasn't crazy about what I found." He begins to read from a small spiral bound notebook. "1: having a compulsive or urgent quality; 2: propelled or—"

Terry breaks in, "Hey, Bill?"

The old man looks up from his notebook, confused or annoyed. "Yes?"

"I think you'll find that all we mean by driven and dynamic is that we want SeaTru to stay competitive in a global market."

"Well, that's all well and good so long as you're taking care of your existing customers."

"Always, Bill. Always. And thanks for that reminder of what's most important about our values and our heritage. No matter how much larger and wider our scope gets, SeaTru will always remain the hometown bank you can trust."

"'Trust,'" Piper repeats. "There's the word that's gone missing. We went from "Seattle Trust Bank" to 'SeaTru.' What does that even mean?"

Terry manages to keep his tone nonchalant. "Our customers and stockholders have been calling us 'SeaTru' for years, Bill. You know that."

"Of course I know. But that's a nickname. We have a *name*. *Have* had since the 1880s."

"Thank you, Bill." Terry shoots a look to someone off stage. The video feed goes silent. "Thanks for sharing your perspective. It's been a unique treat. We'll let you get back to enjoying beautiful Friday Harbor." The old man frowns, says something that can't be heard. He gruffly plucks his mic from his lapel and stands, just as the image cuts out, replaced by the SeaTru logo, its dollar "S" pulsing green to blue to silver to gold.

The crowd begins murmuring, but before they can get too restless Bob Ramirez jumps out and leads them in a "Power of Yes" chant. Terry joins in, smiling and clapping his hands.

Tom decides to beat the rush and heads out to grab some lunch before Maddie can find him in the crowd.

41

•   •   •

Scott Joplin is playing in Maddie's office when Tom arrives back at work a little over an hour later. She hollers: "Hey. Tom, is that you?" He goes to her door. She's eating her regular salad from Mel's. "I guess we missed each other after the rally," she says. "Wasn't that amazing?"

"It sure was."

"Except that stuff with Bill Piper—that was off. I mean, everybody loves Bill, and he means well…"

"Yeah," says Tom. "Like an uncle at a wedding or something. But the other two, Terry and Bob, were both very impressive."

"I know," Maddie nods. "Though Terry's had to work at it. That sort of confidence in front of crowds did not come naturally until he got some really strong coaching."

"Well, it shows."

"You should tell him that."

"Yeah, okay."

"I'm serious. Send him an email, introducing yourself as my EA, tell him about your stage background, and how you really enjoyed his presentation."

"Well, I'm pretty… junior, and I'm pretty new."

"So? I like to hear feedback from all levels."

"Okay. I'll do it."

"Good," she says. Tom heads back to his desk to sort through some receipts from Maddie's last trip. He mildly enjoys puzzling these together, according to a flow chart he found in Maddie's bible behind the "expense reports" tab. When he's done he slides the stapled packet into her inbox on his counter. She'll sign it later. Finally, he starts drafting an email to Torgerson. *She's right. Why shouldn't I?* He keeps it short and to the point but checks it twice for any errors or awkward grammar, then hits send.

Fifteen minutes later his inbox chimes. He alt-tabs to Outlook and sees he has a message from "The Office of the President and CEO." He clicks it open.

Dear Tom,

Thank you so much for your feedback. I really appreciate it. And I'm glad you liked the trombone solo, though personally I think I might be a bit out of practice.

Sincerely yours,
Terry Torgerson.

There's an electronic image of Torgerson's signature over his name. *How cool is that, that he responded personally?* A minute later, Tom's email chimes again. He looks over. It's a message from Wendy Gellibrand, Terry's Executive Assistant. The subject line says: "Please come see me ASAP." There is no interior message.

Tom goes to Maddie's door and knocks. "Hey, I gotta run upstairs for a second. I've been summoned by Wendy Gellibrand."

Maddie arches an eyebrow over her glasses. "What does she want?"

"Didn't say. She just said to come see her ASAP. I sent Terry that email like you said."

"Yeah?"

"Yeah. And he replied right away. Very kindly, actually."

"Good, good."

"Okay, so I'm gonna head up."

"Yeah, don't keep her waiting."

Tom climbs the stairs from 16 to 17 and walks to Wendy's counter in the northwest corner, just outside Terry Torgerson's office.

"Hi Wendy," he says, sounding more chipper than he feels. She holds up a finger, bobbing her head in assent, but not to him. How could he not have noticed that she has a headset on? With striking green eyes, she stares right through him while she listens to the caller. He wonders if she notices how blue his are. She pulls her mic bar down to her mouth and presses a button on the cord to unmute. "Okay. Okay, that's fine. But we're still going to need it by end of day... Yes... By close of business... Okay. Great. Thanks." She presses another button to hang up. Her eyes finally take him in.

"You're Tom. Maddie's new EA."

"That's me," he says cheerfully. *When in doubt, flirt a little.*

The green eyes don't blink. "So you sent this." She pushes a sheet of paper across her counter at him. It's his email to Terry.

"Yes," he says. Flirt mode deactivated.

"Why would you do that?"

"Why would I... send Terry an email?" She nods without taking her green eyes off of him. His guts start to sink. "I uh... I thought it was a good idea. I was really impressed with today's brand rally."

"Why were you there? The rally was for sales associates, and FVPs or above."

"Maddie brought me."

"Maddie brought you," she repeats without inflection, like a prosecuting attorney. "Did Maddie tell you to write this email?"

"Well, actually, she—"

She cuts him off: "So you're going to blame Maddie for both things."

"No."

"Do you know what happens when someone writes Terry Torgerson an email?"

"Um... no." *The less said the better at this point.*

"When someone sends Terry Torgerson an email, I have to print it out for a file, because Terry wants every email sent to him kept on file in hardcopy even though they're already stored on a server as soon as they're received. Imagine how much paper we consume doing that." She waits, as if expecting him to actually imagine it. "Do you know what else has to happen when someone sends Terry an email?"

"I don't."

"Within 15 minutes, either I, or if I'm not available, my assistant, has to respond to that email under Terry's cover, with some sort of personal touch, preferably self-deprecating, so that it doesn't seem like boilerplate. Now I called you up here as a courtesy from one executive-level administrative professional to another."

"Sorry. I... I was sort of working at Maddie's insistence, but..."

"And I work at Terry's insistence."

"Right."

"So we understand each other?"

"Of course."

"Thank you, Tom. I appreciate you coming up to talk with me."

"Of course."

Tom can feel his face burning as he descends the carpeted stairway from 17 to 16.

Fuck.

Fuck this job.

Fuck.

4.

The Business

On Thursday, Tom arrives ten minutes early to the Ban Roll-On Building for his first meeting of Maddie's direct reports. In the windowless conference room, he places a copy of the single-sheet agenda in front of each chair. Attendees, most of whom he met on his first-day tour, begin to gather. With a minute to spare, a huge woman lurches into the room, bringing along a waft of cigarettes. Tom recognizes her immediately from the Lady Sasquatch cartoon doodled on the white board. Mary Saskell is taller than everyone and her frizzy brown hair seems to occupy twice the space around her head. Later, when her agenda items are up, she briefs the team with easy authority, reeling out jargon like some '70s cop-show sergeant. Saskell clearly relishes her role as a cyber security maven. During other managers' briefings, however, she keeps her comments short and guarded.

Al Sherman comes off just as smooth as the day Tom met him, answering all of Maddie's pointed questions, satisfying her dogged curiosity to her obvious delight. He's clearly her favorite.

Tom's attention inevitably begins to wander. He misses his baby Poma, and the long days he used to spend with her on Crack Alley. He hardly gets to see her anymore.

And when, oh when, will he ever get laid again? He and Kona tried about six weeks after she gave birth, but it still hurt her, so they took a break for another couple months. And then, after a specially arranged date night, it didn't hurt, but was woefully awkward, like college students who might be happier as friends. But even thinking about bad sex wakes his dick up. Not good. He's got on thin, silky slacks today. A boner will be impossible to hide. He can't remember the last time he even whacked off.

God, and the sex he and Kona used to have in New York City! She was so eager to please back then, when they both had jobs and could go out whenever/wherever. One lusciously drunken, warm spring night, she let him fuck her quickly between cars on the number seven out to Queens, the bright moon silvering the tracks and the rooftops rolling beneath them.

A few months later some idiots drove a couple planes into the towers.

They're still not sure whether Poma was conceived in the brainless sunny days just before September 11, or in the desperate nights of six-packs and cigarettes just after. Tom can't remember ever taking his eyes off the TV, but Kona swears they shut it off one night and made love in the eerie quiet of their neighborhood: no planes roaring out of LaGuardia, no loud music blaring from the cars swishing by below their open window.

Three-quarters of a year later Tom woke up early to an empty bed. Passing the open bathroom door, he saw Kona sitting in the tub, her digital wristwatch laid out on the white porcelain edge. She held a yellow legal pad and marker.

They took a car service into Manhattan to beat the worst of the morning rush hour. When they got to Roosevelt-St. Luke's, the nurse told them Kona's contractions were too far apart. "Maybe you could go walk around Central Park a little bit to get things going?" she suggested. Kona turned to Tom with such a look of panic that he made the instant decision to crank his charm up to full wattage. If that didn't work, he'd start being difficult.

The charm was enough. The nurse let Kona could stay a few more hours in the curtained-off receiving bed until her contractions were such that they could move her upstairs to delivery.

And of course, the nurse was right. Things didn't really get going until late that evening. The OB/GYN wore a tux, still hoping to go catch the opera after intermission, Lincoln Center being only a few blocks away.

When the male delivery nurse with the tattoo sleeves said "it's a girl," Tom's heart blew up like a carnival balloon

The universe is finally giving me what I want.

"You got a name for this little one, Dad?"

Tom spoke it carefully, like a prayer. "Pomaika'i"

"Pretty."

"It's Hawaiian."

"What's it mean?"

"Good luck."

The nurse slapped Tom on the back. "I like it."

"Pomaika'i Grace Kavanagh," Tom expounded, without adding aloud: *Because luck without grace can be a curse.*

Little Pomaika'i struggled to breathe at first—something the doctor called "grunting." They put her in a clear plastic bassinet and shined what looked like burger-joint heat lamps on her, while gently thumping her chest to clear her little lungs. Tom stood close, murmuring, "You can do this, Poma," her nickname coming naturally in the moment. "Breathe. It's easy. I'm doing it right now. Don't go to the NICU. Stay and be with your mamma and me." Miraculously, his daughter started breathing more easily. "She's a fighter," Tom said to the pretty Indian doctor who began to clean her.

"It's actually quite normal," she replied with a charming lilt. "Sometimes they just find a way."

Tom glanced over at Kona. It looked like somebody had been hacked to death, there was so much blood and gore smeared on the teal surgical drapes. The tux doctor, now covered with a gown, moved into the center of the mess with what looked like a large fishing hook. As he drew a stitch, Kona screamed, "What are you DOING?!"

"We're just sewing up your episiotomy," he answered calmly.

"No anesthetic? *Nothing!?*"

"You're bleeding too much. It's better this way."

"Oh Jesus. OWWWWUHH!'"

They must have given her something topical afterwards because within 20 minutes she was telling Tom to get her a cheese-burger.

"We're going to need you to order food for that," says a woman's voice, used to giving orders… but not Maddie's.

It's Lady Sasquatch and she's talking to me.

Act like you know.

"Of course," Tom replies.

Saskell is staring at him with a curious expression.

Is she suppressing a smile? Does she know I was spacing?

"Let's iron out the details later off-line."

"You bet," Tom agrees.

Jesus, Kavanagh! Stay in the game.

•   •   •

On Friday morning, Tom arrives to find a windowed SeaTru envelope resting in his "in" tray. He tears it open: his first pay-check, more than he's ever made. He sends Kona an email as soon as his PC boots up, adding as a PS: "That's only for one week!"

After work he catches a 43 up the hill. With luck he might beat Kona home.

He hears voices and laughter as he steps into the apartment. He pushes in the kitchen's swinging door to find his wife frying up some peppers and onions in a pan. Looks like she's making his favorite dish: a sort of Hawaiian chicken paella. Her sister sits next to Poma's highchair, helping the baby girl eat. Seeing her father, Poma's eyes go bright. "Daddy's home!" Kona cheers. She's still in her work skirt and blouse beneath her apron.

"That's right!" says Tom. Kona leans over and sneaks a kiss onto his cheek. She whispers in his ear, "I'll have something for you in a minute."

"Mmm. I like the sound of that!" He notes the glass of white wine in her hand, and its match in Hana's. He squats down next to Poma and fake frowns into her eyes. "Give your daddy a kiss!" Instead she gently dabs his nose with a loaded spork of mushed bananas. Kona and Hana burst into hysterics, causing Tom to pull a clown face of outrage, causing baby Pomaika`i to burst into hysterics. "Fine," pouts Tom. "*I'll* kiss *you*." And he presses his lips into her sweet-smelling, golden, Shirley Temple curls. To his sister-in-law he says, "Hiya!"

"Hi yourself!" Hana replies. She's larger than Kona, with a boxier build and a more obviously Japanese face.

"Did I miss the party invitation?" asks Tom.

"Oh, he thinks he's invited," says Kona to her sister.

"Can you at least tell me what you're celebrating?"

"How 'bout the massive money-making man in my life?" Kona replies. "Maybe I'm celebrating him."

"I like it!"

"Here, stir!" She sticks a wooden spatula in his hand, then reaches into the freezer and pulls out their stainless-steel cocktail shaker, gives it a few vigorous shakes, then pours the vodka out over two fat olives already skewered in his favorite martini glass. It's the only one of its kind, a crystal piece they inherited from their next-door neighbor in Queens, an old, gay, black man named Monty who told them it was from the Waldorf Astoria: not the one on Park, but the earlier, more elegant edifice, which stood where the Empire State Building stands now. Tom holds the precious vessel high, exclaiming: "To massive money-making Kavanaghs!"

"Hear hear!" Hana calls out.

The first sip is perfect diamond fire. He looks around the tiny kitchen: wife, baby daughter, sister-in-law. Tom can't quite fathom how easily he's been enveloped since walking in the door. He sips again. He pulls Kona into a squeeze. She lets out a little "Hey!" but surrenders to it. He kisses her forehead. "You love me, don't you?"

"I think I might," she says, finally squirming away, back to the frying pan.

"I gotta go to work," says Hana, standing.

"Oh nooooo!" Tom whines. Inwardly he's glad. He likes his sister-in-law, but sometimes it starts to feel like an all-girls club when she's over. Hana heads out to her shift bartending at the new Irish pub, Clever Dunne's. It's the only way she can put any money away for culinary school *and* afford her rent in the apartment on Queen Anne Hill, which she splits with two other girls.

Kona puts a lid on the paella to let it simmer. "Clean up your daughter," she tells him. "I'm gonna jump in the shower."

•   •   •

Tom has Poma cleaned and changed and is reading to her in the living room when Kona comes out in a short lemony skirt and a flowery sleeveless silk blouse that sets off her slender arms. She wears coral lipstick and her hair in pigtails. He consciously blows out a long breath. She smiles wryly at him, wise to his desire.

"You hungry?" she asks.

"Very much so."

"Then let's get this baby to bed and have some dinner."

•   •   •

Miraculously, they get Poma down by 7:30. They close the kitchen door, talking quietly while they eat so as not to rouse her, though they can hear her cooing occasionally in her crib. She's utterly silent by the time they have their mango sorbet.

"I'm very proud of you," Kona says.

"Thanks, baby."

She looks at him—fully looks at him—in a way she hasn't in maybe a year, since New York, since just after Poma was born. Then she breaks into a merry smile. She's beautiful. He's always thought so, though often she comes off as merely cute. Licking her spoon, she says, "I've got a crazy idea."

•   •   •

They became friends during a temp job Tom was working at American Express down at the World Financial Center. Kona was his nominal supervisor. And, of course, he found her endlessly adorable, with her Raggedy Ann freckles, her Kewpie doll lips, and her tiny perky tits; but he determined to remain disinterested for a whole slew of reasons. First and foremost, it's one thing to fuck the boss when you're an employee, but you've got zero leverage when you're just the temp. But there were a million less noble and infinitely less practical reasons: namely, the half million or so young, fuckable women who peopled his happy hunting grounds of New York City. He wanted them all, or as many as he could have, and Kona hardly seemed the type to be cool with that.

Eventually, however, every eager young New York dick slams into the same granite wall of truth: Manhattan women want men with money. Period. Looks and laughter be damned. The club scene is brutal to true bohemians like Tom. He was constantly fighting above his weight. Dry spells were inevitable and prolonged.

The Kona dam broke toward the end of a particularly long, dead January: the holiday season a slush-soaked memory, spring a farfetched promise no sane person could credit. Innocently, she asked him to join a team happy hour. He pled poverty, persuasively. She stood him the first round, and by the third they were making out in the narrow hall to the restrooms, his eager hand finding its way beneath her black turtleneck to those nipples he'd been musing upon for months.

And tonight, Tom feels another dam finally breaking, as Kona takes him by the hand and leads him into their bedroom. She lights a large candle and several attending votives. He feels himself swelling. She starts to unbutton her blouse. He whispers, "Stop."

"What?"

"Come here." She does. "Kiss me." And she does, with quick, soft searching pecks, growing longer and deeper with each repetition. He loves it when she does this. And he knows *she* knows he loves it. He moves his hands down her slender back and gently cups her butt cheeks. It's all one long kiss now. He glides his hands beneath the silk of her blouse, then pushes her gently away so he can unbutton it himself, slowly, bottom to top. He draws the curtains aside to let her pert breasts touch the open air. She didn't bother with a bra. He bows his head to touch his tongue to a nipple, and she responds with a surrendering "mmmmmmm."

He lies down, opens the top of his slacks. She shucks her panties but leaves her short skirt on as she climbs on top of him, slowly taking him into her. Gently, tentatively, she begins to grind. Tom moves his thumb to the button of her clitoris, but she pushes it away, and picks up her rhythm. He tries again, but again she brushes it away. "Stop," she whispers, not unkindly.

"What am I doing?" he asks, all innocence.

"You're trying to make me come."

"Is this a sin?"

"It's not happening," she says. "This is about you."

"It is?" He's not sure he likes this.

"Shhh," she replies. "Don't make me give you 'the business.'"

"Oh my god," Tom sighs. "What on earth makes you think I deserve 'the business?'" Kona offers this treat so rarely that together they were obliged to invent its nickname.

"Well," says Kona, giving him one last soft kiss. "This is for being my man, my husband, and for taking a job I know you weren't sure you wanted, to provide for me and your baby girl."

"Mmmm," is all Tom can answer.

And with that she reverses herself on him so he can watch her cute, copper-flecked bottom ride up and down on him until he comes, long and hard, inside of her.

This is it. This is what makes it all worth it.

•　　　•　　　•

"How would you feel about me quitting my job?"

"Yeah?"

She pushes herself up from nuzzling in his arm and searches his eyes. "Well, yeah. Hana can't watch Poma forever, and with what I make at the firm, I'd just be covering day care costs, assuming we could even find somewhere to place her. And if I were home with her, I could spend some of that time finding us a new place, somewhere the hell out of Crack Alley. Maybe even a house somewhere."

"A house?"

"A rental house," she assures him. "To start. To see if it's right for us. We need more room. Poma's gonna be running around soon. You want the sidewalks of Crack Alley to be her back yard?"

"Kona."

"Okay, I'm hard-selling. Sorry. Let's sleep on it, okay?"

"Okay. But just know I'm fine with you quitting your job if you think the numbers add up. And obviously I'm also completely fine with moving the hell out of Crack Alley." *Sixty sex offenders in the zip code; 13 on the block.*

5.

Hitting It

T hings are going well for Tom. He's not gonna lie. Of course, he's not gonna shout it from the rooftops either. He knows better than to tempt the Fates. He's hitting a rhythm. Early on he was struggling to stitch the days each-to-each and make sense of them in this new job, this new life. Now the sense is coming of its own accord and he's seaming entire weeks together almost effortlessly as he rolls up on the last days of May.

He can't say there haven't been bumps along the road, and weird ones, too. Like the morning he came in to find that Maddie had organized his entire cube, from his pen and paper clip holders to the binders in his cabinet. But Tom's learning to roll with Maddie's quirkiness. She's the boss, and if she wants his cube a certain way, that's the way he'll keep it. Besides, he must admit her system makes a lot more sense.

Tom is also learning to leverage her fierce reputation throughout the bank. Now when Maddie's junior execs come to his counter, making demands like, "I'm going to need this PowerPoint preso revised as marked and then 20 color copies printed, collated, and stapled for the 3:00 p.m. meeting."

Tom simply replies, smiling, "You bet!" Then he lets the other shoe drop. "But that *is* going to take me off Maddie's urgent project. So, I'll need to let her know you pulled me off."

"No, no. That's… that's fine," heretofore haughty subaltern now frantically backpedals. "I'll find some other way of doing it."

Tom waits until they've gone to nod and smile. *That's right:*

Walk away. I may be a bitch in this prison, but I ain't your *bitch.*

Here's the bottom line: Tom's learning the ropes, obvious and hidden. He's not fucking up as much, and Maddie seems genuinely pleased with the job he's doing. He's hitting a rhythm. Our boy likes rhythms.

Average morning: Alarm goes off. Tom hits the snooze. He's got ten more minutes. Pulls Kona into his arms; falls back asleep. Starts to dream. Alarm goes off again, and he's up. No sense stretching it out. Showers, shaves, gets dressed, kisses Kona, usually still asleep; kisses Poma, *sometimes* still asleep, but more often up and eager to play, in which case he lifts her from her crib and brings her to Mamma and lets *her* sort it out.

He grabs breakfast somewhere downtown: a bagel with cream cheese, an egg sandwich, the greasier and cheaper the better. Nothing's going to beat those soft clouds of fresh Kaiser roll, warmly enfolding sloppy scrambled eggs and crispy bacon that he used to be able to pick up in practically any bodega in NYC.

Today Tom reaches the 16th floor only to find he's forgotten his access badge. He'll have to go to the main reception desk and get a temporary one. He plasters a goofy apologetic smile on his face as he approaches the counter. Count looks up at him stricken, his eyes moist and red-rimmed.

What the hell?

Tom explains the forgotten badge. Count nods and without a word hands him a temp card. Tom thanks him and starts to go when Count says softly, "Tom, wait."

"Yeah, Count?"

"I have terrible news to share with you." Tom stands still and waits for it. "Amy Verducci is dead."

Amy? "Oh," says Tom, and then, "What?"

"I'm sorry to be the one to tell you," Count says.

"Wait. She's dead?"

Count nods.

"When?"

"Over the weekend. A sudden fall, in her home. That's really all I know."

"Okay... Okay, Count. No worries. I'm sure I'll be hearing more. Are you okay?"

"I'll be okay. Thank you for asking, Tom." Count gives him a sad panda look of gratitude.

Tom starts the long, squared-circle march to his cube. At Amy's desk, nothing seems to have changed but the obvious: She's not there. And she was *always* there, oddly upright and vacant: happy bird. He looks beyond her cube into Michelle Fleischer's office, Amy's SVP, who looks up and meets Tom's eyes. Without thinking, he nods. Her eyebrows furrow, but she returns the nod almost imperceptibly.

Mozart's Requiem flows out of Maddie's office. *Well, she's got good taste in music, if not a terribly measured sense of propriety.* Tom goes to sit down, but Maddie calls out to him. "Tom? Is that you?" He's not going to get off that easy.

He goes do her door. "Hey, Maddie."

"Come in."

Tom takes a seat and says, "I heard."

"She fell down her basement stairs," Maddie begins. Tom knows she'll have every currently available detail. "Broke her neck. Instantaneous. I don't think you could safely say she didn't know what was coming, but it doesn't seem likely she suffered any longer than the second or so it took to fall."

"Yeah?"

"Her oldest niece found her. She lived with her sister in a house in West Seattle. She grew up in West Seattle. Lived her whole life there."

"They tend to do that out there." Tom met a guy once who was born and raised in West Seattle, got married, raised his own family there. Got divorced when his kids were grown. Remarried and his new wife moved them into a nice little condo in Belltown. Everyone he knew in West Seattle howled. "How could you do it? How could you move so far away?" "Far" being six miles, maybe three as the crow flies. This guy told Tom he still drove back there to get his hair cut. Tom says none of this to Maddie. Instead he says, "It's like a whole other city out there."

"Are you okay?" She wears a convincing expression of concern. "I know this is a pretty shocking piece of news, and Amy was one of your peers."

"Right." Tom can't remember ever having a non-work-related conversation with his "peer."

"So? … *Are* you okay?"

He can't think of a genuine reason why he wouldn't be. He nods, swallowing.

"Good. Because I have a ton of re-calendaring to go over."

They work for next 20 minutes or so. Once done, Maddie pulls off her glasses, sits back in her chair, and says, "So… obviously, Amy's loss is going to be a huge hit to the executive floors."

"Oh, absolutely."

"I know Michelle Fleischer is personally quite devastated."

"I can only imagine."

"She's also in the middle of putting together some very large pieces of work in market risk. She's going to need help."

"For sure."

Maddie nods. "Now I'm sure someone's going to suggest bringing in a temp, but before they do, I wanted to put your name forward for the job."

"You want me to work for Michelle Fleischer?"

"I think you'd be perfect to help her out in this difficult time."

"But—"

Maddie barrels past the interruption. "She doesn't need some temp sitting useless at Amy's old desk. She needs someone who knows the bank's systems and processes but who is also completely capable of learning on the fly and getting business done in chaotic and challenging situations. That's you."

"Thanks, Maddie, I really appreciate your faith in me, but—"

She lifts her chin. "But what?"

"Well, who's going to work for you?"

"*You* are. I'm not giving you up. I'm adding duties."

"Oh." His gut sinks. "I'll cover both desks?"

"Think you can handle it?" Even though Tom knows Maddie's only being rhetorical, he also knows his doubts won't stop her from throwing him into the fire. She goes on as though the deal is done—and really, it *was* done, before he even walked into her office.

"Obviously, it will mean additional overtime, which I hereby approve in advance for the duration. I'll leave it to you to sort out the details, but for the time being I thought you could sit at your own desk in the morning and Amy's in the afternoon. You'll need to be keeping track of both of our calendars, email, and phones all day, but it's nice, I think, to split up the physical presence. Don't you?"

"Yeah." He tries to calculate how many more hours he's going to be away from his family, and then how much those hours will be worth at time-and-a-half.

"Any questions?"

He's got a million, but Maddie's only going to have the patience to indulge one or two. "What's the uh... What's the time frame on this?"

"You'll start immediately."

"Right. Of course. And it ends... when?"

"You mean when will Amy be replaced permanently?"

"Yes."

"She just died on Saturday, Tom. I don't think we need to rush things, do you?"

"No, I just—no. You're right. Of course not."

•   •   •

That afternoon Tom plants his butt in a freshly dead woman's chair and fires up her computer. He logs in as himself, having already put in a ticket with IT to allow him access to Amy's emails and to emulate her permissions to Michelle's Outlook and directories. For the last hour or more, Michelle has had her door closed. Occasionally her phone line lights up as she makes calls out. Tom has decided to let her answer incoming calls as well, at least until she instructs him otherwise.

Finally, her door opens. As she glides past he can just glimpse the outline of her bra beneath her ivory blouse. Ten minutes later she's walking back, her face a blank study. Seeing him sitting in Amy's chair, she frowns, confused. Tom watches the recollection dawn on her: *on loan from Maddie.* Her expression relaxes, and she manages an awkward nod as she heads back into her office, shutting the door behind her.

When she leaves at 4:30, she stops at Amy's counter, and tries to smile at him, but it comes off as a sort of pinched grimace. "Tom, right?"

"That's right." He feels oddly compelled to stand but resists the urge. Instead, he mindlessly runs his palms over his thighs. "I'm sorry to... about the circumstances."

She nods, brow furrowed. "Yeah, me too. I'm going for the day but... uh, just wanted you to know that I really appreciate you being here."

"Happy to help. Did you want to, maybe, take a few minutes to go over anything you might want me to do for you? Your calendar, email, phone, those sorts of things?"

"I do want to do that, yes, but..." she suddenly stares straight into his eyes. He looks away reflexively.

"But today's probably not a good day," he offers. "How 'bout I put 15 minutes on your calendar tomorrow for us to talk?"

"Make it half an hour. We got plenty to go over."

"Will do."

"Okay then," she says, nodding sharply.

"Right," Tom answers, moronic.

"Okay, I'll see ya," she says.

"Okay then." And he watches her go.

•　　•　　•

It's late. Nearly everyone on the floor has gone for the day. Tom goes to the supply room, finds an empty box, and brings it back to Amy's cube in order to start packing her more obviously personal items: the child-made Jacob's ladder, the over-sized Starbucks mug with Van Gogh's "Starry Night," a hand-made collage of printed family photos.

"You don't need to do that." Lou Sach's EA is standing at the entrance of Amy's cube.

"Oh hey, Darlene."

"I can do this," she says quietly. She stares at the box with a pained resolve.

"You mean Amy's stuff? It's no bother."

"Just leave it," she says, sternly. "I'll pack it later before I leave." She turns and goes.

•   •   •

The next morning Tom works in his own cubicle but keeps an eye on Michelle's emails. In the afternoon he attends an emergency mandatory meeting in the boardroom for "all administrative professionals working on the 16th and 17th floors." Besides Count, he's the only male seated at the expansive table intended to accommodate the bank's board of directors. Wendy Gellibrand stands, arms folded, next to the lectern pushed into the corner. Darlene avoids eye contact with everyone.

A slight, white-bearded man rushes in and looks about the room. He spots Wendy and seems to intuit she's who he needs to talk to. They consult in whispers, then the man takes a seat at one end of the conference table. He folds his hands and regards them solemnly for a pregnant moment. Finally, he raises his gaze and turns it to the woman next to him. From her he slowly goes around the table, looking into the eyes of each and every person. Some ladies engage him in long, soulful, moist-eyed exchanges, while others, like Darlene, only spare him a glance, but the white-bearded man seems satisfied with whatever he receives. Tom knows, intellectually, he's witnessing parlor trickery, but when it's his turn to take in the man's kindly, sad eyes, his shoulders still go soft and he feels a deep urge to let go of a sigh.

"Good afternoon." The man's voice is perfectly measured and warm, like an alto clarinet. "My name is Lowell. And I'm here... Well, I'm here. Full stop. In some ways, it's that simple. More expansively, I'm here to *be* with you, and *perhaps* talk with you, and perhaps share in your sorrow, and, perhaps, share in arriving at maybe just a little bit of clarity. But mostly, I'm here, to listen and to share. That's all… I'm here."

The pudgy, blonde lady who works on 17 in the northeast corner, and whose name Tom can't for the life of him remember, lets out a plaintive chirp. She quickly covers her mouth as tears spring from her eyes.

Nancy, with the way-too-long, way-too-straight cult wife hair, primly raises her hand. Lowell smiles and says gently, "You don't need to do that. Please feel free to speak if you're so moved."

"Thank you," she says. "I just wanted to say that I was up all night praying on this, for Amy and for all of us, and in the morning, I had the most… powerful sensation of… love and assurance, and I knew in my heart that she's with Jesus now."

The room stiffens. Some of the women lean back, others look at their hands. Tom sits stock still. One growls, "Don't start!" It's Carby, the squat middle-aged Italian lady with the frog eyes.

"I'm sorry?" says Nancy, aghast.

"Amy was a good Catholic girl." Carby makes no effort to muffle her pugnacity.

She's old school, thinks Tom. *I wouldn't fuck with her. I forget who told me that Carby's short for "Carbina."*

"She was a good Catholic girl," Carby reiterates. "And she didn't go in for all that born-again thumping. So just leave her out of your dog and pony show."

"All I said was that she's with Christ," Nancy protests to the room. Darlene shoots a look at Tom so cold and murderous he has to look away. "Don't Catholics believe in Christ? I mean, am I missing something?"

"Yes," says Carby. "A shred of common decency."

"How dare you!"

"Just don't start—"

"Let's bring it back to the group," Lowell interjects smoothly. "It's good we're talking about Amy, but I'd like to bring it back to the people in this room."

The fake blonde, EA to the EVP of Home Loans, pipes up.

Tom wants to say her name is Tammy. "She was so sweet. That's what I remember about Amy, just as sweet as a little girl."

"And she'd do anything for anybody," someone adds.

Wendy leaves the room, as if called away on important business.

"I never heard her say an unkind word," murmurs a petite brown-haired woman named Juanita. She looks embarrassed for speaking.

"Never," says Carby.

Gayle, Count's co-receptionist, adds, "She was really sort of a happy little saint." They seem to be going around the room now and the turn has come to Count, but he still looks utterly wrecked and can only manage to shake his head and turn to Darlene sitting to his left. Darlene stubbornly stares at a conference call Polycom sitting in the center of the table.

"Okay," Lowell says, as though offering a conclusion, but Tammy pipes up again, eager to begin a whole new round.

"She was just as sweet and good as a nun." *A nun?* Tammy casually goes on, as though she were chatting in a nail salon. "I don't think she had a boyfriend. I never even knew her to date. All she really cared about were those kids, her nephews and niece. She was like a second mom to them. I don't know what they're going to do without her." There room goes silent processing this.

Suddenly Lowell's turning to Tom. "And what about you? You looked like you wanted to say something."

I did? "Oh… well… just that I… concur with most of what everyone's saying. She was super sweet and I… don't know. I just feel a little weird."

"Why weird?"

"Well, because I didn't know her as well as everyone else here. I'm new on the floor and… well, in some ways I feel like I shouldn't even be here."

"Well, you worked with her, right?"

"Well, yes, of course, but…" *But so did the executives*, Tom wants to say. *Why aren't they here? Why isn't Michelle? Or Maddie? Or Terry Friggin' Torgerson? What's with the tiered grieving system?*

"But…" says Lowell, encouraging Tom to fill his pause.

"But I'm not sure it's right for me to grieve, not knowing her as well as others at this table."

"Everyone has the right to grieve, my friend," Lowell says, like a kindly country pastor.

• • •

By day's end Tom is seriously craving a drink, but first he has to drop some paid bills in the mailbox down on the tower's loading dock. He finds Darlene there, out on the sidewalk sucking on a cigarette and looking out toward the water.

Tom opens with a wry smile. "Didn't know you smoked."

"Didn't know you judged," Darlene answers, blowing some out.

"Not at all. Just wondering if I could bum one."

Darlene squints at him, suspicious, but fishes a cigarette from the pack of Parliaments she holds in the same hand as her lighter. Then they share that always oddly intimate moment of one person cupping another's hand to light a cigarette.

"You used to smoke?" she asks.

"Nah," says Tom. "I'm one of those lucky idiots who can do it whenever he wants and never gets addicted."

"I suppose that's a talent."

"Yeah. Everyone's got one, I guess."

"I'm sorry about yesterday."

"Hunh?"

"About being all uptight about packing up Amy's shit and all."

"Oh, no sweat. You knew her better. I totally get it."

"I didn't know her at all."

"No?"

"Nah. Nobody did. She kept to herself and her family." Their eyes meet again to agree on the shittiness of the situation. Then they both quickly look at their feet.

"How long *you* been here?" Tom asks.

"SeaTru?"

"Yeah."

"Three years," she says.

"Where were you before that?"

"The hospital," she says, pokerfaced.

"Yeah?"

"Five years at Brigham and Women's in Boston."

"You were an admin there?"

"Nope. I was a nurse."

This is great. Tom loves finding out surprising things about people. "You used to be a nurse and now you work as an admin?"

"Yeah."

"Don't nurses make good money?"

"Sometimes… Well, generally, yeah." She's giving him a jaundiced look but is also clearly enjoying this.

"So… I gotta ask."

She gives him a see-if-I-give-a-shit shrug. "So ask."

"Why would you leave nursing to do this?"

"Got sick of people dying on me."

"Ah." They smoke silently for a moment. Then Tom says, "So Amy kicking it must've mucked that plan up."

Darlene blows out her smoke. "The hours are better in this job. Or they used to be until I got assigned to Lou, and he started keeping me to six-thirty, seven."

Tom nods. "I'm starting to know the feeling, straddling two desks."

"I'll bet."

He brushes his cigarette coal off on the lip of a garbage can, rubs it out with his shoe, then drops the dead butt inside the can.

"Look at you. So conscientious." She tosses her live butt sparking onto Spring Street where a truck promptly rolls over it. "I gotta head up and baby-sit Louis." She goes back in through the loading dock.

6.
Risk All-Staff

In their Wednesday one-on-one, Maddie instructs Tom to forward her Friday morning meeting to himself. He pictures her calendar in his head and says, "ERM All hands." *Damn. That's a little scary.*

Maddie nods with satisfaction. "That's right. Jim Verhoeven's meeting. I want you there."

"Shouldn't I be on the invite distribution list for that?" Tom wonders. "Aren't I one of his 'hands' reporting up through you, and temporarily, Michelle?"

"You absolutely are. You should talk to Juanita about that. You're probably just not on her radar yet."

"Juanita?"

"Juanita Bennett. Jim's EA. You need to know Juanita."

"Oh, Juanita. Yes, of course."

Maddie senses bullshit. "Introduce yourself. The sooner the better." She turns back to her screen and starts to type.

"It's just that…" Maddie turns back, glares at him over her glasses, but Tom soldiers on. "The EAs upstairs are a bit… tetchy. I got scolded by Wendy Gellibrand after I sent that email to Terry."

Maddie sighs, shakes her head. "Wendy's a gatekeeper. It's a problem. Always push back a little if you can."

"Right. Exactly." Tom chews his lip, nodding.

Maddie narrows her eyes. "You're not here to be liked. *I'm* not here to be liked. You represent me, so people are going to expect you to be assertive and you most definitely have my permission to be that."

"Understood."

"So talk to Juanita."

"I will. For sure." *But avoid it if you can.*

Tom's new boss Michelle gives him her passwords to her email, her HR dashboard, her payroll login (so he can approve timesheets), and to an interface for an online database called "StreetSweeper Beta 2.2. "I'd like you to pull a spreadsheet from this on a weekly basis." She leans over him to show him how to set the criteria. "It takes a while to crunch so you might want to launch it first thing in the morning and then go work on your own computer outside Maddie's office. Got it?" She turns to face him.

"Got it." He turns away, worried his breath might stink. "What's in the download?"

"If I told you that, I'd have to kill you?" She winks. "Nah, it's just mortgage data. It's an experimental proprietary system which gives a much more granular look at the loans underlying the CDOs we sell into."

"Ah." She has to know he doesn't have a clue what she's talking about.

"I feed it to my quants to play with."

"Now you're just making up words."

"'Quantitative Analysts.' They're my eggheads: post-docs in mathematics, mostly, from MIT and Princeton, when I can get them."

"I bet those guys can party."

"Uh-huh." She slips off his desk and back into her office.

Poking around in the HR dashboard later that day, he learns that Michelle lives on North 75th Street and that her base salary is $195,750 a year. *God damn. And that's not including bonuses or stock options.* Her birthdate is April 25, 1960. A Taurus. His sister Teresa was born on the 23rd of the same year. Michelle is seven years older than him.

On Friday, Tom joins Maddie for the walk across the street

to Benaroya Hall for the Risk All-Staff, to be held in the smaller recital hall, large enough for about 500. Like before, Maddie and Tom part company at the entrance. As one of the CRO's directs, she'll be presenting, and heads up to the stage. Tom isn't able to hide in the back rows this time. Instead he's forced to squeeze into one of the last available seats close to the front. Also, unlike the brand rally, there's no huge projection screen, nor music, nor fanfare, and no one introduces Jim Verhoeven. He simply walks up to the microphone and says quietly, "Is this thing on?" The crowd noise subsides. "Hello, everyone. We've got a lot to cover so let's get started." In measured tones he begins walking through a very straightforward agenda.

"Jim V", as many refer to him, is a smallish man in his 60s. He wears a light gray suit, white shirt, and lime paisley tie. He pushes his golden, wire-framed spectacles up on his thinning sandy hair when he needs to read.

Just before ceding the podium he turns to his directs, who sit, Maddie among them, in chairs pre-placed on the stage. "Just a word of warning: Use an acronym without defining it, that's five dollars. Do it again, and the fine goes up to 20. Deal?"

The directs laugh and nod. Jim turns back to the audience. "I'm going to let you all judge. Last time I did this, I was able to treat myself to lunch at the Metropolitan Grill." Jim introduces the first speaker, a tall guy in his 30s who drones on about credit risk or something. Tom promptly checks out but snaps back to attention when he hears Jim interrupting. "Did you hear that?" he asks the audience.

Several people answer "Yes."

Jim turns to the confused exec. "Barry, you didn't hear that?"

"Uh..."

"You said, 'CRR.'"

"Oh."

"Now, you and I know it means 'cash reserve ratio,' and so do probably most of the folks in this room. But I guarantee *someone* here *doesn't* know." Tom nods. *He's talking about me.* "So..." Jim holds his hand out to Barry, "Five bucks please."

Barry laughs sheepishly and pulls out his wallet. Looking inside, he frowns. "All I have is plastic."

Jim shakes his head. "Figures. The SVP of Credit Risk only has credit cards." The audience laughs. "Okay, Barry. You'll have to owe me. There's a SeaTru ATM right across the street."

Tom thinks, *Hey, isn't "ATM" an acronym? And... come to think of it, isn't "SVP"?* He mentally pockets his reward money. As the meeting goes on, the audience joins in the fun of catching speakers when they slip up. Maddie gets busted during her presentation for saying "SOWs" without providing a definition. Another SVP gets some laughs when he simply hands Jim a 20 before even stepping to the podium. This guy explains how SeaTru's increased merger activity is fueling, in a relentless, positive feedback loop, even more merger activity.

"We have no choice but to be big," says the SVP. "It's a simple issue of volume. If your loan tracking software costs—let's say one million dollars—then if you only write, say, a thousand loans, each one has an initiation cost of a thousand dollars. Simple. But if you initiate ten million loans, then each only costs ten cents."

An SVP named Aurora presents a slide showing the intricate variety of loan tracking systems currently in use after all the recent mergers. She admits, "We call this our spaghetti map." And sure enough, the schematic looks like multi-colored vermicelli flung randomly at the screen. "If we don't manage to untangle and simplify this mess significantly, then our operational risk around loan initiation and tracking will *also* amplify in a positive feedback loop far larger than the one driving mergers. And that's when federal bank inspectors go from friendly donut-eaters to Dirty Harrys." She pauses to let this sink in, then adds, "Discussion of this slide does not leave this room."

Next up is Michelle. Tom enjoys her "preso" best of all. Something comes alive in her face as she presents. Her high, but gently rounded, cheek bones blush pink as Gala apples. *She's literally apple cheeked.* Her eyes flicker with that fire of someone who loves her work as she explains how her team vacuums up money in the narrow spreads of constantly varying interest rates. When she says "LIBOR" she immediately unpacks the acronym: "London Interbank Offered Rate." She describes, with just the right note of pride, her role helping to manage the strategy near and dear to Terry Torgerson's heart: treating SeaTru's mortgage risk portfolio as an asset to be traded like any other. Loans can be bundled and sliced like pepperoni, then sold to secondary markets. It's a win-win for the bank, which profits from the sales while shrinking its exposure by moving loans off its own books and onto the ledgers of Wall Street firms with much larger appetites for risk. Wall Street, in turn, re-bundles them again, reselling them further and further downriver from SeaTru. Her enthusiasm and clarity allow Tom to feel like he understands the subject on some very basic level.

Having deftly avoided any naked acronyms, Michelle playfully shrugs at Jim as she walks back to her seat. Jim stands and chuckles into his hand-held mic. "That's Ms. Fleischer for ya, folks. Grade 'A' perfect as usual, and no misunderstandings about the value of a U.S. Treasury-issued portrait of our 16th President."

"I'd like to leave you with one final thought," Jim continues. "We're hearing a lot these days at SeaTru about 'the Power of Yes.' It's a great slogan, and I understand why Terry and his team want everyone at the bank fully on board with it. For most SeaTru employees, if the Home Loans Division says jump, their job is to ask simply, 'How high?' And that's good; that's appropriate. Home Loans is the largest money-maker we have, and we *are* in the business of making money. But our mission in the Risk Division is a little bit more complex. We are here to make sure the bank does not *lose* money. Right?" He lets the question linger in the room. "So, when Home Loans says 'jump' to *us*, yes, we say, 'How high?' But then, once we have the answer to *that* question, we are obliged to ask a slew of follow-ups: 'What's underneath us?' 'How long is it safe to be in the air?' 'What's our landing strategy?' 'Is a parachute appropriate?' 'What are the risks of not jumping at all?'" Again, Jim pauses to let this sink in.

"'Yes' is indeed powerful, but only if and when 'no' is possible." Jim gazes out at the audience. Indeed, he seems to be looking *through* them, to some future only he can dimly see. Finally, the aging executive nods slowly, abruptly says, "Thank you," then steps from the podium. At first no one claps, but then a smattering swells into a full round of applause.

• • •

Back at the Tower, Maddie and Tom debrief. "I liked him," he tells her. "He was funny in a non-show-bizy way, and no bullshit, if you'll pardon the French."

She waves her hand dismissively. "Please."

Tom goes on, "Doesn't seem like there's anything hinky about him, you know?"

"No. What's 'hinky?'"

"Ah... um. Probably a New Jersey thing. It's like 'weird' or... 'doesn't smell right'— that sort of thing."

"Ah. Well, no, he's not 'hinky.' But he's got his weird points, I assure you."

"Really?" Tom's intrigued. Maddie seems about to dish.

"Do me a favor and close that." She points at the door. Tom does. "First, you have to understand that I think the world of Jim. He's probably SeaTru's number one senior male advocate for women."

"That's awesome."

"He's put me forward for executive coaching, so I can be among those considered as his successor when he retires, which I hope isn't soon but seems like it might be."

"Yeah?"

"Yeah. He barely even lives here anymore. He's got a house on a golf course in Flagstaff. Two of them, actually."

"Two?"

"Right next door to each other. Apparently they're exactly alike, inside and out. He lives in one. His wife in the other."

"Why?" Tom is intrigued.

Maddie shrugs. "No idea."

"You're right. That's pretty weird."

"And that's not the weirdest."

"No?"

For the love of God, woman! Dish!

"No." Maddie's voice drops even lower. She looks at the door. "I'm not supposed to know this. It *can't* leave this office."

"Nothing does. That's my job."

Maddie pauses, perhaps to add suspense. "He likes to give guns."

"He... what?"

"When he particularly appreciates a job you've done, Jim gives you a gun. But only if you're a woman. It's how he shows appreciation."

"He gives you a *gun?*" Tom can't believe it. This is *too* good.

Maddie hastens to explain, "Well, he hasn't given *me* one, but when Vi Johnson backed him up in a particularly tricky round of merger due diligence, he gave her a nickel-plated Glock. She showed it to me once."

"Whoa."

Maddie nods, eyes gleaming. "That's a little weird. Right?"

•　　　•　　　•

Maddie stops at his counter on her way out that afternoon. "Did you talk to Juanita yet about getting on Jim V's all-staff invite going forward?"

"I did not." *Should've known better than to hope she'd forget.*

"Well, make sure you do that before you leave."

Tom's heart sinks a little. "Will do."

Tom reluctantly climbs the stairs to 17 and heads to Juanita's desk, after finding it on the corporate floor map. That must be her sitting there, so petite only part of her head peeks up over her counter: jet black hair pulled into a severe bun. Approaching closer, he sees her nails, long as daggers, perfectly painted to match the plum of her jacket, and he remembers her now from the grieving workshop.

"Hi, Juanita?"

She looks up, blinks at him, says nothing. "I'm Tom Kavanagh. Maddie Dennett's new EA?"

"Ah, Maddie's guy. What can I do for you?" her expression remains inscrutable.

"I had a quick question."

She waits, lifts an eyebrow.

"Well… Maddie's wondering if I can get added to the invitees for Jim's All Hands going forward."

"Is she?"

"Yeah." *What the ever-loving fudge?*

"Why would I add you to an invite list for a team you're not a member of?"

"Well, doesn't Maddie roll up to Jim?"

Juanita gives a quick shrug. "Sort of. So, *she* gets an invite, ad hoc, because she bullied her way into it. But I think we need to draw the line somewhere. If she wants to drag you along, I suppose there's nothing anyone can do about that, so long as there are enough seats for Jim's *actual* team."

Jesus. Tom smiles tightly. "Okay. I'll let her know that." He turns to go.

"So you're threatening me, Tom?"

Holy god, what? He turns back. "I'm sorry?"

"You gonna go running to Maddie? Have her fight your battles for you? Is that how you handle things?"

"No. I—?"

"Fine, Tom. I'll put you on the invite list as a bcc, happy?" Tom can't help but laugh out loud. Juanita frowns. "Something funny?"

"Oh, Juanita, if you only knew the half of it." He takes a half step closer, leaning his arm on her counter. He watches her draw back slightly and relishes it. "Listen," he says in a conspiratorial tone, "I really look forward to working with you in the future. But until then, I hope you do as I plan to, and have yourself an excellent weekend."

Her frown deepens. Her phone begins to chirp. "You've got a lot to learn, Tom."

As he lightly jogs down the blue and green carpeted stairs from 17 to 16, his heart thumps and his face buzzes with adrenaline, but he cannot deny he's happy. He gets it now. If fucking with people is the game, by God, he'll play it, happily and hard.

Back at his cube he powers down his computer, grabs his bag, and heads out. From the main floor lobby Tom jogs down an escalator that leads to the Nantucket, the old bar and seafood joint that occupies the bottom floor of the three-story, 19th-century building nestled in the corner of SeaTru Tower's footprint. He takes the last open stool at the bar—the gods are finally smiling—and orders a dry vodka martini up with an olive. When it comes he drains it quickly and orders another. The bartender asks if he's hungry, and Tom says, "Sure," thinking, *I got at least an hour and a half before I'm due home.* He orders some Kobe beef sliders and a Red Hook.

He's good and lit, with a well-satisfied stomach, when he wobbles out of the Nantucket. If he goes home now, he's just going to have to sober up or go out for more beer. He wanders up Second Avenue toward a blinking neon sign. Closer, he sees it's a pair of animated rolling dice, only the tubes are blown such that after tumbling a few times the dice simply disappear, over and over, ceaselessly, hypnotically. Beneath them a sign reads "Jake's Hard Way 8." Tom's heard about this place. It's sort of legendary. "Don't go in the Hard Way," his friends would warn each other back in the '90s, "Unless you don't care about coming out with the same underwear." "I knew a guy who went in there one night and didn't show up again until three days later… missing a kidney." But Tommy Kavanagh's from the Jersey Shore, not lily-white Washington State, and he has a strict policy about bars: Every joint deserves one round. If after that you can't stand the place, or the place can't stand you, then, by all means, bail. He's explored this policy from Harlem holes-in-the-wall to Deep South, Stars-'n'-Bars honky-tonks. Surely this dive in the heart of liberal Seattle is safe for one drink. Still, he stands outside pondering, even leaning forward to try and peer through the small red and green stained-glass diamond set at eye level in the thick wooden door.

Should I? Why wouldn't I?

Suddenly the door opens and Jim Verhoeven walks out, nearly bumping into Tom's chest. "Pardon me," he says. Tom is stunned mum. His boss's boss holds the door open for him. "You going in, friend?"

"Um... I was thinking about it."

"Well, don't think too hard. It ain't rocket science."

Suddenly grinning, Tom says, "Ain't it?"

"Well, all depends on where you're hoping to rocket to."

Tom decides he better come clean. "I work for Maddie Dennett."

The older man's eyebrows go up. "Do you now? Well, in that case, you'd *definitely* better go in, and I'd better go with you." Jim holds the door open. And as Tom steps inside he thinks, *Damn. This is one weird week that just wants to get weirder.*

7.

Drinking with the Chief

T he stink of stale beer hits Tom like a padded wall. *Is that really "Give me Shelter" playing on an actual fucking juke box?*

"Take that stool there," Jim says, pointing to an open one next to a tiny woman with long, straight, black hair. She seems to have fallen asleep leaning on her palm, in the act of chewing on a cherry red cocktail straw.

"There's only one," says Tom. "Where *you* gonna sit?"

"All I do is sit. Take the stool. Besides Sissy here's likely to be moving on soon. Ain't that right, Sissy?"

The woman cocks open one eye and says, "Yeah, that's about the size of it. Gotta see a man about a horse." And with that she slides off her stool and out into the night. Jim takes her spot, and once situated, lifts a finger. The barmaid, a blonde hair-helmeted Valkyrie, saunters over.

And now Louie Armstrong's "What a Wonderful World." Too perfect.

"I thought we got rid of you," the barmaid croaks at Jim. She seems serious, but they always do, these types. Tom smiles at the perfect absurdity of it all.

"You know what I want," Jim softly growls. "And for my friend here?" He flaps his hand in Tom's direction.

"Oh." Tom grins like a chimp. "Give me a vodka martini."

"Stop!" says Jim. Tom wonders who he's talking to. The older man squelches a demure burp and continues: "Two things. *One.*" He holds up his index finger. "Martinis are made with gin." Tom shakes his head. He's heard this sort of snobbery before. "And two," the exec adds his pinky to the tally, "Consider grimly the risks involved in ordering such a subtle concoction in an establishment such as this."

"Shaddup, you!" yaps the barmaid. "I make the best martini on the West Coast." She turns her glare on Tom. Jim shrugs, makes a hand washing gesture. His warning has been tendered; he is no longer liable for the outcome.

Tom says, "On second thought, give me a Cape Cod."

The barmaid scowls but goes. Tom watches with grateful amazement as she pours three fingers of vodka into a slender tumbler of ice, cracks open a tiny can of cranberry juice, and splashes in just enough to tint the vodka the faintest shade of pink. "Kind pour," Tom murmurs out of side of his mouth.

"The kindest," Jim replies. "Why do you think I come here?"

Tom looks around. The place isn't all that crowded. At one of the extremely narrow window booths—only room for one person to a side—a small, fat man with big square glasses sits alone. He wears a bolo tie, clasped with a carving in Pacific Northwest Native motif: red and black on a white background. Is it a bear's face? Or a man's? Tom can't tell.

"What are you looking at?" Jim asks, not turning his gaze from the mirror behind the bar.

"Just getting my bearings."

"Don't eyeball the Chief," the older man warns.

"Hunh?"

"He doesn't like to be eyeballed."

"He doesn't look conscious," says Tom.

"Even unconscious he's more conscious than you'll ever be. At his throat he wears the sacred image of Sno-qual, Moon the Transformer," intones the Chief Risk Officer, "Who shaped this world at its creation and shapes it still, some say."

Tom suspects he's getting his chain yanked. "How do you know all this?"

"Cuz I talk to the guy," says Jim, sounding more normal. "He's in here every night. The chief will always be here. As long as there's a Hard Way, and there will always be a Hard Way."

"Damn" Tom says in tones of admiration.

"What?"

"You should've been a poet."

"Who says I'm not?"

"Touché." Tom raises his glass. The ice has melted some, the drink's hardly pink at all now. An electric guitar chord thrums twice, a plaintiff harmonica howls, and off launch Waylon and Willie into their classic live cut of "Whiskey River." *This is what I needed,* thinks Tom, smiling at his glass. He starts swaying his head to the beat. There was a honky-tonk in Belmar that played this song every night. He blurts out loud, "That's what I was going to be."

"What?" says Jim, squinting.

"A poet," Tom declares.

"Oh…" After a moment's blip, Jim's back on track. "Well, who says you're not?"

Tom throws his arms out Christ-like. "The world."

Jim sneers at his drink. "'The world.' What in hell does the 'world' know about poetry?" He takes a long sip, then asks, "Were you any good?"

"Do you honestly think that matters when you're a poet?"

"I honestly do. If you're anything, you should be good at it, right?"

"That's the problem. I couldn't tell."

"*That!*" Jim states emphatically, lifting his drink high, as if it somehow illustrates his point. "Is the problem. Nobody—and I mean *no* one—can completely comprehend, to any meaningful degree, their own impact on the world." Tom sits with this one for a while, until Jim finally pipes up again. "You know who can play a helluva trombone?"

What? "Who?"

"Terry Torgerson," Jim answers, nodding in agreement with himself.

"Yeah. I saw that the other day at the brand rally, actually."

"What if he'd stuck with that?" Jim wonders. "What if Terry Torgerson had given his life to the trombone?"

"The world doesn't give a shit about trombone players." *Or poets*, Tom would add, if he didn't fear seeming bathetic.

"Tell that to Branford Marsalis," says Jim.

"Branford plays sax."

Jim screws his face in consternation. "Well which one plays the trombone?"

"You're sort of making my point."

"Which was?"

"No one gives a shit about tromboners."

Jim shakes his head. He won't be gainsaid. "Branford does okay."

"And by 'Branford' you mean the Marsalis brother who plays the trombone, not the sax?" Only after blurting this does Tom realize how dickish he sounds, but Jim doesn't seem to notice.

"Do you honestly want or hope to do better with your poetry than the Marsalis who plays the trombone does with trombone?"

"We weren't talking about me; we were talking about Terry Torgerson."

"Well, you can argue, kid, I'll give you that. As if *that* were a noble goddamned gift. And we were *so* talking about you. Originally."

"Were we?"

"I'm almost sure of it." Jim lifts one finger. The barmaid walks over. Jim lifts a second digit and points it at the bar. And off she goes to make them another round.

"No, no, no." Tom says, slurring it. "I gotta go." He stands.

"One more's gonna kill ya?"

"Shit." Tom shakes his head.

"Come on." Jim pats Tom's abdicated barstool. "We haven't talked about Maddie yet."

"Were we supposed to?"

"Sit," Jim commands. Tom sits, just as his second triple Cape Cod arrives, in all its pink diamond glory. Jim licks his lips upon sipping from his own fresh drink, then purses them a moment before opening the topic. "So… Maddie Dennett…" Tom nods emphatically, as if he knows exactly what Jim means by this, but the truth is, he's swimming, clueless. "How's that going?"

"I'm learning a lot," Tom admits, but he's determined to stay tight-lipped.

"I'm sure you are. She bustin' your balls?"

Tom smiles ruefully. "A bit."

Jim clinks Tom's glass. "It's probably good for ya."

"Yeah. Probably."

"And how do you like working for the bank?"

"It's good. Best job I've ever had," says Tom and means it.

Jim makes a dubious face. "How long have you had it?"

"A month." Tom smiles the smile of an open fool. "It pays better than any other job I've had."

"And that makes it the *best?*" Jim's incredulous. "Hell, the best job I ever had was shoveling pig shit in Nebraska." He sips and seems to see it in front of him. "I knew what I was supposed to be doing and I did it. Just like everybody else who worked with me. I liked them. And they liked me. And that was all the bonus there was."

"I like Maddie," says Tom, surprising himself.

"Me, too," says Jim.

Tom feels lit enough to risk turning tables. He looks at the side of Jim's face squarely. It's wrinkled, sagging at the jowls, badly blotched with liver spots. *This guy's older than he seems at first.* "So, how do *you* like working at the bank?" he asks.

"I'll like it better in my rearview mirror." Jim's jaw tenses almost imperceptibly.

Tom decides to soft-pedal a bit. "I liked how you ran the All-Staff this morning: no nonsense."

"Thanks." Jim turns to Tom. And for all the booze the man's likely to have had, he takes the younger man in with a gaze that's clear and steady. "I truly wish you well with the bank." He lifts his glass, and Tom clinks it.

"Thank you. Thank you very much."

The juke box thunks and whirs, and suddenly Tom Jones is belting out "What's New Pussy Cat?" Tom starts to giggle.

"You all right, kid?"

"Me? I could not be dandier."

Jim leans in and squints at him. "Tell me something about

yourself."

"What's to tell?"

"Everything's to tell. The world. Life. The good, bad, the sacred, the profane."

"How is one to distinguish?"

"One does one's fucking best. So, to start, tell me something good about yourself."

Tom is nonplussed. He was just sort of going with the jokey flow, but Jim's looking at him as if he is dead serious. *Fucking stone-faced drinkers.* "I'm loyal." It's the best he can come up with.

"Okay." Jim nods, carefully considering this.

"I really am."

"That is indeed good. Loyalty's one of the few things corporate money can't buy." He sips from his drink. "My EA, Juanita, she's loyal. She's been with me 14 years. Gave her a Walther PPK on her tenth anniversary."

Tom can't believe it. *Is he actually going to talk about his gun-giving quirk?* He decides to play ignorant. "You... what?"

"I gave her a sidearm."

"Walther PPK?"

"Yeah."

"Isn't that Double-O Seven's gun?"

"Sure."

"I remember reading one of the Ian Fleming books," says Tom. "And someone mocks Bond for packing that piece. 'Bit of a lady's gun, isn't it?' they said."

"It is a bit of a lady's gun," says Jim. "Juanita's a bit of a lady."

"I hear ya. How does she even type with those nails?"

"Rapidly." Then Jim adds: "It was also the gun that Hitler used to kill himself."

The two of them again go silent. "Up A Lazy River" by the Mills Brothers plays. Tom starts to reel. *Where the hell am I?* He looks over at Jim daintily sipping his gin and tonic. *How is his glass nearly empty again? Hell, how, for that matter, is mine?*

"So what do you do when you aren't working for SeaTru?" asks Jim. "Besides writing poetry, that is."

"Oh, I don't write much these days. I'm a dad and a husband, mostly."

"Nice. How many kids?"

"Just one. She's almost two."

"Ah, great age."

"How 'bout you?"

"What? Kids?"

"Yeah."

"Oh sure. Four. Two girls, two boys. Like a damned china set. All grown now."

"Grandkids?"

"Nope. But one can hope. And that's about all one can do. That's the problem. When you're trying to be a parent, you get to do something fun. When you're trying to be a grandparent... you just have to wait." Again, he lifts two fingers at the barmaid.

"Trying must be nice," Tom says wistfully. "For me it's always been the opposite. Spent most of my 20s desperately trying *not* to get the girls pregnant, while still managing to—"

Jim cuts him off, "I get the picture. But not even with your little one? You didn't try for her?"

"Nope. Complete accident."

"Accident? I'm in Risk Management, kid. No such goddamned thing. Just contingencies unprepared for."

Tom smiles and nods, "That's my sweet girl, Poma. A beautiful, out-of-the-blue contingency unprepared for. I was scared shitless when I found out she was coming."

"Why?"

"How was I gonna pay for it all? Didn't have a clue. But my wife and I made it work. We've always been good at that."

"Well?" Jim says, as though iron-clad evidence has been offered. "That's all any kid can ask of his dad. To do his goddamned best."

The drinks show up. Tom swirls in panic. "No, no, no. I can't. I gotta go."

Jim frowns. "You gonna leave a perfectly good drink untouched?"

Tom shakes his head, blows out a long breath. "Fine." He leans forward and takes a long sip through the tiny red straw. He can taste only the flimsiest hint of promise in its bitterness now.

"My god," says Jim, shaking his head. "What a generation of pussies we've raised."

Tom stands abruptly and wobbles. "Seriously, I gotta go." He takes his wallet from his front pocket, extracts a 20, and drops it daintily on the bar. "Hope that's enough." He looks at the bar's countertop, as if seeing it for the first time, then runs his hand across its texture. *Holy fuck, actual fucking marble?* He pats his pockets to make sure he's got everything: wallet, keys, access badge. Then, taking a chance he pats Jim on the back, saying, "Thanks again. I had a blast."

"Fuck you," the old man deadpans.

Tom stops cold. "I'm sorry?"

"You sure as fuck are," says Jim.

"I'm sorry, Jim. Did I offend you?"

"Put that fucking Jackson back in your wallet right now."

"No, no. You're not buying my drinks."

"I'm your boss's boss and I'm giving you an order." Jim finally turns to face Tom. "You understand me?"

Tom feels a flash of anger, and then just as quickly realizes how foolish that is. *The old man's drunk, is all.* "Okay, okay, fine, Grand-boss." He picks up the 20 and pushes it crumpled into his pocket. "Thank you very kindly for the drinks."

"Fuck you," says Jim again, back to the bar mirror, again no hint of a joke.

"Did I offend you?" Tom repeats sincerely, weaving a bit on his feet.

"Not if you finish your fucking drink."

"I will if I can ask a question."

Jim points at Tom's empty stool. "Sit." Jim points at the Cape Cod. "Drink." Jim makes a gun of his pointing finger, points it at Tom, and depresses his thumb. "Ask."

Tom sits, takes a sip, turns to the older man, concerned, like Jimmy Stewart regarding Mr. Gower in *It's A Wonderful Life*. "How are you getting home?"

Again, Jim replies sternly, "Fuck you."

"I will finish this drink if you tell me you're not driving."

"Fuck you," Jim repeats, and takes another sip. "I don't give a fuck if you finish it or not."

"All right. I'm gonna have that nice bartender lady call you a cab," Tom says, and puts his arm in the air to get the bottle-blonde battle-ax's attention.

"Jesus Christ, kid. Where did you learn your manners? From an after-school special? I don't need a fucking cab because I live four blocks away in the Virginia Inn Towers. And I don't need your fucking 20-dollar bill because I make eight times what you do, *before* bonuses and stock options. Why don't you just—" Jim stops himself. There seems to be an entire opera of thoughts playing inside his liver-spotted skull. Finally he grimaces and shakes it all off. "You know what? Leave the 20 and just go. You're right. You're a big boy now and big boys pay for their drinks. They certainly don't let senescent corporate war whores show a paltry fucking kindness."

Tom pulls the 20 back out of his pocket and lays it on the bar. Then he sits and starts sipping deeply on his drink. After a good long while he says, "Honestly? I don't think I remember what 'senescent' means, if I ever knew."

Jim finally smiles, though still tight-lipped. He nods. "Some fucking poet."

"Retired poet."

"'Retired.'"

"Mostly."

Jim lifts his glass, nearly empty again. "To retirement," he says.

"Hear, hear," responds Tom, then adds, "And to friendship."

Jim turns, and squints at him. He looks ready to call shit on the kid again, but instead, he lifts his glass to clink Tom's and says, "To friendship… wherever it's found." Tom nods. Then Jim, says much louder, "Ain't that right, Chief?" Tom looks through the mirror at the squat, black-haired man in the narrow booth. Eyes blink open behind thick glasses, like an owl suddenly alert. "To friendship wherever it's found," Jim hollers. "Eh?"

The Indian answers, high-timbred and clear, "Goddamn right, boss!" He lifts his empty glass in the direction of Jim's. "Goddamn right!"

After that last round, Tom finally left the old man to his gin-and-tonic vigil and staggered his way up to Crack Alley, wondering if he just drank himself out of a job.

8.

Green Fire

The next few weeks are a seemingly ceaseless slog, working for Maddie in the morning and Michelle in the afternoon. Tom figures he's never deserved a happy hour more. Besides, the last two nights he's come home, as early as he could manage under the ever-increasing crush of his double assignment, Kona's been in bed with the covers up over her head. He has his customary brace of martinis at the Nantucket, then considers hitting the Hard Way. The only problem is that he has no idea where he stands with Jim Verhoeven, his two bosses' boss. Since leaving the bar that night under a boozy cloud of acrimony, he hasn't heard boo from the old man. And the not knowing is starting to wrack Tom's nerves. He needs to find out where he actually stands. He should just go. Or should he? He can't decide. He digs a nickel from his pocket. Heads he goes; tails he heads home. He flips it. It's tails. He goes, finds the CRO holding court on his stool next to black-haired Sissy, happily hollering through the bar mirror at the Chief sitting in his regular booth.

After Anna brings Tom a tall, palest-pink Cape Cod, Jim turns to scrutinize him. "So, I come to find out you support not one, but two of my direct reports. How's that work?"

Tom shrugs. "It works. Sorta."

"But how's it going?"

"It's going."

"What are you? A teenager? Give me data: details."

"Michelle's great. She's very nice."

"Unlike Maddie?"

"Oh, I wouldn't say Maddie isn't nice. It's just not the first word leaps to mind."

"Right... And what else?"

"Whaddya mean?"

"What else do you think about Michelle?"

"Nothing. Is there something else I *should* think?"

Jim turns back to his drink, lifts it but doesn't sip. Instead he shakes his head.

"What do you want me to say?" Tom asks. He wonders if he's blushing but figures he's safe in the Hard Way's red neon glow. "You want me to say she's attractive? Is that it?"

"Kid, I don't give a shit what you think about women."

Beware the stone-faced drunk, Kavanagh. Beware. Because you, my friend, are anything but, blathering your blarney until you've sorted your heart out in front of everyone.

"Yeah, she's attractive," Tom allows. "For what it's worth."

"Oh, it's worth a lot."

"Okay, I'm gonna invoke the sacred confidentiality of the bar and ask you, do you have a thing for this woman?"

Jim turns again to face him, pointing a finger at Tom's nose for emphasis. "Let me tell you something, my young friend. I have been married for 43 years. And in that entire time, I have never once been unfaithful to my wife."

"Fair enough. Sorry. Crossed a line. I'm a little tipsy."

Jim waves his hands in irritable absolution. "But!" he says, and now he points his finger at the sky, "As a Jesuit priest once said to me: 'Just because a man is on a diet doesn't mean he can't look at the menu.'" Tom blows a lazy raspberry. "That woman..." Jim continues. "That woman... is the kind of woman that a man abandons any and all sense of decency simply to be with... for as long or as short a time as she chooses to be with him."

"Okay."

Jim ignores Tom's interjection: He's not done. "She is the kind of woman, that whether or not you ever spent any intimate time with her, at the moment of your death, when the angels and/or demons come to take you, and they say, 'But wait. We have an offer: You can live another life if you wish.' Before taking it, you would make sure that you could get the same deal for her."

"Wow."

"That said," says Jim, taking another a sip and licking his lips for emphasis. "I really don't know her very well. She only just joined my direct reports maybe a year and a half ago."

. . .

With those all-too-kindly Hard Way pours sloshing on top of the two huge Nantucket martinis, Tom's pretty lit as he heads up the hill. He's expecting static or silence from Kona and is prepared for either. Instead he finds her in a bit of a party mood, having already polished off half a bottle of white. She's kept dinner warm for him and has another bottle in the fridge. As he eats and drinks, she tells him she's found them a house in Green Lake, but they have to move this weekend.

"It's Thursday," he protests.

"I know, it's a pain in the ass, but we can do it. A lot of our New York stuff is still in storage." His head is swimming; his gut is doing the wine-on-top-of-cocktails crawl. This is too much. He's working ten and twelve-hour days. He'd have to work all weekend to move them, and even then, how would he get it all done? "We can do it," she says, reading his pained face.

"So much for hitting my rhythm," he mutters petulantly into his wine glass, then drains it. Then fills it again.

"We'll be in Green Lake," she offers.

"We'll need a car," he complains.

"I bought one today." Tom puts his glass down and looks at her. She smiles sheepishly. "What? We can afford it."

"You didn't even ask me?"

"I used my money." Tom makes a face at the concept. "I have my own money, you know," she says. "I didn't want to stress you out."

"Too late."

"Please don't stress."

"This is a lot."

"This is life," she responds with a sigh.

He makes another face, skeptical.

"It's a good thing," she says.

·   ·   ·

It was a brutal weekend. Tom worked 13 hours straight, two days in a row, schlepping boxes and furniture up I-5 in a borrowed truck, and unloading them into the new rental house in Green Lake. By Sunday evening he's wrecked.

Bright and early on Monday he catches his new bus, the 16. Maddie's on vacation for a week, so he works the entire day outside Michelle's office. On Tuesday, she's gone, too, to Manhattan for meetings with titles like "Driving the Secondary and Tertiary Derivative Markets Consolidation" and "Maximizing Collateral Swap Modeling."

With the work so much lighter, Tom catches up quickly, and even lets himself doodle some notes for a poem in a comp book he ordered from the supply catalog. He has also started keeping a small pocket notebook for the same purpose. Maddie introduced him to the Moleskine brand and now he's addicted to its subtly superior quality. He jots in his notebooks, big and small, at the bus stop, on the bus, at lunch, and even sometimes in his cube when things are slow and no one's looking. He's trying to capture the simple, the raw, and the fresh: the everyday Seattle things he sees. What William Carlos Williams would call "the gist."

Michelle is back on Thursday. Together they work closely to clean up her calendar. She leans over his desk, right next to him, a single delicate mole pulsing lightly on the skin of her exposed neck. There's a fragrance, floral, but faint: not perfume, he doesn't think, but warm. Is that possible? Can he really smell the warmth of her skin? The poet in Tom rankles. *Anyone who presumes to put smells into words is delusional.*

Tom skips the Hard Way that night, an abstinence which only puts him in more of a party mood on Friday. In his new backyard he grills some ribeyes Kona picked up at Costco, and they chat happily as they eat and share a bottle of Malbec. But Kona falls asleep with Poma while reading to her in her new "big girl bed."

It's 9:30 and still bright outside. Tom fills a flask with green chartreuse and heads out to roam his new neighborhood in the midsummer gloaming. The variety of architecture to be found within even just one small Seattle neighborhood is astounding for anyone who's grown up on the East Coast. In Tangletown, just west of their rental, the houses range from cozy Northwest Craftsmen to overblown Victorians to gargantuan Bauhaus blocks that take up the entire lot and look more like medical/dental buildings than homes. Pretty much the only idea unifying the designs is privilege.

As the darkness sneaks in from the corners of the night, lights on the insides flick on, effusing coziness through the windows. He suddenly wants to know every story each glowing pane signifies, even as he pushes down the bitter ache he feels from the fact that, as things are going, he'll never be able to own a home. He sips some more green from his flask and lets it light up his insides with happy summer Christmas fire. Yup, a poem for every glow, he decides, stalking along the sidewalks in long strides. Brick by brick he'll build an epic about Seattle, a la Williams's *Paterson*.

No! A whole series of epic poems. A multi-volume magnum opus. Each volume encompassing a neighborhood. Tangletown itself will need to run hundreds of pages. How many lives have filtered—are still filtering—through?

He wants to imagine every single one of them. His heart is swollen, is ripe to be ripped open, as though sewn to be torn that way. A tearaway heart.

I should write that down.

With a soft-leaded pencil stub dug from his pocket he scrawls loopily into his mini notebook. "A tear-away heart is a terrible thing."

He's running along Meridian. He's on fire, but unconsumed by it: the burning bush. He's running past the bar where the Honey Bear Bakery used to be. (He had such a crush on one of the girls who worked there in the early '90s, streak of lavender in her soft brown hair, a different thrift-store frock every morning.) But tonight he has no need to seek the solace of the pub and its people. The green has set him loose. He's feral. He's running through the orchard next to Bastyr College. His head hits a dangling apple. He laughs: Pain's just another form of fire.

He sprints to the middle of the grassy field and falls, spreading his arms and legs and goggling up at the sky. He kicks and punches at it, laughing tears of gratitude. He nearly succumbs to the ground's damp softness but abruptly scrambles back to his feet and points them north. He will sleep beneath the sky tonight, but not here. He has his own little plot of grass now. (The chartreuse, he knows, will bring him wild dreams of great beauty and bone-zero meaning.)

He wants to fuck all the women, wrestle all the men. He wants to spin all the children by the arms and sing them stories to set their heads and hearts on fire just like his is, tonight, for no reason, for no one. Who can he share it with? It's nearing midnight. His wife—he has a wife! How absurd is that?—will be dead asleep when he gets home, but his heart will still be on fire. Why does everyone go to bed so early in this town? He keeps pumping his legs northerly. His heart pounds and yearns for yet more pounding. *The stars are wheeling. Close enough to touch.*

Aye, you have the heart of a poet, Kavanagh. That's sure. But do you have the talent? The drive? The will?

William Carlos Williams had the will. He'd scribble out verse on prescription pads between patients.

"William *willed* himself. Can you do that? Or do you just have terminal poet's heart?" Tom realizes he's arguing out loud with himself.

"It's time to go home, brother."

And so he does. When he reaches the soft, newly sodded grass of his backyard, he falls to his knees, stretches out, and dives into darkness.

9.
Summer Running

Does it need saying that Saturday is a greasy, queasy, head-pounding ordeal of a day? And yet, somehow in the afternoon Tom comes up with the ill-conceived notion that exercise is the cure. So, he starts out for a jog around Green Lake. He doesn't even make it as far as the ball fields before he has to run to the water's edge and puke. Wiping his mouth on his T-shirt as he staggers back to the path, he gets some pitying looks from a pair of power walkers. "Fuck you," he mutters, but they've already waddled on.

Hobbling home, he makes a solemn promise to himself. He's going to cut down on drinking and power up on jogging. And not just on weekends. He's got to work it into his weekday routine somehow, or it's never going to become part of his rhythm.

On Sunday Tom plants a small vegetable garden along the eastern fence of their new back yard, reserving the small patch at the bottom of the kitchen steps for wildflower seeds, which he convinces Poma to help him spread.

On Monday, when the alarm goes off at 5:45 a.m., Tom surprises himself by rousting for a run. Behind the blinds the sky looks gloomy: typical Seattle "June-uary" weather. Over a raggy, long-sleeved thermal undershirt he pulls on his *Purple Rain* tour T-shirt. He swaps out the boxers he slept in for some briefs and an old pair of gym shorts. His running shoes are pretty worn out, but he promises himself that if he can make it through this first week, he'll buy a nice new pair at the fancy-pants running shop.

It's maybe 50 degrees when he steps out the front door, with more of a wind than he'd like, but fuck it, he'll warm up once he gets moving. He heads counterclockwise toward the community center. *Once around. That's all. An easy three miles. At whatever pace you can manage.* About ten minutes in, his legs commence complaint, shortly thereafter his lungs join the choir, but at least now he's warm. He's made it to the community center. So far so good. The boat rental hut is coming up. Now he's past that, too.

That's it. That's how it's done, son. One thing at a time.

He sees a woman running across the grass toward the lake path. Fluorescent teal jacket and black hash marks climbing up her gray running pants.

Damn. Nice ass.

Recognition jolts him hard. It's Michelle. He turns immediately, and jogs down to the edge of the lake, quickly bending into a lunge, as if stretching out a cramp. He doesn't think she's seen him. He watches her continue around the lake in the direction he was heading. Now he can't go that way. What if she turned around? It would look like he was stalking her. He turns in the opposite direction, freezes, turns back. He's stalled, smack in the middle of the path. A bicyclist barrels past him, ding-ding-ding-ing. "You're in the wheels lane." Tom can't even manage a proper "Go fuck yourself!" He decides to head in the opposite direction after all, his heart thumping as much from this fresh shot of adrenaline as from the effort of running.

He just keeps going. He's barely feeling it. This is more exercise than he's had in years. He runs past the houses fronting the lake, with their vast porches and their brightly colored ginger-breading and their million-dollar mortgages.

What's the plan? Now you're heading to run straight into her.

So? So why would that be weird? I'm just jogging. She's just jogging. Thousands of people run Green Lake every day.

Fine. Just try and not let your boner show in your gym shorts.

I do not have a boner.

It's at least a chubby.

Fine. It's a chubby. Fuck! Shut up!

Tom narrows his focus. He's picked up his pace considerably.
He's past the church. Now he's past the park bathroom with the
metal prison toilet. His calves are howling. His shitty shoes are
starting to feel like sacks of gravel.

God! Of all days to dress like a hobo.

He's coming up on the old Aqua Theater, where that plaque
says Led Zeppelin once played.

God. Perfect curves. Like some sort of comic book superheroine.

Fuck!

Get it together, Kavanagh!

You *get it together!*

He continues along the main path behind the concrete viewing
stands, and on past the canoe and kayak clubhouse, and leaves the
bathrooms behind, though he really does have to go. He doesn't
want to miss her coming in the other direction. So, even with this
burning in his lungs, and the knife in his ribs, and his bladder fit to
burst, he keeps running.

He's paralleling Aurora Avenue now, halfway around from the
community center. She didn't seem to be running slow. Why hasn't
he seen her yet?

Tom's heard that when you're starting out running, you're
supposed to alternate ten minutes of walking with ten minutes of
jogging, but he doesn't want to be walking when she passes. Still,
he's got to take a break. He gradually slows his pace to walking,
which he does for what he figures is ten minutes. He'll have to remember to buy a cheapo digital watch for next time.

She ain't on this path anymore, dude. She must have peeled off.

Tom gives up. It's a relief, if he's honest. He turns around and
walks back in the direction of the house. Sweat pours down his face.
His shirts are soaked through. He looks like he just dove in the lake.

Back at boathouse he stops to finally piss in the men's room.
Then he takes the short cut over the wooden dock through the am-
phitheater. Some people are running the steep risers of the grand-
stand; others are stretching or just sitting on the concrete risers.
About a third of the way up he sees Michelle rubbing her calf.

Damn. What should I—

Tom shakes away the thought, jogs up briskly, and says, "Hello."
It takes her a moment, but then she smiles. "Hi, Tom! How
are you?" Her cheeks are glowing from the run.

"I'm well. Great minds think alike, hunh?" She tilts her head.
He explains: "I mean like jogging around the lake at the crack of
dawn."

"Ah, right," she smiles. "Yeah, I'm trying to get back in the
habit while the weather's so nice."

"Yeah me too." He glances down at his soaked Prince T-shirt
and dies a little. Michelle winces and grabs at her leg. "You okay?"
he asks.

"Yeah. Just a cramp. Shit." She sucks in a quick breath as the
charley horse grips, then bends over and rubs her leg more vigorously. She looks back up at him. "Sorry."

"For what."

"Cussing."

"You're kidding, right?" he says, grinning. "Did you get enough
to drink?" She looks confused. Again, he hastens to explain, "You
gotta hydrate when you run. Before *and* after."

"Ah. Okay." She inhales deeply, then suddenly lets out the tini-
est, most heart-breaking little yelp. Tom realizes she's started to sob.
Aw shit.

"Hey…" he says, helpless.

"Please," she holds out a hand and covers her face with the
other. Tom looks away, out across the lake. Hills of houses rise
from it on all sides. The breeze on his sweaty back gives him a
sudden chill. He hears her laughing, looks and sees her shaking
her head. "You must think I'm utterly psycho."

"It's been a rough couple of weeks."

"You don't know the half of it."

"I'm sure I don't." Tom takes a deep breath and figures it's
best to quit her company while he's still ahead. "Is there anything
I can do for you?" Inadvertently, the executive assistant tone has
snuck into his voice. He can see she heard it.

"No," she says, her tone changing, too. "I'm fine. I'm just gonna sit here and stretch for a little bit."

"Okay." He's sticking with the chipper voice, for better or worse. And then he's hopping agilely down the steep risers and running along the dock to where it picks up the muddy path back to the main asphalt loop. He keeps up this brisk pace until he's certain she's a good quarter mile behind, then hobbles the rest of the way home.

At work, neither of them mentions their morning encounter.

•   •   •

Tom starts running regularly—early every morning, once around the lake—while trying not to dwell on how eager he is to bump into Michelle again. On Saturday morning he buys some quality running shoes. Test-driving them that afternoon, he decides to shake up his route, doing his best to delude himself that the deviation has nothing to do with the fact that Green Lake will be packed with weekend tourists, and he's unlikely to run into Michelle. Instead, he heads straight down Ravenna Boulevard, down the middle of the stately tree-lined greenway separating the lanes. On a brilliant sunny day like today, if he keeps his gaze forward and ignores the cars and bicyclists on either side, it can feel like he's running through an arbor at Versailles.

At Cowan Park he heads down into the ravine, where the trees form an even richer canopy. Normally deserted, the dirt path today is clogged with jogging groups, pelotons of mountain bikes, and, worst of all, gaggles of dog-walkers, fully halted and blocking the path to chat and watch their mutts sniff each other's butts, as though they were admiring gifted children at play. Tom elbows his way past as another jogger pushes by from the other direction. A familiar jolt hits him. It's Michelle. Tom pegs his eyes forward. Once clear, he keeps running. Maybe he'll get away. But then he hears "Tom!" And he stops. "Hey," she says, jogging up to him. It's unspeakable how good her cleavage looks in that tank top—light sheen of sweat, dew on fruit. "Are you stalking me?" she smiles, panting.

His heart kicks idiotically. "No. How would I…" The dogs, and their fur-less parents, have parted and dispersed.

"I'm kidding, Tom, of course."

"Right." He relaxes a bit. *Idiot, stop gawking!*

"You headed back to Green Lake?"

"Yup," he lies. She must know this, given the direction he was running, but he's shooting for casual.

"Want some company?" she asks, making casual look easy.

"Sure."

They jog up out of the ravine together, and on through the glowing green tunnel of the boulevard. Once they pass underneath I-5, Tom slows down and points a bit south of west. "I'm that way."

"Oh, toward the Latona Pub?"

"Well, yeah, I guess."

"I love that place. Wanna grab a beer?"

"Uh... I'm not carrying any cash."

Michelle reaches behind her and pulls out a SeaTru credit card. "Sneaky back pocket! Come on. I owe you at least a beer for all the help you've been giving me since Amy—" She stops short.

He quickly fills the gap. "Yeah, okay." They walk the rest of the way in silence as a vast tower of clouds rolls over them.

At the Latona, Michelle orders a Hefeweizen, so Tom figures *when in Rome*. When the two hazy brews arrive wearing their lemon wedge caps, Tom thinks of Kona for an instant. He couldn't say why. He lifts his glass in a wordless toast, and Michelle clinks it. "You have a family, right?" she asks, after sipping.

"I do." He tells her about Kona and Poma and their new house just a few blocks away. She tells him she lives near the lake as well. "Yeah? Where?" he tries not to seem too curious.

"75th, a couple blocks in," she says. "Between Orin and Meridian. We got it for a song before things started going crazy in Seattle." She says this as if offering an excuse. "It was a fixer-upper and Nathan did a lot of work on it." Michelle goes on to tell Tom about her husband, a pediatric neurosurgeon.

"What does he do for fun?" Tom asks, half joking.

Michelle smiles sheepishly. "He's an Iron Man competitor."

Of course he is. "Oh." *Christ.*

"I wish I were kidding."

"I sort of wish you were, too." He laughs. "I only *sort* of know what that is, but I still know it's badassed."

Michelle nods. "He runs a hundred miles a week."

"That's about what I do," Tom deadpans. She smiles, eyeing him, touching the tip of her tongue to one of her incisors.

"And then when he competes, he runs a hundred miles in a day," she adds.

"Oh." Tom can't tell if she's bragging or not. She seems pretty matter-of-fact about it. Almost jaded.

"Yeah, so..." She sips her golden cloud. "Maybe needless to say, it's been a little intimidating to take up running again."

"I hear ya."

Michelle tells Tom about how her daughter Bridgette, who goes to Brown, is currently home from school after her freshman year, working as an intern for the state.

"Down in Olympia?"

"Only occasionally. She's with Commerce, which is headquartered in Seattle."

"Ah."

She tells him about her son Jason who goes to Roosevelt, going to be a junior in September.

Tom recounts his days as a stay-at-home dad, watching *Dr. Phil* and *Oprah* and taking daily barf baths. She laughs heartily, utterly unselfconscious in a way she never allows herself at the office. "And your wife, what's she like?" She looks at him directly when she asks, genuinely interested.

"Her name's Kona," he answers.

"What a beautiful name."

"Well, she's a beautiful girl... woman... person."

"'Woman's fine," she says. He feels suddenly shabby. "You'll have to show me some pictures at work next week. You don't keep any outside my office."

"Well, it's not really my cubicle."

"I understand, it just... feels weird, like you're just..."

"Just what?"

"Temping there."

"I am. Right?"

"Right. I'm just... I depend so much on you; it'd be nice to— I don't know—know more about you."

"What would you like to know?"

"I heard you're a poet."

"Who'd you hear that from?"

"Jim Verhoeven, I think? Now how does *he* of all people know that and I don't?"

"Maybe he's a poetry fan."

"Somehow I doubt it."

"I'm kidding. I told him," Tom says.

"Hmmm."

Tom decides not to cough up the Hard Way relationship. "I don't write much these days."

"That's too bad. Are we keeping you too busy?"

"Definitely. Still, I manage to scratch things down when I can. Like William Carlos Williams." She goes blank. "He was a poet, early 20th century. But mostly he was a doctor. He had very little time to write, so he would jot down notes on prescription pads between house calls and at the end of the day squeeze in a few hours at the typewriter after his wife and sons went to bed. He's my favorite poet."

"Really?"

"Really." He gives it a moment, then asks. "Who's yours?"

She grimaces. "Shakespeare?" Then seeing his reaction, "Emily Dickenson?"

"Are you asking or telling?"

"I don't know. I don't know anything about poetry, and your favorite poet's someone I've never even heard of."

"So?"

"So that's intimidating."

"It doesn't matter. With poetry you get to totally go with your gut. If you told me you liked limericks, or filthy haiku written by dirty old Zen monks, I'd have to respect that. That's the rule."

"Whose rule?"

"Kavanagh's rule."

"Okay. I'll go with dirty old Zen monks then."

"Good."

. . .

Next Monday Tom plops a worn, dog-eared, binder-clipped packet of paper on Michelle's desk. "What's this?" she asks.

"That... is my treasured Xeroxed copy of Ikkyū."

"'Icky —?'"

"'You.' Yes. My dear friend and fellow poet J. Wilburn made that for me from his college library's copy." Michelle picks up the worn packet cautiously and inspects it like an artifact. Tom explains: "You said filthy haiku written by dirty old Zen monks was your favorite kind of poetry."

"Did I?"

"You did. I bet you didn't think the genre existed."

"I actually didn't."

"Well it does, and Ikkyū is its master."

"Well, thank you, I—" she looks perplexed. Did he overstep?

He plunges ahead, in for a penny. "Keep it for as long as you want. But that is my only copy. It has all my notes. Which you should ignore."

"I'll do my best. And I'll... get this back to you as soon as possible."

"No hurry."

10.

The Fourth

Tom had hoped Maddie might cut him a break with her half of the workload during his time doing double duty, but no such luck. (If he had someone to joke to about it, he would tell them that he's basically a prison bitch on loan to another bubba who's still expected to service his daddy full-time.) Maddie has loaded him up with PowerPoint decks to develop, intricately linked spreadsheets to build, complex meetings to schedule, and on and on.

One morning she tells him to put together 20 binders for a presentation she and Al will be giving to the Board of Directors' Sub-Committee on Risk. He has to reserve a conference room just to pull all the materials together. Darlene drops by to offer sardonic condolences, and they chat a bit. He tells her how he's been enjoying his late evenings watering the new sod in his yard.

"Why not just let your grass burn out in the summer like everyone else in Seattle?"

"I can't. I haven't had a lawn since I was a kid."

"Where'd you grow up?"

"New Jersey." Darlene arches an eyebrow. "Don't even start. People who make fun of New Jersey have no clue about New Jersey. I grew up in Manasquan on the Jersey shore, and if there's a town more like Bedford Falls, I haven't found it."

"Bedford Falls?"

"The town in *It's a Wonderful Life?*"

"Never seen it."

"You're shitting me."

"Nope."

"You are absolutely shitting me." She shrugs. "Where did you grow up?"

"Kentucky."

"And you live in Seattle now?"

"Kenmore actually."

"Where's that?"

"Right at the top of Lake Washington. You need to get out of the city more."

"How is it up there?"

"We like it."

"Who's we?"

"My husband and I."

"No kids?"

"No thank you. He's a middle-school teacher. He gets his kid fix, and then some, every day."

"And *you?*"

"No desire whatsoever. I've seen what they grow into. Just let it die for Christ's sake."

"What?"

"Your lawn, jackass."

"I can't. It's fresh sod. It'd be like killing a baby."

"It ain't your lawn. Your landlady's just conned you into paying for it."

"True, true." Tom enjoys Darlene's acerbity. She reminds him of Jersey girls; but inevitably she has to cut their bantering short whenever Lou bellows from his office. (It's prison bitchery all the way around.)

One afternoon he happens to knock over Amy's desk lamp and finds a key taped underneath. He tries it in all of the locks in the cube: desk drawers, credenza, file cabinet. Nothing. In the copy room he checks the file cabinets labeled "Market Risk." Still no go. When Michelle leaves her office for a two-hour meeting in another building, he dithers for about two seconds before hurriedly succumbing to temptation—*if you're gonna do it, do it.* In Michelle's office, after closing the door, he quickly finds that the key opens the cherry-wood credenza behind her desk. Personal stuff including a change of casual clothes: jeans, a "SeaTru Fun Run" T-shirt, a fleece jacket, white cotton underwear, and a set of work-out clothes. Buried beneath it all is a dark, nearly black, wooden case. If Tom didn't know better he'd swear it was ebony. *Couldn't be. That's illegal, right?* Tom opens it. Inside, resting on a bed of indigo velvet is the kind of revolver a Wild West gunslinger might strap: metal the color of midnight, inlaid with silver filigree and what looks like—*couldn't be*—a genuine ivory grip. Tom gingerly lifts the weapon, which is slightly oily to the touch. The dedication plate in the top of the box is the same bluish-black metal. The silver engraving reads, "To my straight-shooting Deputy Sheriff of Risk, Michelle McGinnis Fleischer." Tom closes the box, closes the drawer, and locks it. He puts the key in an envelope and puts the envelope in the bottom drawer of dead Amy's desk.

•   •   •

Two mornings this week, Tom's bumped into Michelle running, and both times they've casually decided to finish their lake loop together. Sometimes they talk, but mostly they just run in silence. It feels good. Calm. And it doesn't hurt that they can feel their bodies getting stronger. The only downside for Tom is his ever-growing infatuation. He knows it's stupid, pointless, possibly even destructive: grinding him down in some minimal way, but the jagged electricity of it helps him get through the boredom and soul-suckery of his corporate day, like booze or caffeine without the usual side effects.

At Thursday's Hard Way happy hour Jim V. slides an envelope along the bar to him. "What's this?" Tom asks.

"VIP passes to the SeaTru fireworks show. I can't use 'em. Heading to Arizona for the long weekend."

"Really? Thanks!"

"Enjoy."

Every Fourth of July, SeaTru foots the bill for the fireworks show over Lake Union. Tom's been before but always crowded in with the rest of the unwashed masses clinging to the grassy hills of Gas Works Park. It'll be nice to have some comfortable seats, plus parking and refreshments, as promised by the brochure tucked in with the tickets.

Tom drives the family in the red beater Honda Kona bought into a special lot reserved for SeaTru VIPs. From there it's a short walk to the hulking towers of Gas Works: a steampunk fantasy land of rusting smokestacks, pipes, valves, and gaskets, arranged in an interconnecting confusion. Tom recalls the PowerPoint chart of SeaTru's various loan tracking systems.

Beyond the VIP cordon there are complimentary hotdogs and hamburgers, and freshly grilled corn on the cob. Tallboy cans of Bud are pushed into ice piled into kitschy galvanized steel tubs, and caterers dressed in overalls roam the roped-off section with trays of wine in plastic glasses. Kona seems genuinely impressed. She takes a glass of white; Tom grabs himself a Bud.

Tom spots Maddie with a large, serious, Santa Claus-looking fellow who must be her husband, Harrison. He guides Kona and Poma over and makes the introductions. Maddie, cocked eyebrow, asks, "I thought this was SVPs and above."

Tom is reluctant to betray his hook-up but can't see a way around it. "Jim Verhoeven gave me his passes." Maddie frowns, nodding.

Making their way to the picnic tables, Tom spots Michelle and calls out "Hey, there!" And to Kona, "This is my extra boss, the reason I'm working so much overtime."

"Oh god," Michelle says, shaking Kona's hand. "You have every reason to hate me, I guess."

"Hate *and* love," Kona replies adroitly. "After all, that overtime is coming in mighty handy these days." They each smile, taking the other in.

Michelle gestures to the teenager diddling on a Blackberry next to her. "This is my son, Jason." Jason waves his hand limply without looking up. "He can't be bothered with human interaction lately."

"Where's Nathan?" Tom asks. "I was looking forward to meeting him."

"Dad always works the emergency room on holidays," Jason chimes in, without looking away from his screen.

Michelle explains, "It's his way of giving one or two of the residents a break to be with their families."

"That's awfully nice," says Kona.

"Awfully nice for the residents and their families. Yes." Michelle smiles wryly to show she takes it all in stride. "And my daughter hates fireworks so she stayed at home."

"Too evocative of the actual tools of hegemonic violence, she would say." The kid has finally looked up from his device. Tom is struck by how much of Michelle's beauty he's inherited: the same dark blue eyes, the same thick brown hair, and perfect cheekbones.

From her daddy's arms Poma reaches out to the boy with a finger trailing a string of drool from her mouth. "Guh!" she says.

"Oooh," says Kona. "Someone likes you."

"All the girls like Jason," Michelle shrugs.

Later, when Kona takes Poma for a diaper change, Tom strolls along the concrete bunker-like structures closer to the water's edge. Down on the lower level, practically even with lake, Tom sees Michelle's son surrounded by a gaggle of teenage girls. He's laughing and flirting with them like a rock band manager might schmooze a bunch of groupies: not particularly interested for himself, but still keenly engaged.

It's darker. Almost time for the show. Tom gazes south, toward the downtown skyline glimmering in the deepening blue. A closer pulsing glow catches the bottom edge of his eye. He looks down to see Jason's face partially lit by a lighter. *Shit, kid's firing up a bowl.* Now he can smell it. He's fascinated, but he doesn't want to get caught watching. He's about to go when Jason spots him. The teenager boldly holds the bowl up and waves him down. Tom makes a "no thanks" gesture. As he goes he hears Jason say, "That's my mom's secretary," which triggers a burst of laughter from the gaggle.

Back at their seats, Poma on his lap, Tom feels rattled, then irritated. He can't help thinking that kid might best be served by a swift boot up his ass. He thinks of the story his brother Jamie told about when their father, the principal of their small town's high school, caught Jamie smoking pot on school grounds. "You risk my livelihood and the livelihood of this entire damned family 'cuz you wanna show off for some trim?"

"Naw, dad. I'm sorry. I'll never do it again."

"You can goddamned well say that again. You and me. The beach. 6:00 a.m."

And so it was, that next morning, or so says Jamie: "Pushups and wind sprints until I dry heaved."

"Why didn't you just say, 'fuck that?'" Tom asked.

"And defy the old man? Shit! He just didn't last long enough to teach you what a stupid question that is. Kid, that man was the quartermaster on a ship that delivered by dead reckoning the U.S. 1st Infantry to Omaha Beach. You were ten when he kicked it. Still a boy. And Mom's a coddler. Dad was after making men."

"So what's your excuse?"

"I didn't say he always succeeded, Princess Poetess."

When the fireworks start, Poma goes stiff sitting in Tom's lap. Enraptured? Terrified? Maybe both, but fascinated for sure. The colors cascade across their entire field of vision, so close they can feel them thump in their chests. Tom loves it. He suspects his baby girl does too, even though she clutches one of his fingers tightly in each of her fists. Kona, on the other hand, keeps her fingers pointedly pushed into her ears for the entire display.

Traffic home is murder. It takes them two hours to drive the 25 blocks to their house. Once in the driveway, Kona gently lifts a dead-asleep Poma from her car seat and takes her directly inside. Back in their bedroom, she strips off her shorts, blouse, and bra and collapses into their bed in just her panties. "You coming?" she asks. But Tom knows she means to sleep, and he's restless again.

"Nah, I'm gonna have a nightcap or something." He fills his flask with green chartreuse and heads out, locking the front door behind him. He knows full well where he's headed, even though he doesn't want to admit it to himself. He encounters no one on the dark path around the lake, but in all directions he hears amateur fireworks going off; occasional blossoms of color spurt from Phinney Ridge.

When he figures he's reached the right street, Tom pulls off the lake path and strides up the steep hill, lined on both sides with houses so big and old they seem out of place in this young city. At the top he turns right and there it is: tasteful slate blue with white trim, wrap-around porch ample enough for a cocktail party of 40. Lights still gleam in the living room and in one of the upstairs windows. The moon, nearly full, hangs above. *What a stupidly beautiful house. What an awful lot to want.*

What are you doing, Kavanagh? You gotta stop this bullshit yearning or be consumed by it. You got shit to do. There's a poet somewhere out there in the future you need to will yourself into being, just like Bill Williams willed himself. And who knows? Maybe that could bring you some sort of life you could love. All this goddamned wanting. It's seducing you, sucking you down. It feels huge, and awesome, but it just widens the empty in you. You have a pretty wife who loves you. You have a little girl whom you adore and who adores you right back. You live in the cutest little cottage in all of Green Lake. You don't need an understated mansion with the wrap-around porch to be happy, because if you did, you never would be.

Then and there, staring at that perfect porch, he resigns himself to what he's got to do, and thus resolved, he turns his back on the house and heads back down the hill and around the lake with a feeling of determination bordering on sobriety.

•   •   •

On Monday morning's run, Tom heads south instead of north, catching the Burke-Gilman Trail. He runs west along the ship canal, into Ballard, and then on to Golden Gardens. He goes seven miles or more. He's exhausted but feels fantastic, despite his big sore heart. He knows he's doing the right thing.

He runs every morning now, but never again around Green Lake. It's either the Burke-Gilman, or down Ravenna and through Cowan Park, or just the neighborhoods of Phinney, Wallingford, and Tangletown.

Michelle is cordial at work, even friendly. She doesn't mention not seeing Tom around the lake anymore, or at least not until late one Friday afternoon, when finally, she asks: "You still running?"

One sharp thump of the heart and Tom answers, all innocence: "I am. Yeah."

"Oh, well good."

"Not around the lake though."

"Oh." She's rifling through papers in a tray on his counter, but he knows there's nothing of interest in there. And he knows she knows he knows.

"I'm trying to get more hills in and stretch my distances. And, you know, get some new scenery." He sees her blink at this last comment. *Shit, dick!* "I mean…"

"Oh, no, I get it," she says, still nodding, still pointlessly rifling through the papers. He feels warmth flush over his face, and when she finally looks at him he can see she sees he's blushing.

Fuck it. "I don't think you do."

"No?"

"Can we uh… Can I talk with you privately?"

She frowns. "Sure."

Tom stands and walks into her office. Michelle follows. He looks at the door; she shuts it. He says, "I'm gonna sit. Is that okay?"

"Sure."

He takes the chair facing her desk, but Michelle goes to perch on the small couch looking out over Benaroya Hall. She turns to face Tom squarely. He starts: "I…" She just keeps staring at him. He breathes deep and comes out with it: "I have feelings for you. I know they are not rational; I know they are not appropriate; and I know they are baseless; but I have them, and, in order to deal with them, I have to acknowledge them."

She's completely still. She might be listening to a briefing on overnight LIBOR spreads for all her expression betrays. He keeps going. "I understand these feelings are unrequited and unwelcome." Is he repeating himself? He's not sure. "So… I felt like I needed to take action. And that's why I stopped coming to the lake. I'm... being honest in order to avoid any additional impropriety and embarrassment. Although..." *Although I don't know how you could be more embarrassed than I am at this moment. What the fuck were you thinking, Kavanagh?!?* He shrugs. Utterly at a loss. "Anyway. That's really... all I have. I apologize for... I apologize." Finally, she moves, but only to nod, very slightly. He stands. He's said all he had to say. But her silence compels him idiotically forward: "This is a workplace. We're colleagues. So far, I've done nothing inappropriate, and certainly you've done nothing inappropriate, and so, I want you to know, that you—" He stops, suddenly realizing that the more he tries to sound non-threatening the more he sounds like he is, in fact, actually threatening her.

Fuck!

Michelle nods again: concerned frown, like she's just been told a branch teller's been pocketing cash. "I really appreciate your frankness, Tom. I don't know that... I would've had the courage... to be so honest, if... if the roles were reversed."

Catch that? The roles are not, in fact, reversed.

"It doesn't feel like courage."

"No?"

"No." Of course, now, for some utterly perverse and unknowable reason, being so honest has given Tom a rigid hard-on. It's straining against his pants. Thank god they're corduroy. He's baring his soul in a sad, desperate, and possibly career-killing gambit, and the best his penis can come up with is to betray him like a fat-headed moron. "What it feels like is foolishness," he says.

Without a shred of emotion, she replies, "I can understand that." He's gut-punched. What was he hoping for? What could he possibly expect her to say?

"Again," he fills the void, "I apologize for any awkwardness or inconvenience." *Shit. You sound like a butler.*

She stands. "Well, I think we can let this go." Now she sounds like every manager he's ever had. She goes behind her desk and sits. "And I think we can avoid it in the future. Yes?" She's looking at a Post-it note on her blotter as if those exact words were written on it.

"Yes. Absolutely."

Tom leaves the door open when he goes. After a few minutes, he hears Michelle dialing into a scheduled call with one of her New York market modelers. He feels so paralyzed and stupid. His cock has finally calmed down, but he's left with that gut-twisting, nut-punched sensation of blue balls, which he hasn't experienced since junior year of high school. He stares at his screen, then down at his keyboard. *This is nuts. You're a mess.* Finally, he logs off Amy's machine and walks to his own cube to work the remainder of the day. But even that doesn't help. He knocks at Maddie's door. "Hey, I'm all the sudden really not feeling well. Would you mind if I called it a day?"

"Nope. I don't mind if Michelle doesn't mind."

"She doesn't mind."

Maddie pulls off her glasses to see him better. "You *are* looking a little green."

"Yeah?"

"Yeah. Go home. Get some rest and feel better."

Tom smiles wanly. Maddie's all right, when all is said and done.

•   •   •

When he walks in next Monday there's a young woman sitting at Amy's old desk. "I think her name's Alicia," Maddie says in their one-on-one. "Well, in any case, it's good news, right?

"Sure," Tom almost never disagrees with Maddie now, unless it's clear she wants him to. Besides, it *is* good news. He didn't know how he was going to get through another afternoon at Amy's desk.

"Don't worry. I'll keep you busy. As a matter of fact, I've been holding off."

"Great."

"That said, you shouldn't need to log as much overtime now."

"Right."

"I haven't been crazy about the fact that all of the O.T. you've been logging for Michelle comes out of my budget. I'd like to find a way to charge that back to her cost center if possible."

Tom doesn't know how to respond. It feels a bit like discussing his own price in cigarettes. He stands and says. "Absolutely, I'll look into that."

11.
The Volcano

Tom gave up on the gardens he planted. The one along the back fence is mostly weeds now, though Kona did manage to salvage one or two tomatoes and a couple of stunted peppers. The plot of wildflowers at the bottom of the kitchen stairs grew so thick that it might as well have been weeds. Kona has since cut and placed them in vases around the house to dry. He quit watering the sod lawn out front once he got the August water bill. The next few weeks of late summer sun broiled it into brown thatch, but the autumn rains have since saved it, returning its deep emerald hue, which practically glows in the gray twilight, the only time during the week Tom is ever home to see it.

Seems like the only thing from the summer Tom hasn't given up on is running, which he does now like a zealot, pushing himself farther and farther on longer and longer outings. He often goes in the evenings now. On weekends he sometimes does two-hour stretches. He never sees Michelle.

"Are you training for a marathon or something?" Kona asks.

"Who knows?" he answers, pleasantly enough.

•   •   •

The Tuesday morning after Columbus Day, Tom finds Maddie's office empty and a note from her on his chair that reads: "We have activated the EOC due to volcanic activity at Mt. St. Helens.

Come down as soon as you can. PS: Tomorrow's flu shot day is on the 15th floor. Make sure you make yourself an appointment."

"Not a chance, Maddie," Tom whispers. He quickly logs on to his computer, clears his unread emails, then grabs his EOC access badge and heads down.

The Emergency Operations Center has a somewhat makeshift configuration consisting of several large, attached rooms located in a squat office building just a block south of the SeaTru Tower. Conference calls are taken in a room with a long meeting table. A wall of glass provides a view into the neighboring situation room where a huge bank of monitors displays a dizzying feed of cable news, weather, SeaTru IT systems in real time, plus data center activity, and anything else the team deems pertinent. One screen currently shows a live feed of Mt. St. Helens' summit crater emitting a thin plume of ash, or maybe steam.

Al and Mary sit at the conference table in the war room flanked by key team members, most of whom Tom only knows by face. Maddie sits beside Al and seems to be letting him run the call, which, at the moment, centers on data recovery should Seattle's server farms be compromised. Someone on the line points out in a dubious tone that the volcano is 96 miles away. Maddie chimes in to remind everyone that SeaTru has branches throughout Washington State, and that, additionally, a full-scale eruption could have unforeseen consequences. "Massive mudslides called lahars are actually the biggest concern in the Puget Sound region."

She catches Tom's eye with a head bob and hooks her thumb behind her. Tom follows her into a small windowless room and closes the door. "What's up?"

"Some are rating the likelihood of a new eruption as high as one in 20," says Maddie, sitting and opening her laptop.

"Jesus."

"So I activated the EOC. My first activation since taking over Enterprise Risk."

"So, this is a big deal."

Maddie shrugs. "We're all prepared for it. Al's running the

calls. I'm providing oversight. Everyone's a professional and knows their job."

"Of course."

"I informed Jim V. of my decision at 6:15 yesterday morning. He was fully on board with my call. I didn't see a need to bring you in on the holiday, as I know you've been working a lot of overtime."

"Okay, well I'm here now. How can I help?"

"Right off the bat, I'm thinking if you could get coffee and pastries for everyone. Then get a jump on lunch orders: sandwiches or salads. Something nice. Yesterday we were forced to order a pizza. I'm hoping you can bring things up a notch."

"I'll get on it."

That afternoon Maddie has Tom work a dummy spreadsheet at one of the computers lining the side of the large situation room as she tours three suits—one of them Jim V.—through the facility. "And this is where we take the conference calls. We call it the 'war room.'"

One of the suits asks, "And everyone here is part of the response?"

"That's right. With the extra terminals, people can go about their normal jobs while still participating in event response as necessary. But as you can see, it's a little cramped, and the layout is not ideal. I'm confident we can rectify all of this in the design for the future EOC." Jim V. gives Tom a sly wink as he passes.

•　　•　　•

"Who were those guys anyway?" Tom asks later at the Hard Way.

"Board sub-committee in charge of the new SeaTru Center design. Maddie's keen to finesse her vision for the new EOC, which will be housed within it. Oh, hey, before I forget, these are for you." Jim slides an envelope along the bar. "I can't use 'em." Inside Tom finds four tickets to the Halloween Seahawks game against the Panthers.

"Are you kidding me?"

"Nope. They're not the greatest, but I wouldn't call them nosebleeds."

"Are they SeaTru seats?"

"What's the difference?"

"Well, if I'm going to the Hawks game I might wanna get rowdy, but…"

"But not if you're going run into Terry Torgerson? Don't worry. I own these with a friend at the Washington Athletic Club. He can't use 'em and neither can I. They're on the opposite side of the stadium from the bank's suite. You should be fine."

"Well, in that case, awesome! Should I give you a hug or something?"

"Only if you want a punch in the nose."

•　　•　　•

Next morning, first thing after getting off the bus, Tom heads to the EOC, but Maddie's not there: just Al and a few of his team wrapping up a call. Tom hustles up to the 16th floor of the Tower. Maddie tells him, "I might head down for the 10:00 call or I might just dial in from here. I get more work done at my own desk. I do have other things I have to deal with."

She's bored already. Disappointed the whole mountain didn't blow. "Alrighty then." He turns to go.

"Did you get that shot?"

Shit. Figures.

Tom steps back into her office. "Can we talk for a second?"

"Sure." She doesn't look up.

He sits. "Can I be perfectly honest and candid with you?" Now she looks at him, leaning back in her chair. Tom treads carefully. "I'm just… not sure I want to get the flu shot. I've had one once before several years ago, and I got sick the day after."

"Unrelated. Besides, the vaccines are better now. Less impactful and more targeted. Look, it's not really optional."

"It's not?"

"I need all my direct reports to be vaccinated."

"But it's…" She arches an eyebrow. "…Still my personal decision, right?"

"I don't really see what's personal about it. Your decision affects the health of your coworkers and customers."

"Does my job depend on it?"

"No. But in a way, mine could. As a leader, it makes me look bad if my team's not in full compliance."

"Is someone keeping track?"

"Nope. Just me."

Tom doesn't know what to say. She's squeezing him, and he hates to be squeezed. Ordinarily he'd just suck it up, but he can't see his way around to it. "You're a great leader. I admire the hell out of your leadership."

"Then I'll leave the decision to you." She nods once sharply. "I won't speak of it again."

"Really?"

Maddie shrugs, exasperated. "Of course really. Let's drop it."

"Okay. Thanks, Maddie. I appreciate you hearing me on this."

Maddie's eyes are locked back on her screen. "I got to get back to this."

•   •   •

On the Friday before Halloween weekend, Tom sees a few people in costumes in the lobby and on the elevator but doesn't think anything of it until he ducks his head into Maddie's office and finds her in a brown robe of homespun. "Hi?"

Maddie shakes her head grimly. "I'm a Jedi. It's the best I could think of and still maintain a modicum of dignity."

"Are you telling me folks here dress up for Halloween?"

"Well, *you're* not obliged to, but it's tradition for the executives. Bill Piper started it in the '80s. Claimed it loosened up the staff in front of the customers or some crap."

Delighted, and frankly a bit dazed by the absurdity, Tom makes the rounds. Count at the reception desk is Mozart, complete with a poufy pink wig and 18th-century knee breeches. Gayle, the other receptionist, is Raggedy Andy. Upstairs, Tom runs into Jim V. wearing a very good Woody costume from *Toy Story*. He's got everything right: the plastic cowboy hat, the pull string on his back, and the empty plastic holster.

Tom points at himself. "I missed the memo."

"If that's your story, pardner, stick with it, but it won't cut no ice next year."

"Your costume is… perfect."

"Why do you sound so surprised?"

"I don't know, I just—"

"Juanita rents one for me every year. I don't know what I'm getting 'til the day itself, which spares us both undue anxiety. I kinda like this one though. It's from a kids' movie, right?"

"Yeah." Tom nods, grinning. "It's from a kids' movie."

As often as possible, throughout the day, Tom finds excuses to go up to 17, where he spots Terry Torgerson dressed in a black turtleneck, black slacks, and round, wire-framed glasses. He inquires with a passing EA. "Oh, Terry? He's Steve Jobs." Tom passes Michelle in the corridor. She's wearing some sort of 19th-century man's suit: black jacket with long tails, waist coat, cravat, and high-waisted gray flannel trousers.

"No costume?" she asks, as they are about to pass each other.

He stops and turns, and she does the same. "Didn't get the memo? What's your excuse?"

She lifts her chin, squints, and smiles. "I'm Daniel Brockley."

Tom shrugs his ignorance. "Founder of Seattle Trust Bank?"

Tom reckons Michelle chose this particular costume to avoid even flirting with the tiresome sexist Halloween pitfalls: the naughty nurse, the sexy cat, the slutty cowgirl, et cetera; but as he watches her go, her perfect ass swishing beneath those tails, he realizes that she has failed—or he has, because even in a man's suit from a hundred years ago, the sight makes his cock stir. *Our natures betray us.* Tom shakes his head, grimly. *Well, in fairness, maybe just mine.*

"Oh that this too too sullied flesh would melt."

Wait.

Is it "sullied" or "solid"?

•   •   •

On Saturday they try to dress Poma for a trick-or-treat party at the Green Lake Community Center, but she pitches such a fit once zipped into her Goodwill bumblebee suit that they are forced to relent and let her watch *Blue's Clues* in her PJs.

On Sunday, for Halloween itself, they've hired a bona fide babysitter, since her sister Hana will be joining them for the game. Tom has invited his old college roommate, J. Wilburn, as the fourth. J.'s full first name is "Jethro" but he started using his initial in the sixth grade when he changed to a new, predominantly white school, and the kids there teased him for being the darkest redneck they'd ever met. J. gave up trying to educate them to the fact that Jethro was actually Moses's father-in-law long before he was a closeted cracker on *The Beverly Hillbillies*. Tom and J. started spending most of their free time together in their dorm's basement lounge, studying, shooting the shit, getting high, effusing about Walt Whitman. Since neither of them got along with their assigned roommates during their first semester, they put in for a switch and bunked together until the end of their sophomore year. After that, Tom took a break from school (it would be permanent) and J. transferred to the University of Maryland Eastern Shore, a historically black college, which felt oddly like a betrayal to Tom, though he'd be hard-pressed even now to articulate why. The two wannabe poets kept in touch by sending each other hand-written letters, a habit they sustain to the present even though they live in the same city and have a regular happy hour. J. has introduced Tom to Pablo Neruda, Robert Bly, Mingus, and Ikkyū. Tom isn't sure *what* he's introduced J. to besides his own angsty verse and maybe Elvis Costello.

They pre-funk at the house with blue and green vodka Jell-O shots while they "paint up." Kona goes with a fully blue face while Hana opts for half blue/half white, vertically divided. Tom goes with an upside-down blue handprint over a white base, like one of the orcs from *The Lord of the Rings* movie. J. demurs. "I'd look like something out of *Heart of Darkness*."

Both J. and Hana have, individually and confidentially, expressed their concerns that Kona and Tom might be trying to set them up, but neither Kona nor Tom had actually given it any thought. "You're safe, man," Tom tells his old friend while Hana's downstairs with her niece. "Hana only likes tatted-up, dreadlocked, patchouli-reeking white dudes."

"That's not true," says Kona. "But, I swear, this isn't a set up. I'm pretty sure she's seeing someone."

When J.'s in the bathroom, Hana whispers, "I'm not hooking up with that dude. He's too serious."

"No one's setting you up!" Tom insists, finally irritated. "Besides, J.'s funnier than anyone I know. Don't hate a guy just because he doesn't collect Phish bootlegs."

"Nice," says Kona. "Let's drop it, shall we? We're supposed to be gearing up to watch some—" she shakes her fists in the air and stomps her feet "—FOOTBALL!"

The game's a blast. With the pre-funk, plus another quick round of tequila shots at a bar close to the stadium, Tom's nicely toasted, such that during the game itself he only needs to spend maybe 20 bucks on over-priced beer to maintain. (Hana and J. got chummy sharing a joint on the walk from the bus tunnel.) Kona drinks nothing but water at the game. "Somebody's gotta stay straight, right?"

"I can't think for the life of me why," says Tom.

Having never been to Qwest Field, Tom wanders around a bit during the third quarter, just taking in the crowd, the sea of green and blue. In the south concourse he stops to watch Blue Thunder, sipping on his giant beer. When he turns to head back to his seat, he nearly runs into Michelle, carrying a trough of nachos. "Hello!" he says, but she doesn't seem to recognize him. "It's Tom," he hollers after her.

She stops and turns to face him. A smile of recognition spreads. "You uh… have a little something on your uh…" she points at his face, her eyes shining.

"Hilarious." His heart dips a little. Why did he have to run into her disguised as a moron?

"Enjoying the game, I trust?" She saunters closer, inspecting him closely, as though there were something about him she forgot. It makes his chest tingle.

"I am. You?"

She shrugs. "Not a huge fan. But it was my turn for the bank's box, so I brought my son."

"Well, at least *he* must be psyched, right?"

"Not really. He brought his Gameboy and hasn't really looked up from it."

Tom sighs. Wealth is wasted on such as these. "I don't know what to say to that."

His disgust must register. She squints. "You're a little drunk, aren't you?"

"Hey, maybe. It's a football game."

"I miss you."

He can't believe this. It's like she started up a scene from an abandoned script. "What?" is all he manages.

"I miss you. I miss you working for me. I miss our runs. You're fun. Look at you. You've painted your face for the game. Who does that?"

"Um…" Tom looks around for supporting evidence. "Lots of people. It's a Hawks game. It's Halloween."

"I'm not saying it's a bad thing."

Tom is dumbfounded by her talking to him like this. It's opening a pit in front of him. He decides to yank the emergency brake. "It's great talking to you. I gotta get back to my friends. Enjoy the rest of the game."

Her forehead wrinkles slightly, then she goes utterly neutral. "You too, Tom. See ya soon."

•   •   •

Tom steps in front of Kona as she tries to get in the shower. "Leave it on."

"What? The paint?" She's incredulous.

"Yeah. I like it." He pulls her close.

Into his chest she murmurs, "You're a weirdo."

"I've never had my cock sucked by a blue-faced girl."

She looks up at him askance. "I suppose you haven't lived then?"

"Nope."

She gives him a long, serious sizing-up.

"Help me live," he whispers.

"Hmmm," she says. She unbuttons the top of his jeans, then yanks them the rest of the way open. "Oh my." She lowers her mouth to the head of his cock now poking up above his underwear waistband.

Later, when he's got her on the bed, fucking her hard, he relishes her contorting blue mask of strangeness. She opens her eyes suddenly and says, "I'm not on the pill anymore."

"What?"

"Come inside me if you want but just know I'm not on the pill."

"Why not?"

"It was bugging me. Making me crabby."

"What do you mean... come inside you?"

"Just—I don't know. It's not a big deal."

Tom's so close and so disoriented by the blueness, and the incongruity—the sheer bizarreness—of what she's saying, he quickly pulls out and erupts all over her belly.

Kona draws a circle with her finger through his come. "My goodness," she says, smiling, gazing at his now drooping, still drizzling cock. "I should go blue more often."

12.

The Drain

November owns Seattle outright. When the curtains of All Saints' fall, all clarity and brightness bleed from the sky. With what little light is left at November's end, Seattle slowly circles December's drain. Days will now march past like lumbering ghosts, as the border between day and night softens like bruising fruit into a barely varying sameness. Gray in/gray out. *Shit, this is good stuff.* Tom's scribbling in his mini-notebook. The 16 bus bends at its accordion center in Wallingford, turning from 45th onto Stone Way.

Maddie hasn't said anything about the flu shot, but every day he sees the question hovering behind her eyes. It doesn't matter. He isn't going to do it. He just isn't. He's got to have something, some power to make a simple decision or none of this sacrifice—working this job, supporting his family—means anything, and he really is just an inmate, lumbering the yard, circling the drain.

Jesus, Kavanagh. Smother another metaphor, why don't ya?

At their now regular Thursday Hard Way happy hour, Jim V. has started to trust Tom with some of his Froot-Loopier philosophies. "Let's stipulate. Corporations, at first principles, are risk-mitigation machines: means for individuals to spread financial threats across the group and protect themselves, at least legally, from bottomless liability. The problem is…" Jim's fingers gesture lightly above his glass. "They have grown into something different than humans intended, and most of us don't understand what this transformation means." The older man goes quiet.

Tom knows it's a trick to get him to beg for more. So, after a deep suck on his cocktail straw, he obliges. "And what's that?" Jim stares at his drink. "Come on. Give. What have corporations become?"

Barely audibly, Jim murmurs: "sentient." Tom barks out a laugh. He can't help himself. It's all too wonderfully weird. Jim turns to look him in the eye. "I ain't even close to kidding."

Tom chuckles more gently. "Oh, I know. That's what makes it all the more hilarious and scary."

"Truth is what it is." The risk chief turns back to face the bar mirror.

•   •   •

By the time Tom gets home there's nothing left of the dinner Kona made, so he scrounges in the fridge for leftovers. She storms out to scold him in a harsh whisper. "What's wrong with you? Poma's just in the next room, and I had the devil of a time getting her down tonight."

"I need to eat."

"So eat. Does it have to be Master Chef in here?"

"Fuck. Fine. I'll have a sandwich."

"Don't fucking cuss at me. It's not my fault you're drunk."

"I'm not drunk. I'm hungry."

"Maybe you should've eaten something wherever it was you were tying one on."

"Yeah? And maybe you shouldn't wait until I have my dick inside you to inform me of changes to our birth control strategy."

"What?"

"Forget it!"

"No. Say what you just said to me."

"I said forget it. Non sequitur. You're right. I'm tipsy."

"No, you have a problem with me. But don't worry. The likelihood of you having your dick inside me any time soon just shriveled to zero." She stomps back into their bedroom. Tom eats his sandwich in stony silence at the kitchen table, washing it down with a bottle of beer. A few minutes later she's back out dropping a pillow and a blanket on the kitchen floor. "Please feel free to make yourself at home downstairs."

"Fuck" he mutters, more to himself than her. "Whatever."

On Friday, Maddie informs Tom she has volunteered him to serve on the executive holiday party planning committee. Apparently, it's tradition to throw a small but very elegant reception for the SeaTru senior executives and their staff. The committee consists entirely of EAs, plus the compulsory representative from HR. Tradition also dictates that the party be held in the SeaTru Tower atrium. This makes sense. You couldn't find a more beautifully appointed reception hall in all of downtown. Paved in rose marble, paneled in rich cherry wood, the atrium's ceiling vaults sixty feet above the floor. With the elevator lobby serving as the balcony, it makes a perfect impromptu ballroom. Tom wrangles to get himself on the catering sub-committee to avoid being on the decorating team.

•　　•　　•

Thanksgiving is a disaster.

It all starts the night before, with an impromptu non-Thursday Hard Way happy hour. Then, instead of heading straight home, Tom gets off the 16 a few stops early and checks in at Lenny's for another beer and a shot. Long story short, he's passed out on the living room sofa by 9:00 while Kona's still doing prep work in the kitchen for the next day's feast.

He comes to in the middle of the night on the living room sofa, his mouth a compost bin, his head a beaten anvil. He decides against joining Kona in their bed. Instead, he downs four aspirin with a tall glass of water, grabs a quilt from the closet and collapses back on the sofa. He wakes up to sounds of Poma banging her cup on her highchair. Lurching into the kitchen he finds Kona chopping onions and her sister Hana feeding the baby. "Morning sunshine," Hana half-hollers. Kona says nothing, dumps the onions into a pan to sizzle. "Daddy's a hurtin' pup," Hana whispers to her niece.

Tom nods, grudgingly accepting his joke-butt status. "Please tell me there's coffee."

"There's coffee," Kona says, without expression.

Hana adds, "Coffee's good, but I got something better for what ails ya." Six minutes later, Tom's sitting at the kitchen table, a coffee in one hand and a Bloody Mary thin with vodka in the other. Hana is making eggs. Kona has moved on to crumbling the bread she's been hardening over the last few days.

The Bloody works so well that Tom has two more. Around 1:00 he switches to whiskey and heads down to the basement to watch football while Kona and Hana cook. By 4:00 he's useless again, as the sisters eat while Poma watches a *Blue's Clues* in her bouncy chair next to her dad sprawled on the futon couch.

And again, Tom wakes in the middle of the night, disoriented, in nearly pitch darkness, only the red lights of the DVD player illuminating the basement TV room. And again, he knows better than to try to crawl into bed with Kona upstairs.

Fuck, Kavanagh. Get a grip.

Next morning, he forces himself to run the ravine. Predictably, he pukes in the stream halfway along. Arriving home, he finds a note from Kona saying she's taken Poma to the mall with her sister. Any prior year, she would've rather eaten glass than go shopping on Black Friday.

·　　·　　·

On the second Saturday of December, wearing his marrying-and-burying suit beneath his only—and somewhat thread-worn— overcoat, Tom climbs on a slow-poke 16 downtown to attend the holiday party he helped plan. He runs into Jake the security guy at the loading dock wearing a tux and watching the caterers unload. Inside, decorations and music seem to be setting up nicely, so, still in his coat, Tom steps a couple blocks over to the Hard Way. Not surprisingly, he finds Jim V. there, also in a tux. They chat over a round. Then Tom heads back to the atrium. The best part of being on the planning committee is that he can, and will, charge overtime for all of this.

The evening starts well and improves considerably for Tom when Mary Saskell appears in full evening gown, hair done to the nines, makeup flawless. She holds up a traffic-cop hand upon catching him gawking and warns, "Don't say a word."

"Not even 'gorgeous'?" asks Tom, grinning. "Or 'stunning'? How 'bout 'enchanting'?"

Mary purses her lips in a mixture of disapproval and delight. "Nope. None of those. Where's your wife by the way? I was looking forward to meeting her."

"She's at home. Sitter cancelled at the last minute." A lie is better than copping to the truth: Kona had no interest in coming and he none in forcing the issue.

Later Tom chats amiably with Maddie's husband Harrison, until they inevitably come to the subject of literature, wherein Tom finds the portly man's discursions on Derrida and semiotic analysis in the context of post-structuralist phenomenology to be utterly incomprehensible, and he suspects Maddie's husband knows it, and isn't above bullying a wannabe poet with a barrage of lit-crit jargon.

Well fuck you too, professor.

Tom finally makes his escape over to Jim V., standing next to a smallish woman with gray-streaked brown hair.

"Well, hello, Tom!" Jim exclaims, as if it's been ages. "Glad you could make it. Allow me to introduce my wife, Georgiana." Tom suppresses astonishment. Where the hell was this woman an hour ago when he and Jim were pre-funking at the Hard Way? Tom smiles and takes her surprisingly powerful hand. He recalls Jim saying that she is an ardent potter. Her gaze is blank and clear, like a hawk's.

"Pleased to meet you," Tom says.

She nods. "You as well."

Tom pushes on in search of another beer. "Swing back by when you can," Jim calls after him. "I have one more introduction for you."

Georgiana's gone when Tom circles around again. "Migraine," Jim explains. "She went back to the condo. She hates

Seattle. Always has." He puts his hand on Tom's shoulder and guides him across the crowded floor, placing him suddenly face-to-face with Terry Torgerson, who's wearing what almost looks like a prom tux, medium blue, accented with a lighter blue boutonnière.

"Terry, I got someone I'd like you to meet," says Jim.

"Oh, terrific," Terry says, smiling mildly.

"He works for Maddie Dennett, who heads up Enterprise Risk Services."

"Of course." Terry extends his hand and Tom takes it. It's like shaking hands with the action figure. Tom notes that Jake the security guy is close by, watching. The CEO then nods, indicating that the exchange is over. Jim and Tom step briskly away, and quickly lose each other in the crowd of suits and tuxes and gowns.

And then there's only one gown: midnight blue, an emerald baguette on a silver chain plunging into her unabashed décolletage. "Tom! I want you to meet Nathan." Michelle smiles at him, beckons him closer. Tom hadn't even noticed him, this small, weak-bearded man in a rumpled brown suit—tie loosened, top shirt button undone—but apparently this is her husband.

"How do you do!" Tom offers his hand.

"Just fine. Good to meet you," Nathan replies, slight hint of Brooklyn, but measured, professional. His handshake is loose, careful, and quick: a surgeon thing perhaps. His features are dark, but his eyes are keen. He seems to size Tom up quickly, then scans the room for more interesting subjects, sipping his clear drink on ice. Tom wonders if there is even any booze in it.

"So you're a doctor."

"Yeah."

"Or surgeon, right?"

Nathan shrugs. "And you? What do you do at the bank?"

"Oh. I'm just a secretary."

Michelle leans in. "Not a secretary and not 'just.' He's an executive assistant."

Tom turns to Nathan confidentially: "Secretary."

Nathan nods. "You work for Michelle?"

"I did temporarily while she was looking for a replacement,

but no, I work for Maddie Dennett in Enterprise Risk."

Now Nathan raises his eyebrows, "Oh yeah? I know Maddie." He finally looks Tom in the eye with a sort of questioning smirk.

Tom nods. "Yeah, she's great. Anyway, I better get back to making sure everything's going okay. I'm actually on the clock."

"Great job, Tom," Michelle says, gently patting him where his shoulder meets his chest.

· · ·

Tom finds Mary Saskell with a beer, holding up a wall. "How's it going?"

She frowns. "I'd kill you where you stand for a cigarette."

"So let's go smoke, but first you gotta dance with me." She gives him a skeptical look, but Tom insists. "I mean it, let's boogie." He grabs her beer, sets it on a ledge, then holds both hands out to her. Mary takes them and they move to the floor. At 6-foot-2, Tom's not used to looking a woman directly in the eyes on the dance floor, but in heels, Mary's easily an inch taller. She smiles, shaking her head at the absurdity.

"Thank you," he says.

"For what?"

"For taking this dance. For saving me from the schmoozing, if only for a few minutes."

"Yeah, that's some tiresome bullshit." They dance without talking for a while. At one point, looking over Mary's shoulder, Tom catches Michelle watching him over Nathan's. Out of the blue, Mary says, "You know she adores you, right?"

"What?"

"She adores you."

"Who?"

"Maddie, moron."

"She does?"

"Of course. You can do no wrong in her eyes."

"I wouldn't go that far."

"I would. Use it. Get what you can out of her."

"Like what?"

"I don't know. A raise? Overtime? A promotion? Though she might fight you on that. She's doesn't wanna lose you."

Tom pulls back to see if she's serious and Mary nods at him solemnly. "But remember, it's like the rodeo. You can only ride the kicking bull for so long. No one's lasted longer than a year as her EA."

Later, Tom sees Michelle dancing with Jim V. The crowd has thinned out. He can't see her husband anywhere. He goes to the bar and orders himself another Red Hook.

•   •   •

It's late, at least by Seattle standards, where the downtown sidewalks roll up at ten, even on a weekend. When Tom looks in on her, the coat-check girl tells him she hasn't had a break since five. He tells her to take one and starts trading folks their coats in exchange for plastic check tags. Just one more mild humiliation in the long line of them facing the rare male of the SeaTru admin species. Eventually, Jim shows up with his chit and a droll smirk. "You moonlighting?"

"Making ends meet wherever I can."

"Come by the Hard Way when you're done."

"Just because I'm a coat-check girl doesn't mean I'm easy. "

•   •   •

Now Tom's on his fifth beer, on top of the double Cape Cod foundation he laid at the Hard Way. He hardly cares if the girl ever comes back. He's having fun, joking with people as he hands them their wraps, scarves, coats, and hats. He doesn't care what they think of him, and he suspects, or at least hopes, that some of them might just admire him for not caring. That's what he chooses to believe anyhow. One of the quasi-blessings of living in the Pacific Northwest is the strong taboo against flaunting wealth and privilege. Everyone is only *just* middle class. Not upper—and certainly not lower. To look down on someone stuck in a menial job is tacitly verboten.

Now the flow to the counter has ebbed. Those that were inclined to leave have left, and those determined to stay are doubling down: dancing more vigorously as the band kicks up a rollicking cover of KC and the Sunshine Band's "That's the Way I Like It." Terry Torgerson is spinning his wife like a dervish. Tom remembers Maddie dishing that he married her after the kids flew the nest and his first wife picked up a pills habit.

Now Michelle's coming at him from across the dance floor. He's never seen her walk this way: stalking, one foot hits the floor exactly where the last one left it, making her hips sway as though she's made of ocean. Oh, how he wishes he could strangle these cravings into disappearing.

Disappearing. Dissipation?... Dissolve?

Oh that this too too solid flesh would melt.

Sullied?

Now she's standing right there, only the counter separating them. And now she's leaning over it, emerald pendant glimmering as it dangles, daring him to look down, past it, into... Her eyes shine, her cheeks are flushed, and her chin is lifted in happy—or at least tipsy—defiance. "I think I need a coat."

"I think you do," Tom replies. "Could dip below 50 out there. You got your chit?"

She cocks her head, lifts an eyebrow. "My what?"

"Your uh... little plastic thingy that matches the thingies we hang with your coat."

"Ah... I don't have a chit.

"Oh."

She grins, mischievously. "So, I honestly couldn't give a chit."

Tom nods tightly. He's not having this.

Michelle forces her face into seriousness. "Maybe Nathan has it. He left earlier. Some sort of staffing emergency. So I guess you could say he had to give a *shift*." Her eyebrows go up: *See what I did?*

Tom's still not having it. "Yeah, okay... So, what's your coat look like?"

"It's black. It has these… um… two… things…that I put my arms in. Sleeves, I think they're called. Yeah."

Tom shakes his head. "You're killing me a little, you know that, right?"

"Am I? A little?" She raises her chin again, and Tom realizes the expression isn't defiance, but pride, that of the queen who demands due obeisance. She squints one eye and parts her lips a little, like she's fixing him in a rifle sight.

Tom sighs. "What would you like me to do?"

"What would I *like*?"

"About your coat?"

"Well, I'd *like* you to give it to me. Eventually."

"You're not driving home, I hope?"

"Why? You got a better idea?"

"What's going on, Michelle?"

"I need a coat."

"I know. Black with sleeves." He sighs. "Let me go look for it."

"No. Let me." She knocks on the coat room door to his right, three times sharply, like the law. Tom opens it, and she edges past him sideways, lightly touching her front to his. Then she's lost back in the forest of coats. He follows, bold stripe of dread glowing up his chest. When he finds her, she's pulling a black mink off its hanger.

"That's your coat?" He doubts it.

"Maybe. Help me into it would you." She presents it to him like the spoils of a hunt. He takes it, holds it up so she can slip her arms in. Then she shrugs it on fully. "Mmm, delightful." She nuzzles it to her chin. "Second skin."

"Nothing wrong with your first."

She turns to him. "How would you know?"

"Eyes."

"You disapprove, I'm sure."

"Of what?"

"Fur."

"What makes you say that?"

"You're liberal." She makes a childish face upon saying the

word. It's Tom's first clue to just how drunk she is.

"Well, if you think about how these coats get made, it's pretty damned disgusting, wouldn't you say?"

"I wouldn't say anything," she murmurs. She nuzzles her face deeper. "Feels amazing. Feel it."

"I felt it when I put it on you."

"Did you? Feel it again. What are you afraid of? It's already dead."

"That's not what I'm afraid of."

"Then what?"

"Why are you doing this?"

"Just run your hands over it."

He almost does. He almost reaches around from behind her with both hands, but instead he asks again, in a pleading whisper: "Why?"

She shakes her head dreamily, as though he just asked the stupidest question possible, as if she were the queen and he the condemned man begging to understand his sentence. He reaches out and glides his hands up over her breasts beneath the fur, sighing irrepressibly as he does.

"There, was that so hard?"

She turns to face him, reaches out with one finger and touches the top of his prick pushing stiff against his suit pants. "Well, I guess it is." His hands are at the small of her back, pulling her to him. He kisses her hard and she returns it, plunging her tongue into his mouth. He pushes her back through the rows of coats, until she hits a wall. "Unh" she grunts as he smashes her against it, his mouth still on hers. She shoves her pelvis against his cock. He consumes her neck, he reaches down with his right hand and draws the fur coat open like a curtain. He finds the hem of the black-blue velvet dress and tugs it up, then reaches around to cup her silk-pantied ass cheek. She lifts her leg, and hisses "Yes!" in his ear just before darting her tongue into it. Lightly he brushes his fingertips over the wet silk.

"Take me."

"I can't."

"Oh god!" Her whisper drives deep into his ear. "Do something. Please!" It's the command of a goddess. He finds the top of her panties and pushes it down with the backs of his fingers. For a moment he simply, gently holds the nest of her coarse hair. He can feel her body tense in anticipation.

Oh that this too too sullied solid flesh would…

Ah, fuck it!

He dives his middle finger into her wetness, then slips it back out to touch its tip to her pebble hard clitoris. She bucks against his hand and kisses him harder. He slips his finger back inside and pushes his palm against her clit. She's practically dancing on his hand now. He's barely doing anything. Harder and harder she bucks until she comes, moaning so loudly that he has to muffle her with his mouth.

She slides down the wall on the marble floor, and he slides down beside her, both of them gasping for breath in the close air. They can hear the coat check girl talking at the counter. Who knows how long she's been back? In the dim lighting Michelle gapes up at the ceiling, drawing deep breaths. Tom sees her neck darkly blotched where he kissed—hell, gnawed—her. "I'm sorry."

She turns to him. "You are?"

"Well… sort of."

Silence. Just her breathing. He has to ask. "Are you okay?"

A gasp escapes. Or a laugh. "Am I *okay*?"

"I mean… I sort of got carried away there."

"Yeah. Yeah, it was only *you* that got carried away."

"I just…"

She lifts her hand in front of his face. Pinched between her thumb and finger is a pink plastic coat check tag. "I found my chit."

•　　•　　•

Tom nods to Jake the security guy as he guides Michelle from the party on his arm. *How much might* he *guess?* He waits with her on Third Avenue to flag her a taxi. She even gives him a friendly peck on the check before slipping into the back seat.

Tom gives a thought to the Hard Way but decides to skip it. He has a feeling that if he drinks there, the old man will somehow read it all on his face. He considers taking the 16 local home, but he would have to wait another 25 minutes just to ride it for another 40. He could take a taxi, but he doesn't relish the idea of getting home quite that quickly. So he decides to catch the 358 due in seven minutes. It'll shoot straight up Aurora and he can get off at the lake and walk around.

Every so often, at the bus stop, and later on the bus, he slyly touches his hand to his nose and lips. The smell of her makes his heart thrum. *Her molecules linger on me.* He aches from the tip of his cock all the way up to the top of his gut. *Shit, I'm back in high school. More blue balls.*

"Shit!" echoes a homeless woman sitting across from him, lifting out of her nod. Tom realizes he's been talking out loud.

Tom walks past the boathouse and the old aqua stadium and onto a dirt path into the thicker stand of trees at the very edge of the lake. There, in the drizzling darkness, he grabs at himself with his left hand, while holding his right fingertips to his nose. He hears a runner's steps thopping on the main asphalt path maybe 15 yards behind him. He sees the light from the runner's head lamp dancing in the trees and at once, and with force, he comes, lofting the spurts into the lake.

A minute or so later, he zips up. He bends down to dip both hands in the frigid lake water. Then he heads home, practically sober.

13.

Kavanaghs Overcome

Tom Kavanagh wasn't raised to hate Christmas. Far from it. The house in Manasquan was consistently filled with joyful noise from Thanksgiving Eve until at least the Epiphany on January 6, when, as the youngest, and really the only one who cared any more, Tommy got to put the Wise Men in the crèche. Once, when they were driving past the Presbyterian church in Spring Lake, Tommy asked his mom why *they* had their Wise Men out well before Christmas. Shaking her head in weary resignation, she replied, "That's what Protestants do. They condense and abridge. They demystify."

However, Betty Kavanagh was atypically punctilious about the tree and lights coming down no later than the First Monday of Ordinary Time. (God! How Tommy loved that expression. "Ordinary Time." Sounded like something you stepped out of church and dove into.) Really, he loved all the vernacular and arcana of Catholicism. He loved the kneeling, the standing, the sitting, the standing, and the kneeling again. He loved the prayers in unison— how did everyone memorize them all? He loved how they boomed off the stone walls and ceilings—

"Peace be with you."

"And also with you."

"Let's us give thanks to the Lord Our God."

"It is right to give him thanks and praise."

—like murmurings of some holy monster made of angels.

He loved the rustling of the congregation as they rose *en masse* from the kneelers. He loved genuflection, especially when the middle-aged men did it, stretching their polyester suit pants tight over their fat asses. He adored the silver bowls of holy water resting in hewn rock.

Tom has a favorite memory of church—well, more of a layer of memories—starting as a kid, too young to take the host, having to stay alone in the pew while everyone else in his family filed up for the Body of Christ. (In his mind he sees them neatly in order of age: Terry, Trisha, CiCi, Angela, Mom, and Dad. Jamie's not there, because even in Tommy's earliest memories of church, his brother, the oldest, had already stopped coming.) Tommy wasn't frightened to be left alone—in church he always felt completely safe—but he did feel left out. He longed to take communion as eagerly and earnestly as he longed to join his sisters in the church musicals, maybe playing one of the urchins in *Oliver*, like his sister CiCi. She'd practice her cockney for hours, even though she only had the one line: "Oy, these sausages are stale!"

Communion and the kiss of peace: hands down, Tommy's two favorite parts of the Mass. (As a teenager, he relished the opportunity to momentarily touch pretty girls' hands, all under the approving eyes of Father, Son, and Holy Spirit.) Tommy paid special attention to the words recited prior to communion, because clearly magic was at work. (Later, as an altar boy, during the consecration, he would watch carefully for any signs of the air energizing around the chalice as the priest held the oversized host above it.)

Younger, pre-First Communion Tommy still understood that there was a sort of mutual promise made by the congregation just before they lined up to take the wafers on their tongues. (This was a few years before the rules were altered to allow Catholics to take it in their hands. After that, Tommy once saw a kid slip it into his pocket like he was saving it for later.)

"This is the Lamb of God," the priest proclaimed, "who takes away the sins of the world. Happy are those who are called to His supper."

And everyone chanted back, "Lord, I am not worthy to receive you, but only say the word and I shall be healed."

But not this one time, when his Nana McCleary, visiting from Bayonne, declared loudly, "Only say the word and *my soul* shall be healed," thus finishing slightly after everyone else. Tommy was amazed. She changed it. She added "my soul." Were you allowed to change it?

Tommy asked his oldest sister Angela later that Sunday afternoon. Angela was the scholar, always holed up with her beloved books in the tiny bedroom she had converted from a walk-in closet. Tommy's sister answered in her dreamy, dismissive way, "Oh, Nana's old, Tommy. That's probably how they did it back then, you know, before Vatican Two."

"What's Vatican Two?"

But Angela had gone back to her paperback as though she had forgotten he was there.

Tommy decided he preferred his nana's way of saying it, and that it would be *his* way of saying it too. "Only say the word and *my soul* shall be healed."

'Cuz it's not me; it's my soul.

•   •   •

Number 16. Always the same, over and over. Endless herky-jerky milk run. *Windows dripping with so much human moisture we might as well be under water.* Submarine bus. *What can you do with that?*

Seattle the submarine, Tom jots. *Insipid.*

He's scrawling in his Moleskine with his happy little stubby nub of a pencil: just the right size, with just the right softness of lead, gliding across the paper in a satisfying, only slightly smudgy sort of way.

He's forgiven himself. That should be noted. He would certainly be sorry if he ever hurt Kona; but Kona doesn't know, and Kona's never *gonna* know. He'll live with his sin: let it drip from him, like this condensed breath and sweat of the damned dripping down the bus window, because it's not gonna happen again, and that's *it.*

It's not me. It's my soul.

It's still dark when Tom gets off the bus in front of Benaroya at 7:27 a.m. And it's dark again when he waits for it heading home, across Third, outside the copper-colored Seattle Tower. Days are blurring by him with details only occasionally leaping into focus: Excel sheets, Word docs, PowerPoint decks. Generate, revise, proof-read, print, fill out this expense report, order those supplies, get a signature on this, then route it for these. And then there's Christmas bearing down, looming just beyond that drain of the solstice, which he's losing faith won't suck him in and down for good.

Kona got Poma this great plastic kitchen set, complete with stove and oven and sink and dishes and pans. Girlie's gonna love it. Tom just has to put it together on Christmas Eve. No big deal.

But presents for Kona? That's all on him. And sure, he's got some ideas. He's even already bought her a scarf. And he's work-ing on a chapter of his children's Christmas book that'll serve as a present for both her and Poma, but… it's not enough. He knows this. He has to get something else, more stuff. Just thinking about it bloats a painful balloon in his chest.

His throat is sore. It's been sore for weeks. He's hung over every other day. A week or so ago, Kona said to him at breakfast, "Man, you were pretty messed up reading to Poma last night."

"I read to Poma last night?"

They shared a look, then went back to their coffees. "This is going to get better right? Whatever it is you're going through, you're going to come out of it, yes?"

"Yes," he said, the balloon expanding, pushing hard against his heart.

•   •   •

As a kid, Tommy imagined a soul to be something about the size and shape of his nana's pocketbook. You could carry it in your hand. You could clutch it to your heart. But you could also leave it behind on a car seat if you weren't careful. His mother did that frequently—with her pocketbook, that is.

Tommy loved the church. When he was ten, he decided to be

a priest. Then in sixth grade, after learning more about other religions in CCD, he decided he might be more useful as a prophet. Tommy lobbied hard to be an altar boy, even though his mother would have certainly spared him the duty. Hell, she would have spared him anything and everything. Basketball, baseball, Cub Scouts, maybe even school, if that were legal.

"Oh Tommy, just quit, dear, if it's making you unhappy." And often Tom did just that. Cross-country was a bore, and hard, and there were always going to be kids better at it than him and it made him wonder petulantly why. Wasn't he the one with the long legs? Hadn't he been running the beach since he was twelve? Screw it. He'd do theatre. And make out with the girls backstage while his buddies were puking their lunches in the freezing, late afternoon practices.

Tommy remembers the very first Mass he served. To start, he was assigned a week of weekday mornings, 7:00 a.m., with Joey Snyder as the other newbie, and maybe five old ladies populating the pews. Monday morning, he thought he'd done pretty well, but afterward in the sacristy Monsignor Cooke ordered him to lift up his hands. Tommy panicked. Was the priest going to slap them? But all he did was hold Tommy's fingers in his own large smooth palms and say, "Your nails." Tommy looked and saw them as if for the first time: overgrown, torn, green stuff beneath the edges.

It wasn't long before he was getting actual Sunday masses, at first in the less popular slots: 8:00 a.m. and 12:45 p.m. (the hangover crowd, according to his mother). He preferred being chalice bearer. Sometimes when he had to hold the book, Father Chris, the associate pastor, would sway backward and forward so precariously that Tommy seriously feared the rank-breathed hippy would eventually topple on top of him.

Tommy only quit serving once he realized he would never get scheduled for Midnight Mass, the altar boy's Super Bowl. That privilege would always go to the St. Denis Parochial School boys.

•　　•　　•

Kona has been threatening to go to Midnight Mass this Christmas. She hadn't exactly been raised Catholic, but her mother's parents converted when she was around twelve. For the life of him, Tom cannot fathom what might possess a pair of Nisei Japanese, who had both spent their adolescence in internment camps, to convert to Roman Catholicism, and in Honolulu of all places. But the mysteries of faith abound, or so his sainted mother would say between civilized sips of her Cutty Sark rocks and delicate puffs from her Parliament slim. If Kona wanted to go to Midnight Mass with her sister, who was Tom to object? But he'd be damned if he'd join them. He wouldn't even waste his breath explaining that, to dyed-in-the-wool-every-single-Sunday Catholics, Midnight Mass was what St. Paddy's Day was to true Irish: an amateur-hour dog-and-pony show for toe-dippers. He'd put together Poma's play kitchen instead.

Christmas was so perfect and easy when Tom was a kid. Well, until his dad died. The Christmas after that sucked. And the one after *that* sucked even worse. He was down in the basement playing his brand-new Atari console. Even though he had only owned it for five hours, he already knew that his favorite cassette was "Combat"— the one with the biplanes and clouds you could hide inside. He toggled and thumbed his joystick happily, until he heard someone stomping down the stairs. She came and stood right over him, uncomfortably close in her Jordache jeans, which she bought for herself with the money she made waiting tables at HoJo's. "You're one selfish little shithead, you know that?" Her cigarette dangled dangerously next to his face.

"I know no such thing," Tommy countered defiantly. But his guts got tighter whenever Trisha came at him. She was five years older, and nasty as a gutter rat to anyone who dared cross her.

"What the fuck, Tommy? What the ever-loving *fuck?*"

"What did I *do?*" He gestured as emphatically as he could with both hands still working the controller.

"*Seriously?* You sit there playing that dumb game and you *seriously* ask me that?"

"Yeah. I seriously do. What did I *do?*"

She sucked in on her cigarette and said, "You know *what?*"

She blew the smoke up to the ceiling as if looking to the heavens for some relief from her frustrations.

"What?" His eyes were pegged to the screen.

"I'm done with you. Never come to me for anything ever again. No favors. No change from my tip jar so you can go buy Big League Chew. No help with laundry. Nothing. I'm d-o-n-e *done* with you."

"What?... Did?... I?... *Do?*"

"You *know* what you *did*. It's right in front of your fucking face."

"I DON'T!" he was full-on whining now, but he was also almost at high score.

Trisha leaned in, spewing sour cigarette breath as she half-whispered, half-hissed: "Every single one of us agreed not to ask Mom for anything big. We all knew she wouldn't be able to say no and that she'd put herself in hock trying to give us all everything we wanted. So... *small* stuff. We were all supposed to ask for *small stuff!* Cici asked for a sweater. Terry, an E.L.O. album. Angela asked for a Crown Books gift certificate. I asked for an Amoco card, which I would pay off myself, though Mom did give me 40 bucks along with it, which was too much and really sweet and that's the goddamned *point!*" Trisha expertly crescendoed. "She can't stop herself and you knew that and yet you asked for this stupid video game that cost TWO HUNDRED BUCKS!"

Tommy couldn't say anything. This was a crucial moment. The enemy biplane had gone behind the clouds. He was blind to his hunter.

Trisha bent down to scream right in his face, "TWO HUNDRED BUCKS!"

"I didn't ask for this from Mom," Tommy replied, surprising even himself with his calmness. The enemy plane was falling behind.

"Then who *did?*"

"What?" When was she going to leave him alone so he could concentrate?

"I *mean*..." she said, drawing it out with menace, "If you didn't ask for it, then... who... *did?*"

"Well, *I* asked for it. But not from mom."

"What?"

"I wrote a letter to Santa."

Except for the staticky pops and hums of the game, the basement went silent. After a moment, Trisha asked softly (bad sign). "Are you kidding me, Tommy?"

"No?" Was this the right answer?

Again, she exploded, right in his face: "ARE YOU FUCKING KIDDING ME?"

Tom faced her and tried to top her rage. "NO!" But he couldn't even match it. And he'd lost his game. His plane shot right out of the bright orange sky.

Trisha was relentless, more like an irate mom than his mom ever was. "You are eleven years old!"

"So?"

"So?... *So?*"

"Yeah, so?"

"So what eleven-year-old on the planet believes in Santa?"

Tommy shrugged, defiant, always happy to argue the nuances. "I don't *not* believe in him."

"You know what?" she said quietly again, coming in creepily close. Tom tried to ignore her, but she was like a gun barrel pushed up against his head.

"What?" he said finally, but it wasn't the defiant question he intended.

"I'm done." She turned and pounded up the stairs.

Tommy stared at the "game over" screen for a full minute, wondering what he had done. Would they really go into hock because he had thought his mom might think it cute he still wrote to Santa? He started another game, but the fun was ruined. He could never play that console again without feeling a pit in his stomach. By spring he had traded it to Mark Lardieri for a stack of *Playboys*. And Trisha, true to her word, didn't speak to him directly for three Christmases and all the ordinary days in between.

By then Tommy was 14 and the last kid living at home. The great Kavanagh diaspora had begun. And on it still goes: siblings forever scattered in all directions as if blown apart by an ever-exploding A-bomb. Over the next decades they fled to the far flung reaches of the continent, even the globe. (Chasing what? Everything? Anything? Nothing at all? All of it: whatever worked as the rabbit.) They went to New York City, of course, but, hell, that was nothing—Penn Station was just up the Long Branch spur of the New Jersey Transit line.

They went to Chicago, too, and LA, and San Fran, Austin and Boston and D.C. An ashram outside of Telluride for Terry. CiCi lived with a mambo percussionist in Miami for a while. Before that, she spent a year in Liberia with the Peace Corps, coming home only briefly to tell tales of heart-eating wizards and machete amputations. Tommy watched the scattering with wonder from the safety of junior high and high school. His brother and sisters went just about everywhere, doing just about everything, with everyone: smoking, screwing, dancing, drinking, couch-surfing, and Dead-following. Generally consuming life. "All things in moderation," his brother Jamie would opine ebulliently, Cutty rocks in one hand, American Spirit in the other. "Including moderation."

Tommy took such vigorous pride in his heritage: pure Irish on both sides, with maybe just a touch of Welsh, some said, from his father, to keep things interesting. In an essay for eleventh grade social studies he wrote, "There are so many of us, we have taken over the world. This is how we have finally beaten them, our oppressors and enslavers, the English, our murderers and torturers. We took their language and we tortured it in turn, making it sing in ways they never even dreamed of...

"Being Irish," he concluded "Has never been about winning. It is about losing so hard that we overwhelmed and overcame. The Irish overcome."

He was so proud of this essay that he brought a Xerox of it to his brother, tending bar at the time in Manhattan. (Back in the mid-'80s, a 17-year-old as tall and shaggy as Tommy could drink beer with impunity in an East Village dive so long as he knew the bartender.) Jamie read the essay during quiet times, laughing so hard at points that cigarette smoke erupted though his nose.

"Oh, this is good, kid. This is rich."

•   •   •

Tom has a last Hard Way happy hour with Jim V. before his boss's boss heads to Arizona for Christmas. Tom wonders if having two identical houses right next door to each other comes in handy with all the kids and kids' spouses visiting, but instead he asks: "Why did you make a point of introducing me to Terry Torgerson at the party?"

"What? Don't you want the totem pole's top face to know yours?"

"I got the impression he wouldn't be able to pick me out of a lineup if I robbed him at knifepoint."

"Probably not," Jim agrees. "Of course, there are days when I get the feeling he might prefer to see me in a lineup, or better yet, prison orange."

"How come?"

"My job is to tell the truth." He turns to face Tom. "Now, I understand that's not everyone's job. Not even most people's job. But it's mine. And the truth ain't exactly an asset in today's banking industry."

"Why not?" From everything Tom hears on the official SeaTru party line—the company intranet and all-staff emails—banking's better than ever: cheaper, more accessible and equitable, generally helping more people

But Jim isn't biting. "Kid, it's Christmastime. Let's keep it light."

Tom nods and raises his glass. "To light!" They both drink. "What do you do for Christmas? I mean… Do you buy everyone in your family a bunch of presents?"

"Sure. I pay Juanita a thousand extra in cash under the table and she takes my credit card and orders gifts for everyone. And everyone's happy."

"Including your wife?"

"*Especially* my wife. She loves Juanita's taste."

"I'm getting my wife a scarf."

"A scarf's good."

"It's not enough."

"No." Jim looks down at his drink as if he expects it to do something unusual. "A scarf is something you get your mother."

"My mother's dead," says Tom, instantly unsure why. It actually gives him a pang. It's been a year now. For days he wept.

"Yeah, so's mine." Jim replies, gruffly. "What's your point?"

Tom shrugs. "Sorry." They stare at each other in the mirror behind the bar: each remembering his own mother.

Jim tries to get back on track. "She's the one for you, right?"

"Who?"

"Your wife, dumbass. What's her name? It's unusual, pretty."

"Kona."

"Kona." Jim savors the word. "Hawaiian?"

"Yeah. Her mom is from there."

"And she's the one for you, right?"

"Well, yeah. She's my wife."

"Okay, so put some skin in the game and get her something that shows her that she's the one."

Tom sighs.

The next day he goes to the jewelry store on Westlake Plaza, likely the priciest place he could go, but at this late date, why search for bargains? In the second glass case he finds it: a gold mesh choker with an emerald center stone meant to hang right at the divot of the throat. It's two paychecks. He doesn't hesitate. He puts it on his brand-new SeaTru credit card, the one he holds in just his name, the one for which he gets the statements emailed instead of sent hard copy. Kona will never know just how much he paid. But she'll suspect. And she'll be awed. And that's how you do it, right?

•   •   •

Christmas comes.
The drain is circled...
Goes.
...and passed.

The scarf was a hit. Kona also loved the story chapter, or claimed to, from Tom's book-in-progress *Candleshire*, about a brother and a sister who live in a town under a Christmas tree. Kona reads it Christmas night to Poma, who also seemed to like it well enough, except she kept flipping pages and asking, "Where-uh pitchers?"

"They're coming," Tom promises from the kitchen. "I just need to find someone to draw them."

The necklace, on the other hand, went over strangely. He had waited until Poma was busy playing with her new kitchen playset, then he pushed the wrapped package with his toe toward Kona, sitting on the living room couch. She looked at him then picked it up slowly. Because of its shape and size, she knew it contained something special. Once she had unwrapped it, the store's embossed black box confirmed her suspicions. She tilted the lid open and stared inside.

"Well, what do you think?"

"It's..." She just stared. No expression. Nothing.

"Yeah?"

"Gorgeous."

"Are you going to take it out?"

She took it out.

"Do you love it?"

She looked at him as if the question didn't make any sense. "Sure."

"Sure?"

"I love it."

"What's the matter?"

"Is this a real emerald?"

"Of course."

She shook her head. Tom kneeled down in front of her. "Listen. I want you to know that I've been fucking up." She looked up at him. "Well... you already know that. What I want *you* to know is that *I* know I've been fucking up. But that's gonna change because it's *got* to change. I'm committed to us. I'm committed to this family. And I'm gonna change. I have plans. I'm done with the poetry and that shit. That's over."

"Why?"

"'Cause it's time to get serious."

"What's not serious about it? You were always serious about it. I like that stuff. I like that you do it. It's part of why I picked you."

She picked him. That's how she looks at it. He never realized that before. He doesn't remember picking anything. "Look, that's... I don't want to argue about it. That's not the point of this. The point is, I love you. You're the one."

Her eyes were filling with tears.

"What? Why?" he asked

"But I know you love me."

"Okay. But sometimes it's nice to show it, right?"

She nodded and said all too softly, "Okay."

"Okay. So are you going to put it on?

"How much was it, Tommy?"

"Who cares?"

"I care. *We* care. We should care. We shouldn't be blowing money. We should be saving it."

"This isn't a 'we' thing. This is a '*me*-giving-*you*-something' thing."

"That's a 'we' thing."

"Don't worry about it. You deserve it." He rubbed her calf.

She held the necklace up to stare at it again, then said, "Okay," and set it back down in its box, nodding once, sharply.

"You're not going to put it on?"

"Not... right... now. I just... just give me a break, okay."

"I can't believe it."

"I'm sorry."

"I thought you'd be thrilled."

"Tommy, don't you understand? This, whatever it costs, could've gone toward a house. This is a down payment, or a good chunk of one."

"We'll get the goddamned house. One necklace, more or less, doesn't matter."

"Of course it does.

"You can't think in narrow terms. We'll get there. Broad strokes."

"Bullshit, broad strokes. You don't walk ten thousand miles in broad strokes. You walk it one step at a time. That's the only way."

"Well it isn't my way."

"What the hell is your way?"

"Merry fucking Christmas."

.   .   .

That entire night in the East Village dive, way back in the '80s, Tommy had held down the corner of the bar nursing beers his brother fed him. Finally, the regulars had been thrown out under the unholy bright closing-time lights, and Jamie had tipped out the cocktail waitress and the busboy and had locked the front door and turned the lights back down. Then he poured two shots from a bottle of sambuca chilled in a mini-freezer below the bar: so cold that when Jamie lifted the bottle off the glasses with a flourish, the liquor flowed down in a slow, syrupy rope.

"What are you so down about?" Jamie held out two cigarettes, one for himself, one for Tommy.

"Who says I'm down?" Tommy let Jamie light his. ("Always let a bartender light your smoke," his brother had taught him, along with several other lessons in public-house civility that would become obsolete in the coming millennium.)

"You sat there all night, nursing your beers like a Campfire Girl, all the while ignoring the bevy of hot Manhattan ass eye-fucking you."

"None of that ass was interested in me. They knew how young I am."

"They knew and didn't care, shit-for-brains. This is New York Fucking City."

"And I'm in love with a Manasquan girl." It was true. Her name was Shelley, and apparently she'd been in love with him since junior high. This discovery had singularly shocked Tom into requiting her feelings. Why not? She was lovely enough.

"Fuck," Jamie said, blowing smoke in disgust. "More's the pity. You need to get out of that somnambulant town as soon as you can. Spread your wings. Join that diaspora you talk about in your essay. Fuck or fight everything you find."

"You laughed at my essay."

"I sure as fuck did. It was hilarious."

"It wasn't meant to be hilarious."

"It was about the goddamned Irish. How could it not be?"

"Fuck it."

"'The Irish overcame.' I fucking love it."

"Don't start."

"'Don't start?' You hit the nail on the fucking head. 'Overcame.' That's *exactly* what we did. We left that boggy island, and everywhere we went we came and came. We came so hard that you can't throw a stick from Woodside, Queens to Queensland, Australia without hitting some Paddy Bogtrotter or some Paddy Bogtrotter's son or daughter." That's how Jamie talked when he sipped sambuca after hours: like a natural goddamned poet. "Every goddamned one of us is the sorry result of some other poor Mick overcoming."

14.
Presidents' Day

K ona watches him eat the meatloaf that she and Poma had three hours earlier. "What would you say to me getting a job?"

Tom doesn't miss a beat: "I'd say, 'Are you going to make enough to offset the ensuing cost of day care?'"

She smiles, expecting this tack. "To which I would reply, 'No, but...'"

"To which *I* would say—quoting the great Pee-wee Herman, 'Everyone I know has a big butt.'"

She's still smiling. This must be important if she's indulging him so cheerfully. "I won't find the job of my dreams right away. I have to get back in there." Tom chews and nods, serious. "If I can find something, doing what I want to do, maybe part time at first, maybe as some sort of intern, and if I can make enough to offset what it'll cost to put Pomaika'i in day care, then maybe it's something we should consider."

"Okay. Maybe it is."

"Good. Then I'm going to start putting out feelers."

"Feelers are good."

•   •   •

Nearly no one's been around work the entire "dead week" after Christmas. New Year's Eve day is especially mellow, just the way Tom likes it. He leaves at three. Kona makes them a nice dinner, and they get Poma to bed by seven, then head down to the TV room to stay up and watch the ball drop. They don't make it. Tom wakes on the futon couch to find Kona asleep in his arms, some sort of infomercial playing on the TV. He kisses her forehead and picks her up to carry her to bed, but before he makes it to the stairs she rouses and slides like a cat from his arms to climb up on her own.

•   •   •

Today there were 82 more seconds of sunlight than yesterday. Tomorrow there will be 87.

Tom is locked.

The job was supposed to solve his problems: net him enough to support his whole family, and yeah, maybe, ideally, his creativity too. Instead it's gunking up everything, like some speed-sapping computer virus. He's bored shitless. Can't bring himself to write, though he orders himself all different sorts of pens and pencils, Post-its and paper, which he then buries in his bottom desk drawer, like he's hoarding for the office-supply apocalypse.

Then Maddie's back from the holidays, and with her she's brought a hard-on for her new favorite threat to global enterprise security: pandemic flu. She subscribes to all the relevant journals, watches all the latest webinars. She scrupulously avoids inquiring whether Tom's gotten his shot, but the question lingers in the air like rot.

He's strolling on the sidewalk back from the Second Avenue Starbucks one drizzly morning when a pair of bicyclists, a middle-aged man and woman, nearly run him down. "What the fuck?!" he hollers.

"What the fuck yourself?" yells the man.

"This is a sidewalk!"

"So?" The woman barks.

"So ride on the fucking street!" Tom froths. He's stunned at his rage. It's all out of proportion, and it feels fucking great.

"We'll ride where we want. Thanks," the woman smugly calls

over her shoulder as she rides down the wheelchair ramp onto the street, not sparing so much as a glance for oncoming cars. Tom wants to soak his hands in their blood. He heads back to work with the amped chemicals of a savannah near-kill coursing through his veins.

•   •   •

Today was 112 seconds longer than yesterday.
Huge.

•   •   •

Kona's found the perfect job—at least that's what she's calling it: a paid internship with the layout department of a nationally affiliated agency. Tom is a little surprised. "I guess I didn't know you wanted to design."

"Well, you knew I always liked art and drawing and doodling on the computer and stuff." There's that slight sharpening of her tone that's warning him he should probably let it go. He ignores it.

"I knew you liked to do art, but I thought, you know, as an *artist*—like I do writing. Not as something you'd make your living at."

"Would it be so terrible if I did?"

"Not at all." They eat in silence. Poma babbles and plays with her mushed peas. Every so often Kona helps her get a spoonful in her mouth. "It's sort of awesome though…" Tom says. "That you got a paid internship doing exactly what you want to do, like… right out of the blue like that."

Kona puts the spoon down and stares at him. "Yeah. It is."

"So, I'm imagining… some strings got pulled?" Kona waits. "Like… long ones… like from Hawaii?" She waits. "It's gotta be helpful having a dad heading up one of Honolulu's biggest firms."

"Sure is. Though, as you know, Dad's more on the accounts side of things. I'll be on creative. And if I don't earn my keep, all the connections in the world won't keep me in that job, let alone move me up the ladder."

"Ah, the ladder."

"Make your point, whatever it is."

"My only point is it's good to know people."

"I'm good for this job. I'll work hard and learn a lot."

"I don't doubt it for a minute."

"So what's your problem?"

"I don't have a problem."

"Really?"

"Really." He eats. Lets a minute pass. "I'm just saying it's good that you're plugged into the good ol' boys network from the get-go."

"Are you fucking kidding me?"

"Don't cuss in front of Poma."

"Fuck you. *You're* gonna lecture *me* in the advantages of privilege?"

"Really?" Tom acts shocked. "We're gonna play the whole Seattle 'More-Discriminated-Against-Than-Thou' game?"

"How are you discriminated against *at all?*"

"You are so missing my point."

"What *is* your fucking point? 'Cuz it sure as fuck sounded to me like the tall, attractive white guy was casting aspersions on how I got this job, which is going to help us eventually buy a house and have a better life." Tom shakes his head as though the notion were absurd. "What? Were you planning for me to just stay at home forever, greeting you at the door every night with your slippers and a cocktail?"

"Why are you— How did I become this asshole you hate?"

"By being an asshole."

He can feel his face flushing. He looks over at Poma, who gawks back at him with a confused, hurt look, peas drooling from her open mouth. "You know what?" he says, but he doesn't have anything more to say. Instead, he pushes up from the table and grabs his hoodie hanging by the back door, which he is careful not to slam on his way out. At the end of the driveway, he checks his pockets to make sure he has his wallet. He heads south to Lenny's on 54th. They'll understand him at Lenny's: working-class guys.

Fuck! Let's face it, white trash boozers, whining about Seattle liberals like me and my now upwardly mobile, mixed-race family.

It'll be perfect.

And tomorrow he'll beg forgiveness, or she will. And whoever is begged will beg it in return, so that each will be at least half-forgiven. And half will have to do.

Time being.

It's a game of seconds.

Billions of them.

●　　●　　●

By some lucky break, Kona finds a day care with an opening close to her new job. For Tom, it all happens in a blur. Suddenly he's riding the 16 downtown each morning with his kid on his lap and his wife by his side, like some middle-class working family fucking cliché. By the end of January, he's climbing the walls. So, on one Thursday morning's ride in, he asks Kona if she'd mind taking Poma home by herself that evening. She doesn't bat an eye. "Go have some fun. You deserve it." It almost seems like she means it.

After work, Tom pushes the Hard Way's heavy door open to find Jim V. locked in a huddle of concentration with Anna the barmaid and a construction worker absurdly dwarfing the barstool on which he is perched. A bestickered hard hat dangles from his belt. His hair is the color and stiffness of broom straw. Jim splits his attention between inspecting the face of a dollar bill and squinting up into the hulk's eyes. "Waiting on you, Anna," he says, without sparing her a glance.

"I know, I know. I'm thinking. Don't rush me."

Someone farther down the bar hollers, "Anna, what the hell?"

"Hold your horses!" she snarls over her shoulder. "Aw, hell. Four eights!" she says, before stomping away to fill the barfly's glass.

The hard hat keeps his dollar folded in quarters and scrupulously close to his chest, while he scowls at Jim as though contemplating the best way to pluck him limb from limb. "Five fours," he mutters.

"You're a lying sack of shit," Jim replies casually.

"Careful, Shylock. I'm an awfully damned *big* sack of shit, whether or not I'm lying."

"Point taken." Jim gives his bill a last lingering glance before slipping it in his shirt pocket. "Seven sevens."

"Fuck that."

"Yeah?"

"Yeah."

"So call it."

The giant bellows down to Anna. "Seven sevens, he says!" She rolls her eyes as she dumps the head off a draft. Back to Jim he says, "I'm gonna call you, old man."

"Are you?" Jim makes a show of looking at his watch.

"Why wouldn't I?"

"Can't think of a reason."

"'Zactly."

"Other than the ten straight you already lost to me."

"'Seven sevens' even sounds made up. It's a made-up fucking bullshit bid."

"So… call it." Almost daintily, Jim sips.

The worker seems about to, but finally shakes his huge head. "Fuck it. You can afford to lose and I still gotta pay the bus fare to Renton."

"Your call." Jim plucks the single from the man's thick, scarred fingers. "Just don't whine later."

"Fucking bankers," the guy mutters. "Liars and cheats."

Jim nods sagely in agreement. "If you only knew, my honest and hard-working friend." Tom wonders how wise it is for Jim to be needling this guy. "I bet you bank at SeaTru."

"I got an account there. So?"

"How'd we get you in the door? No, don't tell me. Free checking."

The guy shrugs. "You guys offer the best deal."

"There."

"What?"

"Right there." For emphasis, Jim V. points a finger into the man's massive, sheet-rock-dusted chest. Tom tenses. "*That's* where we're fucking you."

"It's a good deal," the guy practically whines. "Better than anything the other banks are running."

"It's a sucker's bet," Jim assures him. "Peanut butter we put on the traps."

The hulk glares at his dregs: a half-empty schooner of beer and a rocks glass with what looks like the leavings of a Goldschläger shot. Softly he says, "It works for me."

Tom's just as surprised and disheartened. He's always admired SeaTru's free checking. Other banks make you keep a 500 minimum balance. Who has that kind of cash to leave fallow?

Jim continues: "Every other bank hated our guts for that free checking offer, until they realized why we were doing it."

"Providing a service," Tom chimes in. "What a concept."

Jim winces at this stupidity. "It's not a service, dummy. It's a poor tax. You think we make money on the interest spread of your lousy minimum deposit—in today's market? Or do you figure we're getting rich charging you a 25-cent fee every time you write a check? He turns back to the hardhat. "How many checks do you write a month? Fifteen? Twenty?"

"Sure. Why not?"

"So that means with regular checking we'd make maybe five dollars, tops, off you every month."

"Okay. That's five dollars I'd rather keep."

"Sure, sure. Now how many of those checks do you bounce?" The hard hat glares at him, but Jim pushes on. "See where I'm going? Let's say you hit the low side of the average and only bounce one, every three months or so, at a rate of 20 to 40 dollars in NSF charges. You wanna do the math, or should I?"

Tom jokes: "We were promised there would be no math."

Jim ignores him, presses on. "A rubber check every quarter means that instead of a measly 60 bucks a year in fees, now I'm taking at least a hundred, if not more like three, just because I convinced you it was a nifty idea to carry a near-zero balance in your checking account, and you bought it."

The construction worker sighs, pulls out the wallet he's been sitting on, plucks a 20 from it. "Put that shit away," says Jim. The older man meets the huge man's eyes squarely. "Anna, Ronnie's on my tab tonight."

"You're the boss," she says.

"Check out Mr. Businessman," Ronnie growls. "Admits to my fucking face he's been cheating me for years, and then thinks he's gonna make it right by paying for a few lousy drinks?" The man is marble in his menace. Tom wonders if he's going to have to wade into a bar fight. Suddenly, and in unison, the banker and the hard hat break into wide grins. Ronnie shoves out his huge, scarred paw, and Jim shakes it eagerly, patting the man's vast back as Ronnie pushes up off his stool and shuffles out onto the street, basking in his gratis happy-hour glow.

Tom takes the open stool. A moment later his signature pale pink Cape Cod appears, unbidden, in front of him. He sips it in silence. Finally, looking at Jim through the bar mirror, he admits, "I really think you might be fucking nuts."

Jim shrugs, sips. "The world is fucking nuts, my friend. I live in it."

"And make money off it."

"That too."

"I had no idea about that free-checking scam."

"Kid, that's cake icing. Real crimes are in home loans."

"Wait. What? I thought we were making home loans more equitable. More accessible, to everyone."

"More's the pity."

"Why?"

Jim calls out, "Anna, how's that adjustable-rate mortgage working out for ya?"

The barmaid hollers back. "I love it!"

"Hear that?" he mutters out of the side of his mouth. "She loves it... Wait 'til the rate resets in two years and her monthly nut doubles."

Anna comes to their end of the bar, swiping it down, grabbing Jim's empty glass. She's eager to talk. "I pay less now on my new house each month than I did in rent on an apartment. Gil's talking about building me a deck come spring."

"Gil's her boyfriend," Jim explains, once she's stepped away. "On disability and nursing a Percocet problem. If he winds up building her a deck, I'll eat my hat."

"So Anna gets a house with her doped-up boyfriend. That's a bad thing?"

"Yes, it is." Jim rubs a hand down his weary face. "Look. We used to say 'no' to people who couldn't afford to buy houses. I mean, that's the basic definition of what a banker did. The old joke was we only loaned money to people who didn't need it. It was harsh. People got locked out. But it worked. For hundreds of years it worked. Now? Now we give loans to everyone. 'Give?' Shit, we practically force 'em." He lowers his voice as Anna comes closer. "And if you're like her, and we think you might not be able to pay it back, then we charge you more for it. A *lot* more. And we call it 'sub-prime.' And then we sell it off to Wall Street, shifting the risk off our own balance sheets and onto the books of the big investment banks hungry for risk: Goldman Sachs, Lehman Brothers, what have ya. They love these shit loans, because they can charge so much more for them. They cut 'em into slices, and then they shuffle all the slices into different CDOs like cards from different decks."

"You owe me five bucks!" Tom blurts.

"What?!"

"Acronym without definition." Tom savors his small opportunity for smugness.

Jim lifts his chin, thinks back through what he just said, then nods. "Collateralized Debt Obligation. There. That help clear it up for ya?"

"Not really."

"All you need to know is that instead of labeling these sausages 'sub-prime,' due to the shit they're made of, Wall Street calls 'em 'Triple-A' premium."

"If it's as bad as that, seems like the shit should eventually hit the fan."

"Kid, the fat money's on the shit never coming *near* the fan."

"Well, maybe the fat money's just the smart money. Isn't it true that real estate prices, overall, never go down?"

"Who told you that?"

"Um... well? Pretty much everyone, constantly, since I was a kid."

"Yeah."

"So are you telling me that's *not* true?"

"Yeah, not really."

"When have real estate prices significantly declined?"

"There was a decade-long dip in the 1930s."

"The Great Depression?" Jim nods, solemnly. "You're suggesting we have another Great Depression coming?"

Jim's tone stays sober, measured, in contrast to Tom's rising outrage and incredulity. "I'm suggesting we got *some*thing coming. I'm suggesting that my eternal truth trumps your eternal truth, that real estate prices never go down."

"What's your eternal truth?"

Jim turns to Tom, utterly sad and resigned. "There's never been a bubble that didn't eventually burst."

"And you're saying you know how to stop this coming crash?"

"I'm saying I know how to bring it to a head more quickly and possibly more painlessly. But mostly, I know how to make money off it—a bona fide tsunami of money—by betting against mortgages. My problem is I can't find anyone willing to stake my bet. The fix is in."

Tom likes Jim, but he doesn't buy for a second that there's some big conspiracy his boss's boss has stumbled onto. It saddens Tom to think how inevitable it seems for cynicism to set in after a certain age. Tom shrugs. "Way of the world, I guess."

Jim shakes his head slowly but vehemently. "In the '90s, we used to write maybe 30 billion a year in subprime mortgage lending. 2005 will see *600* billion, the vast majority of which will find its way to the Street as sausage filler." Tom tries to say something, but Jim holds up a finger. "Now. If I were to graph what I just told you—" in spilled beer Jim V. finger-paints a graph line that sky-rockets upward, "—and then I were to lay over it another line tracking the incidence of mortgage fraud, what do you think that would look like?" In answer Jim draws another line of beer swill paralleling the first. "SeaTru's in the shit-selling business. And since shit doesn't grow on trees, it has to be manufactured. Putting us in *that* business, too, which includes the flat-out fraudster who pushed Anna's ARM on her, knowing full well she'd almost certainly default on it in less than three years, putting her *where* exactly? On the streets maybe? But, hey, who cares? By then it won't be *his* problem. Or *our* problem." Jim lifts his drink in a sloppy toast "To the power of Yes!"

"You want another?" asks Anna, swinging by.

"Only for the last ten minutes," Jim growls.

"You want one or not?"

Jim nods. "And get one for young Plato here too."

"Shouldn't the house of cards be toppling?" Tom asks.

Jim shakes his head again. "Someone would have to have fat money staked on that outcome, someone willing to sell the mortgage market short, like you'd short-sell a stock. And no one's currently in that position."

"I thought there was a market for everything. Invisible hand and all that."

"You're talking about free and fair markets. You might as well talk about unicorns that shit rainbow gold. The mortgage short-selling market does not exist."

"Can it be created?'

"You'd need money—and I mean lots of money."

"Ain't you rich?"

Jim shakes his head wearily, "Kid I ain't even close to that kind of rich. You'd need hundreds of millions to even start. And you'd need some sort of hedge fund with the right access and lawyers. And you'd need to convince them that the mortgage market is as toxic as I'm telling you it is, which means you'd need data."

"Like StreetSweeper."

Jim stiffens. He slowly turns to Tom to take him in squarely. "What do you know about StreetSweeper?"

The younger man shrugs. "Wall Street custom data interface: gives real-time looks into underlying mortgages. I used to do data pulls for Michelle Fleischer from it."

"Yeah?" The old man's gone stone sober.

"Yeah."

"They gave you a login and password for that?"

"Nah. I used hers. I was just working for her temporarily."

Jim nods. Tom drains his ice.

Tom likes Jim but wouldn't swap shoes with him. He can't stop thinking of how much the old man reminds him of Old Man Gower in *It's A Wonderful Life*, especially in the version of the world the angel Clarence makes George visit, where George doesn't exist, where his old boss Mr. Gower is weak and old, soused and bitter.

•   •   •

Maddie's mood seems to have gone the way of the weather: dark, cold, and blustery. The pan flu conference call she had Tom set up devolved into a technical clusterfuck. For unknown reasons, the audio wouldn't stop feeding back, with Maddie's opening remarks looping over and again in a virtual echo chamber between Seattle and the remote rooms in Chicago and L.A. Tom did his best to fix it, but the techs on the help line finally instructed him to restart the call from scratch, adding another ten minute delay. Maddie slammed her binder on the table and stormed out of the room. "I'll be in my office when you get this shit fixed."

Later, Maddie makes an explicit point of asking Darlene to help her with a complex spreadsheet because, as she says to her within Tom's hearing, "My guy isn't quite up to the kind of pivot tables I need." The sad fact is, it's true. Tom really doesn't know shit about pivot tables.

The succession of petty fiascos is humiliating, but Tom's getting used to that. Valentine's Day comes as a perfect example.

Tom happens to be walking by the front desk when Count calls out to him, "Oooh, Tom. Are you heading back to your desk?"

"Sure am." He always tries to stay chipper with Count. It's good to keep the front desk folks on your side, and, conversely, Count and Gayle always seem to go out of their way for him. Count turns to the credenza behind him and puts his arms around a huge bouquet of blood red roses. "Can you take these back to Michelle? Alicia's not picking up and Michelle's on her line."

Tom briefly thinks of making an excuse but realizes it's impossible. "Sure," he says, taking the unwieldy bouquet. Their cloying fragrance enfogs him immediately. He feels like a fucking idiot schlepping them, like some medieval page on errand for the lady of the manor. Alicia's at her desk after all, filing her nails and ignoring her chirping phone like some '60s sitcom cliché.

"Count called back about these," he says, sounding like a scold.

Alicia smirks. "Yeah, I don't answer the phone when I'm on my break. Are those for me?"

"No, Michelle. From Nathan, I'm guessing."

"Well, go ahead and take 'em in," she says, just one more person utterly fucking comfortable bossing him around.

Tom feels his way into the office with his feet. "You want these on your table?"

"Sure," she says. He sets them down and steps back to find her staring at him.

Unable to come up with anything cleverer, he says, "They're very nice."

She shrugs. "Nathan subscribes to a service. I get a delivery on our anniversary, my birthday, Mother's Day, and Valentine's Day. Like clockwork."

"Wow. Smart."

"You think? Oh, and white roses dyed green on St. Paddy's Day." Tom makes a questioning face. "He's a Jew. From New York. Figures it's some sort of holy day for us."

Tom shrugs. "Maybe. Me? I tend to keep my head down. No sense crossing swords with amateurs."

"Long time no talk."

He lowers his voice, hoping Alicia can't hear. "Probably for the best, right?"

"Well, I wish you wouldn't be a total stranger."

"Well, that's what I am, aren't I?" Michelle frowns. "Sorry." He stumbles on, "I just... I don't know... I gotta get back to Maddie. She needs some stuff printed out for her 11:00."

Michelle's mouth twists for an instant, like a cruel queen's, then she snaps back to dead neutral. "Yeah. Of course. Get back to Maddie."

•　　•　　•

Maddie's been piling so much on top of him lately that he comes in on President's Day to catch up. He's got about 30 binders to put together for an upcoming pan flu presentation to the risk sub-committee. (Maddie reminds him that she doesn't like it when people say "pan flu." "It sounds like you're trying and failing to say 'Pan flute.' Just spell it out. People take it more seriously if you spell it out.")

The 16th floor is dark when Tom gets to it on Monday morning. He decides not to turn on the overhead fluorescents. He sort of likes working in just the light of his desk lamp: makes him feel Bob-Cratchity, cozy and forlorn. He starts opening the files that will go into the binders as tabbed inserts. The printing alone should take him to lunchtime. Around eleven, the overheads blink on. Someone else is on the floor.

About 15 minutes later he walks to the printer room to pick up his first batch. He sees it's Michelle's office light lit. His chest tightens. He dithers for a few seconds, but ultimately decides to go over and knock. She looks up. "Just wanted you to know that someone else was in the office so you wouldn't... I don't know... be freaked out by the noise or something."

"Well, thank you. I appreciate it."

"You bet."

"Glad you decided not to be a stranger." She gives him a smug smile.

Tom nods at the point scored. "Okay. I'll see ya later." He goes back to the printer, grabs his packets, and takes them to a conference room so he can spread out.

Tom slips deep into assembly mode, moving from binder to binder, laying hole-punched section after hole-punched section onto the unclasped metal prongs. Over his years of temping, Tom developed a system of scoring each new assignment with how difficult it would be to train a monkey to do it. This task would score big monkey points, although, truth be told, Tom really doesn't mind. He relaxes into the repetition and lets his mind go pleasantly clear. If he wanted, he could daydream a bit, but he prefers to stay blank. He's a happy cog, "a useful engine" in the parlance of the *Thomas the Tank Engine*, which Poma has started watching. He knows what he's supposed to be doing, and he's doing it.

It's almost just enough.

15.

The Monaco

A lmost.

And then she's there, leaning against the conference room door, watching him with an amused look on her face, thrilling an ice pick into his chest. "Hi," she says.

She's wearing a brown suede skirt, slightly shorter than the blue and gray suit skirts she wears on regular days. Its hem falls just above the knee instead of just below. (She has the knees of a 17-year-old.) Even the fact that she's not wearing any makeup is arousing: her beauty more striking in starkness. Good thing he's wearing jeans, 'cuz he can already feel his dick swelling.

Christ almighty, Kavanagh!

Tom goes back to slipping the hole-punched pages onto the binder prongs, one after another. He finishes a row of ten, then allows himself to look up at her again, still standing there, still watching. "Can I help you?" he asks.

"You're the one who looks like he could use a little help."

"You offering?"

Cutesy pained apology face. "Uh… not really?"

"Ah." He goes back to collating.

"We never really talked after the Christmas party," she says.

"Were we supposed to?"

"Why wouldn't we?"

He doesn't answer.

"I don't think you need to ignore me quite as much as you've been managing to." He has no idea if he's putting these binders in order anymore. It doesn't matter. *Just look busy.* "I like you. I have fun with you. I don't see why we can't be civil."

"I'm totally down with that."

"You're 'down' with that?" She mocks him like a teenager.

"I'm just not sure what you want from me." *Now you just sound pathetic.*

"You want me to want something?" She tilts her head and smiles, her bare arm akimbo at the spot where her short suede skirt meets her sheer white T-shirt.

"What do you want to hear? That I liked you? Felt strongly? Fantasized about you and frankly still do? Does that help you get through the day?" *Dammit, his dick's hardening again. Why did he have to start confessing things?*

She squints. "What does that look like, I wonder?"

"What does *what* look like?"

"Your fantasy."

"Stop."

"No, I'm curious. How does it play out?"

"Just go, please."

"Do you take me in the office? Or at your house? Do we go to a hotel?"

This isn't happening.

"Do we fuck or just fool around?" It's unnervingly unreal, her calmly asking these questions across the wide expanse of the conference room.

"Jesus! Seriously! What do you want from me?" His chest expands suddenly with all kinds of hope for answers. "Who *are* you?"

Calmly, like a conscientious professor handling a troubled student, she answers, "I'm the woman you claim to fantasize about. And I want to know how it works."

"How it 'works'? It *doesn't*! I'm fucked up. I may have done irreparable damage to my marriage." A lump swells in his throat as soon as he says this.

Now she's frowning: flirt mode deactivated. "I'm sorry. I didn't know."

"It's..." How did he become such a drama queen? "It's probably not as bad as I make it sound."

"It's just... I'm sorry," she murmurs. "You made me feel something, for that brief moment and..."

Oh god...

"...and it was special, and I thank you for it." She seems about to go.

"Don't you worry?" Tom calls across the room. "Aren't you afraid?"

"Sure. I worry about nearly everything. I worry that my own marriage has gone completely stale; that my son's a drug addict. I worry that my daughter will grow to hold me in contempt, if she doesn't already. I worry about my job..." She throws her arms wide, "Everything... but when I think about how you made me feel... that night at the Christmas party, I..." she shakes her head, smiling bitterly. "I worry that I'll never feel that way again." She turns.

Fuck. "Don't... Not yet."

She turns back, takes a full step back into the room, and closes the door. The entire volume of the space suddenly electrifies. His body flushes from toe-tips to crown. Now she's rounding the long, polished cherry wood table, closing the distance between them. Now she's standing right in front of him, half a step too close, gazing at his chest—eye-level for her—saying, "Christ. You're shivering."

"Shuddering."

"No... You're shivering. Why?"

He doesn't want to answer.

"Why?"

"I can smell you."

"Oh," she shrugs. "Sorry?" He shivers again. "Oh my. You're like a racehorse or something."

"Or something."

She gazes up into his eyes.

"You need to run."

"It's been a while since I've been running."

She shakes her head slowly. "No... that's not what I mean. I mean...." She trails a finger down his chest, "...release." He lets out a breath, long and ragged. He doesn't try to talk, because he's afraid he can't. She puts the tip of her finger to the tip of his penis, rock hard, pointed straight up beneath his jeans. "I owe you that much." Leaning forward, she puts her mouth on his neck and whispers onto his skin, "One release." She undoes the top button of his fly. "Then we're square." The head is already poking up and pushing out a bead of clear fluid. Like a doctor spotting the problem, she says, "Mm-hmm. There it is." She pops another button.

"Oh god."

She grabs his cock fully in her fist and starts working it up and down.

"Oh, holy Christ... This is... this is..."

She kisses him, softly, lips open. "What?" she says into his mouth. She pulls back, looking at him questioningly, as if she really expects an answer. All the while working him up and down, just the perfect amount of grip. *How does she know?*

"I am not..." he starts to say, "I can... not."

"Cannot what?" Her expression is deeply curious, pure interest of science.

"...do this. I cannot... do this. I am not... "

"I think you can."

"Please..."

"Can," she says, grinning. She looks down. He does, too. More pre-come has oozed out, delicate lubricant in her light touch. "I think you can... just... about..." she looks him in the eyes. "Now," she says, and grips it harder, stroking down swiftly. He comes. Hard. She dodges the first arcing spurt, letting it soar far across the corporate carpet. He jerks again and again. And each time she giggles and dodges, aiming his cock to the side, until he's spent. "See?" she says. "You were holding on to a lot there."

With his pants falling off his hips he's suddenly embarrassed. He hikes them up and buttons his fly, while she watches, amused.

"So... now we're even."

He shakes his head, disbelieving. "Right... but..."

"But what?"

"But how am I not going to want more of you?"

"How much more do you want?"

"Are you kidding?" He pulls her to him. Kisses her deeply. She melts willingly, then pushes him back and looks down at his crotch, bulging to life again. "Damn. What are you, a teenager?"

"I could fuck you where you stand."

Michelle shakes her head slowly, solemnly. *Oh fuck.* His heart sinks. He's gambled too far. Crossed a line. She never had any intention of ever going *that* far.

Guessing his thoughts, maybe, she holds up one finger. "Not here." His heart rebounds almost painfully, suddenly soaring somewhere over Third Avenue.

"Okay." He pulls her to him.

She pushes back, lifts a second finger. "And not without birth control."

Oh! "Of course not."

"So... Might I suggest a plan?" She gazes into his eyes questioningly.

"You might."

"How soon can you finish up here?"

"Soon."

"Do it. I'll finish back at my desk. At..." she looks at her watch. "...11:45 we'll meet for lunch at Sazerac. Do you know it?"

Tom has never eaten there, but he's made several lunch reservations for Maddie. "Sure. The bottom of Hotel Monaco."

Her eyes brighten. "Very astute. I'll buy lunch. And you can come up with something for dessert. Good?"

"Good."

At the entrance to the drugstore on Third and Pike there's an old homeless guy selling *Real Change* newspapers from the front basket of his Rascal scooter. Tom's seen him before in the Hard Way. On his way out, with his box of condoms in a white plastic bag, Tom shoves a dollar of his change into the old guy's cup and waves a "no thanks" at the paper offered.

Tom marvels at his feet moving forward; but then, how could they not? You can swear to yourself that you chose your direction, but, regardless, your feet always stay pointed at the grave, due north death.

Where's your stupid notebook when you need it?

"In my back pocket like always," Tom mutters, under his breath.

So why not jot the note? "Due North Death." It's pithy enough.

"Fuck you." Tom doesn't notice the hunched Asian lady scowling at him as he passes.

•　　•　　•

Tom picks nervously at a Niçoise salad. His stomach is roped tight, and besides, he doesn't want to get shit stuck in his teeth. At Michelle's suggestion, they split an exquisite bottle of French white.

They talk about art. They talk about beauty. Or at least that's how it seems to Tom. He's really not sure. He can't seem to pay attention to anything but her face and his aching hard-on. They talk about travel, and how little of it Tom has done. Never seen Europe. Never seen Asia. Nothing. Puerto Vallarta once, being the farthest he's ever gotten, for a morose spring break. "Still, I had it better than some. When my father was young, the only way a man of my means could travel was by joining the service."

"What do you mean, 'your means'?"

"You know what I make."

"So make more."

"Why didn't I think of that?"

"Why *do* you work as an admin?" This conversation is not going in a direction he'd prefer. "I mean, I'm assuming you could move up the ladder if you wanted."

"Not really. I don't have a diploma."

She seems genuinely shocked. "You didn't graduate high school?"

"No. What?... No. I didn't graduate *college*. Left after my soph-omore year."

"Oh." She still seems puzzled, just less so.

"For the record, I graduated high school early. I was taking college courses as a 10th grader." *Fuck, Kavanagh. You are one pathetic douche.*

"Okay. So you didn't get a degree. Go back and get one."

"With all my free time?"

"I got my master's when I was pregnant," she says, casually forking a hunk of salmon. "And I had a three-year-old running around." She smiles, swallows her bite, then says: "Sorry. Am I being a dick?"

•   •   •

Michelle consumes him in that hotel room. And he recipro-cates. There's a brilliant boldness to their give and take, each of-fering, by some marketplace miracle, exactly what the other most wants.

Later, spent and glued to each other under the high thread-count sheets, they plummet into the deep blackest of naps.

He rouses in half-darkness to find to her circumscribing one of his nipples with her tongue. And then they're fucking again. Then room service for dinner and an awkward call home, which thank-fully goes straight to voicemail: "Hi. I got sucked into another big project. I'm gonna grab a quick drink somewhere afterward. Blow off some steam. Then head home. Love you. Bye."

Michelle whispers in his ear: "Blow off some steam?"

He hits "end call" and turns to her. "I really gotta go."

Michelle falls back, spreads her limbs beneath the sheets and scowls at the ceiling. "That's it? You're gonna fuck me three times and then split?"

"No."

"No?"

"No," he rips the covers off. "I'm gonna fuck you *four* times and then split."

•   •   •

The dash clock reads 10:57 p.m. when Michelle drops him at the bottom of the hill that leads up to her house. He figures the half-mile clockwise hike around the lake ought to help him pull his thoughts together.

At the boat rental shack, he turns off the path and heads out to the edge of the dock. He doesn't need to put his hands to his face. All he can smell is her. All of her, all over him. The smell of her hair in his hair. Her skin on his. The taste of her tongue still lingering in his mouth. He can't go home like this. Impossible. Insane.

So, he jumps—shoes, clothes, coat, and all—into the black water beyond the edge. It's great how freezing it feels. He figures that on his long, soggy walk home he'll have time to work up a lie about falling in.

16.
The Fever

He calls in sick the next day. He isn't, but he doesn't want to see Michelle, and he doesn't want to work, and he doesn't want to ride the number 16 milk run downtown with his wife and toddler daughter. He doesn't want to do anything but sleep. He's got a bunch of sick time saved up, so what the hell? "Mental health day." Isn't that what they call it?

He naps most of it away in the bedroom/office Kona has created in the basement next to the TV room. She said she thought it would be nice to have a place for guests; but Tom can't help suspecting she also wanted to give him somewhere other than their shared bed to pass out drunk. She painted the walls and ceiling a corporate beige. Staring at it most of the day, he decides it's a very un-Kona-like choice of color.

The next day he actually *is* sick. It started around midnight: in bed with Kona he began feeling chilled and restless. So he crept down to the beige room so as not to disturb her. The faint burning in his sinuses flared to a full blown four-alarm fire by 2:00 a.m. Now it's the middle of the black night and he's sneezing and coughing up vast, viscous quantities of snot. As dawn begins to brighten the window he finally falls into fitful sleep, cut through with scraps of dream he can't quite thread together.

Bed spread thread shreds.

Words drained of meaning circling around and round.

Poet don't know it.

Tom drinks from an old camping thermos Kona was kind enough to fill with ice water before leaving. (She called in sick for him today, too.) He refills the thermos at the utility sink next to the washer/dryer in the unfinished part of the basement. He also uses this sink to piss in, not caring to climb the precarious stairs to the bathroom.

Gotta do something about those soon, or Poma's gonna take a tumble and crack her head open on the bare concrete at the bottom.

The walls are beige.

Cracker head open bare bottom.

There's a computer in a cheap, varnished blonde credenza pushed against the interior wall of the office, which is beige.

Pushed blonde.

On the computer in the credenza is the internet, on which there is pornography. Tom considers availing himself of this modern convenience, as Tom is especially determined to assiduously avoid the calling up of memories of the Monaco.

Acid juicy.

Instead, at first, he tries to show some masturbatory loyalty by attempting to conjure visions of Kona, but that proves much too much effort. On the internet, however, there is porn: quick and easy.

He's no better on Thursday morning. If anything, he's worse: head detached and ringing. Maddie calls him right back after the voicemail he leaves calling in sick. "Are you drinking enough fluids?"

He croaks, "I am."

"You sound horrible." He's glad she thinks so. Best to be convincing. "I won't take this opportunity to emphasize that this is exactly why flu shots are so important."

Are you fucking kidding? "It's not the flu. It's a sinus infection."

"Should I be worried?"

"Worried?"

"Should I be looking for your replacement?" *What in the ev-er-loving fuck?* "There's a lot of stuff piling up. I'm just wondering if I should get a temp in." She pauses, as if considering it. "Anyway, that's not your concern. You just get better."

"Thanks, Maddie."

"You take as long as you need."

"Thanks, Maddie." He hangs up, gut sinking, brain tumbling backward sideways into yet more dream-fever foolishness.

Late afternoon. Can hear Kona banging around upstairs. Feels lonely for her, and for Poma, but dares not attempt the stairs. And Kona keeps the kid with her so as not to disturb him. Sweet of her.

He spends the whole weekend this way. Kona and Poma gone for hours, time and time again.

Even the stupid ceiling is beige.

Why did she paint the ceiling?

At night the room turns gray as the walls leech their beigeness.

Phone rings. *Beige.* Morning. Phone rings. Monday maybe. *Though these could be Tuesday beige walls.* Phone rings. Clock glows red: "9:47." Phone displays gray LCD: "SeaTru." *Has to be Maddie.* Not her direct line, though. Conference room? *Fuck.* Phone rings. *She's ratcheting.* Should answer. *Tell her I'm coming in tomorrow for sure.* Phone rings. *Even if it isn't true. Buy some time.* He grabs the receiver, puts it against his head. "Hello." Throat throbs.

"What are you doing?" Woman's voice. *Not* Maddie.

"I'm sorry?" he croaks.

"You hiding or something?"

…?

"It's Michelle."

His heart punches him once from the inside. He actually winces. "What are you…" He can't manage anything else.

"How long are you going to stay away?"

"I'm not… I'm sick."

"Yeah. I can hear that. I'm sorry."

"Well, it's not your fault."

"No?"

He says nothing. *Fuck.* For all he knows, maybe it is.

Can't remember how he gets off the phone with her, but it's lying next to him off the hook when he wakes up in the bright-beaming, late-morning sun. Wonders if it happened. Seems unlikely. Hell, preposterous. "I've been thinking about you," she had said. "A *lot*." He could swear she had added that.

And that he had pleaded: "I can't do this right now. I can't… talk to you. I'm sick." Must have sounded pathetic.

"I understand. But I'll see you again, right? You're not going to just disappear, are you?" Voice soft, smooth, like the inside of her thigh.

"You'll see me."

"Feel better, okay?" *Not imagining the way she had said* that. *At least don't think so. "Feel better, okay?" So sweet, so filled with genuine concern, just like a new girlfriend would say it.*

Fuck that.

"I know. I *know*," he says out loud.

Fuck you. You "know"? You know shit. This woman is not your new fucking girlfriend.

"You don't think I fucking know that?"

I have no idea what you think, you pathetic fuck.

"*You're* the pathetic fuck."

Silence.

Sleep.

Sunbeam lights the floating motes. Out of nowhere: *No one has ever fucked anyone like you fucked that one in that room at the Monaco.* His cock gives an instant nudge, single soft knock at a door.

Unbelievable.

He fucked that woman. He fucked her. That gorgeous—*married: And* you're *married, too, asshole*—woman. He gives in, finally picturing it all over again, working himself until he explodes all over his sweat-salt-stained sweatshirt.

Fuck.

"I'm lost," he says out loud.

Some truth, finally.

Sleep.

When Kona comes to check on him that night, he tries to pull her into a hug, but she easily pushes him down. "You stink."

"But I put on a clean shirt." It's true. He did it in the late afternoon, finally replacing the one he'd been wearing for three days.

"You still stink. Like..." she gives it some consideration. "... Sick homeless person."

"Gee, thanks."

She shrugs. "Truth hurts. Or in this case, reeks. Get better. Then get a shower. Then get better some more. You need rest." She disappears upstairs into sounds of cooking and Poma playing.

This box is beige.

As is only just.

•   •   •

On Wednesday he's finally strong enough to go in.

Well... not really. But the problem is he's run out of sick time. If he stays away any longer his paycheck will shrink. If he stays away any longer, Maddie really might replace him, whether she adores him or not.

He's kitten-weak climbing onto the bus with Kona and Poma. The number 16 bounces and jounces the whole slowpoke ride in. At the symphony Starbucks, he treats himself to a cranberry scone and grandé drip before heading up to the 16th floor.

Maddie is surprisingly gracious in their first one-on-one, giving him just a few minimal tasks for when he's done digging himself out from over a week's worth of missed emails. She doesn't mention the flu shot, but Tom suspects this is only because she feels supremely confident that her point has been driven home.

Once, in the corridor near her office, he passes Michelle. She nods at him, friendly. No one observing would ever guess at what they were doing to each other eight days earlier.

He's made it to the end of the day. He's on the elevator and the brushed metal panels close to offer him his slightly blurred reflection. A hand darts in, the doors recoil with a jerk. Michelle steps on. The doors close completely. She's behind him, pressed against the back of the car as it descends. He can't see her but can feel her breathing. His head spins a little. He's sure he still has a touch of fever. The car slows, and just before they hit the lobby, he hears her say:

"I'm still hungry."

The doors part. She strolls out past him and is gone.

17.
Logistics of the Future

We live in the future.
And the future lives in logistics.

That's what Tom's training module says. And turns out, it's true. Tom himself is currently living in a future where he's fucking his ex-interim boss from behind in a hot tub in a Snoqualmie Falls Lodge suite. And what got him here?

Simple: logistics.

How we communicate.
How we get things done.

It was the day before St. Patrick's Day when he got an email from an address he didn't recognize: GiveAChit@hotmail.com. The subject line read: "Happy Belated President's Day…" He dismissed it as spam at first, but a secondary sinking feeling prompted him to open it: "… or maybe I should say, 'Happy Early St. Paddy's?' I know it *could* be. Get yourself an anonymous email and reply. We'll go from there. Yours…"

Logistics.
They're everywhere.

Tom's vision went grainy for a moment, like a photo taken decades ago with low-light film. He hit delete. Then went to his deleted folder and deleted it from there.

For the executive assistant,
executive communication is key!

What could be truer? How could you have closer communications with your executive than plunging inside her? It's scalding bliss. The hot tub opens onto the bedroom, so that through the balcony's sliding door he can see the vapor rising off the falls as the spring runoff roils to froth and mist on the rocks below.

Logistics break down barriers.

On St. Paddy's Day he found a kelly green Post-it note stuck to the back of his mail-room cubby. In anonymous block letters it read, "SEND EMAIL." He made sure to tear the Post-it through the letters themselves, twice. Then he tossed half of the torn pieces into the mail room's recycle bin and the rest in the bin in the break room.

The day after, he got an email from MFleicher@seatru.com, Michelle's regular work address. The subject line read "Open Position Opportunity." He sneered at the audacity. He considered deleting the message unopened, but felt compelled to understand just how big a risk she was willing to run. He had to have some scope on the crazy. So he double-clicked:

Dear Tom,

Wondering if you would be interested in meeting informally to discuss an interim out-of-class position opening soon on my market risk data management team.

Perhaps a coffee next week some time? My calendar's up to date. Just send an invite for a time that works for you. I'll make sure Alicia accepts it.

Thanks!
Michelle Fleischer
Senior Vice President of Market Risk
Seattle Trust Bank

That afternoon he caught her in the elevator lobby. "Really?"

he hissed, desperate to keep his voice low. "A work email?"

She smiled at him. "Oh, you saw that. Good. Have you sent Alicia a time?"

"Hell no. It's totally traceable."

She frowned now, perfect picture of innocent bemusement, as if there were cameras on them. *Holy shit, were there?*

"Are you okay, Tom?"

"No, I am not."

"I can tell you it's an entry-level position. I know you don't have deep experience in the field, but as I recall you did do some similar work in New York... with American Express." His head swam. The elevator opened.

"Yeah, that's right. I worked on a currency exchange database."

"Great. That's what I thought." She stepped on, pushed her floor. "Look, I gotta get to this meeting, but send me an invite for that coffee next week, and we'll go a little deeper."

Fuck!

"Fine," he said, petulant teenager. And just as the doors closed, she touched the tip of her tongue to the corner of her mouth.

•   •   •

At the symphony Starbucks he cooled his heels five, ten, fifteen minutes. Finally, nearly half an hour late, she stalked toward his table with a faintest glimmer of a grin. She ran a hand under her skirt as she sat.

"Maddie expected me back at my desk five minutes ago."

"Oh, I ran into Maddie on the way over: told her I was running late and might hold you up."

Tom frowned. "Do not drag Maddie into this."

"Into what? Oh, the job opportunity? Well, I know she likes you, but if it works out, she'll have to understand that it's better money and a better chance for your advancement."

"I'm not gonna take your bullshit job."

"In all seriousness," she said. "You could train on the job. You could get the company to pay for undergrad courses at the U and finish your degree in finance. And then you could get a master's. The U has an excellent night school program."

"You got it all mapped out. And I'd report to you?"

A White Witch of Narnia smile spread across her face. "Not officially, no. But you *would* be spending a lot of time directly under me." He covered his face with his hands. "What?"

"We gotta stop."

"Do we?"

"Please?"

"Seems to me, we need to find a better way to communicate."

Logistics is communications.

He made up his own quasi-clever anonymous email address: MonacoRunner2005@juno.com, and he replied to hers.

Once you know what your executive wants, it's time to deliver.

Oh, he's delivering. He's got his right middle finger gently but firmly brushing her clit while his left middle finger twirls her left nipple, and she pounds her ass back against him: again, again, again.

The logistics of birth control have proved a bit harder to overcome. He needed to find a way to keep condoms on hand without consistently killing the momentum of each ripe opportunity by going to the store first. So he kept a supply of them in his desk at work, until the day he came back from the men's room to find Maddie crouched in his cube pawing through his drawers.

"Looking for something?"

"I need some goddamned Wite-Out. Why is this one drawer locked?" She tugged at it futilely as proof.

"Oh, I keep my wallet and phone in it sometimes."

"You worried about someone stealing your wallet off the executive floor of a bank? Jake does a circle every 90 minutes."

Tom shrugged. "Force of habit, working in New York and all. I don't have any Wite-Out, but I do have this." He offered her a correction tape dispenser. "Just press it to the paper and drag it along any line you want to blank out. Way less messy." Maddie eyed the dispenser dubiously but took it and ducked back into her office.

Tom sat, concentrated on breathing, waited a good minute before taking out his keys, unlocking the drawer and reaching to the very back to grab the four-strip of condoms hidden there. These damned things have become his oppressor. He hates how they feel, always squeezing and constricting, or riding up wrong: banal emblems of guilt, always reminding him of reality. How is *reality* the point of any of this? Right now, fucking her in this hot tub, his cock is getting Indian burn.

**Logistics are the future,
but the challenges are ever-changing.**

"I want you to come in me," she gasps.

"I'm wearing a condom."

"You know what I mean."

Fuck.

He can't do it. He pulls out; tears it off. Works himself with his hand, staring at her rippling spine, hoping for the best, encouraging himself with the notion of how delightfully different it is to come *on*, instead of *in*; and there it is, shooting up across her shoulders.

She stands abruptly and grabs a towel. "Okay. That's one way to do it," she says, wiping awkwardly at her back.

"I hate these fucking things," he whines, the dead soldier dangling from his finger. He flings it at the waste can and it sticks like a gecko to the hanging lid that's supposed to open on impact.

**Logistics are the future,
but meeting ever-changing challenges takes communication.**

They are lying in bed, her head snuggled into the crook of his armpit.

"If you could do anything you wanted, what would it be?"

She turns to look at him and says, all seriousness, "I think I just did it."

"No. I mean… for a living."

"Oh, yeah. No," she says, frowning. "I probably wouldn't want to do *that* for a living. Might take all the fun out of it."

Tom looks up at the ceiling. "I don't want to be an admin all my life."

"I wouldn't think you would."

He turns to her. "How about you? If you could have any job, make as much as you want doing it, what would it be?"

"What makes you assume I'm not doing that already?"

Tom's taken aback. He never suspected someone could be happy in an office job, no matter how high up the corporate ladder one had climbed. But Michelle seems serious. "That's awesome," he says. And he's close to meaning it. "So you're happy?"

"Well," Michelle shrugs her beautiful, smooth shoulders. "Happiness is like money, isn't it?"

"How so?"

"Can you ever really have enough?"

Tom gives this some thought. It doesn't really add up for him, but he doesn't want to tell her that—doesn't want to break this current spell of quiet honesty between them. Instead, in utter earnestness he asks, "What would make you happier?"

She gazes soulfully into his eyes. "You really want to know?"

"I really do."

"To not be quite as sore as I am right now… so that you could fuck me again."

"Ah." He feels his dick swell. "Well, think I might know a cure."

He pulls his shoulder out from under her and kisses her lips, then drags his tongue down her neck to a nipple, then works his way farther down.

Logistics are the future, but…

Now, in the future, after making her come hard with his mouth and her doing her best to return the favor, she's riding him in reverse, watching herself in the mirror facing the bed, her dark brown hair falling around her shoulders, lustrously lost in the re-

flection of herself fucking. Tom's staying hard, but with the condom and the amount of sex they've already had, there's no chance
in hell he's going to come. Curious, he reaches with the fingertips
of both hands and touches both of her ass cheeks.

"Yes," she says, as if answering a colleague who just asked her
to coffee. So he holds her up a bit, a cheek to each hand, as she
bounces on him. It's a perfect ass. Can this woman possibly be in
her 40s? "Yes," she says again, same distraction.

> ...recognizing the ever-changing environment
> is the best way for an executive assistant
> to meet the constant challenges of logistics,
> and consistently overcome them.

He casually creeps a thumb to her ass crack. She makes no
sign of noticing. Now his curiosity is earnestly rising as his cock
goes stiffer inside of her. This she seems to notice, letting out a
light sigh and quickening her pace. He sits back and enjoys this for
several strokes, then cat-killer curiosity gently nudges his thumb-
tip in and finds her puckering anus. He simply rests it there. "Yes,"
she says again.

This is wrong. He knows that. This is nasty. And fantastic.
This is living. This is what you are absolutely supposed to do with
life. You grab for it. You take what's offered. You bite the goddamned apple. Because that's what goddamned apples are for. It's
why goddamned God put them in the goddamned garden in the
first place. This is how happiness is pursued.

He pushes it in. She pounds him harder, faster, until she comes,
over and over, yelping like a puppy.

But he doesn't come. There's no way he's going to come. Not
with this desiccated latex chafing him. Not with as many times as
he has come already. He looks around at the amazing room. Feels
the amazingly soft, smooth sheets under his ass. He could never
afford to stay in any place like this, let alone use it only for a few
hours of fucking. When she had put down her credit card at the
check-in counter, he whispered in her ear. "I'll split it with you."
She shrugged dismissively, didn't even bother to turn around.

"Money's the least of our worries."

"But—"

She held up a hand. "We'll sort it all out later."

**In the business world,
in the world at large,
yours is the reality you create.**

Inspiration comes to him. He pretends. Simple! He's rather convincing, if he may say so. And the rubber makes covering his tracks a breeze. Why had he never thought of this before? Maybe because he never had to?

Logistics are the future.

More future. Sprawled in bed again.

"What do you and Nathan do?"

She doesn't answer. Darkness has begun to gather in the room.

"Hello?"

"What are you talking about?"

"I'm talking about you and Nathan."

"You are not seriously asking me how I fuck my husband?"

"What? No! I'm talking about birth control."

She turns to look him in the eye. "What do you *think* we do?... We use condoms."

"Oh."

He lets some future slip by.

"How often?"

"Really? So we *are* doing that?"

"Nope." He'll let it drop. That said, he's not going to placate her with small talk. He lets the silence go long.

The future is forward.

He can be as mysterious as the next guy. He figures she's forgotten, maybe even drifted off. But then: "Fridays," she says.

"What?"

"We do it on Friday, if we do it at all."

"Oh... So... pay day?"

"Cute." Suddenly a heavy down pillow thumps on his face.

The key to satisfying your executive's needs...

He flips her on her back. Pins her. "I think in the case of *this* limited partnership, we'll need to negotiate a somewhat more aggressive fee structure."

... is as simple as pushing forward.

18.

Hurricanes and Hotels

Poma turns three.

Really?

Of course. That's how the future works. It's ravenous and relentless.

Poma turns three, and she loves *Blue's Clues* even more than she did in the past, but now, in the future, she *also* loves the large color foam alphabet puzzle her daddy helped her put together on the floor of the unfinished part of the basement, and she loves the color "dark pink"—not "pink," mind you—*dark* pink. You might call it magenta, but you'd be wrong, and Poma would let you know. Tom attempted such foolishness once. She cocked her head and firmly corrected him, "No, Daddy! Dat's dark pink!"

You wanna argue with the future? You go right ahead.

Her hair has darkened, now just on the brown side of blonde. Her blue eyes have transmuted as well, to mostly gray, sometimes green. Tom had hoped they'd stay bright blue like his, but hopes don't live in the future.

Poma likes it when her daddy rubs colored chalk on the bottom of his fist and stamps Blue's paw prints on the basement's cement floor. "A clue! A clue!" she shouts, just like on the show. She likes Elmo too, of course, but she's not crazy about Dora. "Dumb" she mutters when it comes on and promptly exits the room. She also doesn't like scary stuff, and almost anything on the TV can be scary. Certainly the news, which Tom likes to watch when he gets home. "Daddy. News too scary."

"Don't I know it, kiddo. Still, Daddy likes to watch it, so go upstairs if you don't want to." But she doesn't go upstairs. Instead she straddles his lap facing him, blocking his view by combing his hair back with her dark pink comb and putting it in barrettes, the color of which you should be able to guess.

Oh, and kid's a fish. Absolutely loves her swim lessons at Green Lake Community Center's indoor pool. These lessons are always a time of extra tension between Kona and Tom, so maybe it's a good thing he misses them at least half the time, either working late for Maddie, or drinking with Jim, or fucking Michelle in some random downtown hotel room. When Tom does show up, Kona prefers him to be the one in the pool with Poma, but Kona goes regardless and watches from the bleachers, because of that one time at free swim when they were all in the pool and Tom thought Kona had her, and Kona thought he did, and instead Poma was at the bottom of the water, three feet deep. "Drowning," Kona later asserted. But Tom feels this is an overly dramatic interpretation of events.

"She was exploring." Turning to his little girl, he asked, "Weren't you, darling girl?"

Poma nodded solemnly.

In any case, she does her parents proud, both of whom grew up within walking distance of separate oceans.

And the spring, being future, blurs by.

•　　•　　•

Tom takes the family to the Fourth fireworks at Gas Works again, but without SeaTru VIP passes. They decide to bike down from the house this time—Tom towing Poma in a trailer Kona picked up at Value Village. The three of them spend the day on a blanket with the unwashed masses, trying not to get too sunburned waiting for it to get dark enough for the fireworks to finally light up the southern skyline. He and Kona take turns keeping Poma occupied: walking her down to the lake to dip toes in the frigid water and marvel at the practically naked teenage skinny-dippers in their soaking shirts and underwear.

Getting home afterward is a total clusterfuck, even though they thought they were being smart by biking. Tom's confidence that Poma will quickly fall asleep in her trailer—which Kona made extra comfy with a blanket, pillows and Poma's favorite stuffies—is dashed as soon as he clears the crushing crowds outside the park and begins pedaling the steep climb to Wallingford. Poma immediately starts screaming to get out. The poor thing is four hours past her bedtime and badly sunburned despite their best efforts with the SPF 50. Tom soldiers on, standing to pedal, and cutting sharply between the blaring red brake lights; but when he hears the screaming stop and the trailer zipper opening, he knows he's in real trouble.

"Poma! Stop it! Sit on your *bottom!*"

Where the hell is Kona?

Suddenly the bike lurches forward as he loses 40 pounds of deadweight. And then comes the caterwauling: abject pain and terror. He leaps off his bike and runs back to her, but Kona has already scooped her up, inspecting her gushing raw hamburger knee. "Shhh shhh shhh," Kona coos. "You're gonna be okay. It's only an owie."

"Daddy made me fall!"

"No, no. It's not *daddy's* fault. *You* broke the rules. You never *ever* get out of the trailer while it's moving. Never *ever*. And this is why." The kid lets loose another shriek of existential rage. Tom knows exactly how she feels.

They trudge slowly home, Tom pushing Kona's bike, and Kona pushing his with Poma back in the trailer. She's barred her father from touching it. And now, of course, she's sound asleep. Maybe six blocks from their house, Kona mutters, "Why can't you stop fucking up?"

He stops dead in his tracks. "You're kidding, right?"

Kona pushes the bike past him as he gapes at her, frozen where he stands. She continues down the hill and out of sight.

Finally, he climbs onto her bike, far too small for him, and coasts down to the lake.

On Aurora Avenue he finds, to his mild surprise, a new bar, the St. Andrew's. Inside is a lively post-fireworks crowd. They have an entire wall of fancy scotches, so he orders a Macallan 12 and an IPA back.

He winds up closing the place, barely able to walk, let alone pedal Kona's puny pike. He pushes it back to the lake and passes out in the soft damp grass.

Dawn comes early in the midsummer Pacific Northwest. He gets home just as Kona's making coffee. He showers, shaves, gets dressed, fills a thermos with coffee, and heads to the bus stop. He'll grab an egg sandwich downtown.

Tom has begun tracking hurricanes for Maddie as one of the extra duties he's assigned himself as an honorary officer of the Disaster Response Team. It helps him feel like more than just a glorified secretary, sans the glory. NOAA's hurricane tracker site shows that a tropical storm named Cindy has formed in the Gulf of Mexico. Cindy later makes landfall as a minimal hurricane, dropping five inches of rain on Louisiana. She also spawns a couple tornadoes, floods some coastal areas, and kills three people, but still, all in all, pretty minimal. No SeaTru assets affected.

However, later that same day, Dennis forms in the eastern Caribbean. Over the rest of the week, Tom watches as it crosses Grenada and intensifies into a Category 4. According to Dennis's projected trajectory, as of Thursday, he could easily hit Florida, where SeaTru has 250 branches. Based on Tom's briefing, Maddie decides to put the EOC on alert. This gives Tom a bit of a glow: Maddie seems to genuinely appreciate his updates and analyses. He's not fooling himself. He understands that there is someone else on the team whose job it is to do this sort of monitoring and reporting. But that person, whoever they may be—and Tom's not exactly sure: someone who reports to Al Sherman probably, but whoever it is, they don't have direct access to Maddie like he does. Maybe there's a way to grow in this job after all.

Through most of mid-July he tracks a hurricane named Emily. She's a biggie, quickly dwarfing Dennis as she enters the Caribbean. At one point she blooms into a full Category 5, the earliest such monster ever recorded in the Atlantic. The news sites and blogs are ablaze with speculation about how global warming might be ratcheting these storms, but Tom does his best to keep his analyses sober and free of alarmist speculation. Besides, Maddie's still pretty zeroed in on pan flu as her apocalypse of choice. No sense trying to convince her to switch horses.

Emily crosses the Yucatán Peninsula as a Cat 4 before hitting Mexico's mainland at Cat 3. She winds up killing 14 people.

Could be an interesting summer.

•   •   •

Tom gazes south from a balcony of the Westin Hotel. Rainier hovers on a billow of blue mist, looming vast behind the downtown skyline. Is there any city more naturally beautiful than Seattle in August? A barely perceptible breeze strokes his skin like a silk dress. What's the old joke? "Seattle's like your really hot girlfriend who's sick most of the time."

They've started running together again. They meet early, nearly every weekday morning at Green Lake, in front of the lifeguard stand. They don't talk. Instead, they push each other's pace in a silence punctuated only by their breathing and the slap of their shoes on the asphalt or the crunching gravel.

It would be difficult to quantify how happy these runs make Tom, how much they elevate him throughout the day. He doesn't even need to see Michelle at work, and often doesn't. For him the runs are an almost sufficient stand-in for sex. Almost. For Michelle, only sex is sex, and she wants it at least once a week, ideally more.

Thursdays work best for her, just after work, like today. He's giving it a good half hour, maybe more, and then he'll head out. That's the system. Michelle rents the room. He knocks on the door maybe 20 minutes later. Once done, she showers and leaves first so they're never seen together.

Fact is, he's in love. He hasn't said as much, but he's shown it, in and out of bed. And he's not who he used to be when he used to be in love. He's grown. He's not some impatient kid, fawning over and losing some supermodel-wannabe obsession like rich-titted Kirsten to some Brown-alum, Wall Street douche. No, he understands that, to some degree, falling in love involves a calculation (a calculation on the fly, but a calculation nonetheless) of what next steps exactly give you the best chance of capturing the happiness you have chosen to pursue. He further understands that this coming change is going to require a plan to sell this shit sausage to each of their existing families. In order to have what he really wants, he's going to have to be patient, and he's going to have to plot his course to the prize: waking up to Michelle every day, sharing a house with her, both of their families finally coming to a place of acceptance that the two of them were meant to be together; that this was inevitable; that sometimes it takes time to find your soulmate or whatever the fuck you want to call it.

Sometime after 7:00, Tom crosses the Westin's vast open lobby. Someone's playing "Witchcraft" on the lounge piano. The temptation bubbles up to order himself a meditative martini and sip it from one of the low-slung couches, but he doesn't break stride, deciding it's wiser to head home while the hour's still reasonable.

"Well, howdy pardner." A familiar man's voice, but Tom can't think who would know him here. He keeps walking. "Mr. Kavanagh!" More insistent.

Shit, it's Jim V.

Tom turns to find his older friend sitting in an overstuffed chair. "To what do I owe this serendipitous pleasure?" Jim asks, casually reaching for his highball.

Tom goes with breezy. "Why Jim Verhoeven, away from the Hard Way on Thursday? Is this the end of times?"

Jim shrugs, as easily at home in this upscale hotel lobby as he is in his usual Pike Street dive. "I'm meeting with my investments guy. You?"

"Me what?" Tom decides not to sit, then instantly pins this as a mistake.

"What are you doing in the lobby of the Westin at..." Jim checks his watch. "7:15 at night? Don't you have a young family?"

"Indeed, I do." His brain is blank. He's got to cough up something.

Think, Kavanagh. Be a poet. Prince of liars.

"Poetry." He blurts.

Jim arches an eyebrow. "Poetry?"

"I know, right? There was a reading earlier, and one of the poets invited us up to his suite for a drink. I'm lucky to get out of there, actually. They were starting to get shitty."

"So can I implore you to join me for one last libation?"

"Ah, no. Tempting, but like you say: young family at home."

"Indeed." Jim raises his glass in toast to that.

•　　•　　•

Tuesday, Tom notes that Tropical Depression 12 has grown into a Cat 1 over the Bahamas.

Wednesday, he logs onto the NOAA site to find it's been given a name, "Katrina." He briefs Maddie.

On Thursday, Katrina hits land a few miles south of Fort Lauderdale, where SeaTru has five branches and a regional mortgage processing center.

On Friday morning, Katrina has been downgraded back to a tropical storm, but some predictions for her future path include major population areas along the Gulf Coast. Tom feels obliged to report this to Maddie, albeit reluctantly. One of the areas is the nightmare scenario: New Orleans. Three weeks prior Maddie had brought in an expert from the University of Washington to brief the EOC team on how vulnerable New Orleans could be to a direct hit by a hurricane, sitting as it does in a bowl mostly below sea level: massive Lake Pontchartrain to the north, the great Gulf of Mexico wrapping from the east around to the south, plus the full final force of the entire 2,300 miles of the mighty Mississippi pushing right through the city's center. Tom knows Maddie's going to fixate on the nightmare scenario and rev there all day and longer until subsequent updates convince her that the coast is, literally, clear.

On Saturday, he wakes to find that Katrina has grabbed back her hurricane status: Cat 3. New Orleans has begun mandatory evacuations in St. Charles, St. Tammany, and Plaquemines Parishes, with orders for voluntary evacuations going out for Jefferson and St. Bernard Parishes. He passes all of this along to Maddie, and in 20 minutes gets a terse email back. "Yes. Thank you. Monitoring situation from multiple sources but do appreciate you staying on top of this of your own accord. Would you be prepared to book me travel to the area if/when I determine to go?"

He answers back right away, "of course," but he doesn't hear back from her for the rest of the weekend even though he sends her three more capsule updates.

Just before going to bed Sunday night, he goes online, but the situation looks well in hand. All proper precautions are being taken. Mayor Nagin has issued a mandatory evacuation for all parishes of the city. The Superdome had been opened as a shelter of last resort, but nobody really believes it will come to that. The U. S. Army Corps of Engineers issues a statement. "Everything that can be done is being done. The levees are holding as they were designed to hold, and the massive emergency pumps that push floodwater out of the wards below sea level are working tirelessly, just as they were designed to. There is every reason to believe that the citizens of New Orleans will dodge a bullet."

19.

Big Easy Derringer

Why do people say that: "Dodged a bullet?" Why is that even an expression? Never, in the now centuries-long joint history of humans and bullets, has one ever been fired from a gun and subsequently evaded by a person. If a bullet misses, it wasn't aimed at you in the first place. Bullets are too fast and stupid to be dodged, and humans too slow and stupid to dodge them. So, no, New Orleans didn't dodge a bullet. Instead, the Big Easy took Katrina like a .44 slug to her gut and then went into shock from the force of its impact.

And then the wound went septic.

Tom and Kona watch mute and stricken as the news plays out on the idiot box, just like they did during those days in September four years prior. Only this time there's no chain-smoking or Budweiser guzzling. This time their daughter plays 15 feet away with her giant alphabet puzzle in the unfinished part of the basement. They watch families of poor black people wave bedsheet flags of surrender to the circling voyeur-copters. They watch people wade chest deep through filthy water toward a highway on-ramp. They read the word "HELP" chalked on the edge of the rising water, as people crowd into swamp boats to navigate past bloated floating bodies. Next morning, they watch the president peer bewildered from his Air Force One window: 30,000 feet not quite high enough to hide him from the flood's devastations.

Now the president's on terra firma, addressing a press gaggle, congratulating FEMA executive Mike Brown with an instantly in-famous "Heckuva job, Brownie!"

Later. People shooting people for trying to cross a bridge.

Later. Snipers firing on the evacuation of a hospital.

Later. Night again. Jumpy footage from a blacked-out Super-dome: aural intimations of mayhem and rape in rabbit-run tun-nels.

It's when they watch an older black man, still tethered to his oxygen tank, waiting on his roof to be rescued, that Kona finally loses it, recalling her own emphysemic grandfather.

People literally can't breathe.

Something leaves Tom at that moment. Some sort of faith—a trust—just goes out of him and leaves him wondering why he ever had it in the first place.

And it's not because of a hurricane: a bullet dodged, and then not. It is because of a human failure, really, a collection of failures, of people. Strike that. Failures of a *People*. A failure of Americans. We can only believe in our *own* happiness. We can only believe in our *own* future prosperity and freedom. The game *has* to be zero-sum. Someone *has* to lose for winning to have any meaning. And you have to believe that *you* will win. That's how games are played.

Why *are* we so convinced that we *are* such a noble people? Why do we want to believe things that aren't true and believe them fiercely in the face even of our own sure death and the death of people we love? Maybe we weren't designed to be anything other than credulous fools. Maybe believing's all we're really good at.

"The levees'll hold."

"Housing prices will rise."

"Goodness prevails."

"Your true love will find you."

"You will win. You will win. You will win."

All good stuff to hold on to in the moment, and what do we have but a moment? But what if *your* moment happens to be lis-tening to the approach of taunting howls bouncing off the tunnel walls of a pitch-black Superdome and you're just trying to find your way back to your mom and sisters? You can't just trust to luck. All luck is fool's luck.

Where are the Americans everyone knew and talked about when Tommy was growing up? Where is James, begetter of Kavanaghs? And where are all of those men and women like him? People who rushed to help others and sailed across an ocean to punch Nazis in the nose because—yeah, sure—it was the right thing to do, but also for the sheer righteous fun of punching Nazis? (Though in the end it wasn't so fun for James. Tom's mom used to tell the story of how his dad was hiding out in Manasquan, on leave from the European Theatre, praying to God he didn't get sent to the Pacific, when news broke of the unthinkably huge bomb they dropped on Hiroshima.) Still, Quartermaster Kavanagh and his ilk didn't look away from the horror, they faced up to it.

But Tommy's dad ran out of time too early. And where are the rest of them? The Americans? Friends to the world: laughing a bit too loud, grinning a bit too wide, and not giving a royal shit who cares? The men for whom the notion that money made the man was laughable if not downright pitiful and filthy? Where are they? Extinct? Endangered?

Are we better than this? Than what this idiot box is showing us about ourselves? We have to be. Better than this. We're better than this. Say it over and over, often enough, and through Goebbels' magic, it becomes true, right?

Better than this.

Better than this.

You better believe it.

You better.

Tom finally shuts it off and takes Kona by the hand upstairs, where they talk earnestly in their cozy living room, empty of any electronic screen. Tom tells his wife about wanting to do something different with his life: maybe getting his teaching certificate, maybe opening a bar. (Kona gives him a dubious look on that second option, and he admits it's probably a bad idea.)

Kona tells her husband about wanting to grow in her career but also strengthen their family. In the back of his mind Tom wonders what she means but lets it go.

They wind up making love, in the sweet quiet darkness of their bedroom. "Do you have any condoms?" she whispers.

Panic leaps through him. He pulls back to look at her. "What?"

"I know. It's stupid. Why would you, right? It's just I wish you did. I'm still off the pill and I know how you feel about taking chances."

He relaxes. "It's okay," he says. "I promise I won't do anything stupid."

"Suit yourself," she says and pulls him back into her.

•   •   •

Maddie flies to Florida as soon as Tom can get her on a commercial flight. She's eager to get on the ground, eager to walk the walk of the talk she's been talking for her entire tenure as the head of Enterprise Risk. As she's said in countless meetings: "People need food, water, and shelter in the aftermath of a devastating event. Absolutely. But what's next on their minds? They need to be sure they can go to the nearest ATM and get as much money as they need to get them through. These machines need to be stocked just like store shelves, only the logistics are trickier. Security for the armored cars needs to be arranged. Currency needs to be procured, transported, and installed, all during a time, and in an area, where movement is restricted at best and security is, by definition, compromised."

As annoying and callous as she can so often be, Tom can't help feeling proud. Maddie is putting herself on the line down there, as close to ground zero as she can get. He can't think of anyone better suited for "manning" SeaTru's response.

When she returns ten days later, she seems changed: older, thinner, just generally smaller. She spends most of the day in her office with the door shut. On Tuesday she works from home.

At the Quarterly Risk All-Staff, Jim V. makes a special point of congratulating Maddie on her handling of SeaTru's Katrina response. Afterward, he takes her to a one-on-one lunch at the

Metropolitan Grill. She comes back wearing an almost girlish, but also confused, expression. "Can you come into my office. Just whenever you get the chance?" When has she ever been so solicitous? He goes straight in.

"What's up."

"Close the door?"

"Of course."

Tom waits for Maddie to speak. She always speaks first. He never has to show the initiative. But here she is, staring down at her immaculate desk, utterly mute.

"Everything all right?"

"He gave me a gun," she says, finally looking up.

"What?"

She pulls out a small box of polished blonde wood. She places it carefully squarely between them like a triggered time bomb. It's a surprisingly small box: maybe ash, maybe birch, exquisitely inlaid with what look like tiny ivory lozenges. *But they can't be ivory, can they? Mother-of-pearl maybe? No. Too yellowish.*

"There's a gun in that?"

"Ostensibly."

"You haven't opened it."

"Oh, I've opened it. I'm just not sure it's a gun."

"What do you mean?"

She pushes it over to him. It's clearly an old thing, not just made to look old. The hinges are so stiff, he has to sort of pry it open. Inside, on a bed of vermillion velvet, lies a tiny palm pistol.

"Oh, it's a derringer!" says Tom.

"Yeah."

"It's actually quite beautiful. May I?"

Maddie makes a "be my guest" gesture. Tom lifts it gently from the case: heavy little death nugget. It's lovely. He's half tempted to crack it open to see if there's a round in the chamber, but he's also quite certain there isn't. Hell, do they even make rounds for something like this anymore?

He looks up, catches her eyeing the tiny weapon like a cat might a mouse she's lost interest in killing. "Don't you like it?"

"Should I?"

"It's beautiful."

"Other women got... *guns.*"

"This *is* a gun. What makes you say it isn't?"

"Well, look at it. It's tiny. It doesn't even have a trigger. How would you fire it?

"Oh, no. It has a trigger. See? Right here: this smooth little lever, laid against the grip. May I?" Maddie shrugs. Gently with his thumb, Tom draws the hammer back to the cocked position, which causes the little metal lever to jut out a little. "Then you just squeeze to fire. But I won't do that." He carefully releases the hammer and places the pistol back on its velvet bed. "It's very sleek and unconventional. It would be used by gamblers or con artists, often one and the same, or ladies, so maybe all three and the same. Something you'd see on a paddlewheel riverboat. Or rather, you *wouldn't* see it. Not until it was fired. And maybe not even then. See how it fits in the palm of your hand?"

"So, an assassin's weapon?"

"No. Not accurate enough. It's the weapon of someone who doesn't like to fight but may have to. It's the weapon of someone who... manages operational risk." He looks up at her and grins. "Yeah. It's kind of perfect for you."

Tom gently tugs at a ribbon tab at the top of the box and a false lid drops to reveal an inscribed metal plate:

"Fabriqué par Du Maine et Fils, New Orleans, 1854"

"Look! Did you see this? It's from New Orleans. It's an antique." He pushes the case back to her so she can read.

He's sold her on it. Maddie remains delighted for the duration of the day. But she does go home early, again, exhausted.

•   •   •

On Halloween, Tom comes to work as Jim Morrison: long ratty brown wig and a peasant blouse open to his belly button. An absurdly huge belt buckle barely holds up his black faux-leather pants, which are, he comes to find after a few hours, grievously uncomfortable. His thighs stick to the insides, and by lunchtime his crotch has developed a noticeable (for him at least) ripe cheesy smell.

Maddie doesn't come in that day.

•　　•　　•

Things with Kona have softened.

A part of him insists he should be honest with her, right here, right now. He's fallen in love with someone else with whom he sees his future. But it's also true that he hasn't even come close to having this discussion with Michelle. (They don't do much "discussing.") So in the absence of a clear path forward, there's no percentage in tearing his current family apart.

His younger, idealistic self, would make the break right now, of course—and what? Maybe find some one-room apartment to live in while he sorted it all out. But he's grown since his 20s. And grownups compromise. Why has that become a dirty word? Grownups find workable ways forward.

And here's the dirty secret: Ever since he's made this internal decision to go with the flow, his life at home has been happier. Because he's been less eager—or, depending on how you look at it, less desperate—for sex with Kona, she's been initiating more often, and then it's less his fault somehow that he's double-dipping: less of a sin or, really, not a sin at all, since she *is* his wife and it's *her* who wants sex from *him*. Who is he to withhold just because he's in another relationship with a woman, *herself* married and having sex with *her* husband every (convenient) Friday night?

This is what grownups do. They wait; they exhibit some patience. They work a plan for their future happiness. And the fact that he's maintaining a viable marital relationship with Kona in the meantime can only bode better for their future as they parent Poma separately, right? And let's face it, the way she's been making love to him lately has been super sweet.

Shortly after Halloween, Kona comes to Tom with her plan for Thanksgiving. She and Hana will take Poma to their parents' house in Hawaii. Her folks are paying for the three of them to come. Tom is, of course, welcome, but Kona didn't feel comfortable asking her folks to pay his airfare too. Does he want to come? It's pricey but well within their own budget for him to join. She'll understand if he can't get the time off.

Tom says he'll think about it. But over the next day, he comes up with a plan of his own. It involves something he's been contemplating ever since spring: part of being a grown-up, something he would have never considered doing even just a few years ago—but, looking at his situation from all sides, he sees how it would solve a lot of problems, large and small, trivial and crucial.

So, he tells Kona he'll pass. He's better off banking the money it would cost to fly and the vacation time, too. He's fine spending the holiday alone, getting some quiet time by himself for a change. It's better.

He drops the sisters and his little girl off at the airport that Saturday before Thanksgiving. He goes home, reads, rides his bike, makes a healthy meal, limiting himself to one bottle of wine, plus a small green chartreuse nightcap. He's in the bath by ten and in bed by eleven.

The next morning, he gets up before the sun and joins Michelle at the lake for a run. After their loop, they walk a cool-down mile to his house. Looking around their modest living room for the first time, she's utterly charmed, or claims to be. "Your wife has made the coziest room I've ever seen."

"Thanks." He doesn't really want to talk about his wife.

Michelle goes to use the bathroom. A couple minutes later he hears the shower running. He pushes the door open. Through the clear plastic parts of the New York subway map shower curtain he can see her soaping up her body with Kona's loofa.

"Hi."

"Hi, sorry. I was kind of stinky," she says, water dribbling from her lips. "Wanna join me?" He strips, gets in. They play.

Out of the tub and drying off, Michelle throws her towel around Tom's neck and begins pulling him into his bedroom. He stops.

"What?" she asks.

"Not in that bed."

"So where? On the couch? In your kid's bed?" There's a hint of nastiness in this but not enough to turn him off.

"There's a bedroom downstairs," he says.

"You're not making me go down to your basement. It's just a bed, Tom." Tom doesn't move. "Forget the condom," she says.

"What?"

"Fuck me on this bed without a condom."

"You're kidding."

"I didn't say you could come inside of me, but——" He's already pushing her back, into the bedroom, on to the bed. He shoves inside of her immediately. "Oh my!" she says. He starts to buck. She pushes him up off her and puts one finger in his face. "Now don't be an idiot."

"No."

"You can*not* come inside of me."

"I won't. I won't."

"Don't be stupid."

"Any more than I already am?"

She slaps his face, hard, still smiling into his eyes. "I mean it!"

"I know!" he says and fucks her harder. It feels so good to finally be inside her with nothing between them: so smooth and warm, so real. He's so close, and he wants so badly to just give in to the burning, utterly evil temptation. (Could he pray for a clearer confirmation of the wisdom of his Thanksgiving break plan?) Soon. Soon. He's dangerously close. He pulls out. Goes to jerk himself to climax, but she gasps, "No" and quickly turns over and crawls to him, beautiful tits dangling. She takes him in her mouth, into which he explodes.

Later she's staring at the ceiling from Kona's pillow. "I can't see you for the rest of the week. My daughter flies in on Tuesday. And it's all family stuff after that."

"Understood."

•   •   •

"That was some gun you gave Maddie."

Jim nods. Sips his G and T, then asks, "She show it to you?"

"Of course. I'm her trusted lieutenant."

"Why do they always do that?"

"What?"

"It's meant to be a discreet recognition."

Tom shrugs. Having beaten Jim to the bar, he's two overly kind Cape Cods ahead. "I suppose they're proud of the recognition. Maybe wanna share the weirdness of it too."

"What's weird about it?"

"You kidding?" Jim remains stone-faced. Apparently, he's not kidding.

"Well, for one, why guns?" Tom asks. "And for two, why only women?"

Jim gazes at himself in the bar mirror, lets out a long-held sigh. "You know what, kid? Even if I thought I could explain it to you, I still wouldn't."

"Fair enough."

"She like it at least?"

"Hard to tell. I'm not sure she got all of your symbolism."

"What symbolism?"

Tom figures his leg is getting pulled, but the old man just stares at his drink. Tom shrugs. "She's different since she came back."

"How so?"

"Older? Worn somehow. I don't think she's in condition for field operations. Or not anymore. Maybe it was a job for Maddie in her 40s, not her 60s."

"Careful, there, kiddo. You're flirting dangerously with ageism." Tom shrugs again. "But, yeah. You're right. Most of the shit we're called upon to do is a much younger person's game. And by the time you have the wisdom to do the right thing, you no longer have the strength."

"We still talking about Maddie?"

"Maybe." Jim finally looks at him. "Maybe not."

"Well, don't look at me; I'm just a secretary."

"No such thing." Jim turns to him. "What's your percentage in all this?"

"In what?"

"This," says Jim. He throws his arms wide. "The big canasta. You looking to get paid? Laid? Famous?... What?

"Happy."

"Happy?"

"I'm looking to get happy."

"Shit kid, you think any of us got any choice in that?"

"Just me. I think I get a choice if *I* get happy. Or I like to think so. I get to pursue it, at least. It's my constitutional right."

"You're confusing the Constitution with the Declaration of Independence. It's a common mistake, but a sucker's bet."

"So, I'm a sucker. Like the Irish, there's one of us born every minute."

"You're a goddamned cock-eyed optimist, is what you are."

Tom shrugs. "I thought you knew."

After a silence Jim says, "Ever want to change it?"

"Change what?"

"The world, dummy."

"You think you can change that? *You*, of all people?"

Jim scowls. "What do you mean, 'me of all people'?"

"You're the Man."

"I'm the what?"

"The Man."

"And you're what? Some Black Panther from the 1960s? 'The Man'?"

"What are you even talking about? 'Change it'?"

"Okay," Jim says, holding his hands as if framing a scene. "Very simply, imagine a world where mortgages were priced appropriately so that the *customer* was best served instead of rich assholes like me."

"I thought such a world was unicorn shit."

"Imagine yet further a world where you got paid to make that happen."

"You're saying there's some mythical job, that I'm qualified for, in which I can change the world to make it better for work-ing-class people?'"

"I'm saying there is. Yes."

Tom gives a rueful grin and shakes his head. "You really do think I'm a sucker."

"What I need is data," says Jim. "To which I don't currently have access, but I believe you might."

"What do I have access to that you don't?"

"StreetSweeper."

Tom goes stiff. A prickling ripples across his skin. He tries to shrug nonchalantly, but it ends up more like a slow-motion spasm. "Michelle owns that app."

"You think I don't know that?"

"So… why not get your data from her?"

Jim sips. Through the bar mirror there's a ghost of a smile on his face. Tom's guts turn over. He worries he's blushing, but what's the difference in this red neon shithole. He decides to bite the bul-let. "What are you trying to get at, Jim?"

"Well, you know her, right?" The old man keeps his tone in-nocent, his cards close.

"I worked for her for a little bit. I wouldn't say I know her."

"You think she gives a shit?" Tom turns with a questioning look. "About the world," Jim explains.

Tom's face burns. He's never thought to think this way about the woman he's been fucking with gusto since spring. The woman he believes he loves. "What's it matter what *I* think she thinks?" Why is there a lump in his throat?

"I like to get all perspectives."

They sit in silence. Tom doubts he could lift his drink at this moment.

"Corporations are risk mitigation machines," Jim finally says, out of nowhere.

"Okay." Tom really doesn't want to hear the spiel tonight.

Jim persists, as if talking to himself, or a multitude of ghosts. "Their sole reason for coming into being was to spread risk among individuals and protect them legally from bottomless liability."

The old man nods, as though he's piecing it all together for the first time. It's a convincing performance, but Tom's done enough theatre to recognize the craft when he sees it.

"But… there's something antithetical to humanity in the very idea of risk mitigation. That's why corporations are the most de-humanizing institutions in existence. Human beings are evolved risk buccaneers: We sail risk and go a-pirating with it. We didn't evolve just to simply mitigate it. We *revel* in risk. It gives us pleasure in and of itself. Like sex." Tom looks at him, but Jim doesn't seem to notice and he doesn't miss a beat. "Sex, in and of itself, is a *huge* risk, but we savor it *because* it's risk. Indeed, the riskier the sex, the more fiercely we enjoy it." Jim drains his drink and places the glass softly back on the bar.

"Why do I get the feeling I'm being worked?" says Tom. "And not gently?"

"Nothing gentle about work, son. Not if it matters."

20.
The Cut

On the day before Thanksgiving, Tom enacts his plan. Maddie's out all week, but just in case, he notes his 2:00 p.m. medical appointment on her Outlook calendar. He cuts out at 1:15 and catches a 12 up to Pill Hill. At the Seattle Urology Clinic's check-in desk, the receptionist directs him to a room where he changes into a hospital gown.

When they met about a month ago, Dr. Stephen Fine told Tom in no uncertain terms: "You will look back on this decision as one of the top five best you ever made." Tom asked about potential downsides. "Like what?" the urologist asked.

"Like, is there any chance it might make me impotent or affect... performance or enjoyment? This actor I met once told me it would and that's why he'd never get one."

Fine arched his eyebrows. "An actor? This is the expert you consult?" He shook his head. "No chance. We don't go anywhere near anything that could affect any of that. Besides, hasn't anyone told you it's your brain that does most of the heavy lifting in that department? I thought you were going to ask me about real potential risks."

"Like what?"

"Like it not working, your tubes growing back, that sort of thing."

"Okay?"

"Ten thousand to one."

The fact sheet said the patient could drive himself home if he wished, but that most prefer someone else to do it, so Tom has J. pick him up when it's all over. He's the only one in Tom's life who knows about "the plan." On the way out, Tom stops at the receptionist's counter and requests a printed bill. The charges total to $878.39. He pays with his SeaTru credit card, for which he gets his statements online only.

Back in his own living room, propped on his own couch, Tom melts with gratitude as he watches J. pull a bottle of 12-year-old Macallan from his knapsack. "There are some nice lowball glasses in the cabinet over the sink. I'd get them, but..." Tom demurely points at his crotch.

J. grabs the glasses and pours. They clink, and J. says, "Well, you did it. No more Kavanaghs."

"Trust me, too many are already. You know our history. We overcame."

"When are you going to tell Kona?"

"When it makes sense to."

"You don't think she should know sooner than later?"

"She's always said she only wanted one kid."

"Always?" J.'s face is a blank slate. "What does she say now?"

"Why? What've you heard?"

"What have *I* heard? What the hell *would* I hear?"

"I don't know. You were the one that had to go and make things awkward."

"How's that?"

"Dating my sister-in-law?"

"'Dating' seems way too formal a description."

"Fine. Fucking?"

"Well, that *is* less formal."

"Hope you're enjoying yourself."

"It'd be a pity if I weren't."

They drink in silence for awhile. Tom can feel J. staring at him, which is weird for both friends, since J. has never been big on direct eye contact. For a moment, Tom considers telling J. all about the whole insane affair, but he chokes off the impulse. He doesn't want to put his friend's loyalties under stress, and perhaps more crucially, he doesn't want to know what J. would think of him.

"What's going on, Tommy?"

"In what regard?"

J shakes his head at Tom's awkward phrasing. It's a an obvious tell, and they both know it. "You're not being you."

"How is that possible?" Tom understands he's sounding like a first-year philosophy student now.

"I wish I knew, maybe I could help you. It's like you've left yourself behind or something. Certainly left the rest of us—Kona, most of all."

"I love Kona."

"Clearly. And yet somehow deeply enough to keep her in the dark about the possibility of having another kid with you."

"People have trouble having kids all the time."

"That's not Tommy talking."

"Who is it then?"

"I don't know. Maybe someone making a plan without filling the rest of us in?"

"What?!" Tom can feel his face burning. It doesn't matter. He's not changing his mind about this. He can't. He already got the goddamned procedure. "I gotta keep moving forward in my life, J." *The future is forward.*

"Makes sense. Do any of us get to go with you?

"Listen. If you wanna know the truth of it, it was Kona who began the bullshit around birth control. One day she just stopped giving a shit whether we used it or not, like she wanted to get pregnant but didn't want to *talk* to me about getting pregnant."

"Man, that sucks. Must've felt like your part in that decision was being taken away from you?"

"*Again*, yeah."

"Again? What do you mean?"

"Wasn't my decision to get pregnant the first time."

"Dude!" J. looks truly stunned. "And you had nothing to do with it?"

Tom is silent.

"And it all worked out so horribly for you, right?"

Tom holds the silence for as long as he can, then he holds out his empty glass. "Do you mind?"

J. pulls the cork from the bottle and fills Tom's glass with another inch of Scotch. As Tom sips deep, J. says, "I don't know what to tell you, man. Mostly because I honestly don't know what's going on with you. But I feel like I have to remind you that sometimes we have very little choice in the best things that happen to us." Tom nods. His throat is suddenly so swollen that he can't swallow his whiskey. It just sits in his mouth and burns.

"But we can choose to burn it all away."

"Yeah."

J. doesn't push any further, and Tom can't bring himself to offer up anything else. Maybe more than anyone, he needs J. to think well of him. After another few minutes of sipping in silence, Tom's friend finishes his whiskey and goes.

And over the course of the next couple hours Tom finishes the bottle.

•   •   •

Through Thanksgiving and Black Friday, Tom recuperates in a soft cloud of loneliness and boredom. He manages to abstain from testing out the modified plumbing until Saturday morning, when he finally gives in to curiosity and sheer horniness and calls up some vanilla porn on RedTube. The fact sheet from the clinic says: "Your initial post-procedure ejaculations might contain some blood or 'rusty residue': this is normal." And sure enough, the dirty T-shirt he uses to catch it shows little brown flakes; but it feels so good to know there are no other differences and even that difference will go away soon.

In the afternoon, he goes for a long walk, after which he sends an email to Michelle's secret address. "Want to go for a short run tomorrow morning? I have an early Christmas present to give you."

The reply comes hours later. "Can only be short one. And we can't do the lake. My daughter's in town and likes to walk it."

Tom replies: "Burke-Gilman."

The sky is just filling with gray light when she picks him up the next morning. They drive to Gas Works and run out to the Ballard locks and back, stopping for lattes and scones at the cafe at the bottom of Stone Way. Tom pulls the invoice from his running pants pocket and pushes it across the table. "Your Christmas present, early."

She unfolds it and reads. "I don't get it."

"It's the invoice for my procedure. Official documentation: I'm a gelding."

"What's it supposed to mean to me?"

Tom shrugs one shoulder. "Simple: no more condoms."

She frowns and lowers her voice. "You did this so you could come inside of me?"

"Well... sort of. Among... other reasons."

"And what? I'm supposed to pay this?"

"What? *No!*" He's surprised she's taking it so oddly, but he's eager she sees the humor, so he adds: "Unless you want to." She shoots him an evil look. "Kidding, kidding." *Fuck.*

They walk back to Gas Works without talking and drive up the long hill of Stone Way. Stopped at the light at 45th and Stone, Tom looks over to see Nathan on his bike. "Oh shit!" Tom instantly slides down in his seat below the window.

"What is it?"

Tom hooks his thumb in Nathan's direction. Michelle's eyes go wide in horror. "Turn your head. Don't look at him!" Tom tells her.

"What's the difference?" She hisses, face locked forward. "He's going to see the car. He's going to see me!"

"So?"

"What if he knocks on the window to say hi or something?"

"Really? Would he do that?"

"Maybe."

"Nathan?"

"Okay, fine. But what do I do if he sees me?"

"You honk and wave. That's it. Easy."

"Oh shit. This is it."

"No! It's not. Just relax."

The both stare at the traffic light dangling above them. Finally, it turns green. "Don't peel out, just accelerate normally." She pulls forward slowly. "Well a little faster than that. Christ! Just be normal. Pull into that parking lot at Woodland Playfields when you can." They quickly leave Nathan pedaling behind. Michelle turns into the lot, throws the car into park, and slinks down below the window. But Tom sits up normally now. "We don't have to act like spazzes. He's not going to see us in here. There are at least 50 other cars. And we're facing away from the street."

"What if he sees the license plate?"

"You read license plates when you're biking?"

"This is crazy," she says, but she sits up normally.

"You're right. We have to be more careful. We've been so lucky so far. The only other time I thought we might be blown is when I ran into Jim V. at the Westin one time after we used it. But, still, we've been lucky. We need to be more vigilant. Okay?" He looks over at her. She's staring through the windshield with a stricken expression. "It's okay," he assures her.

"No." It's a sort of croak.

"Come on, Michelle. Nathan didn't even see—"

"Fuck Nathan. It isn't okay. It isn't fucking okay, Tom. You ran into Jim V. at the Westin?"

"Yeah, but months ago. Back in the summer."

"August."

"Yeah, okay."

"You fucking *idiot*… *I* ran into Jim V. at the Westin after coming out of our room."

Fuck.

"Tom."

"What?"

"Tom look at me."

He looks at her. "Listen to me, Michelle. Jim doesn't know shit."

"It's over."

No.

He says it out loud.

"Yes. Jim Verhoeven knows. He's known for months."

"No way. Can't be. I have drinks with him nearly every week and he's never even given the slightest hint he suspects." *But he did, didn't he? He did hint.*

Michelle turns on him. He's never seen her eyes like this: feral, scorching, her face a mask of rage. "You have *drinks* with Jim Verhoeven every *week?*"

"Well, not every week. On average, maybe—"

"What the bloody *FUCK?*" This last word is so loud it literally rings in his ears.

"He doesn't know."

Her chest starts to heave. "You're a fucking idiot."

He rushes out words to placate her: "I'm telling you, he's practically senile. He's an old drunk. That's all. He likes to blather, and he likes me 'cuz I like to listen, and—"

She grips the wheel and shakes it like she's trying to rip it from the steering column. "STOP!" she screams, then, letting go of the wheel, says quietly, "Just... fucking... stop!" She shakes her head rhythmically, side to side, and keens like a mental patient. "This is it. He's coming for me. He's gonna try and sink me."

"No. No. This is Jim. He loves you."

"He doesn't *love* me, Tom. He hasn't loved me since he pulled me on his team and I didn't hew immediately to his doom-and-gloom rhetoric. He's soured on me like he's soured on selling mortgages to the Street. He's latched on to the notion that CDOs are poison and he's got this revisionist history that I'm responsible for the bank's deep position on them. But I haven't even been in place long enough to be responsible."

"Trust me. He's not trying to sink you."

"*Trust* you?" She turns and screams at him: "*Trust YOU?* How the fuck can I trust you, Tom? You're his goddamned fucking *drinking* buddy!"

"I don't give a shit about him."

"I don't give a shit if you give a shit or not."

They stare at each other, wordless for a weird moment, then she reiterates, calmly, "It's over."

"No."

"You need to get out of my car."

"Michelle."

With crisp, clipped words, as though talking to a dog, or a servant with poor English, she says: "You *need*... to be a *man*... and get the *fuck*... out of my *car*."

She starts the engine. As soon as he's out and clear of the car, she revs and jerks back out of the space, shifts to drive, and squeals away.

It's not more than half a mile to his house but, of course, it starts to rain. Pathetic.

He puts the vasectomy invoice at the bottom of the carved Salish bentwood box that J. gave them as a wedding gift. Kona never showed any interest in it, so he took it for his own and kept it in his desk in the beige room. As far as Kona knows, it holds his old pocket notebooks, which are coded in a sort of shorthand and barely legible anyway, but beneath them he keeps some odds and ends he'd prefer her not to see, like the R-rated pictures of rich-titted Kirsten he can't quite bring himself to throw out. He masturbates to these morosely then heads upstairs to soak in a long, hot bath.

·   ·   ·

She breaks off all contact. No replies to his emails to her secret address.

His first day back at work, before even wading through his own email in Outlook, Tom checks Michelle's calendar. She's in. She has meetings, but he can no longer see what they are, or where, or with whom. She's clearly reset his access to "busy/free" only. He checks to see if he can open her inbox. No dice. This is serious. She's given this thought.

On a whim, he "alt-Cs" the URL to Streetsweeper 2.0 from

an Outlook note he keeps on it. He tries Michelle's login and password to this. It opens. Looks like she forgot about this one. He pokes around to check if he has the same access he did when he was downloading data for her. He does. He quickly logs out.

•   •   •

He's barely laid eyes on her in December. He finally gives up. Sure, he feels the hole she left inside him. But he's also got a fucking life to lead—a job, a family—so *fuck* her. Grownups don't nurse broken hearts like teenagers, they fucking fix them or cut them loose. They pursue happiness elsewhere. They do whatever it takes. His regret is nothing to what hers will be. He's sure of that. Dead sure. So, he can wait. Let her come to her own dark realizations.

In the meantime, Christmas goes extremely well with Kona and Poma. He's written them a new chapter of the *Candleshire* story, and they love it.

Christmas night, under the tree, for the first time in a long time, he and Kona make love. Without even thinking much about it, he comes inside of her. And she hugs him close after, like she never does. Afterward, lying next to her, staring up through the branches, the colored lights and shining ornaments, he supposes that sometimes—given time—some things repair.

21.

The Memo

Tom takes the dead week off. It was an easy decision. Maddie's out the whole week anyhow, and since Christmas comes on a Sunday, the bank is closed the following Monday. So it's only going to cost him four vacation days, and he's got plenty banked.

The day after Christmas, he and Kona take Poma tubing up on Snoqualmie and everybody has a blast: Christmas carols in the car, hot cocoa in the lodge afterward. Family. Is there anything better, when it's working?

That night Tom sends an email to GiveAChit@hotmail.com. Subject: "Let's Talk." There is no reply.

Late on the night before New Year's Eve he takes a flask of green chartreuse and walks the lake. Just past the midnight of Green Lake's clock, he walks up the hill, turns right, then turns to face the huge blue and white house with its splendid wraparound porch. He breathes in. Then very slowly lets it out. He tugs his Moleskine notebook from his breast pocket. With his trusty pencil stub, he scrawls a single question mark on a blank page, then he tears it out and folds it under the windshield wiper of her car.

•   •   •

First day back of the new year, 2006: unbelievable! Who in their right minds, listening to Prince play "1999" back in 1985, ever thought 2006 would be an actual thing?

Tom spends Tuesday and Wednesday in blissful near-solitude at his cube. On Thursday morning he is surprised to hear music coming out of Maddie's office. She wasn't supposed to be in this week. He drops his backpack and boots up his machine. The music goes off, and Maddie hollers out, "Tom, is that you?"

He goes to her door. "Hey, Maddie."

She doesn't glance away from her screen. "Come in, shut the door, have a seat." Once he's done all three, she turns to him. "What have you heard?... Anything?"

"About what?"

"So... nothing?"

"I guess not."

She slow-blinks her annoyance. "You ever read *The Puget Sound Business Journal?*"

"Not really. No."

"*The Seattle Times?*"

It's his turn to be irritated. "I read *The Times*, Maddie. I just don't subscribe to it."

"Maybe you should. Their front page is about our layoffs."

Fuck.

"They were supposed to roll out Monday," she says. "But somebody leaked it."

"Christ. Is our team affected?"

"Yes. But the layoffs are only half the story." She turns her screen to him so he can read the digital front page of *The Puget Sound Business Journal*. It has a picture of Jim Verhoeven, with a headline: "SeaTru Risk Chief Warns Board."

"Read the pull quote," she says. Tom starts to, but she tells him, "Go ahead and read it out loud."

He reads it aloud. "'If we continue writing high-risk loans, the results could be disastrous for the bank,' Verhoeven warned in his memo to the risk management sub-committee. 'My credit team and I fear that we are considering expanding our risk appetite at exactly the wrong moment and potentially walking straight into a regulatory challenge, precipitating criticism from both the Street and the board.'" Tom looks up at Maddie. "How did they get

Verhoeven's memo?"

Maddie answers: "Someone leaked it of course."

"Who?"

"Who knows? Does it matter?"

Of course it matters. "I guess not," he says.

"All we know is that concurrent with that leak to the *PSBJ* was the leak about the RIFs to *The Times*, so..."

"Same leaker."

"Almost certainly."

"When do..." Tom doesn't know how to put the question. "Can you..."

Maddie frowns. "Spit it out."

"Well... when would it be appropriate for more information about the layoffs to be shared more broadly?"

"Do you want to know who's being let go from my team? Is that what you're trying to ask? Not you, I can assure you of that."

"Well, that's a relief."

Is it? What would the severance package look like? And then the unemployment to be raked in on top of it? A RIF notice might've been a godsend.

"You don't get out of here that easily. Mostly compliance took the hit in our group. Kathy Smith Johnson and about half her team. The other half will report directly to me for now until I can find someone to run them. But we're still holding off on the actual rollout 'til Monday. HR says we legally can't do it any sooner."

"Understood. Strictly confidential."

She nods. "In the meantime, you need to get me with Jim V., face time preferably, but a phone call would do, I guess. I don't suppose we'll get more than 15 minutes."

Back in his chair, Tom sends Juanita an email requesting Maddie's face time with Jim. He gets no reply. He goes about his work, but Maddie is soon poking her head out. "What's the word on Jim?"

"No word yet."

"Call Juanita."

Smothering his frustration, Tom picks up the phone and dials. It goes straight to voice mail. He hangs up. "Straight to voice mail," he tells Maddie.

"You didn't want to leave a message?"

"I already sent an email."

"What about going up in person?"

"You think that's a good idea?"

"You think I'd mention it if I didn't?" Maddie pulls her head back in her office. Tom lets out a long sigh, stands, and heads for the stairs.

No one on 17 meets his eye as he passes. Juanita is on the phone. An uneven conversation rumbles behind Jim's closed door: Woman close to shouting and Jim muttering curt replies. Juanita says into her phone, "I need to put you on hold for a second." She punches a button and lifts her chin to Tom. "And you need what exactly?"

"Maddie sent me up to see if she can get some time with Jim today."

"Not gonna happen."

Jim's door bursts open and Michelle blows past them without a glance. Jim watches her go with a rueful look then turns to Juanita and says softly, "Please hold all my calls. And clear what you can from the rest of my day." Without a glance to Tom, he turns back in and closes the door. Juanita gives Tom an "are-you-still-here?" stare.

He nods, politely. "Thanks anyway, Juanita."

That afternoon, Maddie forwards Tom an internal memo, for SVP-and-above-eyes-only, itemizing organizational changes going into effect immediately. Jim Verhoeven has been placed under a new Chief Operating Officer, Greg Governale, brought in suddenly from one of the Manhattan mega-banks. All of Jim's directs will now roll up, through a dual reporting structure, both to him and a business unit of the company. Tom asks if that means Maddie's dotted line to the CIO Jerry Croft just went solid. She makes a face and turns back to her screen: his cue to excuse himself.

He leaves his desk as close to 5:00 as he can and heads directly to the Hard Way on hopes of finding Jim V. there. Sure enough, he's perched on his regular stool.

"In every hole, if you must know," Jim says once Tom has his Cape Cod.

"In every hole what?"

"Is where they're fucking me."

"Ah."

Jim gives Tom a scrutinizing look. "You're like the rest of 'em."

"How's that?"

"You think I'm the leak."

"Can you not see how that thought might occur?"

"Shit, kid. I got better things to do than perpetrate some penny-ante corporate skullduggery."

"Hmmm. When last we spoke, it didn't sound like pennies comprised the ante. By your description, someone would need millions, if not billions, to create a mortgage-shorting market."

Jim nods, almost appreciatively. "So you *were* listening?"

Tom shrugs. "So, if you're not the leak, who is?"

"Could be any number of folks. Could be someone who feels threatened by me, things I know."

"Like what? Who?"

"Who knows? Maybe Tom Kavanagh. Maybe Michelle Fleischer."

Tom's bristles at the poke but resolves to remain opaque. "Interesting. Now what would cause you to pull *those* two names from a hat?"

"Well, remember, *I* didn't put them *in* the hat." Jim shakes his head slowly for emphasis. "No, sir. It wasn't *me* who did that."

Tom sneers, but pushes on, determined to meet this game with his best moves: "And what exactly do you think you know?"

"Two beautiful young people. There ain't a lot to figure out. I never had too much trouble with simple math."

"And now, because you think you know something, you want me to do something for *you*. Is that about the gist?"

"Not even close."

Tom leans in, close, so only Jim can hear him. "You want me to pull down the Streetsweeper data. You so much as said it the last time we drank together."

"Might be what you heard, but not even close to what I said."

"I don't get paid enough to get involved in your nefarious corporate bullshit."

"So it's payment you want?"

Tom freezes. Little pinpricks float across his face. "I didn't say that."

"You didn't *not* say that. Hell, who knows *what* you're saying? Do *you*? I sure as shit can't tell." Jim sips his drink, cucumber cool. "Tell me something, kid. And be honest. Tell me that's *not* what you want. Because getting paid in this world—this world of nefarious corporate bullshit, as you call it—is always within the wide realm of possibility. Tell me you're pure. Blameless. Disinterested. Tell me you're just watching the game and not *in* it. Tell me you have nothing to lose and no interest in finding out what there is to gain. Tell me that with that handsome, young face of yours and keep it straight, if you can."

"Fuck you."

"Yeah?... Pass."

"Seriously. Fuck you, old man. I'm done with you."

"You sure?"

Tom stands and drains his ice, leaving Jim calmly nodding at his drink.

•   •   •

"We need to talk."

Michelle looks up from her desk. "Nope. Not true," she replies. Chin slightly lifted, eyes amused, but deadly, she watches Tom close the door behind him. He sits in the chair across from her. She immediately stands. "So that's the play? After hours? Not a lot of people around? 'What can she possibly do to stop me'?"

"Please." He stands and walks to the window, waving a dismissive hand at the idea of him being some sort of bully. He really doesn't have plan. What was he going to do? Plead his love? Curse her name? Call her a bitch? A cunt? He walks to a plaque on the wall and makes a show of inspecting it, and then the picture next to it: a lone Polynesian woman paddling her canoe down the slope of a huge breaking wave. Michelle rounds her desk and stands next to him. "I love her," she says. And *fuck! There it is!* His dick swelling again. "What is it you wanted from me?" she says, right under his ear.

He goes back to the chair and flops into it. "Decency," he says, in a tone her teenage kid might employ.

She goes and perches on her desk in front of him, her blue skirt hiking up over her teenager knees. "You wanna keep fucking me?... Is that it?... Is that all?"

"I want you to talk to me."

"Is that what you want? Talk." She leans toward him, reaches out, and firmly grabs his cock, which is now—great traitor of his heart—high-carbon steel. "Not talk, I think... I think... you want to come inside of me. Yeah. I think that's what the whole vasectomy deal was all about. You accomplish that feat, and somehow I become yours." She releases his swollen prick and leans back. He can see where her nylons cover her panties now.

Aw, fucking hell.

"How do I even know that you had a vasectomy for real?" She's wearing her White Witch smile, now, eyebrows arched, in feigned curiosity.

"I—"

"Oh, that's right. You showed me the 'invoice.'" She puts quote marks around the word with her graceful white fingers. "How official... and efficient." She squints at him, coolly scrutinizing the emptiness inflating him. Then, completely deadpan, she asks: "Why don't you just take what you want?"

"What?" he says, so softly he barely hears himself.

"Why not just take what you hope to own?"

"No one owns anyone." Now louder, "What the fuck is wrong with you?"

Smiling, shaking her head as if rousing herself from a silly bad dream, she pushes to her feet and circles back around her desk to sit. She begins leafing through the binder she was reading when he barged in. "You are literally nothing, Tom," she says, not looking up. "You really should try to understand that. If you were a pawn, you're taken. You're off the board."

His face burns. At least a minute passes. Finally, she looks up at him, as though surprised to find him still here. "Would you mind shutting the door on you way out?"

"Yeah," he says. Then "No." As if it's important that he answer her question correctly. Then he goes, shutting it behind him. He has no choice. Obviously, everyone has understood that for a lot longer than he has.

He's nearly to the Hard Way when he sees Jim lurch out into the misting rain.

"Hey!" The old man turns but then turns away and heads in the opposite direction. Tom dashes across the street against traffic and slips momentarily on a rain-slick manhole. "Hey! Wait up!" Reluctantly Jim slows his pace, pulls a pocket umbrella from his overcoat, and opens it over his head. Tom catches up in three long strides. He puts his hand on the older man's shoulder, but Jim shrugs it off. "Will you just stop for a goddamned second?"

Jim growls, "What do you want?" at Tom like he's confronting a change-begging bum.

"I'm in."

"You're in what?"

"StreetSweeper. I'll get you the data." Jim stares at him then turns and continues walking. "Hey! Did you hear me?"

"I heard you."

"What? You want me to beg now?"

"I want you to use your head. It's clear you're not right now. You're being driven by some other organ. If I were charitable I'd say your heart, but I ain't charitable."

"I've thought it through."

"Bullshit."

"I want to change things. I'm with you. I'm in this game."

Jim squares off with him, looking up into Tom's eyes, his glasses rain-spattered, his irises rimmed red. He looks from one eye to the other as if inspecting Tom for genuineness. He sneers, turns away, resumes walking.

"What?" Tom's openly pleading now, shuffling sideways with the old man to keep up.

"You don't have the first clue," Jim barks over the hardening rain.

"What do you want me to do?"

"I want you to be angry. I want you to be resolved. I want you to understand the sacrifice and the struggle."

"Fuck, dude. I'm angry. Okay?"

"I want you to see red."

"Okay."

"Right. When you see red, you'll know. And you'll be ready."

"What does that even mean?"

Jim stops so suddenly that he heaves forward then backward. Once he finds his balance, he turns on Tom one last time. "When you see red, you'll know." Then he's walking away again, and this time Tom decides there's no point in following him.

22.

The Download

E veryone's out of town.

Maddie's at a conference. Jim V. took some sick leave according to Darlene, who heard it from someone on 17, who heard it straight from Juanita. Michelle? Well, who knows? She's just not around. When Tom casually asked Alicia about it in the copy room, she just nodded and smiled in her oddly leering way and said, "Oh, Tom. You know that if I told you I'd have to... kill you."

Even Kona's gone. On Friday night she came home telling Tom about some emergency pitch session she got pulled into next week in Chicago because the assistant art director on the project got mono or something. So starting Tuesday, Tom's stuck babysitting Poma and figuring out the day care gaps until Kona gets back. He's not just a little bit pissed about it, but what can he do? Bitching won't do any good, that's certain. And he understands how much of a dick he'd be if he did.

He's intimidated at the prospect of spending so much time alone with his baby girl, though she's hardly a baby anymore. He's lost his chops as a stay-at-home dad. Three-year-olds talk back and slam doors (a pet peeve of Tom's: "Scream if you want, but how is this the *door*'s fault?"). Three-year-olds relish refusing to do things and take great pride in doing that which they know they shouldn't. In short, they exhibit nearly all of the more troublesome features of Kavanaghs.

On Friday night Tom offers an extra hour of TV to convince Poma to take a bath. She was supposed to have one Wednesday night, then Thursday, but he couldn't manage anything more than getting them both dinner, reading her stories, then falling asleep with her in her bed, waking up around midnight, cramped and confused, then heading into to the kitchen to clean up as best, and as quietly, as he could.

The good news is, he's managing. It's hard, but it's good hard. The kind of hard work should be. And the cherry on top of this episode of single parenthood? He hasn't drunk more than a beer or a glass of wine each night. He's been sleeping all the way through the night, no headaches, no mouth parched like a sun-blanched toad carcass.

Per her directive, Tom has whipped Poma's bath bubbles to a tower of froth and is sitting with her as she tunnels through it. They alternate scooping the bubbles onto their faces and pretending to be Santa, "Ho, ho, ho. And what do you want for Christmas, little girl?"

"We just had Crismus."

"So? It's never too early to want things."

"You're not Santa."

"Sure I am."

"No, you're not.

"Yes, I am."

"NOOOO!!!" she screams and pushes a wave of bubbles at him.

In normal voice he pleads, "Okay, okay. Let's not get upset about it."

"I'm not upset. You're not Santa. You're Daddy."

"Okay. Fine."

"Santa's not sad. He's happy."

"What?" But Poma sinks below the bubbles. Then, an un-nervingly long moment later, she spouts up through them like a breaching whale. He asks again: "Poma. Why did you say that?" She ignores him. Hanks of foam float momentarily, falling back into the tub. "Pomaika'i *Grace*." He sing-songs.

Her head reemerges, eyes blinking away the soap. "Don't call me that!"

"Pomaika'i Grace," he calls to her again. Then adds, "Lucky girl!" She likes that.

"What?"

"Why do you think I'm not happy?"

She shrugs, suddenly twelve, "How should I know?"

• • •

He fights back tears when he picks Kona up from the airport. He hugs her longer and harder than Poma does. On the drive home when she asks him how it went, he tells her, "Four and a half of the best days of my life."

"Yeah? That's a pretty precise count there."

"Well, I ain't gonna lie to ya. I was counting pretty goddamned precisely."

It's just him daydreaming on the slowpoke 16 into work on Monday. Kona took a comp day to stay home with Poma. He fantasizes his life if he didn't have to sail the corporate slaver. He'd still have to make a living, sure, but what if he could do it from home, like he keeps hearing people can. What would he do? Maybe he could teach? But part-time. Not full-time. His father was a teacher turned principal and his mother had nothing but horror stories. Maybe he could do it part-time though, like at a community college or something. He could teach poetry or theatre, or his wheelhouse: the nexus of both. Who would be more qualified than the guy who sold out five nights straight playing the good doctor from Paterson in *This is Just to Say…* at the Winnipeg Fringe Festival?

You think cushy, fun jobs teaching arts at community college just drop like ripe fruit? What kind of courses do you think they actually teach at those schools? It's vocational stuff: mathematics, English-as-a-second-language, business statistics. Those kids want jobs when they get out. Jobs like the one you're riding this bus to. They don't want to learn about theatre and poetry. They want to eat, and have families, and houses to raise them in.

He realizes he's grinding his teeth and both of his hands are balled into rage fists. He concentrates on breathing and unballing.

He decides to reward his forbearance by indulging himself with his favorite fantasy: the dream house, which he designs in his head, mostly when he can't sleep. It's situated in the city, on a double lot, never to be sub-divided to crowd in a McMansion like is happening lately with nearly all the double-lots in Green Lake and Wallingford. From the outside it looks almost Victorian. But only almost. It's not as big as Michelle's, but it's close. It's got a room just for a piano, though maybe there's a bar in there, too. He'll call this the conservatory. There's a mediation room, because Kona's always wanted one. Poma's room is vast and sunny, but it is on the same level as his and Kona's. (Somehow the interior of the house is divided into modern spaces even though the out-side is pure 19th century.) Of course, he has his own study, with an old-fashioned standing globe and a chess set and lots and lots books on hardwood shelves, but not cheesy, stuffy, leather-bound books. No, these are books that he's read or *will* read: novels, and volumes of poetry, and the complete works of Borges, Twain, and Atwood. (He's really starting to dig her.) There's a guest room—no two. And maybe another room for another kid.

What?

Why not?

'Cuz you're a eunuch.

We can always adopt.

He mutters "fuck" to himself out loud.

"Hey, buddy. Excuse me." A huge, white-speckled work glove pushes a small, bright red thing in front of Tom's face. "I think you dropped this." Attached to the glove is a giant of a man, blond hair bristling from beneath his ball cap.

"What?"

"I think this is yours. Fell out of your bag or something." It's some sort of clear red plastic ovoid capsule.

"Oh... uh, no. That's not mine."

"Are you sure? It's red."

"It's what?"

"I'm just saying it's red. Bright red. You'd know if it's yours or not."

Suddenly Tom recognizes this guy. It's Jim V.'s liars' poker partner from the Hard Way. Randy or Robbie. *Ronnie!* That's it.

Instinctively, Tom takes the red plastic thingy. "You're welcome," Ronnie says then shuffles to the back door and gets out at the next stop.

Upon closer examination, this candy-apple-colored plastic lozenge turns out to be a flash drive. Tom finally gets it. This is the follow-up to Jim's cryptic prediction: "When you actually see red, you'll know it's time." Tom is supposed to load StreetSweeper data onto it. Smart. A thumb drive means no file transmission trace like there would be with an email. Dread passes over him like a rolling cloud. This is real now. The old man wasn't bluffing or blustering. He has taken his steps, and now, to keep it going, Tom has to take his steps. Will he keep it going? Whatever this is?

He slips the drive into his pocket. And that's where he keeps it. Every morning he transfers it to a fresh pair of pants like some sort of lucky token: a rabbit's foot or a buffalo nickel. At odd moments during the day, he idly worries it between his thumb and fingers.

And every day is another day. Up at six, then the three-way power struggle to get the family out the door and to the bus stop on time for a sleepy, jouncing ride in, and then Tom's at his desk, plowing through emails, Maddie's first then his. Then PowerPoints and spreadsheets, binders and expense reports. And Maddie needling him when he least expects it: "Did you get those SOWs signed? Is the pan flu preso draft ready for review? Have you thought about this? Did you see that you didn't italicize the word 'imperative' on page six like I asked?... You did?... And are you prepared to live with that or should we reprint all of the packets?"

"What would you like, Maddie?"

"It's not about me, Tom. It's about the job. Is the job done to your satisfaction? Are you satisfied with that work? Because you're right, maybe in the end it's just the two of us who'll notice, and I've already told you that I can live with it. But what about you? Are you willing to let it slide and get in the habit of making mistakes like that?"

And so the packets get reprinted.

And then one day, on the ride home, Kona taps his shoulder. When he turns to her he sees her eyes are bright but also cautious. "I have good news," she says.

"Give."

"I'm no longer an intern."

"They fired you."

"Tee hee. Very funny."

"Give!" He gives her leg a gentle pinch.

"Ow!" She socks him back in the arm. "They hired me full-time."

"Yeah?"

"Yeah." She stares across the aisle and out the window as the bus rolls over the Aurora Bridge. He follows her gaze. The Cascades are snowcapped purple tsunamis frozen in time. He turns back to look at her. She nods as if reassuring herself. Tom can't remember seeing her more beautiful. Poma squirms on his lap and nuzzles into his neck. "Yeah." Kona repeats. "I mean, it's kind of a big deal."

"Yeah?"

"Yeah, a promotion, and I'd be sort of running my own team."

"Holy crap. Is it a raise?"

"Yeah, it's a raise." She tells him how much: about ten grand more than he makes a year, and a tiny ice pick pushes up into his solar plexus. He smiles and makes a show of widening his eyes. "That's amazing! That's... we gotta celebrate."

"Okay!"

"They giving you bennies too?"

"Well, yeah. They offered health care, but I told 'em I'd stay on your plan. SeaTru's got better coverage."

At least I'm good for something

That night they order in Thai and split a bottle of wine. After putting Poma to bed, they make love, then turn in, but Tom's restless, so he sneaks out of their bedroom, slips on some Crocs and a coat, fills his flask with green chartreuse and walks.

This is it.

Things are happening for his family. They're on their way. They'll be able to buy a house now. For real. And not out in Federal Way either, but here, in the city, maybe even somewhere close by.

Well, shit. Why not this house we're in now?

They should make the landlady an offer. Except the basement stairway is a death trap for toddlers, and it's too small if they're going to have more kids.

What?

Well, that's what Kona wants. That's clear. She hasn't come right out and said it, but she lets me fuck her without any birth control, so…

Can you not even see how fucked you are?

I'll tell her. Not now, but soon. She just got a job and a raise and a promotion. Why would I want to ruin her triumph?

Indeed, why?

•   •   •

Happy hour is ruined now. He can't go to the Hard Way. He'd have to admit to Jim that he's chickened out or, at the very least, stuck in some very serious dithering.

He sees her one day, after work, on the elevator. Just the two of them, all the way down. They don't speak. Each in a separate corner. He can smell her though. And it reminds him that, as shitty as she made him feel in the end, she also made him feel alive. And he deserves that. He deserves to feel alive. Deserves to engage the pursuit. He just flat-out deserves more. Of everything. And there aren't that many ways left for him to get it. And he's bored. He's flat-out fucking bored. His life was supposed to be more interesting than this. He wants to take the two steps to her, push her against the elevator wall and drag his tongue down her neck into where her blouse opens; but instead, when the doors open on the lobby, he stays on as she gets out. She offers the briefest questioning look, and he nods at her as the doors close. *That's right, bitch. I'm not done for the day.* He pushes 16.

Back at his cube he uncaps the flash drive and boots up his PC. Once he's got Windows, he pushes the drive into the computer's

USB port. His computer begins to whir; a bright window opens with simplistic graphics, ugly orange and purple. The StreetSweeper login screen opens. The user box blinks at him expectantly:

Login: _____
Password: _____

"Holy damn! The drive's preloaded to go directly to the site."
Of course it is. It's all preloaded. Isn't that fate's quintessence?
Careful, Kavanagh. Now's no time for the poet to turn philosopher.

He stares at the StreetSweeper login framed by the garish custom macro: a scrap of software hand-crafted to disintegrate an industry.

Is it so wrong to want to be a hero? Or so crazy to think that you might actually be able to pull it off? That circumstances might just align to make it possible?

He types.

Login: <u>MMFleischer</u>
Password: <u>NMBJ58618689$</u>

Her husband, herself, and her kids' initials, then years of birth, all in order of birth, plus a dollar sign to satisfy the character requirement. He's playing her family like notes against her. And doesn't she deserve it? Such a stupid fucking password. Anyone could've cracked it. Live a banal life; leave a banal password.

He stares at it for a moment. With his right middle finger he strikes the enter key.

Nothing.

In fact, the screen seems to freeze momentarily. When he moves the mouse the cursor moves, but when he clicks nothing happens. But then he hears the internal disk drive of his CPU click hard, twice, then whir, and the StreetSweeper application runs through a series of screens so quickly Tom can't read them. Then, just as suddenly, the display stops on the login screen. A new window opens: "Download complete." Then another window opens on top of that: "Please remove external drive." Tom tugs it from the USB port, caps it, and slips it back in his pocket.

And that's it.

•　　　•　　　•

Every morning he rides the 16 in with his family, stiff with nerves, expecting Ronnie to reappear at any moment and demand the drive back. Or is Tom supposed to get it to Jim directly? Should he write Jim an email? No. Any electronic strings between them, no matter how innocuous, could be incriminating. And he can't call because Juanita always answers the phone.

•　　　•　　　•

A week goes by.

•　　　•　　　•

The Federal Home Loan Mortgage Corporation known as Freddie Mac announces it will no longer buy the riskiest subprime loans. Is this the first noticeable ripple? An echo of the first shots fired?

•　　　•　　　•

Another week goes by.

•　　　•　　　•

How will he know when the tsunami starts?

•　　　•　　　•

Weeks and *weeks* go by.

•　　　•　　　•

Al Sherman invites Tom to come by his office in the Ban Roll-On Building. He closes the office door when Tom arrives, and

Tom takes a seat. "I've been meaning to ask you about something."

"Shoot," Tom says.

"I'm wondering if you might be interested in a position as a disaster preparedness coordinator, which I happen to know will be opening up on my team. It's entry level. A little more than you're making now, probably, but no overtime, so the money's likely a wash, but there's opportunity for advancement a few years down the road. Would that be something you're interested in?"

"Uh… sure."

"Then I think you should apply. It should open early next week."

A new job. A new direction. This could be huge. "Am I qualified?"

Al smiles, leans back in his chair. "No. But we'll make it train-as-you-go."

"Have you talked to Maddie about this?"

Al twists in his chair. "I gotta tell you, Tom. I don't think that's my place. I can advocate for you, but you have to decide whether or not it's a step you want to take."

Tom takes the idea to Maddie. She peppers him. "You understand this is an exempt role, right? You'd be making a little bit more money, but you wouldn't be able to work overtime. It's a salary. You'd make what you make no matter how many long hours you put in. And the hours will be long, and if there's an event you'll be on call. You might be working around the clock. You get that, right?"

"I get it."

"You won't have my ear, not directly, or my protection. I mean, you won't have the imprimatur of my office, do you understand?"

I get it. I won't be your cell block bitch anymore, with all the protections that affords me.

"You saw the layoffs. All SVP's have an EA so that role's essentially protected, but if a corporate decision should come down to shrink the Office of Emergency Preparedness, I can't step in and help you personally."

"Well, that gives me a lot to think about."

"Take your time."

Tom takes his time.

Tom doesn't tell Kona.

Tom doesn't answer Al.

Tom doesn't do anything about the thumb drive.

Tom waits.

He's hitting a rhythm again. A quiet one. Hearing nothing from Jim, he figures the old man has let his better angels guide him. Not telling Tom is kind of dickish on the SVP's part, but Tom understands that this is how things are often done. If anything, he's grateful. The world will not explode on his watch, or if it does, it won't have been him lighting the fuse.

He dodged a bullet.

Even so, every Thursday he hits the Hard Way at 5:15 p.m. like clockwork, but Jim's never there. So, Tom usually only has the one drink and moves on, mostly to home, but sometimes to another bar downtown, or Lenny's in Wallingford.

He waits.

Spring should be coming soon, if you believe in that sort of thing. Tom could swear this time last year there were already blossoms on the cherry trees but, inspecting the ones in front of the Green Lake Library, he finds nothing but pregnant buds. And he remembers Ikkyū's admonition:

Chop the cherry tree open

You'll find no soft flowers

But spring breezes bring myriad blossoms

So... he waits. Hearing nothing from Jim, never seeing Ronnie again, Tom decides the grownup thing to do is maybe forget all of it ever happened.

One night, Kona tells Tom that she has stepped down from her role as manager at the advertising firm.

"What?"

"It's okay. I'm still making the same salary, which was really cool of them actually."

"But why?"

"Well, I didn't tell them the real reason. I said that I wanted a year or two to get my hands really dirty on all aspects of creative. And they seemed to buy it."

"Well, what's the real reason?"

"Well… come on, Tommy. It's now or never don't you think?

"Now or never for what?"

"To have another baby."

23.

The Elbow

Tom managed to put her off last night, to convince her that he hasn't given the subject of another kid any thought at all; and he wants to be a grownup, and grownups take time and care with decisions, right? So he asked for a month. A look of doubt crossed her face, but then just as quickly a smile returned. She shrugged. "Okay. Fine. Let's talk in a month."

That was three weeks ago. Kona seems to have decided to make a game of it. She ambushes Tom with sex, and he does his faux best to evade her entrapments. He loves it. When she does manage to bag him, he makes sure to make a show of not coming inside of her. And she makes a pouty disappointed face but then shrugs and slithers out from under him to go wipe off.

He's got to figure out a way to not lose this girl. Fact is, he's starting to fall in love with her. Or maybe just deeper. It's a puzzle he's having trouble working out. He didn't realize you could fall like this: over time, while you were just living a life. How could a word like "aging" having anything to do with falling in love?

So, he's got a week, maybe more time if he can figure out a way to buy it. When you're patient, when you can find yourself mindfully watching the days go by, one after the other, sometimes you can catch a rhythm. And sometimes that rhythm can bring you to a point of inspiration.

That's the theory anyway.

• • •

Coming back from the copy room, he grabbed the phone over his counter. "SeaTru Enterprise Risk Services, this is Tom."

After a pause, a man says, "I'm sorry, *who* is this?" Tom looks at his caller ID display. It reads "Puget Sound Business Journal."

"This is Tom. Who's *this?*"

"Tom who?"

Tom's focus sharpens. "Who is this?"

"This is Anthony Nellam with the Puget Sound Business Journal. What's *your* last name, Tom?"

"What can I do for you, Anthony?"

"Enterprise Risk Services, is that what you said?"

This guy is clearly fishing. He's got a number and he's running it down, trying to figure out who it belongs to, because... why? A chill creeps up Tom's neck. "Anthony, do you have some business I could help you with?"

"Well, yeah. I think maybe so."

"Can you hold on for a minute?"

"Sure, Tom."

Tom presses the hold button and walks around his counter so that he can sit at his computer. He pulls up Google and enters "Anthony Nellam Puget Sound." Sure enough, the first hit is an image of a smiling, light-skinned black guy at his desk on a news floor. Tom puts the receiver back to his ear and hits the button next to the flashing red light. "So, what can I do for you, Anthony?"

"Did you just Google me, Tom?"

Jesus.

"What can I do for you, Anthony?"

"Well, Tom, since you have the advantage on me, you can start with giving me your last name."

"Anthony, what's this in reference to?"

"StreetSweeper."

Tom's fingers go numb where he's gripping the phone. He looks around. *Where the fuck is my water bottle?* His throat is suddenly as parched as bleached bone.

"Tom?"

"Yes." His tongue has gone so fat that the word has a lispy quality, and the rest comes out sluggishly: "I honestly… think you have… the wrong number, Anthony."

"Honestly? You think so?"

"I have another… call coming in. I'm gonna need to let you… go now."

"Whoa, come on, Tom. I'm just trying to—" Tom hits the orange call-release button, and his ear fills with the comforting hum of dial tone.

After stewing, staring blankly at his keyboard for a long time— but just how long he couldn't say—Tom, on impulse, pounds out an email to Jim V.

Subject: Happy Hour – Today – 5:00 p.m.

Message: I am in urgent need of a drink with you, due to a phone call I received this morning.

At five sharp he logs off and heads over, heart pounding, to the Hard Way. The stools are mostly empty, and Jim isn't squatting on any of them. Tom asks Anna the last time she's seen him.

"Jim who?"

Unbelievable. "Jim V… Jim Verhoeven?… Older dude. Thinning red hair running gray on a high forehead. Works at the bank?"

She nods and says, "Gin and tonic."

"That's him."

"Hasn't been in for a while."

"Well, if you see him, tell him he needs to talk to me."

"And who are you?"

"Jesus, Anna, I've been coming in here for two years."

"Yeah, vodka-cran. Hell if I know your Christian name though."

"It's Tom. Just tell Jim he needs to talk to Tom."

"You got a last name."

"Just Tom is fine. Trust me."

Ann shrugs and moves on. Tom tips her a ten in hopes it puts a pin in her memory.

•　　•　　•

Kona's flirtations have faded, and ominous clouds have again gathered above the Green Lake bungalow. At dinner, and on bus rides in and out of the city, she keeps her conversations with him short and informational. He finally calls her on it. "Look, baby, I know you're frustrated with me, but the God's-honest truth is I haven't been able to give this the thought it deserves. I got massive shit rolling down at me at work."

"We all got shit at work," she says nonchalantly as she fills the dishwasher.

"Not like this."

"How would you know?"

"Because you're better than me, okay?"

She stops loading and turns to him. "What does that mean? What did you do that could be so much worse than what I might be doing? You're a secretary for chrissakes. How much damage could you possibly do?"

Tom falters. It's like she pulled off the blindfold to let him see the edge of the cliff he's been marching along. *Only the nation's complete financial collapse, that's all.* "I hope I—" He can't finish. What the hell can he tell her about any of it? "Look, I just— Don't worry about it. I'm gonna fix it." He's been anxiously monitoring the markets, stock and bond, for any new precipitous activity. So far everything seems normal.

"What's broken, Tommy? Can you tell me that much?"

"I can't. I really can't."

She shuts her mouth tight, shakes her head, goes back to loading the dishwasher.

•　　•　　•

Tom hits the Hard Way again. Again no sign of Jim, but he does find the old man's hard hat buddy, Ronnie, bellied to the bar. When Anna slides Tom's Cape Cod in front of him, he tells her to set Ronnie up with another round. When she delivers the

Goldschläger shot and beer back, she points to Tom, and Ronnie turns, glares at him as if trying to place the face, then nods a curt, expressionless thank you. About ten minutes later, when the stool next to the big man clears out, Tom takes it.

"I don't usually go a second round," says Ronnie, sipping his schnapps. "Gonna be fucked up on the bus home."

"You'll be fine. Enjoy it."

Ronnie takes a long pull on his beer then kills the remainder of the schnapps. "I'm gonna go for a smoke."

"Cool. Can I bum one?"

"Sure. Come on."

The big man fastidiously places a coaster over his beer to hold his place at the bar. Tom does the same with his Cape Cod. Out on the sidewalk, Ronnie draws two cigarettes from his red pack of Marlboros, transfers them to his left hand as he slips the pack back into his pocket with his right, then he backswings, with stunning quickness, to bitch-slap Tom across the face. A high-pitched bell sizzles in the back of Tom's skull. It's oddly bracing and utterly humiliating. Ronnie nods as if the smack affirms an understanding between them. He sticks the cigarettes in his mouth, draws out a Zippo and lights both, then gently holds one out in his huge paw to Tom.

"Is that from Jim, then?" Tom touches his cheek.

"Naw, that's from me for making me do errand-boy work."

"So, what's the errand."

"To tell you to shut the fuck up, stand the fuck down, and never try and contact him, or me for that matter, again."

Something's rising in Tom. "Got it."

Ronnie pulls an envelope from his jacket and pegs it to Tom's chest with his index finger. "That's a half strap. You know what that is?"

Tom meets the other man's eyes cold. "Not a clue."

"Well, a strap of Franklins is ten grand, so you do the math."

How could this get more insane?

Don't ask.

"What's it for?"

"Fuck if I know or care." Ronnie pushes his face in close. "I like you and all, but I ain't keeping my finger here all day." Tom grabs the envelope, slips it down into his pants pocket. "Good boy."

"Did you get your own half strap?"

Ronnie cocks his head, narrows his eyes, then suddenly smiles. "We're done."

Tom pushes it on impulse. "You got kids?" The big man stops smiling. "The next time I see you, Ronnie, I think I'm gonna get to your throat with something and open it." The big man's chest starts heaving. "I'm from Jersey, Ronnie. I've met mobsters. You? You're not a mobster. You're just some guy getting paid. You ain't killing anybody, and you ain't even spending the night in jail for a public sidewalk beat-down on some Jersey prick who deserves it."

"Keep talking, kid."

"You tell the old man he talks to me, in person, or I do him fully, publicly."

"I don't have any plans to talk to anybody after you."

"Then make some. Or see yourself involved."

"Oh, so you're threatening *me?*"

"Geez, Ronnie. I already promised to kill you next time you laid hands on me. Bet your ass I mention your name to the cops if it comes to that. And don't you think that's just what they live for, giving the really big ones a proper shit-kicking?" Tom can see Ronnie knows he's right, so he eases up. "Just pass the message and we're square."

"I ain't doing shit for you."

"Just pass the message." Tom flicks his cigarette sparking into the street and walks away, shaking, but not visibly, he hopes.

What the fuck is wrong with me?

He gets off the 16 at Lenny's, throws back a shot of Cuervo Gold, and walks the rest of the way home. Opening the front door, he finds Hana, his friend J., and Kona sharing a bottle of wine in the living room. They all avoid Tom's eyes. Kona's clearly been crying. "I guess I'm not invited to the party. Anyone mind if I grab a beer?" He heads past them into the kitchen, pulls a bottle out of the fridge, opens it, swigs half, waits a beat, then heads back into the living room. Hana already has her coat on and J.'s giving him a helpless look.

"You guys heading out?"

"Yeah, we're gonna catch a movie."

"Enjoy."

Hana goes, leaving the front door open behind her. Kona takes her glass and the bottle into the bedroom. Tom tosses an open-armed "whatthefuck?" gesture to his friend, who is shrugging on his leather jacket.

"Dude. No. I tried with you; you blew me off. I am *not* getting in the middle of this shit-house crazy bullshit of yours now."

"Seriously?"

"Seriously."

"Nothing?"

"Zip."

And then J.'s gone too.

Tom waits a minute, then stands at the bedroom door. "You're mad at me."

"Not even close."

"You're sad at me."

"Okay. Closer."

"I get it. You wanna make babies."

"Fuck, Tom... just don't."

"I wanna make babies too."

"*Don't.*"

He goes and takes her glass and sets it on the end table. He kisses her head. "I mean it. I've made my decision. I want another kid."

"You're drunk."

"Not even close."

"*I'm* drunk."

"Is that a problem? Will that freeze up your fallopians or something."

She shakes her head petulantly. "Doesn't work that way."

Tom tells her again: He's decided. Then he proceeds to fuck her, hard, and comes inside of her to prove it.

．　　●　　●

They're both pretty hungover the next morning, Tom especially, since he got out of bed around midnight and took a bottle
of Maker's out onto the front porch steps, sipping straight from
the bottle, sitting in the darkness. He'd killed about half of it when
he finally headed downstairs and put the envelope containing the
half-strap in the carved Salish bentwood box of keepsakes.

Kona's asleep on his shoulder on the bus ride in, while Poma
begs and begs for him to go through the flash cards he's made for
her. He shuffles them ostentatiously and displays them at random
for her to guess at.

"see"

"here"

"go"

"now"

"time"

To be a smart ass, and to make his girl giggle, he's also thrown
in a few ringers:

"plinth"

"serendipity"

"pneumatic"

Kona shakes her head on his shoulder, murmuring, "*I* don't
even know what a plinth is."

"Neither do I," he replies. She pinches him.

"Ow."

"What, Daddy?"

"Mommy pinched me."

"Oh." Poma does too.

Later they are standing, waiting to cross at a corner a couple blocks from Poma's day care center downtown. Poma tugs at
Tom's arm. "Let's gooooo!"

"We got to wait for walking man."

"There's walking man now. Let's goooo."

"We still have to look both ways. No matter what." Tom looks
right, then left. There's a bicyclist zooming down the hill toward them.

Asshole's not going to stop.

He feels Poma move forward. He tugs her back away from the curb, and then for some reason, or no reason at all, he elbows out with his left arm catching the bicyclist on the side of the face and sending him skidding sideways into the back of a car parked on the far side of the street. "Let's go." He grabs Poma's arm and they cross.

Kona's right behind them, running to catch up. "What happened?"

"He clipped me. He was too close." He yanks at Poma who is now holding back, doing her best to gawk.

And now the bicyclist is up and hobbling toward them screaming, "HEY! WHAT THE FUCK, MAN!"

Tom pumps his legs forward, turns only his head, and shouts: "You clipped me! You ran the light!" But his voice doesn't come close to matching the other man's outrage.

"You *elbowed* me in the FACE!"

Tom's halfway down the block now, not stopping. He yells over his shoulder, "Not how it happened!"

Kona has caught up and is hurriedly crabbing sideways next to him. "Why don't you just stop and talk to the guy?"

He stops. Squares on her and snarls, "You want me to stop and talk to the guy?" The sides of his vision are crowding with red.

Kona's sees something in his face which scares her. "No. Just go. Keep moving."

They deliver Poma to her day care in choked silence, unbroken even when they part ways to head to their jobs.

24.

The Table

*F*inally.

Spring is here. The cherry blossoms are snowing pink and white.
No need to chop open the trees.
Yet.

Tom's taking his 10 a.m. coffee break at the symphony Starbucks, scribbling in his Moleskine with trusty nub. Now someone's looming over him. Tom looks up, finds a friendly looking black man grinning at him, Patagonia fleece over a loosely knotted knit tie.

"This is just to say…" says the guy. Tom waits. He feels like he should know this guy, who seems about to go on, but doesn't. Still smiling, the guy repeats: "This is just to say…"

"Sorry?"

The man nods, encouragingly, as if egging Tom on. "This is just to say…"

"I… oh… um—"

"It is you, right?"

"Uh, yeah…"

"The doctor poet. William… something Hispanic…"

"Carlos."

"Carlos?"

"William Carlos Williams."

The man points at Tom, beaming. "Exactly! That's you, right?"

"That *was* me, yes." Tom can't believe it. It's not often he gets recognized from his one-man show *This is Just to Say...* about the Paterson, New Jersey poet, but it did happen once or twice, especially back when he was performing it.

"You doing any shows lately?"

"Nah. I... don't really act anymore."

"What about writing? I mean, you wrote that show too, right?"

"Oh yeah. Well, I still do a little bit of writing, but... got a day job and all now."

"Yeah, where at?"

Tom points south. "SeaTru."

"Yeah? Doing what?"

"Executive Assistant. I'm a glorified secretary. Sans the glory."

"Hah! Well, damn. Guess we all gotta grow up sometime, hunh?"

"Yeah."

The man pulls out a chair at Tom's table and sits. "So, with that in mind, what can you tell me about StreetSweeper?"

Tom freezes. A nut of nausea begins climbing his throat. He pushes away from the table and stands. *That's* where Tom's seen him, the *Puget Sound Business Journal* website photo: Nellam, Anthony. "You're stalking me? That's fucked up, dude."

"Tom, I'm doing my job. We all have jobs, right? If I'm stalking anything, it's StreetSweeper. I'm not the one that put your phone number in with it."

"Who did?"

The reporter shrugs. "You tell me?"

Tom grabs his coffee. "Just stay the fuck away from me."

Nellam casually stands in front of him as he moves to go. Tom looks him up and down. Nellam grins. "Should we duke it out?" He does some quick and goofy shadow punching. "Right here, right now, in the symphony hall?" Tom steps to the side and walks past him. The reporter hollers at his back, "I don't know if a fight is what you want, Tom. Newspapers may be struggling and all, but we still buy ink by the barrel." Tom is pushing open the door to the street when Nellam calls out, "Happy Administrative Professionals Day!"

What?

The elevator.

Fuck. Please God let Maddie have forgotten.

Seems like she has. The morning passes with no mention of it; but then, sure as shit, come 11:45 a.m. she's at his counter with her coat over one arm and her purse in the other. "Got plans for lunch?"

"Nope."

"How's Sazerac sound to you?"

Like warmed-over regret.

Over lunch, Maddie admits to forgetting about Secretaries' Day until this morning when she saw Louis give Darlene a bouquet of flowers. "Not the sort of thing Louis Saks is going to do without a damned good reason."

"No." *Fuck that asshole.*

"I figured I'd spare you the flowers," she says.

"I appreciate it." *You could've spared me the whole fucking farce.*

"This way you get to eat and I get to discuss that opportunity Al offered you. He says you never applied for it."

"No. I... it didn't feel like a fit."

"Nonsense. Of course it's a fit. I certainly hope you didn't feel like I was discouraging you." *Only emphatically, and in no uncertain terms.* "He's extended the posting. If you want it, you should put in your application."

"Who would work for you?"

"You think you're irreplaceable?"

"No, I just..."

"We'll find somebody for me. And yeah, sure, maybe we should do that first before moving you into that new position. But I would never want to hold you back."

"Thank you, Maddie."

Tom's phone rings after lunch; the caller ID reads "Liz Mitchell," one of the EAs on 17, though Tom forgets exactly whom she supports. "Enterprise Risk Services. This is Tom."

"Tom, Liz Mitchell calling on Greg Governale's behalf." The new COO, Maddie's new boss's boss, the guy they brought in to clean up the Jim V. memo mess.

"Hi, Liz. You've actually dialed my direct line. Would you like me to connect you through to Maddie?"

"No. I'm calling for you, Tom. Greg would like to see you."

"Um. Okay. Now?

"Right now, yes. Please."

"Okay, uh… remind me where you're located."

"On 17." *Well duh.* "Right next to Terry's office in the northwest corner."

"Right. Well… okay. I'll be right up."

Tom knocks gently on Maddie's open door. "Hey, uh… I just got called up to 16 by Liz Mitchell."

"Greg Governale's EA?"

"Yeah, I guess he wants to see me."

"*You?*"

Tom shrugs. "That's what she's telling me."

Maddie turns to her phone and punches the hands-free button. Liz picks up after one ring. "Hi Maddie."

"Hi Liz. Does Greg have a minute?"

"Well, actually, he's just stepping into a meeting."

"That's what I understand. Apparently with one of my people, Tom Kavanagh."

"That's right."

Maddie shakes her head, confused, but keeps her tone cool. "He needs Tom, not me?"

"That's correct."

"Any idea as to why?"

"None whatsoever, Maddie."

"Okay. Thank you."

"You bet, Maddie. Bye-bye."

Maddie punches off, frowning. She shrugs. "I got no clue." She finally looks up at him. "Well, I wouldn't dawdle if I were you."

"Nope."

As Tom passes Terry Torgersen's office, his EA, Wendy, gives him a brief appraising glance then quickly goes back to her screen. Tom steps up to Liz Mitchell's counter. She's a large, blonde woman with kind eyes. In other circumstances, Tom might try to strike up a friendly conversation. "Hello, Liz. Tom Kavanagh here."

Liz nods, avoiding eye contact. "Great. Let me take you to the room." She walks ahead of him down the row of offices. Tom follows her into a small conference room where Greg Governale, tall, with well-coifed silver hair, stands and puts out his hand. Tom shakes it, looking past him to see Michelle sitting next to Jim V. She gives Tom a quick glance, her blue eyes as cold and unfathomable as the North Pacific, then she lets her gaze rest on the wall opposite. Across from them sits a crisply dressed Asian man, and back from the table, against the wall, stands Jake the security guy, hands thoughtfully folded at his crotch, looking for all the world like he couldn't possibly know how to snap a person's neck.

Just breathe, Tommy. That's the first thing you did when you came into this world.

Yeah. But this time, try to do it without screaming and shitting yourself.

"Why don't you have a seat?" says Governale from behind him. The COO sits at the table's end and indicates with an open hand, "I believe you know Jim Verhoeven and Michelle Fleischer." Tom makes a point of fully taking in both as he sits across from them. Jim gazes soulfully back at him, nodding ever so slightly like he's suffering a slight palsy. Michelle stares at the blank white legal pad in front of her, her face a marble study in dignity impugned. "And this is Kevin Dong, he's with our HR department."

Ah, it's come to that: the Gestapo in the room.

Dong nods curtly, clear-eyed and eager as a cat. Tom decides to say nothing. *Exactly. Wait and see. Don't make the first move.*

Governale sits back, content to wait, and the rest seem content to follow his lead. Dong finally flips open a thick portfolio. He peels back a page, then another, then a third, then lets them all float back down. "Why do you think you're here, Tom?"

"Here?"

Exactly. Play as dumb as humanly possible. That's what the mook Guidos on the Jersey Shore taught him: the half-connected Italians who ran the pasta parlor in Belmar where he got his first job bussing tables when he turned 14. He'd bike to the job from

Manasquan through Spring Lake, five and a half miles there, five and a half back, five days a week, all summer. He was alone in the front of the house, folding napkins, when the health inspector came in between lunch and dinner shifts. When the guy started to question him, Tom shook his head, acted like he didn't speak English. Then the guy switched to Italian. Luckily, the night manager Marco DeDeo showed up just in time. Afterward, he gave Tom's cheek a fat pinch and said, "Good boy. Never say shit to nobody, specially some hard-on with a badge nosing around. You act as dumb as possible." Marco gave his tie knot an adjusting touch in the reflective chrome of the cigarette machine. "And in your case, Tommy Boy, it won't be much of an act."

Dong makes a face, shakes his head, then reiterates, slowly and condescendingly, "Why do you think you are here, *in this room*, Tom, with the Chief Operations Officer and these other senior executives?"

"I don't know."

Dong flips the first sheet and tucks it underneath the oxblood folder. He circles something with his fountain pen then states flatly, "StreetSweeper."

Tom makes no response.

"What does that mean to you?"

"Beyond the obvious, like… something that sweeps a street?"

"What do you know about StreetSweeper in the context of your job?"

"Oh." Tom says it as though *now* he's tracking, albeit only barely. "I think I remember that being the name of a… sort of… online data tool, which Michelle Fleischer had me work with occasionally when I was temporarily her admin assistant."

Dong blinks at him. Tom returns his stare as stupidly as he can. Marco DeDeo would be proud, if he isn't dead and dumped in the Meadowlands by now. From the sheet, Dong reads: "StreetSweeper is a proprietary online tool for analyzing the most current and comprehensive mortgage data available. On February 21—nearly two years since working for Michelle Fleischer—you logged onto StreetSweeper, extracting and downloading a very specific and substantial data set. You then, some weeks later, leaked this data to multiple media outlets, including *The Puget Sound Business Journal*, possibly at the behest of financiers looking to short the mortgage market, a strategy, which if successful, could have collapsed the U.S. and world economies."

After a long, long moment, Tom decides to offer one word. "No."

Mistake?

"'No'?" Dong's face is an Acting 101 class mask of incredulity.

"I don't know anything about what you just said. It sounds absolutely bat-shit crazy, if you want my opinion, which I'm sure you don't." Tom shoots a scanning glance past Jim. Was that a hint of a smile on the old man's face?

Dong pounces. "You haven't been talking to *The Puget Sound Business Journal?*"

"I may have talked to a guy; told him he has the wrong number, that sort of thing. I haven't been... leaking any——"

Governale cuts in: "But you *have* been talking to them?"

"Some guy called me asking for information."

"Information about what?" Dong demands.

"Now that you mention it, I think he may have said 'Streetsweeper.' but he was hard to understand over the phone." *Fuck. What are you doing? The* one *thing the Guidos told you....*

"What about when he met you in person at Starbucks this morning?" Dong now arches his eyebrows like a soap opera actor. A perfectly spherical void begins to expand within Tom's intestines. He feels like this burgeoning black hole could consume the room—the entire tower—if he doesn't get it under control.

"I told him to go away," he says.

Dong nods, faux friendly, "Your contact at *The Journal*. You told him to go away. You didn't want to talk to him?"

"He's not my contact. I didn't *know* him. So, no, I didn't want to talk to him."

"Why not?" Dong lets the silence dangle this time. He finally has the advantage and knows he's unlikely to lose it. "Why did you come onto the 16th floor after hours on February 21?

"Don't know." Tom adds a shrug. "Don't know that I did."

"The badge access log tells us you did."

"Sounds like the log tells you that *someone* did."

"We also have cameras, Tom. It's the 21st century." Tom can feel his face burning. "Let's be clear. We're not here to determine *if* you did it. That much is clear from the preponderance of circumstantial evidence."

"Circumstantial..."

"Evidence, nonetheless." Dong leans back. "No, Tom, we're more about the *why* you did it. What did you hope to achieve? And who were you working with?"

Tom resists the urge to look at the others. He's not interested in implicating or impugning anyone. Not *yet*, at least. He first needs to know where he sits in this game.

"Tell me about this picture." Dong pushes a blue file folder across the table. Tom opens it. Inside is a screen grab printed on a sheet of plain, white 8 ½ by 11. Tom and Kona are wearing Kerry/Edwards 2004 T-shirts— "A Stronger America"—and Poma, a plump two-year-old, sports a floppy denim beach hat with a big Kerry campaign button stuck to the front of it. The photo looks for all the world like it could have been staged by the campaign itself. A handsome mixed-race couple with their soulful, golden-locked, Asian-eyed toddler, staring openly, wondrously expectant, into a better future. J. shot it at a friend's fundraising barbecue in West Seattle.

Tom, though he's seething, smiles and shrugs. "You have a picture of my family."

"At a John Kerry fundraising event."

"Okay?"

"Are you an idealist, Tom?"

"I have no idea what that means or what it would have to do with what you're accusing me of."

"An idealist is someone who acts on the belief that they can change the world for the better. Is that you?" Tom glances at Michelle. She's been watching him but now quickly looks down. "Or did someone pay you a large sum of money?" The half-strap Ronnie pushed into his chest flashes to mind. Without wanting to, Tom glances over at Jim, but Jim's not looking at anything: just sad eyes swimming behind his glasses. Dong persists. "Tom? Did someone pay you to download the StreetSweeper data?"

"I feel like… I shouldn't say any more to you."

Silence. It goes on for a while. Greg Governale starts tapping his forefinger lightly but with an insistent rhythm. "Jim, did you have anything you wanted to say?"

The old man is slow to rouse. He lets out a weary sigh, and only then does he move his hands from their folded monk's position, placing them palms up on the table. "What can I say? I'm sad." Without looking up, Michelle nods in sad agreement.

"You mean disappointed?" Governale asks. He seems perplexed.

"Well, yeah, but really?… Sad. I feel sad… Listen, I know Tom a little bit. He's a good guy." Jim looks at him. "Tom, you're a good guy. I don't know why you did this, but I can maybe guess, and I can also maybe understand your reluctance to explain, but… I don't know… I'm just sad."

Tom resists smiling, or worse, laughing out loud. *This amazing, bald-faced fucker. I'm out of my depth with this dude. He's the Yoda of corporate fuckery.*

Governale leans forward. "Well, a case could be made, Jim, that the data Tom stole might be used to support the thesis *you* presented to the board, that the loans underlying our CDOs aren't sound enough to support their triple-A ratings."

Jim nods. "Yeah I know." He looks Governale in the eyes. "Honestly, I *wish* I had full and free access to this data at the time, so that I could've shared it with the board to convince them, but I didn't understand the sort of granularity StreetSweeper was capable of until very recently."

Michele looks at Jim, seems about to say something, but stays quiet. Jim turns to Tom. "I'm sorry, son." Tom smiles at him. He can't help it. The old man's audacity is astounding and impressive. Tom finds himself once again admiring his friend in spite of every reason to loathe and despise him. But then a pang hits him: This guy never cared anything for him, played him like a pawn from the very beginning. Tom stares down at the table to steady himself. *Do not do this now. Do* not *let these fuckers see your fucking emotions.*

Michelle speaks. "Obviously, I'm disappointed, too, but as much in myself as anyone. I should have kept tighter security over my password to the StreetSweeper tool. *Oh, you gorgeous, ruthless cunt.* "The bank forces us to renew our system passwords, but StreetSweeper was independent and in test mode, so they never prompted me to change it, and I never did." She gazes at Tom with open compassion. He wants to crawl across the table, push her down to the floor, and strangle her. She seems to see this in his eyes because something in hers, almost imperceptibly, sparks. *She is secretly enjoying the fuck out of this. She's probably sopping wet right now.* She turns back to Governale. "It was a crazy time when Tom was working for me." She glances over to Dong, careful to include all key players at the table. "My own executive assistant had died suddenly. I was so emotionally fraught and unavailable that I never got to know Tom. Had I, maybe I would've been able to understand his own emotional state, and thus possibly been able to head off his behavior somehow, or alert someone to it, or at the very least, tighten my own security. But I guess I was too distracted to even do that."

Governale holds his palm out. "I appreciate what you're saying, Michelle, but I'm pretty sure there wasn't anything you could've done to deter this young man from his actions once he chose to embark on them." He turns to Tom. "Obviously nobody here wishes you ill. But deeds have consequences."

"You gonna fire me?"

"Let's not get ahead of ourselves."

Dong pipes up. "That hasn't been determined yet. Your cooperation now could go a long way toward mitigate——"

"Am I under arrest?"

Dong scoffs, "Please. This is not a legal proceeding."

"Am I free to go then?"

"Well, you *work* here right?" Governale is losing his cool. "We're in the middle of a meeting are we not?"

Tom replies calmly, "I have work to do for Maddie. Plenty of it..."

Governale practically spits. "Your work for Maddie is done." He stands and leaves the room abruptly. Jim V. and Michelle quietly follow him out.

"Go home, Tom," says Dong. "You are suspended with pay until further notice. You are not to log onto any SeaTru devices or systems during your suspension. You are not to talk to anyone inside or outside of the company about the content of this meeting." Dong slides a paper to him with these instructions printed on it in legalese and tells him to sign the line above his name.

"And if I don't."

"You're done immediately. Fired for cause. No severance. No vacation payout. No unemployment benefits, and the option of criminal charges will almost certainly be pursued. Aggressively." Tom signs the paper. *What's the difference? I'm fucked anyway. Might as well keep my bennies.*

Jake the security guy escorts him down to his cube on 16 to collect his stuff. Maddie isn't there, and Tom is glad. In the elevator down to the lobby, Tom catches Jake observing him in the reflection of the brushed steel of the closed doors. "All in a day's work, huh?" Tom says, smiling lamely. Jake's reflection raises his eyebrows as if to consider the question, then, still pokerfaced, nods agreement.

25.

Fool's Check

Tom looks good. Different. You probably wouldn't recognize him if you had worked with him at SeaTru. His hair is a good inch longer and he leaves it wild and shaggy now. He's even got a glossy, mostly black beard going: the stray straggles of gray only serving to give him an even handsomer, weathered, dark-Irish, Daniel Day-Lewis kind of vibe. He's keeping incognito, wearing mirror shades and a Mariners cap turned backward, cargo shorts, T-shirt, and Teva sandals. Call it his loosey-goosey comfort wear for the summer. He's sipping an iced latte at one of the symphony Starbucks tables. He's been staking out this spot with some frequency these last few weeks. It's far enough from the SeaTru Tower to be relatively safe from awkward unintentional encounters, but close enough to hope he might catch sight of one of his big fish.

He's biding his time, finally playing the long game. For far too long he mistakenly thought he was just watching some fascinating chess match. Then he got moved, played like the pawn he always was—advancing sluggish single spaces while the Bishop and the Queen zipped deftly around the board. Were they working together all along? Seems unlikely, but isn't that what a pawn *would* think? If Jim and Michelle wanted to team up to grab the data off StreetSweeper for profit and/or idealism, then who better to trap into covering their tracks than the idiot, love-struck, high-minded poet-puppet, strings easily jerked by naïve notions of seduction, revenge, easy money, corporate ascendance.

You're mixing your metaphors, Kavanagh. Is it chess or puppetry? Pick a tired trope and stick with it.

He spent two full days overhauling his bike, all the while talking to himself and polishing his confrontation fantasies to perfection. He pulled off his old mountain treads, so old and worn that the steel webbing was wearing through the side walls, and replaced them with beautiful, fresh, black street tires, because how often did he really ride on rough trails anyway? With chain lube and an old toothbrush, he completely detailed his chain and cassettes, front and back. He's even bought some new bike shorts—not the super tight kind, mind you; he's not quite ready for that and doubts he will ever be—but a baggier pair with form-fitting interior webbing. He's also sprung for new lights, front and back, for night riding. He's really getting into it. He had forgotten how fun it was to simply ride a bike and lean into the long swerving downhills. A different part of your brain engages, one that Tom hasn't plugged into in forever. Running tends to numb Tom out, but when he's riding, the back of his brain is constantly scanning for the circumstance that could kill him: the car that pulls out suddenly, the chunk of loose asphalt that could send him flying, the car door opening, the pedestrians crossing without a look or a care.

Tom's fantasy conversation with Jim always begins with one word: "Why?"

From his Hard Way bar stool, phantom Jim counters: "*That's* not the question. The *question* is: why *not?*" Tom shakes his head, shifts gears, pedals harder while Jim explains. "The center can't sustain. These fraudulent mortgage securities are bound to collapse eventually. I'm just accelerating the process."

"Why involve *me?*"

"Simple. I'm too old, and weak, and compromised by comfort to perpetrate revolution. But that doesn't mean I don't recognize it as a necessity. I just can't sit and wait for the young, dynamic, and relatively innocent to realize what they need to do. I need you to *do* it—*force* you to do it—if necessary."

"Doesn't forcing people to do good almost always lead to evil?"

"See? You don't need to worry about a job, kid. You got a career at the fortune cookie factory whenever you want it."

"Fuck you! And fuck your high-minded excuses. You're profiting from this devastation, plain and simple." Tom shouts this out loud. He doesn't care. He's on a bike, rocketing along the Burke-Gilman trail at 25 miles an hour.

In the Hard Way of Tom's heart, Jim pushes that half strap of cash forward with the tip of an accusing finger. "Sure, kid. And as I recall, I ain't the only one."

Tom smiles, rueful, and downshifts to pedal past a slower cyclist. "But why *me*? Surely you knew other folks with StreetSweeper access. Clearly you did, because you didn't even bother to ever collect the thumb drive." Tom's finally catching a clue. "Shit! You never *needed* the thumb drive, did you? You only needed a fall guy."

"And kid, you could not have been more perfect," Jim sips from his ever-half-full lowball, then licks his lips. "Look, we're all part of it, the grand story. Even the frauds, backstabbers, and cheats like me, just as much as the dreamers, patsies, and cheaters like you. You think I'd ever have the guts to a bed a woman as astounding as Michelle?"

Tom shakes off the fantasy and yells, "You're full of *shit*, Kavanagh!" A couple riding tandem in the opposite direction gawk in alarm as they pass. He hollers up to the green leaves racing overhead. "Massively packed *full!*"

Phantom Jim rants on. "And when that enormous volcano blows, swallowing all of Puget Sound in mud and ash, we'll *still* have been part of it." He lifts his glass. "I'm optimistic."

"Shit," Tom murmurs to himself. "It sounds exactly like him. I should write all this shit down and make a play about the fucker."

A "play?" You should write a "play?" Yes! Absolutely. And when you're done, you should twist the script into a roll and feed it to a big, blue, office water cooler bottle and toss it into the sound. Working title: Bullshit Message in a Bottle.

"Why not?!" He shouts again to the trees, grinning like a maniac, hands thrown wide to the sky. He grabs the handlebars and digs back in, building speed.

But he can't talk to Michelle on his bike. It has to be in the "beige room," gripping his dick as he plunges into her in his head, hissing in her ear. "Who are *you* in all of this? Which moves did *you* make on the checkered board?" And always the same reply.

None.

And so into her again he slams. "Were you in on it? Did you profit?"

Slam…

"Who *are* you?"

Slam… slam…

"This is *my* mind. You *have* to tell me."

Slam…slam…slam.

He shouts it out loud, down in the beige room, no one home to hear him. "Tell me!"

Slam…slam…slam…slam…

"Who the fuck ARE you?"

Slam…slam…

In the beige room.

slam…slam…slam…

slam…

It's getting old.

That's why he's waiting here at the symphony Starbucks. He wants real world answers. One of his prey *has* to walk past, eventually, and when they do, he's going to put them under the bare, bright, torture-room lightbulb of reality.

He can wait.

The day they sent him home, he told Kona they suspended him with pay because HR suspected him of sharing with work colleagues advance news of the layoff. He figured this had the ring of truth because it's something that actually happened to a colleague of his back in the early '90s. Kona frowned, trying to figure it. "So is Maddie pissed at you?"

"No. Maddie didn't know about it."

"Are you're saying you did it? Why would you do something like that?"

"Baby, I… don't make me talk about it. The less you know, the better."

"Really? How is *that* true?"

"They got no hard proof, baby. Just a suspicion 'cuz I was outside this exec's office door when he blabbed about it on a conference call. So, really, it's this EVP's fault, not mine." This was all pretty close to what happened with his friend.

"Maybe. But since when has what's right, and who's really at fault, ever been the deciding factor? Who can they most afford to blame? That's the question." Tom shook his head, but she went on glaring at him. Finally, she said, "I guess all we really know at this point is that you're out of work."

"Administrative leave. I'm still getting paid."

"For now."

"Whatever." He kicked back in his chair, big show of nonchalance. "Bottom line: I'm handling it. It's all going to work out. So... relax."

Kona's voice went very quiet, "Don't ever fucking tell me to relax."

"Fine. Fuck it. Don't relax."

And like that, she was gone from the room.

But Tom really didn't care. He still doesn't, recalling it. Something's releasing for him. He's acting on instinct more now, and his instincts feel perfect.

So, he stakes out the SeaTru Tower as often as he can. He's managing a couple hours in the middle of the day about three days a week.

He's had a lot of time to consider. *Should I get a lawyer?... Should I get a gun?* Neither option seems completely unreasonable or, for that matter, completely sane.

A blue suit walks past with a stiff, slightly hesitant gait. Approaching from the opposite direction, a woman in business attire gawks when she recognizes the man's face. She smiles and nods, and the man gives an awkward little wave.

Holy shit, it's Torgerson.

Tom stands and follows, tossing his latte cup into a garbage can. He doesn't want to run, so he just manages to make it across the street as the light is turning. He follows the CEO into the

SeaTru Tower lobby at a good distance but, seeing his chance, he hops into his elevator just before the doors close. *What exactly is the plan here?* The car climbs. Various other passengers get off at various other floors. Tom's slightly shocked at his luck when the last of them gets off at 10. When the doors close completely, he says: "Hello, Terry."

Torgerson looks over and gives a single awkward jerk of his head. "Hello there."

"No reason you should remember me, but we've met."

Another quick nod, plus a look of seriousness. "Help me place the face."

Tom tugs the red emergency stop button. The elevator jerks to a halt and an old-fashioned clamoring bell sounds like the ones that used to set kids free from class, only it doesn't stop, and Tom knows his time is limited. "I'm the StreetSweeper, Terry."

Torgerson frowns. "I don't know what that means."

"No? Maybe you don't. But maybe you should. Do you know that the mortgage market is about to fail catastrophically?"

"I do not." The banker is on firmer territory now. "What's the plan here?" he asks, matter-of-factly, as though working his way through a checklist he learned in some security workshop.

"Terry, let's not try to put things in boxes right now. And you know what? Fuck that. I'm not calling you 'Terry.' That's some bull-shit. I'm going to call you 'Mr. Torgerson' if that's okay with you?"

"Sure." Terry's nodding rapidly now, like a bobble head. He stops suddenly, when he realizes he's doing it.

"I mean, I still work for you, technically, and you're the head of one of the country's largest banks after all. It's absurd that someone like me would call you by your first name."

"You can call me whatever you want."

"I'm going to call you Mr. Torgerson, Mr. Torgerson."

"That's fine. Can you tell me what you hope to achieve by trapping me here?"

"How are you trapped? I only want to talk to you."

"Are you saying I could push that emergency stop button back in and we could be on our way?"

"I don't know. Should we fight about it, Mr. Torgerson? Should we have a tussle over this button? Do you like your odds? Do you calculate that you might have less to lose than me? If you'll pardon me saying so, you and your team have been consistently pretty lousy in properly evaluating risk."

A jaded voice squawks over the intercom: "9-1-1 What's your emergency?"

Tom smiles at Torgerson. "You want to tell them? Or should I?" Tom bends down to the speaker and shouts, "The imminent collapse of the U.S. financial system!"

The voice replies with astonishing institutional blankness, "Say again please."

"Just tell me what you want," Torgerson tells Tom.

"I want to be your Marley's Ghost. I want to convince you to change the direction of SeaTru. You know what? Fuck that. Seattle Trust Bank. What's-his-name—Bill Piper—was right: You should've never changed the name."

Torgerson shrugs, defensive. "Folks have been calling us 'SeaTru' for decades."

"That's not the point. Let them call you what they want, but you should use your grownup name. You're a bank, for chrissakes. You're not Starbucks and you're not Walmart. Hell, a big part of your *job* is telling people 'no.'"

Torgerson stiffens. "So you work for Jim Verhoeven."

"Please. Verhoeven's worse than you."

"How is that?"

"Jim lies to friends. You just lie to yourself. And your customers. And America."

Torgerson shakes his head sadly. He says, "I don't understand," like it's another bullet point on the security seminar checklist. *Try to evoke their sympathy. And whatever you do, don't tell them you understand.*

"Mr. Torgerson, I know under the current specific circumstances I seem like an extremely unreasonable person, but really, believe me, nothing could be further from the truth. My requests are simple. One: fewer mortgages. Just reduce your intake for a while. Heck, you could do that easily and effectively just by asking for proper documentation instead of writing mortgages up on a wing and a prayer. Two: audit the mortgages you've already written, paying extra attention for fraud.

"I need to stop you right there."

"Do you?"

"Well, if only to tell you that those two steps alone would cost the bank billions."

"But if you do them, you might still have a bank, right?"

Torgerson shrugs. "Maybe. Or maybe our stock will plummet and we'll be swallowed by one of the New York megalodons currently circling our boat."

"'Megalodons'?"

Torgerson sighs. "Giant prehistoric sharks."

"Ah, very nice," says Tom, always happy to learn a new word. "So you're saying if you do the decent thing—hell, the *prudent* thing—you might get bought by a bigger bank."

Torgerson pushes on, eager to be done: "What are your other demands?"

"Three: stop trying to be a category-killer brand. Before you actually wind up killing the category."

"And?"

"And... that's all."

"Should I be honest?"

"Completely."

"There's no going back on our branding. If we don't move forward, we die."

"Like a shark. Like your megalodon."

Torgerson shrugs.

"Who says?"

"I say."

"Why?"

"Because I'd *rather* we die, as a bank, than be the same as we were in 1905."

"So, it's about you."

Torgerson's jaw clenches. He's close to closing this conversation down, but Tom presses: "I want you to remember you said that, Terry. I want you to remember that you'd rather the bank die than not be what you wanted it to be."

Torgerson stares blankly ahead.

He's done.

Hell, we're both done. But Tom can't just leave it.

"What happened to us, Mr. Torgerson? The Americans? My father was a combat veteran who became a teacher who became a principal; your father was a teacher who became a band director. I bet he served too, right? These men had jobs that mattered to people and made the world better by the intangible, nonmonetary wealth they passed along. But us, we're only satisfied if we're accumulating more cash. Why is everything about growth? Why is growth the goal? You know what the definition of unlimited growth is, Mr. Torgerson?"

Torgerson says nothing. He's looking at the elevator floor now.

"Do you?"

Still nothing.

"It's cancer. The definition of unlimited growth is cancer, Mr. Torgerson. That's what my father died of. How 'bout yours?"

Torgerson looks up at him, stricken. Through sheer nasty luck, Tom has clearly hit a nerve.

"We're Americans. We can make things, right? We can do better. We've done it before." Tom stops. He realizes he's spouting meaninglessness, like a politician or an athlete after the game. He could be saying the Pledge of Allegiance for all the difference he's making to Torgerson. He turns and pushes the red stop button. The insane ringing ceases immediately. He pushes the floor 15 button, and the car begins to ascend. As soon as the doors open, he hops out, turns left, and runs for the stairwell. He understands this will limit his options. The doors lock on the inside. From regular fire drills, he knows that the only time the stairwell doors unlock is when an alarm has been triggered. You need a badge to get back in, and he doesn't have one. He'll need to go all the way down to the street lobby to get out. Seeing no better choice, he starts down to 14, then 12 (the tower being one of those superstitious buildings that skips the 13th floor). At 10 he starts to hear noises from below: men hollering. He stops. Listens. He hears walkie-talkies too. They're getting closer.

He heads back up. He remembers that every tenth floor is open for people who get trapped in the stairwell. He'll head for 20. He can hear their footsteps now, loud and fast. He starts taking the stairs two at time. He trips at one of the landings, slamming down hard on a stair corner, cracking his knee on the metal lip of the concrete tread.

Fuck!

He can feel blood flowing down his leg: warm, thin syrup. He pulls his right sandal back on, but it flops uselessly. The straps are blown. He crawls up to the landing at 18 and sits to inspect the damage. The cut is bad. Could need stitches. But right now the blood pumping from it is a worse problem. He might as well be sprinkling breadcrumbs. He pulls off his shirt, mops up what he's dribbled already, then ties the shirt tight around his knee. He kicks off his remaining sandal and gingerly climbs the last two flights barefoot, knee throbbing. The makeshift bandage does its job.

He pushes the door open onto 20. Inside it's carpeted and quiet. He hobbles, knee squawking, to the elevator bank, where he faces another choice. Take one of the three elevators running express down to the street lobby, or take one of the three on the opposite side, which make local stops up to 40, where he could transfer again and go all the way to the top floor, 54.

Tom realizes he's trapped. If he takes an express car to the street lobby, security's almost certain to be waiting for him. If he takes one of the up cars, he's just ratcheting himself higher into the trap. He has an idea. He looks around but doesn't see what he's looking for. He limps around the corner and there it is, mounted on the wall right next to the ladies' room. He doesn't think twice. He reaches for the red panel and yanks at the white t-shaped tab that reads "Pull Down." An electric klaxon whoops; white strobes flash for the deaf, and Tom smiles, knowing he just made two magical things happen. Now, all of the stairwell doors will be open, and the public access ways of the entire building are about to be crowded with hundreds of evacuating decoys.

Options.

He bangs through the stairwell door and gingerly gimps his way down to the 18th landing, which is already filling with people. A woman gapes at his naked chest and bare feet. She sees his knee. "What happened to you?"

"No time," he yelps and pushes past her. He's almost to 17 when suddenly he's face to face with Wendy Gellibrand. He whips around and heads back up.

"Somebody *stop* him," she yells at his back.

What were you thinking, moron? Heading down into the 17th and 16th floor stairwells after flooding them with all of your SeaTru colleagues? Tom flashes on all the guns that must be, at this very moment, sitting useless in the desk drawers of so many of SeaTru's women exec-utives, planted there by Jim V., as though he were some mutant hybrid NRA Johnny Appleseed.

He climbs slowly, painfully, pushing, as best as he can, past all of the office workers evacuating in the opposite direction. He curses them, blesses them. As badly as they are blocking his escape, they're also blocking his pursuers. He finally makes it to 20 and heads for the elevators. He'll take his chances in the lobby now that the alarm has caused some covering chaos. He pushes the down call button.

"Elevators are off limits!" A guy wearing an orange vest is pointing at him like Smokey the Bear. His pristine white hard hat reads "Floor Warden." "You gotta use the stairs. Evacuate to five flights below your work floor."

Tom points at the shirt tied around his knee. "I'm badly in-jured."

Floor warden shakes his head. "It's not safe. Plus, the firefight-ers need to move around the building."

Tom's panic surges. What if the fire department has already called all the elevators back to the lobby? What if that happens automatically? He's good and royally fucked if so. A bell dings and the indicator light glows above the doors for the middle car. He lets out a huge breath. To the floor warden, he hollers: "Fuck off, hall monitor!" The doors open and Tom smiles to see his buddy Jake the security guy.

Wait.

Jake pushes against Tom's bare chest what looks like a small black cell phone. A deafening crackle claws into Tom's sternum and shakes him like a doll. He can't catch the slightest gasp of air. The mad crackling goes on for exactly forever, then suddenly stops, releasing Tom into Jake the security guy's waiting arms.

26.

Back Office

Tom huddles in the corner of the elevator, desperate to get his breathing back to any sort of normal. He hardly notices Jake zip-tying his hands. His skull aches as if someone directly hammered the world's worst hangover into it. He looks down at the two tiny circular burns on his chest about an inch and a half apart. It looks like he was bitten by a voltaic vampire. And *man*, they itch. He goes to scratch, and finds his hands bound tight.

Fuck!

The inside of his mouth tastes like it's been painted with molten copper. "Shit, Jake, you didn't have to electrocute me."

"You know I work for a living, right?"

"So?"

"So, do us both a favor and shut your fucking mouth."

The elevator opens on the lobby. Jake yanks Tom to his feet by the zip tie. "Ow! Mother*fucker*, Jake!"

Jake pushes right into Tom's face. "I said shut it." He turns Tom around and shoves him briskly through the lobby confusion. A brace of uniformed guards approach, questions on their faces, but Jake waves them off and pushes Tom around a corner into a stairwell Tom didn't even know existed and down one flight into a starkly lit corridor. Halfway along, at a plain, gunmetal gray door, Jake stops, pushes Tom against the opposite wall, points at him like a dog. "Don't move."

"Don't worry."

Jake unlocks the door with a key he pulls from a bunch on his belt, then he shoves Tom into the small windowless office. "Sit," he says, pointing at a chair set between two desks. Tom sits. Jake pulls a pair of handcuffs from a drawer. Looping one cuff through Tom's zip tie and closing it, he closes the other through the eye of a bolt sunk deep into the surface of the desk.

Tom splays his bound hands, ultimate victim. "Are you kidding me, man?"

"Does it seem like it?"

"Why are you so mad at me, Jake?"

"Because you fucked up my day, asshole. My day, my week, my year."

"That wasn't my intention."

"Your intention? What the fuck was that? To kidnap my client?"

"*Kidnap?*"

More to himself than Tom, Jake mumbles, "CEO of a Fortune 500 corporation riding elevators alone. 'Insisting.' *I* should have fucking insisted."

"It's not your fault, Jake."

"My watch. You got to the king on my fucking *watch.*"

Tom doesn't know what to say. He's miserable. He hates that Jake hates him so much. How is that every fucking move he manages to make fucks something up he didn't even know *could* be fucked up? He wants his friend—well, his friendly acquaintance, but in any case, this guy Jake whom he always thought he could be friends with—to understand. He swallows and begins to speak, more to the wall than anyone. "Did you ever find yourself foolish enough to believe that if you could only talk to the right person and reason with them, convince them of what the right thing to do is, they might actually do it?"

"Nope. Never." Jake plucks a small walkie-talkie from his belt. He presses a button to talk. "Base 1 this is Husky 1. Copy?"

A moment of silence, then a burst of static. A female voice. "Husky 1, this is Base. Go ahead."

"I have the elevator perp. Subdued and in my office on G-1 in the STT. Over?"

"Copy that Husky 1. Nice work. Over."

"Standing by awaiting further instructions. Over."

"Uh... copy that. We're still dealing with the alarm. Over."

"Almost certainly a false pull by the perp. Over," says Jake.

"Okay. Copy that. I'll let fire response know. Over."

"Okay. Out." Jake places the radio on the desk in front of him and stares at it.

"The fire alarm was a dick move," Tom says. "I realize that now."

"Just please... *please* shut up."

After a minute or so, Jake leaves, the heavy door slamming behind him.

Tom can't remember feeling shittier. He's practically naked. His chest throbs and itches. His knee howls. His head is still throbbing and flaring with strange colors from the zap Jake gave him. He's utterly parched but also fiercely needs to piss. *Fuck!* There is a hollowed-out pit in his core. He's doomed. Seriously. Like hop-off-the-Aurora-Bridge doomed.

After about ten minutes, maybe 15, Jake returns, sits, and swivels his chair to face the wall. "Really?" Tom asks.

Silence.

Tom persists. "What are we doing here?"

Still no answer.

Tom yanks his zip tie, rattling the cuffs against the bolt. Jake does not turn, but he holds up his Taser and fires off a deafening crackle of arcing blue. Tom goes quiet. But eventually he can't help himself. "Are you going to call the cops or what?"

"You're asking me to call the cops?"

"Well, *you* can't arrest me, can you?"

Jake spins to face Tom. "Sure as fuck looks like I can."

"Not even the cops can hold someone indefinitely without a charge."

"I love this. A lesson in legality from the guy who just held an innocent man captive. You don't think I have charges?"

"He's hardly innocent."

"Oh, no, no. Don't start with that bullshit."

"What bullshit?" But Jake only shakes his head, disgusted. Tom decides to push. "*What?*"

"Asshole, do you forget? I was in the room when they laid out the charges against you. Stealing data to blow up the financial system. What kind of idiot anarchist does that kind of shit?"

"It didn't happen. Not like that. In a way, it didn't happen at all."

"'It didn't happen at all?'… 'In a way'?" Jake's expression is pure odium.

Tom tries to explain. "What happened—what *is* happening—all the shit that's raining down now and will continue to rain down—all of it would have happened with or without me." *And maybe that's the worst insight of all.*

Jake shrugs. "I don't care."

"I have to pee," says Tom.

"You'll have to hold it." Jake spins back away from him.

Jake's walkie squawks. Then a male voice, older. "Husky 1, this is Husky Leader."

Jake straightens in his chair and pulls the unit from his belt. "This is Husky 1; go ahead."

"Bring your friend to 16."

Jake pulls the walkie away from his face to scrutinize it. Then looks at Tom. "Say again. Over"

"Bring the perp to 16. They'll take it from there."

"My instructions were to wait for SPD. Over."

The other voice goes prickly. "Well, obviously, those plans have changed. Get him the fuck up to 16. Now."

"Roger that. In or out of cuffs? Over?"

·   ·   ·

When Count looks up from the reception desk to see Tom, shirtless and bedraggled, (*but cuff-less, thank Christ*) all he can manage is a strangled, "Oh no!" He hurries into the back room, reappearing a moment later with a green T-shirt, which he hands to Tom. "It's left over from our big Sarbanes-Oxley compliance push."

"Thanks." Tom pulls it on and looks down at the front:

¡xoS s,♠ nɹꞁ𝔢aS

"They're expecting you in conference room C." Count searches Tom's eyes for answers.

"Thanks." Tom turns to Jake behind him: "Shall we?"

"No 'we,'" says Jake. "You're on your own again. I assume you know the way."

No one looks out from their cubes as Tom squares the circle to conference room C. Within he finds Maddie, Mary Saskell, and Greg Governale all seated at the table. "Come in, Tom," Maddie says. "Have a seat." Tom sits, then practically collapses into the all-too-comfortable Aeron chair.

Governale says, "You're a lucky young man, Mr. Kavanagh."

Tom makes a mental survey of all of the parts of his body currently screaming. "Am I?"

"Thanks to Maddie and Mary Saskell's InfoSec team, we have a better understanding of how the StreetSweeper data was downloaded."

Tom blinks. "Okay."

Governale's lips tighten. He seems keen to rip Tom a new one, but instead says quietly, "Turns out it was earlier than we thought. And it wasn't you."

"So... you're saying it turns out... what I told you was true?"

"Yes."

"It was Verhoeven," says Maddie.

Tom looks over at her. "That's what I figured."

Maddie nods, maybe a bit sadly. She points at Mary, who opens a file and explains: "Jim Verhoeven, or more likely, someone working for him, was using a backdoor into StreetSweeper as early as six months before the download from your machine." She slides the file over to him.

"And you know it was him for sure?"

"We found the data and trace records of the logins on his personal laptop."

"And how," Tom asks, "did you get access to his personal laptop?" Mary stares at him, the slightest hint of amusement dancing in her eyes. "Right," he nods.

"Bottom line is, Verhoeven is done here," says Governale. "Done with the bank and done in the industry."

"Because you fired him?" Tom asks, even though he knows the answer. Governale stares at him stone-faced. "Don't tell me," Tom goes on. "You let him pull the rip cord on his golden parachute. Well, good for you, and good for him. That, plus what he makes shorting your CDOs, should see him all the way through retirement. Win/win/win, right?"

Governale pushes up from the table and mutters, "I'm done here." He turns to Maddie and jerks his head at Tom. "I leave it to you how best to proceed." Mary excuses herself as well, giving Tom a sly wink on her way out.

Once it's just the two of them, Maddie asks, "When can you start?"

"Hunh?"

"Back to work. I'm hoping Monday at the latest." He's not sure he's hearing this right. "Understand, you won't be working as my EA."

"No?"

"No. Part of the deal I struck is you're not to step foot in the SeaTru Tower."

"Oh. Yeah. Well... I can... understand that."

"You'll be in Second and Seneca."

"Ban Roll-on Building."

"Right," she says, frowning. She clearly hates this nickname. "Working for Al in Emergency Preparedness."

"Wow."

"Congratulations. It's a promotion."

"Jesus... Thank you. I don't know how to..." Tom can barely talk. The painful lump in the back of his throat feels close to choking him. "Maddie, you..."

"What?"

"You really saved my bacon."

"Mary and her team did that."

"They wouldn't have done it—couldn't have done it—without your air cover."

Maddie shrugs. "I'd do that for anybody on my team."

"I believe it."

"So don't thank me. Thank the team. Do it with your hard work. And staying clear of trouble."

"You got it."

"And, also…"

"What? Anything."

"In a few months it's going to be flu season."

"Yeah?"

"You'll be getting a shot, yes?"

The air pixilates before his eyes.

Amazing.

"Of course," he says. "You bet."

27.
Fall Out

Tom's hauling the last of the boxes up the basement stairs from the beige room. It's almost over, this second backbreaking move in two years. When their landlady showed up one Saturday with a new dryer from Costco, Kona mentioned they were trying for another baby. Kona says the woman got a weird look on her face and then, just before leaving, told her that they would need to be out by the end of the year. Without blinking, Kona replied, "Oh, I think we can be out of here earlier than that."

And sure enough, within two weeks she had found them a place in Shoreline, not quite as adorable, but bigger: three bedrooms, a more workable kitchen, and much more kid safe. She's over at the new house now, with Hana and J. (still claiming to be casual, but nobody's buying it since they're practically living together). Tom's just got these banker's boxes left, full of old notebooks, manuscripts, and other small stuff.

The big news is that there is no news. The mortgage market hasn't crashed. If anything it's expanding. If Jim V. and his ilk are out there trying to short it, they're likely shitting their pants right now because, as far as Tom can tell, the subprime market is only expanding. At least that's what Tom gathers whenever he reads the financial news, which isn't often. That's not his job. His job is to keep an eye out for natural disasters that might impact the bank's operations and, so far, the 2006 hurricane season has been significantly less active than the year prior—the Year of Dennis, Emily, and Katrina.

Bottom line, the economy has not faltered and does not look likely to. Tom figures maybe all those execs and eggheads in all those glass towers from here to Manhattan, and on to London, Frankfurt, Hong Kong, and Tokyo—maybe they know a thing or two after all about keeping the system stable and profiting themselves in the process. Maybe. All Tom knows for sure is that he's happy to be out of it, happy to be working in his safe little cubicle in the Ban Roll-on Building, reporting up through Al Sherman, at least three levels of org chart between him and Maddie. His family is working again. He and Kona have never been happier together. She's grown a little concerned that they haven't been able to conceive another child, but Tom figures he's got time to figure that out too. Right now, it's working.

As he schleps boxes, Poma plays on an old Fisher-Price bulldozer she found in a pile of toys Kona is giving to Goodwill. She's a little bit big for it, and both sets of wheels are fixed so it doesn't really steer, but she's having fun anyway. She's rolling around the empty house as fast as she can and steering by whipping her whole body along with the toy in whatever direction she wants to go. Currently she's racing a circuit run around the entire main floor clockwise: living room into Mommy and Daddy's old room, through the bathroom into Poma's old room, past the basement door into the kitchen, then back into the living room. Round and round she goes. Tom is reminded of the famous Big Wheel tracking shot in *The Shining*.

"Hey Daddy, lookit!"

Tom glances up from the bottom of the basement stairs to see Poma roll past, precariously balanced skate-boarder style, with one foot on the bulldozer and the other propelling her forward. "Baby girl, that's not meant for standing on."

"I'm fine!" she shouts back.

He adds a box to his stack and starts up the stairs. Poma rolls to a stop at the open basement door, standing now with both feet on the plastic bulldozer.

"Poma. Please put your bottom on the seat, not your feet."

"You rhymed."

"Just do it please."

"You're a poet, didn't know it." She wobbles a little and grabs the door jamb with both hands. Tom drops the boxes. She cries, starts to fall. He clambers up the last remaining steps, stumbles on a box, but manages to stretch out and push her back into the kitchen where her bottom hits the floor with a thud. His left foot slips off the stair tread, and when Tom grabs at the flimsy chair rail bannister to steady himself, it tugs right out of the brackets; and now he's tumbling backward, his head hits a stair, his feet flip over him. He's sliding backward down the steps, reaching out to slow his tumble toward the bare concrete so he doesn't crack his—

•　　•　　•

Poma's crying.

In his face.

He can't see her.

•　　•　　•

She's right next to him.

He doesn't want to open his eyes. The light stabs him when he blinks. A sharp wet knife is stabbing him in the back of his head, on the right side. It hurts so bad he wants to barf but he's afraid that barfing will make it hurt worse.

"Wake up daddy. Wake up."

•　　•　　•

Poma's crying.

•　　•　　•

Now she's giving him big, drooly kisses, hurting his head when she grabs it to kiss him. He's got to do something.

Open your eyes, asshole.

He opens his eyes, and the stabbing light punishes him for it. He needs to barf. Random colored bolts shoot across his field of vision.

This is not good.

No, it's not.

Get to the hospital, asshole.

•　　•　　•

Crack your head open.

That's how they used say it when Tom was a kid. "Don't do that. You'll crack your head open." Like it was an egg. An egg that could crack. And all the goo inside could run out, humpty dumpty-like.

Crack your head open.

•　　•　　•

Kona's talking to him. He's at the hospital.

He's fine. They've pretty much told him that. Sure, a little bit of a concussion, and they needed to shave the spot on his head where they gave him some stitches, where he cracked his head open. Only he didn't really. No humpty-dumpty goo came out. Just blood. He's fine. Still, they want to keep him overnight for observation.

Kona's talking to him, but she's not looking at him. Instead, she's looking just above his head, as though he were wearing a halo, or a top hat, or something. It's weird. But only just a little bit. She's telling him that everything's moved into the new house.

"Oh good."

She's telling him that Poma is proud of herself for saving her daddy.

"She should be."

She's talking very calmly and evenly, as though she's trying to keep things calm and even. It's weird, because she was in the room when they told him he'd be fine.

"So, you're sure you feel okay?"

"I do. I do. It hurts, but… some of the weirder parts, the bright-colored flashes and the nausea, and… that's gone now."

"Good." Her gaze meets his, then instantly shifts back to that magic spot above his head. He suddenly realizes she's been crying.

"Hey!" he says. She looks at him. "I'm going to be alright."

"I know." She looks away.

"So… turn that frown upside down, yo."

"I need to talk to you." She looks at him squarely again. *Oh shit.* Now he's tracking. She's angry about something. Really angry. What is it this time?

"So talk."

"I don't want to do it with you in a hospital bed."

"I'm fine."

"On the other hand, I don't want to wait. I'm done waiting."

Now he's irritated. "I told you I'm fine. What do you want to talk about?"

She reaches down next to her. He follows with his eyes. She's pulling something from an old Gap shopping bag. What the hell is it? Oh, his Salish bent-wood box.

Shit.

She opens it.

Fuck.

She pulls out a photograph, old school, like you got back from the Fotomat booth. She carefully, almost respectfully holds the edges with her fingertips. She turns it to him: rich-titted Kirsten, tugging up her sweatshirt to display for the camera just how rich her tits are. *God, what a gorgeous, inhibition-shattering smile she had.* "This?" Kona flaps the photo, like she's drying a Polaroid. "This, I couldn't give two shits about. I don't care what you jerk off to, even if it *is* an old girlfriend." She flicks it away onto the floor.

"This on the other hand," she pulls out a manila envelope. From it she draws the half-strap that hard hat Ronnie forced on him so many months ago. She holds it up and stares at him with a fierceness. "*This* is, like, thousands of dollars. In cash. *This* worries the fuck out of me." She tosses the neat stack of bills away as well. It flops somewhere on the floor next to his bed.

Good lord, woman. That's five large. For the love of Christ, *pick that up.* But of course, he doesn't say a word. Every muscle is stiff with fear.

"And this…" She's reaching back into the bag. What could it possibly be? But of course, as soon as she pulls it out—single folded sheet of white paper—he knows.

"Kona…" he whispers.

"Don't," she says, shaking her head. She makes a great display of unfolding it and holding it out for him to see: the invoice from Seattle Urology. "Nearly nine hundred dollars. Out of your own pocket, I'm guessing. Or whose? Someone else's? I mean, your amazing SeaTru health plan would've covered it, but no. It had to be a secret, right?"

"I'm… of course… I'm…"

"Of course, shut up." He was wrong. She's not angry. Not now anyway. She's something he's never seen before. Stunned, resolved, distant, but burning. She looks like she could slice a man's throat. She looks like she could eat a beating heart.

"I fucked up."

"You what?" she hisses. He locks down again. Every muscle rigid. She goes on, measured and venomous, "All those times you fucked me, came inside of me, trying for a baby. 'Trying.' Every single one of those times, you knew it was useless. Every single one of those times, you lied. You fucking lied… inside of me."

"Fuck," he says. It comes out of him like a defeated sigh. She is silent. He lets her be silent. But he can only bear it for so long. "Please, Kona, please hear me."

"No." She stands. "J. is going to pick you up when they release you tomorrow. He's offered to let you crash at his place for a few days until you can figure out other arrangements."

"What are you talking about?"

"You know exactly what I'm talking about."

"Please give me a chance… to get my shit together. To make this right. All of this. I can make it all right, again."

"It was never right. I'm done. You're broken."
She goes.
He exhales. Long and ragged, like it's his last breath.
She's right.

28.

White Buffalo

T om is late.

Egregiously, perilously.

And fuck if he didn't have a plan this time: catch the bus from Northgate Transit Center instead of trying to drive downtown. Not only would he avoid traffic, but he'd also skip all the hassles of parking (not to mention the expense—upwards of 20 bucks an hour). But as the cherry on top of all of that, he figured that—and maybe this was where his cleverness overreached—because the interview was for a job with the Transit and Mobility Division of the City of Seattle's Department of Transportation, it would be a great introductory nugget to mention off the bat that, of *course*, he took the bus.

Of course.

Of course the 41, which was scheduled to arrive at NGTC at 3:05 p.m., didn't. The next run, due at 3:15 p.m., didn't appear until 3:28 p.m., and now traffic on I-5, which he assumed would be clear heading southbound this time of day, is moving only slightly quicker than a Sodo parking lot after a Seahawks game.

Ordinarily, Tom loves busses, much prefers them to driving his little red deathtrap of a Honda, which he tends to use only for his grocery runs for the family. Transit is almost always less stressful than driving. Except when you're late. Which by his best calculations he's sure to be, by at least ten minutes, if not 20.

Fuck.

This particular articulated coach just now noses its way past the 50th Street Tangletown exit: the one you'd take if you wanted to, say, have a beer at Lenny's or cruise past the cute little cottage he, Kona, and Poma shared back in the day.

Fuck.

Like he needs that squeeze on his heart right now, as if he hadn't already walked through most of the past decade with a huge hole blown through his middle. As if there weren't times, some seemingly endless, when his anguish crowded everything else out even, at times, his very will, such that sometimes it didn't seem like he was making his way through the world so much as the world was dragging him dumbly, numbly through it, a broken needle through the grooves of a worn-out record.

Dumbly, numbly. Too much rhyme.

Fuck that. No time.

Concentrate, Kavanagh. Get your goddamned shit together!

Busses have been the focus of Tom's fate so often lately that, really, why *should* today be any different?

When he first met Kimberly she was driving the 11:15 p.m. 358 to Aurora Village, easily one of the roughest rides in the city. "More business gets transacted on the 358 between midnight and 8:00 a.m.," she used to joke, "Than the rest of the city does all day."

Tom had just moved into a mother-in-law apartment in Haller Lake and was using his bike to get around most of the city, expanding his range when needed with the bike racks all Metro buses had mounted on their fronts. He had to wrestle a bit to get his wheels into the rack that night, and he wound up slamming the locking lever down a little bit harder than he needed to. As he climbed onto the coach, he heard the woman driver say, "Hey! Go gentle on my rack there, dude!" She was—damn!—cute as a deep-dish apple pie with her round cheeks and wry smile. Pushing out from under her forest green Metro beret were bright purple dreadlocks, big as thumbs.

"Oh…" he said. "Sorry."

Her face stayed neutral, but her eyes gleamed. "Or at least take me to dinner first."

Tom couldn't think of anything.

Fuck!

He wanted to kick himself as he walked back to one of the few open seats. And then he had it. But he'd have to wait to play his second chance. Forty blocks later, he pulled the string and walked up front. "This is my stop coming up."

"Congratulations."

"Well, I only say that 'cuz I wouldn't want you to pull away with my frame still locked onto your rack."

"Nope," she said, arctic deadpan.

"What? You get to make a joke, but I don't?"

"Correct."

"Damn. That's cold."

"You have no idea."

"More's the pity," he said.

She finally cocked him a glance. "Sorry, dude. I only fuck black guys."

It was like a sock to the gut. "Well, that seems racist."

She braked to a stop and threw the door open. "Nope, it's prejudiced. 'Racist' is something different. Look it up."

The next night he caught her run even though his bartending shift ended an hour earlier than usual. Once aboard the bus, he sat in a seat just behind and across the aisle from her.

"You're wasting your time, Tall Drink. I do not date customers."

Tom grinned innocence. "So let me ride for free."

She shrugged and shook her head, as if to say, "Funny, but not quite funny enough."

He kept riding, kept sitting close, all the while observing the warm buzzing in his chest growing stronger. And then, just like that, he decided to stop. He still needed to ride her bus, of course. After all, it was the run that came after his shift was usually over, but he stopped sitting near her, stopped talking to her except to say a friendly "hello" when he got on and "good night" when he got off. He just had to let it go. His heart wasn't up for any more breaking. And besides, he actually dug her as someone to talk to, and so, in that eternally trite and twisted irony, he talked to her less.

The bus he's on now, the 41, downshifts and whines to a stultifying, stupidly slow crawl as it begins the south-bound climb of the Ship Canal bridge. *Fuck.* This bus is going to make him late for the rest of his life. He's not even sure he wants this job. He only applied for it because when you're on unemployment you have to apply for three legit gigs a week. Tom determined to only put in paper on bona fide cherry gigs: Starbucks, Vulcan, the Gates Foundation, King County, or the City itself. Just not Amazon. Never Amazon, no matter how good it pays.

Fuck Amazon.

"Fuck 'em all!" is what he swore when he finally got shit-canned from SeaTru in the Big Shit-Canning of 2007. The crash came after all, after everyone stopped expecting it, and all those execs and eggheads in all those office towers from Seattle to New York to London to Tokyo were left with very little but their own shriveled dicks in their hands—while, presumably, Jim V. and a few others made a filthy fortune when their short-selling ship finally came in.

Wave after wave of layoffs had washed away most of the bank's workforce in the months following SeaTru's stock finally hitting the shitter. Not long after that, one of those New York megalodon mega-banks swam in and gobbled up the 130-year-old local thrift for pennies on the dollar: more mercy killing than hostile takeover.

Tom got paid a nice severance along with everyone else. Mind you, not as good as what Maddie and the other senior executives hauled in, but still enough for him to not to have to work for six months, especially the way he was living then: alone and close to the bone in a studio apartment in Eastlake with a baked potato, broccoli, and a single beer for dinner most nights.

Sure, the divorce left him with a small nut of monthly child support to hit, but it wasn't much. Kona, on the advice of her attorneys, decided not to press that point in order to limit Tom's custody. At the time he wasn't really in a position, either financially or emotionally, to put up much of a fight.

In 2008, after Obama got elected, Tom determined to kick Seattle's dust off his feet and ditch out of town for good. Or if not for good, then for the foreseeable. He rejoined the grand Kavanagh diaspora and went—where else?—East. To New York City first, to crash for awhile on his sister's couch in Tudor City for the holidays and beyond. When the weather got warmer, he headed down to the Jersey shore to tend bar with his brother Jamie in a classic upscale Toms River fish house.

But life with Jamie inevitably, and quickly, drove him into the dirt. He'd lost his East Coast Irish knack for sustained and prodigious day in/day out boozing. And the sex he was managing to have ground him down as well: bagging married women, sneaking down solo from the City to their expansive beach houses for quick, easy lays with the tall and handsome—but undeniably aging—boy they knew from high school, or, more often, the boy they knew from some friend who knew him. Only the truly courageous and committed can live the lewd life of an aging shore rat for long. Whatever efficacy it held in salving his sore, empty heart only served to make it grow sorer and emptier in the end. It wasn't passion he was missing in his life; it was Poma. And yes, Kona too, but he knew that any hope for having her in his life ever again was gone, daddy, gone. To live without his daughter, however, became an impossibility.

And so back to Seattle he went, ditching the debilitating diaspora for good. He worked office temp jobs and odd bartending shifts. He pieced it together. He didn't need much to stay in the studio apartments and spare group-house rooms he managed to score for three months, six months—heck—even a year or two sometimes. And any spare hours he could cobble together he spent with Poma. He went to every recital, every soccer game, and every practice. He didn't have the time to date and didn't want to. He was making his half-life work somehow.

Then Kona asked him to lunch. Which never happened. They saw each other all the time, but only in the context of co-parent-ing: school plays and teacher conferences. They weren't friends outside of the family held together for their eight-year-old.

As soon as they sat, and the waiter began pouring their waters, Tom asked, "What's going on?"

"Can we order first?" she asked cheerfully.

"I'd rather not. I've got a kind of a gut-twisty feeling, frankly."

"It's nothing terrible."

"It's not?"

"I don't think so." Kona took a prim sip of her water, then added, "But you're not going to like it."

"You're getting married." Tom figured it had to be that. Poma had mentioned some guy Kona had been seeing over the last year. So, it had gotten serious. Who was he to kick a fuss, even though it made him a little nauseous? He'd fucked up everything. Besides, it wasn't like he paid alimony, and he wasn't likely to be getting out of what little child support he *did* pay. Hell, he didn't *want* to get out of it.

"What?" She seemed almost insulted. "Who would I marry?"

"What's-his-name. Dude you've been seeing, Teegan, or Keegan, or whatever his name is. Tall, red-headed, fit dude."

She made a face. "You mean Phelan?"

"Whatever."

She shakes her head. "We broke up a month ago."

"Oh, well. Sorry."

The waiter approached, but Tom told her they needed more time. "Just tell me," he said to Kona.

"I have an opportunity. With my dad's firm. Creative Director."

"That's great. Your dad's firm?" For a moment it didn't add up, then sudden comprehension knifed into his already twisted guts. "In *Oahu?*"

Kona's face was a perfect fun-house mirror of his own appalled expression. Clearly it pained her to see him in pain, but he didn't give a fuck. "You're screwing me. You know that. You have to know that. What does... How does Poma feel about this?"

Kona shook her head. "I would never talk to Poma about this before talking to you."

Oh, no, he thought. *You don't get to hide behind your decency on this.*

And then it happened. Whatever it was that was holding tight in Tom, just like that, it broke. And when it broke it hurt like hell, but it also felt like yanking out a rotten tooth or popping a dislocated shoulder back in. And as soon as the pain passed, there was such a huge wave of relief that he had to fight back tears. This woman wasn't trying to fuck him over, or get revenge, or whatever it was that divorced men since time immemorial have contrived their ex-wives to be doing. She was only trying to do what was best for her and her daughter—*their* daughter. And in some stupidly shining, sad, sappy epiphany straight out of the stone church of his childhood, he realized he loved her, this woman, this mother, former-wife of his. *Kona.* But he didn't need to keep being in her way. And if it meant spooning out a hunk of his heart and handing it over to her so she could be free and try for what she really wanted, then over to her he would spoon it. He would do anything to make a tiny piece of what was wrong right.

"Okay," he said, swallowing. There was no way he'd be eating any goddamned lunch.

"Okay?" She seemed genuinely shocked.

"Yeah. Okay." When the waiter came, Tom ordered a double vodka martini up with olives. He sat and drank it while he watched Kona eat.

A few weeks later he was signing an amendment to the custody agreement. He'd get Poma in the summers. What he didn't know—couldn't know—was how many summers there would be when she wouldn't come at all. He wouldn't force the issue. Poma deserved to be free, too. Someday, maybe, she'd understand, and maybe she'd hate him a little less. And maybe hate wasn't even the word. "Contempt?" Nah. "Pity?" Nope. Poma didn't seem the type. Tom didn't dare go near his biggest fear, namely that his daughter didn't have much feeling at all for him anymore. Whatever she felt, that spoonful of his heart he handed over at lunch that day would never be his again. He would never be whole.

The 41 lurches, throwing him against the girl in the brown hijab sitting next to him. "Sorry," he murmurs, but she's got earbuds in.

He's wearing his old, gray, marrying-and-burying suit, the jacket always unbuttoned nowadays because, truth be told, it doesn't really fit him anymore. It's also got a small but noticeable tear over the left breast, like he's been sitting shiva. Long story short: suit's seen better days. High time he got another, before the next marrying or burying or, for that matter, job interview. But where's the cash for *that* coming from? Unemployment benefits?

Here's a thought, Kavanagh: Maybe you should actually try and get hired for this job.

Maybe I should.

The bus pulls off onto the Denny/Stewart exit, grinding down into yet a lower gear as it crawls past REI. Tom wonders who can afford that place anymore.

Every single asshole who works at Amazon.

Right.

The administrative coordinator position up for grabs at the City starts at 50 grand a year. He could do better elsewhere—the ever-accursed Amazon, for instance, starts its EAs at 90—but there are perks that come with working for the City that are otherwise hard to come by: solid-gold bennies and, after a year, a whole bureaucratic process they have to go through before they can shit-can you. Amazon's all-but-stated business plan is to burn out its hires within five years. Tom wants to know where all those people go once the benighted behemoth is done with them. Do they stay in Seattle to increase the population of over-entitled, under-engaged douchebags, or do they beat feet back to where they came from?

Jim V. beat feet.

Maddie filled Tom in over beers a couple years ago at the Atlantic Crossing in Roosevelt. They meet for drinks every other month or so at this prefab demi-dive. For some reason, Maddie relishes how hard the place pretends to be an East Coast Irish bar: precisely the same reason Tom detests it.

The way Maddie heard it, SeaTru's ex-CRO was blind drunk, a state he occupied with increasing frequency and for longer durations lately. One late night walking home from the club, along the perimeter of the golf course, he mistook his wife's condo for his own, an easy error, as they were smack next door to each other and essentially identical. When his key didn't work, he broke a small pane of glass to undo the dead bolt. That's when his wife fired the Desert Eagle he had given her several decades prior. One booming blast from that hand cannon put Georgiana Verhoeven on her butt and blew a hole the size of a salad plate out of her husband's back. If SeaTru's former Chief Risk Officer knew what hit him, he didn't know for long.

The 41 noses onto a surface street. It has ten blocks of downtown traffic to push through before it dives into the bus tunnel at Convention Place. Once rolling underground, things should move a bit quicker.

He scrawls this in his pocket notebook. *The heart-shaped hole in the middle of his everything.* It's a Moleskine knock-off. He can't really afford the real thing and doesn't currently work somewhere he can order it from the office supply catalogue.

Two Christmases ago, he sent Poma a completed draft of *Candleshire*, his children's story about the brother and sister who woke up in the village under the Christmas Tree. He had the manuscript printed on special, thick, cream-colored paper, which he then had bound into a leather book with those fancy hand-marbled inside covers. On the title page he penned a note apologizing for the lack of illustrations, but she could rest assured his heart was in the right place, and that he never gave up on the idea of finishing this story.

He never heard back. He knew he shouldn't be surprised. She was a teenager now. She probably set it aside unopened. Still, he tried calling her that Christmas, but Kona didn't pick up her phone. So he stewed, eventually letting the anger, which was lurking below, come up for a drink. And then another. And then a bender's worth, stretching almost until New Year's. He drank until his anger at his little girl felt appropriately pathetic. And then he quit drinking for good.

He made it until St. Paddy's.

That summer was one she didn't come to Seattle. Instead, she attended an arts camp in Estes Park, Colorado.

He's in the bus tunnel now, Westlake Station. Barring a tunnel-jamming stall, he's got fewer than five more minutes on the bus, then a three-minute jog up the hill to the Seattle Municipal Tower at Fifth and Columbia. Or is it Cherry? It's one of the two. (Jesus *Christ* Made Seattle Under Protest.)

For about three years, Tom had a steady gig working as an administrative coordinator at a pharmaceutical company. But, of course, the board of directors decided to shutter their Seattle research site and pull everything back to California. Once again Tom scored enough severance and unemployment bennies to put together a year of not really working: bartending for cash only or occasionally working as a banquet server. That was what he was doing—making rounds with a tray of champagne at a swanky happy hour in the Four Seasons' Georgian room—when he felt something brush against his waist. When he turned, for the first time since the disasters of the mid-Zeros, there she was, dreamily gazing up at him. "Why, Mr. Kavanagh. I had no idea how fetching you'd look in a tuxedo."

Thump.

"Oh. Well… hello, Michelle. How nice to see you!"

"Is it? Really?" There it went, her tongue tip to her teeth edge. Classic.

"Of… of course, it is," he stammered. "Why wouldn't it be?"

A Cheshire Cat grin, a wheeling gaze around the room in which she found absolutely nothing of interest, and then, ever delicately, she liberated a bubbling flute from his tray. She looked him fully up and down as she guzzled the entire glass. Then, after an adorable gasp for air, she said: "You look fantastic."

He nodded, smiled grimly. He was at least 25 pounds heavier than the last time she laid eyes on him. He was going gray at the edges, and that patch up top, which was already running thin in the mid-Zeroes, had broadened to a full-blown bald spot. "You, more truthfully, have not aged a single moment. What's the secret? A charmed portrait of you aging in your attic or frequent baths in babies' blood?"

She gleamed, visibly rising to his nasty flattery. When she

shrugged, she somehow managed to use her whole body. "Just good, clean living, I guess."

"Yeah, okay. Well..." He gave his tray an indicative lift. "I should circulate. Been a pleasure."

"What? No. Fuck that. Have a drink with me."

"I'm working."

"So, finish working and have a drink with me."

"I'm here until the end of the party."

"I can wait."

"I have plans."

"Bullshit."

It *was* bullshit. And his dick swelled a little admitting it. He agreed to meet her at the oyster bar inside the hotel. Over single malts, he regaled her with stories about his jobs, various and hilarious; his divorce; how the stitches in his heart still tear whenever he thinks of the time he's forever lost with his daughter. She offered boilerplate expressions of sympathy, utterly unconvincing, which was fine by Tom. He didn't care to be convinced. Her rich plum satin dress clung to every curve.

Her own life since had proceeded pretty much perfectly. She was now a senior partner at an investment firm that occupied the top floors of what was supposed to be the new SeaTru center. Her husband, the pediatric neurosurgeon, was still practicing, but now also on faculty at the U as well. They had bought a ski lodge in Telluride and several apartment buildings on Phinney Ridge and in Roosevelt, close to where the light-rail station will be. Tom had to wonder where the money for all that came from. Her son had graduated college, and after a few stints in rehab, finally found a place for himself with the Peace Corps in Liberia. Tom pictured the kid holed up in a grass-roofed hut, finally able to get as blissfully baked as he always really wanted. Michelle's daughter was Maria Cantwell's senior legislative aide for healthcare and engaged to her counterpart on Mitch McConnell's staff.

"Stretching a hand across the aisle, is she?"

Michelle scrunched her shoulders. "She's a realist."

"You'll be a grandmother soon."

A flash of genuine panic crossed her face, quickly banished with a glassy-eyed smirk. "Bite your tongue, motherfucker." Tom nodded, stayed mum. Biting his tongue had finally, and thankfully, become a permanent part of his skill set. "Listen," she said, squirming on her stool, "I'm bored with catchup chitchat."

"I'm sorry about that. But can I ask you one serious question?"

"Shoot?"

"Were you working with Verhoeven the whole time?"

She frowned, as though trying to understand what he was asking. "I worked *for* Verhoeven. He was my boss."

"I don't mean officially. I mean in his scheme to topple the mortgage markets. Were you in on that? Were you his partner? Were you one of the short-sellers?"

For a moment she just stared at him. Then she said, "It's almost flattering that you would think that. I want to say yes."

"Well, then say it, if it's true."

"Here's what I know for sure..." she grabbed his leather jacket and pulled his cheek to hers, her voice hot and wet in his ear. "I'm going to get a room. You're going to come up to it with me. Understand?" She pushed back to look up into his eyes. He remembers thinking: *This is how it all cycles around, if you let it. This is how, if all you do is watch your life happen, all your sexual revenges come true.*

"Wow," he said. "That's the kindest offer I've had in months."

"I don't doubt it."

"So, you're not going to answer me."

She shrugged, coquettish. "It's a dumb question. But I'll fuck you, for sure."

"I really do have plans."

"No. You really don't."

He shrugged, shook his head, and slowly pushed up off his stool.

Her smile remained plastered. But above it, the eyes went cold. "You think I'm joking?"

"I do not. I do not think you're joking. No."

"You think you're better than me."

"I... so long, Michelle. I wish you all the... I wish you... everything."

He was nearly to the door when he heard her say, "You're still nobody." He smiled and nodded, but he did not turn around.

The 41 finally pulls into Pioneer Square Station. Tom takes the bus tunnel escalator stairs two at a time. The extra effort will absolutely cause him to sweat right through his shirt, but what choice does he have? He'll just have to keep his jacket on during the interview.

Up on the street, a homeless guy steps into his path and begins a spiel about needing light-rail fare to Columbia City. Tom makes an "I got nothing" gesture, then notices the guy's ancient, thread-worn T-shirt, torn at the pits:

We're making
A difference.
Seattle Trust

He suspects the Gods of Fate and Overt Omens have finally overplayed their hands, but just to be on the safe side he tears a five from his wallet and palms it into the guy's hand as he shakes it. Then he pushes on, up the hill, and into the Columbia Center, Seattle's tallest building with its sheer walls of Darth Vader glass.

Keep pushing, Kavanagh. Ain't much farther now.

One night, after his St. Andrew's bartending shift, he climbed on the 358 and his deep-dish-cute, purple-dread-headed crush said, "Enjoy the ride, Tall Drink. It's your last with me behind the wheel."

"What?"

"Changing routes on Monday. I'll be driving the night owl 7 up and down Rainier." His sudden sadness was shocking. And it must have shown on his face because she got serious and said, "Hey, I'm a bus driver. It's not like your puppy died."

"Yeah," was all he could manage before heading back to an open seat, far past the accordion joint. A block before his stop he pulled the string and stood to get off through the back door. But the back door didn't open. "Back door!" he shouted.

Over the intercom: "Oh *hell* no. You come up front and say goodbye proper."

Goddammit, but he shuffled up the aisle.

"Or," she said off the mic, as he came within earshot, "You could be a gentleman and buy me a send-off drink."

Unbelievable. Where does the universe come up with this idiocy?

After Kimberly checked in and punched out at the transit center, they drove her jeep right back down Aurora. Tom thought Craig might still be serving a few lingering regulars at the St. A's, but when they got there it was dark and locked up. Kimberly offered to get him high instead. They pulled into a far corner of the parking lot next door and shared a joint next to the food co-op.

Chatting and laughing, they were soon making out, hot and heavy. Before long she was rubbing her hand over his cock, hard beneath his jeans. And soon after that she had him unzipped and was jacking him gently. And then, after a particularly lovely and deep French kiss, her mouth left his, and she went down.

He pulled away. He could hardly believe it himself.

"Seriously?" she asked.

"I... I'm... I'm sorry." His head was swimming. He hadn't smoked weed in ages.

"What is up?" She was genuinely confused.

"I... too fast."

"You're kidding me."

"It's just... I'm... fuck!"

"Dude. What's going on?" She asked with real concern, like maybe he was running a fever or something.

"I... like you."

"I like you, too." She shook her head in bafflement, then shrugged and dove for his cock, but he took her chin and lifted her face to his.

"I don't... I have... fucked things up with people I have genuinely liked in the past. Hell, I've fucked things up with people I've hated."

"So?"

"So, you're in the first category."

"The what?" He suddenly realized, with relief, that she was pretty high too.

"You're one of the people I genuinely like."

"Well, good! You should." She reached for him again. He stopped her.

There they were, just sitting in her Jeep Wrangler, in the food co-op parking lot, his cock out and still fully at attention. The store had been closed for hours, but he still felt oddly, and sort of wondrously, naked. The feeling did nothing to calm his dick down. It was absurd. He sighed, lifted his face to the sky, but it wasn't the sky, just the gray upholstered ceiling of Kimberly's Jeep, two inches from his face. "Fuck."

"You want to go home?" she asks, again making him sound like a kid sent to the nurse's office.

"No. I want... to be a better person."

"Oh Christ!" She said it with pure disgust.

"What?" he turned to her.

"Man, I hate that shit. 'Better person.' Somebody starts talking to me about being a 'better person' all I want is to run as far away as possible. Lord save me from people trying to be 'better people.'"

"Why?"

"Why? Better than what? Better than who? And why? How 'bout, just be a *person*. Ain't that hard enough?"

"Yeah... okay."

"Yeah?" she inspected his expression, with a glint in her eye.

"I guess."

"You guess?"

"Whatever. I know I like you. I know I want to get to know you."

"A'ight," she said, in a *Well, duh. What's-stopping-you?* tone.

"'A'ight'?" he asked, as if to confirm her permission.

"Yeah. A'ight."

He nodded. Relieved. "A'ight then." He felt foolish.

"So let's take our time. Get to know each other."

"Okay."

This woman is amazing.

"But in the meantime," she said, suddenly back in bossy bus driver mode, "Would you please do me a favor and take your cock-sucking like a man?"

Tom shortcuts through the Columbia Tower "wormhole": a series of connecting tunnels and escalators leading to the Seattle Municipal Tower itself. He first learned about Seattle's wormholes working temp jobs in the '90s. There are parts of downtown where you hardly ever have to come up to the rainy streets.

He's not desperate, but he should try and get this job if he can.

He's not their dad—Gaius and Octavius. He will never be that. Doesn't want to be, even if he could. And they don't want that, either. They're Kimberly's kids, through and through. But all that said, he finds himself doing all sorts of "dad things" with and for them. And they come to him with all sorts of dad questions and problems. What is he supposed to do? Refuse? He does his best and keeps his tongue in his cheek, often half-bitten through.

He finds he's not bad at it, being a not-dad. He gets a particular kick out of teaching them specific East Coast Irish schtick—things they would otherwise never know—like hitting the table with the bottom of your glass between clinking your toast and taking your first sip. "That's for the dead," he told the younger one, 'Tavius, when they were on the back patio of the St. Andrew's one summer evening, waiting for Gaius to be done with drama camp. Tom was having his summer usual: Glenmorangie Nectar d'Or with a splash of water and an IPA back. 'Tavius was having a Coke with a maraschino cherry in it—two actually—special gift from Mark, one of the bar's two ex-soccer-pro owners.

Death had been on his family's collective mind that summer. Tom's best friend J., who had married Kona's sister Hana in the late Zeroes and had two daughters with her, died suddenly of a heart attack in February, and the entire extended family—from New Rochelle, New York to Columbia City, Seattle to Oahu was bereft. Losing J. had punched another hole through Tom, and he wondered how many more of them his Swiss cheese heart could sustain.

Oddly, the persistently irritating presence of 12-year-old 'Tavius buoyed him like nothing else, as if being annoyed was somehow life-affirming. He watched the kid, sipping his Coke and squirming in his patio chair, never quite able to get comfortable in stillness. Tom felt like he could die tomorrow and the world would be all right for the simple fact that this kid existed.

Kona and Poma flew in for the funeral. Tom was one of the pallbearers, as was Kimberly's older boy Gaius, tall and strong for 15. Later, at the wake, which Kimberly graciously hosted, the brothers chatted up Poma, whom they were meeting for the first time. Aggressively flirting would be a better way of putting it. Both boys seemed to have been triggered into adolescent overdrive by Poma's golden curls, green eyes, and burgeoning curves. Tom could tell, watching through the kitchen pass-through window, that Poma was getting increasingly aggravated. She finally stood.

"Where you going?" 'Tavius asked.

"To find some grown-ups."

"Why?"

"Because you're talking about my body and I'm right the fuck in front of you."

"Ohhhh!" they both howled in unison.

"She got spunk," 'Tavius told Gaius. Of the two of them, 'Tavius was the socially savvier, always eager to act five years older than he was.

"Fuck you," she told him flatly. She was five inches taller. He made a face like she'd hit him for no reason.

Gaius played the intervening voice of reason. "A'ight listen. There ain't no cause to be a bitch."

"Fuck you too," she said, turning to him.

Tom was almost sure it was time to weigh in, but he'd been burned before stepping to Poma's protection. She was either going to handle this or she wasn't.

"Why you gotta be like that?" 'Tavius asked, now serious.

"Because you guys are treating me as a sexual... thing."

"What? We were complimenting you," said Gaius.

"No, you weren't." She looked from one to the other. "I'm not that to you two. I'm never going to be that to you. Do you understand?"

"What *are* you then?" asked Gaius. He seemed earnestly curious and confused.

As if were the most obvious thing in the world, Poma replied, "I'm your sister."

The brothers looked at each other. Tom worried they might break into laughter. But they didn't. And then Gaius turned back to Poma and said simply, "A'ight." He held out his hand as a peace offering. Poma took it and shook. Then she offered her hand to the younger brother.

But 'Tavius regarded it with deliberately manufactured disdain. "You ain't my sister."

"I am though. And I will be. Forever." She withdrew the hand and walked away.

"She trippin'," Tavius said to her back.

"Shut up, fool," his brother said.

Tom remembered thinking he'd never seen anything quite so extraordinary in his entire life.

That Christmas, Poma sent him back the bound edition of *Candleshire*. Carefully inserted in between every few pages were slightly less than page-sized watercolor illustrations. They weren't professional, but they were perfect. They were hers. And it was all in there, every key moment: the Icicle Queen casting her initial curse, the Bitter Shelf Elf bickering with the PTSD Toy Soldier, the marriage of the NYC Taxi and the Space Needle, the Lazy Maid-a-Milking taunting the Piperless Piper, and, of course, the culmination of their journey, the Disco Angel at the top of the tree. It's a fundamental fact of life, which only grows starker as a person ages: the Christmas-movie miracles aren't real. They never happen. And yet here one was, sitting in his open hands.

Something washed over Tom that holiday season and beyond. It wasn't a flash flood; it was an ever-rising tide. It took days, weeks. The boys and Kimberly noticed it.

"What do you have to be so happy about, old man?" 'Tavius asked, especially fond of taunting Tom. He threw words like "fat," "old," and "white" at him like sparring-partner punches. And Tom gave it back as good as he could. The brothers had different bio-dads, and while Gaius had rich, dark skin like his mom, 'Tavius's was nearly as light as Tom. So, when he would pop off

302

at his not-dad, Tom would often slap back with some dig on 'Tavius's for-all-practical-purposes whiteness. Who knows why he did it? Just one of those provocations that seem to leap all too easily from a father-figure's mouth into a young man's ears, as if natural selection insists a certain quotient of assholery be passed on to preserve the primordial soup of patriarchal stupidity. Usually it would slide off the sly kid's back, but one time 'Tavius was simply not in the mood and shot back, "I'm blacker than you'll ever be, you dumb drunk Mick."

Tom grinned. The defiance in this kid made his heart sore with love. "Touché, my boyo," he said kindly. "With that spirit of rebellion, we'll make Black Irish out of you yet."

"What's that make you?" asked Kimberly, passing through the kitchen with a basket of laundry. "A white nigger?" 'Tavius hooted like a frat boy, and Kimberly winked at Tom as she headed downstairs.

Tom glides up the escalator to the main floor of the Seattle Municipal Tower, which opens out to a lobby of soaring walls of glass to the south, west, and north, like a space-age cathedral. The bustle of people moving up and down and all around him has become denser, louder, more animated, and more multicolored. Instead of just corporate attire, he's seeing Levi's and Carhartt, reflective orange vests, dreadlocks and afros, Kangols and hijabs, and yet oddly, as the people become more diverse, they also start to strike Tom as more familiar. Faces leap out from the crowd. Everyone in Seattle is starting to be someone he half-recognizes, whether he actually knows them or not.

He finds the elevator bay with express cars to the 40th floor. From there he'll take another elevator to 43 for his interview. An elevator opens and spews a clown car's worth of people into the tight lobby. He waits for the last of them to get off, then boards the empty car and presses "40." As the doors close, a large black arm reaches in and sends them recoiling back. A truly huge woman steps on, wearing unfaded denim overalls over a thick, gray, woolly sweater, like she'd be comfortable unloading a freighter down on the Duwamish Waterway. She smiles widely. "You sure dressed up today." She says this like she's seen him every week for the last 20 years.

"Yup," he says, returning the smile as naturally as he can. The doors close and they start their ride up. There's something about her presence, her sheer hugeness and amicability, that feels vaguely supernatural. He's getting the good kind of goosebumps. "Job interview," he adds. Maybe some of her powerful positive mojo will rub off on him.

"Congratulations!" She grins like he told her he's won the lotto.

"Well, I haven't gotten it yet."

"Well, congratulations on getting an interview." It's a good point. The hiring manager told him they had received over 400 applications for the position.

"Thank you. I guess it *is* hard to get one with the City."

"Yes. It might behoove you to revisit the Legend of the White Buffalo."

Oh boy. "Yeah?"

She nods sagely.

"I don't... I don't believe I know that story."

"That's why I say it might behoove you to revisit it."

Tom decides it's unwise to point out he can't revisit what he's never visited. He decides instead to make a stab at levity. "Maybe this job is the White Buffalo."

She shrugs. "Or maybe *you* are."

"Like an endangered species, right?"

Again, she shrugs, narrows her eyes on him. "Up to you."

The doors open on the sky lobby. He waits for her to step off, but she gestures for him to go ahead. He takes a few steps, then turns to say goodbye. The doors have closed. She must not have gotten off after all.

As weird as this strikes him, sunlight beaming from his right tugs him onward. In the wide band of windows ahead, all of Beacon Hill and most of South Seattle stand foreground to the great mountain beyond, wearing its wisping disc of cloud as a toupee. He knows he's late, but he can't help himself from approaching the view. He looks down and sees I-5 and I-90 running together below, pumping cars through myriad capillaries. A cherry-red helicopter rockets in from the west and lands with breath-catching quickness on the Harborview emergency-room helipad. *Somebody's having a worse day than me.* The streetcar crawls up Jackson toward Little Saigon. Everywhere Tom looks things are moving. It's like that Richard Scarry children's book *Busytown* with the foxes and pigs and bears all bustling around, plus the little worm, always somewhere to be found.

Am I the worm?

Nice try.

When he first came here, Seattle was just a city you moved to when you wanted to go somewhere you were certain no one you knew had ever gone, but also somewhere you were hearing great things about: Equity theaters plentiful as bookstores, and new music that would blow your skull open. It would be your home for as long as you decided to make it that.

Now.

It's a city on the rise and permanently so. No more boom and bust (and Tom had seen both, at least twice now). Somehow—and somehow slightly sickeningly—it was going to be only boom from now on. Seattle, city of the world, city of history, to be mentioned in the company of Athens and Rome, London and Beijing, Buenos Aires, Amsterdam. (Tom thinks of the pot shops sprouting like moss on Aurora and Airport Way. *Yeah, Amsterdam.*)

But is it true? Is this city something special? Or is that just more solipsism on his part? *The city where you find yourself is the city of the world.* This is how you think when you're an American male of passable paleness. You get lucky enough, often enough, starting with how and when you were born, and you start to think it ain't the luck, it's you. Anywhere you go, anyone you meet there, is special. Lucky. Like you.

Lucky, lucky you.

Who knows? Depending on how this interview goes, this city of the world might be printing his paycheck. That is, if he can manage to get to this interview before they give up on him.

But he can't take his eyes off the view: steel and rubber, bone and blood, anxiety and anger, and idiot hope. Busytown.

There's still a gist in all of this. A poem.

Hell, maybe even a series of poems. An epic. One he could will himself to write like Doc Williams. He's not dead yet. He says out loud, albeit in a whisper: "Fuck. This city keeps making me love it."

You're late.

"I need to catch my breath."

You don't have time for this.

His breath mists the glass: "Who knows what I have time for?"